Martina Murphy has been writing for as long as she can remember. She is the author of twenty-three previous novels under various versions of her name! Her books have been translated into many languages and include the YA award-winning *Dirt Tracks* and the Impac long-listed *Something Borrowed.* She also writes plays and is a qualified drama teacher. She lives in Kildare with her husband, two adult children and a dog.

W0007737

The Bone Fire

Martina Murphy

CONSTABLE

CONSTABLE

First published in Great Britain in 2024 by Constable

A CIP catalogue record for this book
is available from the British Library.

ISBN: 978-1-4087-1886-5

Typeset in Bembo MT Pro by Initial Typesetting Services, Edinburgh
Printed and bound in Great Britain by Clays Ltd, Elcograf S.p.A.

Papers used by Constable are from well-managed forests
and other responsible sources.

Constable
An imprint of
Little, Brown Book Group
Carmelite House
50 Victoria Embankment
London EC4Y 0DZ

An Hachette UK Company
www.hachette.co.uk

www.littlebrown.co.uk

To you, dear reader — but most especially to those who've loyally accompanied me on this twenty-seven-year writing odyssey

Glossary

AFIS	Automated Fingerprint ID System
APT	Assistant pathologist
Cig	Short for *cigre*. A common nickname for detective inspectors as *cigre* means 'inspector' in Irish. Pronounced 'kig'.
DCS	Detective Chief Inspector
DDU	District Detective Unit (unmarked cars)
DG	Detective guard
Debs	A graduation dance attended by sixth-year students before they go on to college.
DI	Detective inspector. Often referred to as 'Cig'
DO	(Detective Officer), used on p.59
DPP	Director of Public Prosecutions
DS	Detective sergeant
FLO	Family Liaison Officer
GDPR	General Data Protection Regulations
GNECB	Garda National Economic Crime Bureau
IP	Injured party
IRC	Incident room co-ordinator
NBCI	National Bureau of Criminal Investigation

NSU	National Surveillance Unit
PM	Post-mortem
RSU	Regional Support Unit
SIO	Senior investigating officer
SOCO	Scene of crime officers
SO	Suspected offender
TE	Technical examination

And Peig – I have shivers even explaining it. *Peig* was the name of a book many Irish teenagers of a certain generation had to study for their Irish exam in the Leaving Certificate. Even though Peig (in real life) was apparently great craic, her book was - for Irish teens anyway – the most depressing thing they would ever read. Set on the Blasket Islands, it is a bleak story of survival that some-how is very boring.

Prologue

Eamon

The stars and colours are amazin', the way they zoom and pop and zing. They hurt, though, these colours, because as they fade, as the fireworks go out of them, his head booms like the shock of coming home.

He doesn't quite know what's going on and he's a man who likes to know. One fella came asking about the cattle and there was something about him, something very feckin' odd, but because he was selling a few cattle and because this man was offering a good price, he ignored all his instincts.

Ever since he was, what?, maybe eight years old, he's prided himself on his instincts.

They've been letting him down bad this past while, though, first with herself and now this.

'What the feck is going on?' He manages to speak through a mouthful of blood and broken teeth. He's hanging on to the fence for support.

'Don't you know?' The man who'd come about the cattle leers into his face.

'No, I don't. Have a bit of mercy. Haven't I just lost—'

1

'Mercy? You're a man to talk about mercy? Don't make me laugh.'

He wonders then if that bitch . . . But, no, she wouldn't. She couldn't.

'Who are you?'

And the man bends down and whispers in his ear and he understands then.

He knows that the bitch has broken the law.

And he knows that this is the end of the road for him.

He barely feels the kick as he falls to his knees, as he topples into the soil of the stony field.

But the colours dazzle as his life unspools . . .

1

Day 1

I'm walking through a house that looks like mine: the hall and the doors are in the same places but the colours are different. More vibrant. Yellow walls. Blue walls. Blood red walls. Blood? It drips from the ceiling and onto the floor. Plip-plop. And there is a ticking sound. Tick-tock. And I stand, frozen, wanting to run, but my feet are stuck. Up ahead, my son Luc is carrying my grandchild, Sirocco, and the tick-tock grows louder, and I try to call out to him to be careful, and even my voice doesn't work so I reach for him and my arms are heavy and then—

SMASH.

I jerk awake, heart pounding. I've knocked the clock radio flying across the room where it has landed with a weak 'bleep' on the floor beside the door.

'Sorry,' I call out, because I know my mother, who sleeps in the next room, would have heard. But, of course, my 'sorry' only makes her scuttle from her room into mine.

'What was that noise?' she whispers, looking quite odd in her childish Donald Duck-patterned pyjamas, a gift from Sirocco. I don't know why she's whispering - there's only the two of us in the house.

3

'I knocked over the clock radio.'

'A bad dream?'

'No.'

She knows I'm lying. Leaning against the door frame, she says, 'Lucy, you need to do something about this.'

'Haven't I got sleeping tablets from the doctor?' Pushing myself up, I flick on my mobile. It's five in the morning. There's not a hope of finding sleep now. I shove my feet into my runners, which are lying at the side of the bed. 'Cuppa?'

'At five in the morning?'

'No, at seven. I was just going to put the kettle on now.'

A smile tugs at the corner of her lips. 'Nothing wrong with your sarcasm anyway,' she says fondly, as she follows me, Donald Duck slippers flapping on her feet, along the hallway to the kitchen. On the way, we are forced to navigate towers of boxes, some open, their contents spilling out all over the floor, while others are sealed.

'When is Luc ever going to sort that stuff out?' I toe one of the closed ones.

'Isn't he doing his best?' My mother is never one to bear criticism of her grandson. 'It's an emotional thing to go through all his dead father's papers.'

'He barely knew Rob.' I fill the kettle. Saying it makes me feel mean. Rob, my robber husband, the person we'd all mutually despised, had only gone and tried to save our lives just over five months ago. He had died in doing so and now, well, it's hard to know how to feel about him. The papers and radio shows at the time had had a field day. 'Convicted Fraudster Hero,' one paper had proclaimed, in a rather confusing headline. There had been debates on talk shows about bad people who had done great acts.

For years, I had got used to being flippant and snarky about Rob, but now there's a tug on my heart that says he probably wasn't the monster I believed him to be.

My mother settles herself in a kitchen chair and studies me, head to the side. 'Still . . .' she says.

'Still,' I agree, pulling down two cups.

It's disconcerting to have all the boxes in the hall, though. Luc had brought them home two weeks ago, after Rob's estate had been settled. Everything except a few photographs had been left to him. So far, from what I can tell, it's a lot of flashy bad-taste clothes, a pile of papers that detail the pitiful savings in Rob's bank accounts, a laptop with a password none of us can figure out and copious stunning photographs of the Mayo coastline.

And that was it, the sum total of Rob's time on earth.

And although Luc is cold-shouldering me, at least he's in good form with everyone else. Of late, he even seems quite buoyant. It makes me hope that he's moving on from Rob's death.

I fill the teapot and pour us both a cuppa. My mother looks tired, probably because I keep waking her. I watch her add five heaped teaspoons of sugar to her cup.

'Mam—'

'I can't drink early-morning tea without sugar.' She shuts me down, then says, 'I thought they gave you, you know, counselling in the guards.'

'I did it.' And I had, dutifully trotting out the whole story of my home being invaded by a man with a grudge against me. How my ex-husband had taken the hit. How I'd been powerless to do anything. I'd told the story until I was numb. I'm an expert in recounting tales of brutal deeds, having spent years going to court and trotting out other people's traumas, so I'd employed the same techniques to my own narrative. 'I am fine. I can do my job. It'll just take time for the dreams to stop.' Then I add, 'It's like when you treat a wound and put a plaster on it and it takes a little while to . . . heal.'

My mother is pleased with that. 'I get it. Oh, that's good.'

After the case I'd been working on at the time had been put to bed, William, the DI, had insisted I take a few weeks off so I could sort myself out, and I had gone on holiday. I had never been so bored in my life. I'd come back and engaged with An Garda Síochána's services. They're allegedly there to help any guard who'd been through a trauma in the course of their duties. Honestly, that's about 90 per cent of us, but only a few seek help. And it's mainly the desperate. No one wants to see their career skydive because other people think they can't cope. I only did it because I knew William would insist on it, would check up on me. And it worked. I'm fine, mostly, except for the dreams. My mother seems to have bounced back from the events of that night, as has Luc, though our relationship has shifted a little on account of what he found out about my previous life as a detective in Dublin during the attack. I'm hoping it'll settle in time.

My mother finishes her tea. She has the impressive ability to drain a scalding hot cuppa in seconds. 'I'll go back to bed.' She yawns widely. 'I'll lie on in the morning.' Crossing towards me she drops a soft kiss on the top of my head. 'Night.'

'Night.'

She leaves, nimbly hopping over large brown boxes, and I hope I'll be as agile when I hit my seventies. Carrying my tea over to the window, I watch the sun creep over the hills and paint the sky scarlet. All is silent as a new day breaks open.

***

Sometime later the lyrics from 'Wake Me Up Before You Go-Go' playing at full volume rouse me from where I'd fallen asleep at the table. It takes a second to adjust before I realise that the music is my work-phone ringtone.

My knees crack as I hobble into my bedroom to where I'd left it on my locker. 'William' is the name on caller display and part of me sings. My boss, DI William Williams. He hasn't side-lined me because I've received trauma counselling. Something has happened and he wants me on his team. Another part of me dreads the news of what tragedy has unfolded.

I swallow, press answer. 'Cig? It's Lucy.'

'There's been a fire at a house on Slievemore. The chief fire officer believes it might have been deliberate. And we've a fatal-ity. We're locking the scene down.'

My heart judders. I know people out that way. 'Any idea of who it is?' I fight to keep my voice steady.

'Not yet. See you in ten.'

I tell him I'll be there in twenty minutes.

2

By the time I arrive at the scene, the sun is creeping up in the east. Though we've had a very bad start to spring, June is doing its best to make us think we might have a shot at summer.

I park my new car a little away from the cordon. It's only a few months old and I do not want it smelling of smoke. I would have taken a DDU – district detective unit – vehicle from the station but it was quicker to come direct. William is not a man who likes to be kept waiting. Jordy, a sergeant in the Achill station, is the guard on duty, responsible for preserving the scene and the log book. He looks beat, not used to being roused so early from his bed.

'Lucy,' he wheezes, as I arrive up, 'how have you been?'

'Grand, Jordy. Yourself?' Even as I'm asking, I'm scanning the area. The mountain, Slievemore, rears up like the crest of a wave about to engulf the graveyard, the deserted village and the few occupied houses scattered along it. The closest residence has been reduced to a blackened ruin. Two fire brigades and two ambulances are in attendance. The blaze appears to be in its dying throes.

'I'm good.' Jordy thumbs to the house. 'The place is gutted. It was ferocious, I heard. Deliberate too, they think.'

'And the ambulances?'

'One child. Found upstairs. He's alive.'

'Aw, Jesus.' After signing into the scene, Jordy allows me through.

As I approach, having donned the forensic suit, which, as usual, is enormous, the residual heat from the fire meets me like a wall while the smoke finds its way into my eyes. I recognise the residence: it's a holiday let, belonging to my mother's friend Lorna. It was a pretty cottage, aimed at tourists, with its whitewashed walls and bright red door. The walls are black now, the windows blown out, the door charred and falling, revealing the gaping hole of the interior. The lads from the fire brigade are still on alert in case the fire decides to kick off again. Until the heat dies, anything can happen. The stench of damp and smoke hangs heavy in the still morning air. The building groans, dying, creaking and straining. Water trickles down through the destroyed shell.

I fire off a quick text to my mother looking for Lorna's number just as I notice a tall figure making his way across the grass towards me. Even under the mask, he's recognisable. It's in his assured walk, in the scrutiny of his ice blue eyes. I wonder suddenly if he has any bad dreams. Will he have bad dreams about this scene? Of all the members on the team, he's had more than his fair share of trauma. With a nod of greeting, he launches straight in, 'They reckon another few hours and they'll be able to let us enter,' he says, his eyes raking over the smouldering ruin. 'According to the fire officer, the body of the victim was located in what we believe was the kitchen area. The person was on the floor, in the middle of the room. Right now, they've no idea how the fire started, but because it took so fast, they reckon there must have been an accelerant used.'

'Accelerant? With a child in the house?'

There's hesitation, which is not like him. Then he says, 'Two children. One alive and one . . .' He looks skywards and heaves a sigh.

Of all the things I've encountered in this job, I'm still staggered at the depths of horror out there. 'Where are the parents?' I swallow my upset.

'We haven't found any.'

I don't respond to that. Chances are we might find a parent, dead somewhere in the vicinity, after taking their own life and deciding to take the children with them. Or maybe having drunk themselves into a stupor and been unable to react when the fire started. 'How is the child that's alive?'

'A bit of smoke inhalation but he'll be all right.'

He'll never be all right. This moment will sear itself on his soul in ways that will be hard to predict. The 'why' of it will be the thing to brand him. Whatever the 'why' is.

'So, two things.' William is back to business. 'I need you to talk to the man who called nine-nine-nine. He lives across that field.' He points to the next house over, just a white blur in the distance. It's a rented house too and I don't know who lives there. 'Also I need you to find out who—'

My phone rings, blaring out the Wham! song

William raises his eyebrows as if to say who the hell is calling me on my work mobile.

I glance at the screen and recognise the number. I flick it off but it immediately starts up again. Jesus, I think, why can't she just answer a simple text message?

'Mam,' I say into it, as William makes a tsk sound while glaring impatiently at me. 'Can you please just text me back and—'

'Why do you want Lorna's number? Has something happened?

I'm sorry, but if something has, I don't think you should be the one—'

'If you don't give me her number right now I will arrest you for obstructing a garda inquiry.'

Beside me William splutters out what I think might be a laugh. 'You wouldn't.'

She's right. 'Her holiday home is on fire,' I snap. 'Now can you—'

'Oh, my God, Lorna said there was someone renting it. A long-term lease. She was delighted and—'

'Mam.'

She stops abruptly and rattles off Lorna's name and address. Then, as she's expressing her hope that everyone is safe, I hang up. 'The owner is Lorna Long, Keel,' I say to William. 'Do you want me to go and talk to her?'

'Yes. Better do it straight after you talk to your man over in that house. It might give us an early ID on who was living in the place. There's no car outside that we've found yet. When is Dan due back?'

'Day after tomorrow, all going well.' Dan is my work partner and right now he's in hospital, having tripped over a garden urn that he hadn't known was there. It's a long story involving his partner's mother who has just moved in with them. He'd suffered bad concussion and a bruised elbow.

'Grand. Right. Give Kev a shout, get him out of bed. Tell him to set up the incident room and pull the usual team together, depending on who is available. We don't know what we're looking at yet, but if I was a betting man, I'd say we might have arson resulting in a murder, along with an attempted murder on our hands.' He shoots a sideways look at me. 'Are you all right with that?'

'Sure.' I pretend I don't know what he's referring to. I tap my notebook, which I've jammed into the pocket of my rain jacket. 'I'll get going.'

'I'll give you a call when we get the all-clear to go in. The more eyes the better.'

'Yep.'

'And, Lucy,' I turn back to him, 'on your way out, tell Jordy to tuck his shirt into his trousers, for fuck's sake. When the bloody press get here, they'll think some middle-aged country bumpkin is in charge of the perimeter.'

Jordy *is* a middle-aged country bumpkin, I'm tempted to say, but instead I answer, 'I'll have a word. See you later.'

He tips me a salute and saunters off in the direction of the fire officer.

3

Two children. Who the hell would set a fire with two children in the house? What sort of a person does that? Did whoever did it know that the children were there? And where was the mother or father? Will they be found on—

A volley of small stones hits the windscreen as my car slides on a tight bend. I'm driving too fast. Slowing down, I think it wouldn't be great to crash my brand-new car so soon after buying it. The lads in the station would have a field day.

Five minutes later, I pull up outside the home of the person who had reported the fire. From this vantage point, I can clearly see the plumes of black smoke drifting away across the mountain. Small flickers of flame, like miscreant children, leap up from the blackened ruin and are immediately quenched.

It takes five minutes to get an answer from the occupier, who rattles about inside, looking for a key, I think, before eventually pulling open the door.

'Lucy! Hey!'

For feck's sake. I face the man who'd broken my heart when I was fifteen and who, through a series of misfortunes, has featured in my life ever since. 'Johnny. You live here now?' I don't know where to look as he's wearing nothing but a short silk dressing-gown tied loosely with a flimsy belt.

'For the last four months,' he says, lounging in the doorway. 'In fact, since my marriage imploded I haven't settled for too long anywhere. It's been hell.'

'Indeed.' I take out my notebook. 'Pity you were such a shit to your wife and daughter. Now, I've a few questions for you regarding—'

'Is this part of your interview technique?' He feigns shock. 'Going about insulting your witnesses?'

'No. Reserved especially for you.'

He laughs a little and opens the door wider. 'You'd better come in, I suppose. D'you want a cup of tea? Or some toast? It's very early to be working.'

I'm surprised he even knows how to do toast. Johnny Egan had always been a bit too much about Johnny Egan to bother with the normalities of life, and for some reason I'd found it wildly attractive. 'No.' I follow him down his hall as he leads the way to the kitchen. 'Thanks anyway. I just want you to tell me anything you remember about seeing the fire earlier.'

'*I'm* having toast.' Rubbing a hand through his messy blond hair, he gestures to a kitchen chair. 'You can sit there. It's clean.'

'Good to know.' I perch on it, ready to leave as quickly as I can. 'What time did you notice this fire?' I keep my tone professional.

He pops two slices of bread into his toaster. 'Are you always like this? Straight down to business?'

'When I'm doing my job, yeah.' I wait a second, then add, 'This isn't a social call.'

Chuckling, he pulls butter from the fridge. 'About half five,' he says, sniffing the butter. 'I was after finishing a design for a house out in Ballycroy, and I was just heading to bed and I saw this reddish glow. At first I thought, you know, it was a lantern or a torch but, like, it was red and it sort of kept ebbing and flaring up. I went outside and there was a smell of smoke in the air so I figured it had to be a fire.' He pokes a finger into his butter and takes a cautious lick. 'That's fine.' He's referring to the butter, which he sets on the table. Then to me, 'I called nine-nine-nine and the girl on the other end of the line said she'd send someone out and I went to bed.'

It's only Johnny who could report a fire, then go to bed. Still, it's always been out of sight, out of mind with him. 'You saw a glow about five thirty, rang it in and went to bed?'

He must hear the incredulity in my tone because he answers a little defensively, 'I've an early start in the morning, which is earlier now, thanks to you. And sure,' a shrug, 'I'm not a fireman.' His very pale toast pops and he slathers it with half a block of butter. He offers me the plate. 'You positive?'

'If I had any regrets about refusing the first time, I don't now. It looks rank.'

'Your loss.' He bites into one of the slices.

'Do you know who lives in that house?'

'It was a house?' His jaw drops, exposing masticated bread. 'Aw, Jesus, I thought it was one of the bonfires for St John's Eve. They seem to be everywhere this year. Was anyone hurt?'

He'll find out soon enough. 'We think so but we haven't been into the scene yet. A child was taken to hospital, though.'

There's a moment of disbelief before he puts his toast down and shoves his plate away. 'Jesus. Sorry, I've been a dick. What is it you want to know?'

'If you know who lives there?'

15

'I'm out most of the time. Could be a woman . . .' he pauses '. . . or maybe a man. I saw a man there a few weeks back.'

'Can you describe him?'

'It was a while ago,' he says. 'I don't know. Big fella. Physically strong, I mean. He was walking up the drive as I was driving past. It was the day I was meeting Akins and Co for a redesign of their offices, so I can check the date.' He spends a moment locating his phone. 'June the second,' he says, and I jot it down.

'What was this guy wearing?'

'Nothing that stood out. Jeans, I think, and a black jacket. He had jet black hair, because I remember thinking, I bet that fella's dyed his hair.'

Takes one to know one, I feel like saying. Instead, I close my notebook and stand up. 'Thanks. I'll be back if I need anything else.'

'Sure.' He smiles a goodbye and for the tiniest of seconds my heart flutters, like baby kicks.

Trying to ignore it, I march with purpose out of the kitchen and into the hall. I'm about to open the front door when he calls out, 'I was wondering . . . how are you? You know after . . . well . . . everything?'

The question catches me by surprise, and I stall, swallowing a sudden lump in my throat. I turn around slowly. 'Fine.' My voice is a croak.

'Right. Good.' Another shrug. 'It's just . . .' he pauses again, not sure maybe if he should, but finally blurts out '. . . you look tired.'

'It's six thirty in the morning, Johnny.'

'Yeah, I guess.'

Awkwardly, 'Thanks for asking.'

'Anytime.' Awkwardness over, he turns back to his toast.

4

As I knew she would, my mother has already rung Lorna to break the news because Lorna is waiting for me when I pull up to her house.

'Lucy!' She runs to greet me as I make my way up her drive, then trots alongside me, breathlessly firing out questions. 'What's been happening? Your mother rang and we weren't sure whether to go up to the cottage or to stay here. But your mother said you'd call. Oh dear, this is terrible, terrible. What's happened?'

The woman is as thin as a rake, but strong-looking, with the quick movements of the perpetually nervous. Chattering about how awful this all is, she leads me into her tidy but overly fussy kitchen. Knick-knacks vie for space on the shelves – ceramic hens, paper hearts, St Brigid's crosses, cheap ornaments and an alarming number of photos all featuring hens of different hues.

'How bad is it?' She finally comes to a standstill beside her kitchen table. Before I can answer, she calls, 'Denis, Lucy Golden is here.' Then, to me, 'Sit down. I'll make some tea.'

'There's no need.'

'Denis will want tea anyway.' She scurries over to the sink and fills the kettle. 'Sit. Go on. Sit.'

As she's whirling about getting cups and making toast, Denis arrives into the kitchen, freshly washed and shaved. He slides in beside me.

'How's Lucy? How's your mother?'

There's no rush with him. It's like he sucks Lorna's panic out of the room. His breath smells of mouthwash.

'She's grand, thanks. Ye were very good letting her stay after the . . . attack.' Even now, I have trouble referencing it.

'That was a terrible how-do-you-do.' Denis shakes his head. 'The poor woman was half cracked with the shock. Fair play to you all moving back into that house.' He waits a beat, then asks, 'So, our house? Badly damaged?'

Lorna turns towards me, eyes huge with anxiety.

I brace myself. 'I'm afraid so.'

'Oh.' That's Lorna. 'Oh dear.'

'The house is destroyed,' I say, as gently as I can. 'I'm sorry.'

A shocked silence broken only as Lorna sits down heavily on a spindly kitchen chair.

Denis stands and squeezes her shoulder, 'It's insured, let's not worry.' He turns to me. 'And our tenants? Are they all right? Any idea what caused it?'

'That's why I'm here. I need details of who was renting it from you.'

'You mean they're not at the house?'

'Look, you'll read about it soon anyway, but we believe there was a fatality and—'

Lorna covers her mouth with her hand. 'Not the mother? Not Moira?' She looks in horror at Denis.

'Will you let Lucy talk?' Denis admonishes gently. He turns to me. 'A fatality?'

'Yes. We have no ID yet. One child was pulled alive from the upstairs bedroom and . . .' like William, I find it hard to say '. . . one child we think is dead.'

They both inhale sharply. Lorna stifles what I think is a sob.

I let them take that in before adding, 'It's terrible, I know. How many people were in the house?'

'Three,' Denis confirms. 'But . . . well, I think Moira told me only . . .' he frowns '. . . the day before yesterday the children were going to be away today, that they were going on a sleepover last night. Are you sure?'

'We don't have an ID on the body in the kitchen yet. The firemen thought it might be a child but . . . we don't know.' Even as I say it, I know it's crap. The firemen do know. 'Who did she tell you was taking them last night?'

'She didn't. I just passed her in the street and said to her that she had her hands full with them and she said she'd enjoy the break when they were on their sleepover tomorrow. And I just laughed, the way you do.' He sounds bereft.

'The children are Bren and Ella,' Lorna jumps in. 'Bren is about four, chatty little chap. And Ella is the opposite, never talks but she's a lovely little thing. About five or six, I think. And Moira, she's the mother. Is she not . . . ?'

'We haven't found her. Would she be in the habit of leaving her children alone?'

'She loved those kiddies.' Denis is very definite about that. 'She'd never do anything to hurt them.'

'But we don't know for sure,' Lorna chimes in, 'do we, Denis?'

'Well . . . no,' he concedes. Then, swallowing, he says, a little defensively, 'Look, she would be collecting seaweed in the mornings on the beach, to sell. Early, like five or so. I'd see her some

19

mornings – I'd be taking pictures for my calendar.'

Denis brings out a calendar of photographs each year and sells it for charity at Christmas.

'I don't know what she did with the children those mornings,' he continues. Then, ruefully, 'I didn't ask her because, well, it's not my business and she was great with them and . . .' His voice trails off. 'Maybe I should have.'

I refrain from commenting. Of course he should have, but that's easy to say in hindsight. 'Were you on the beach this morning?'

'I was, but I didn't see her. She might have gone to a different one.'

'Okay. Thanks.' I fire off a text to William. He'll probably send someone to check the beaches. Refocusing on Denis and Lorna, I ask, 'Is there anything you can tell me to help trace Moira or her next of kin?'

'Moira Delaney,' Denis says. 'A Limerick girl. I'm not sure from what part. Though that was her married name. She was trying to change everything to her maiden name, she told me, but I can't remember what that was.'

'Long shot, but would you have a picture of her?'

Lorna looks to Denis.

'No,' he says, and, weirdly, I'm not sure I believe him.

'You sure?'

Beside him, Lorna appears to stiffen. 'How would we have a picture of her?'

I leave it a beat, but neither of them fills the silence. I won't pursue it – it's not relevant just now anyway. If Moira was in her thirties, I'd expect her to be on social media. Facebook is probably too dated. Instagram might be my best bet. I open my account, never used except once upon a time to keep an eye on

Luc. Under search, I key in Moira Delaney and, of course, loads of profiles pop up. The pictures are tiny. And most of the profiles are private. 'Have a quick look there and see if you can recognise her.' I hold my phone towards Denis.

He gives me an incredulous look. 'Neither of us is a spring chicken, Lucy. Even with our glasses those pictures are a blur.'

'A blur,' Lorna chirps.

I revert to Facebook and Twitter just on the off-chance, but looking for a Moira Delaney is like searching for a needle in a haystack. Finally, I key 'Moira Delaney', 'Brendan Delaney', 'Ella Delaney', 'Limerick' and 'Bren' into Google. 'Anything else you know about her?'

'She came from Limerick but moved west after she married. Then her marriage broke up. Not long ago, I don't think. She went back to Limerick for a short while, maybe family there or something, but she returned here because of the little girl. She was in school here. And I think her and the father were discussing him seeing the children more or whatever.'

'Husband's name?'

They look at each other and shake their heads.

'She was an artist,' Denis suddenly remembers. 'Not that famous, I don't think. Her pictures were the sort of ones that you don't know exactly what they are.'

I put in 'artist'. And bingo. One entry.

'You certainly know a lot about her,' Lorna remarks, and her tone makes my senses pop. She's looking oddly at Denis.

'I know what she told me when she moved in,' he says. 'Sure didn't I help her with her boxes and it nearly killed me?'

He holds her gaze, and a moment passes before Lorna tears her eyes away from his. 'I think we might have a reference for her somewhere.' She crosses to a dresser and pulls open a drawer, setting free a sheaf of papers that cascade to the floor. 'Marvellous,' she mutters, almost with a sob, as she bends down to sift through them.

Being here is like stepping into warm water and finding an unexpected cold current underneath. I don't have time to analyse it because, for now, all I need is information on Moira. I flick my attention back to my Google search.

Moira Delaney is one of our selected artists for the inaugural Peter McCroy bursary. She is developing a body of work, set in the natural landscape, which she said will expose the hidden dangers of the seen world. As well as that she will use bodily—

Blah. Blah. Arty claptrap that no one understands. I scroll down and, yes, a headshot! It was obviously taken when she got the bursary. If it hasn't been Photoshopped, the woman is stunning. There's an ethereal quality about her. Delicate and otherworldly with luminous skin and large, sad brown eyes. Her hair, midnight black, falls about her face in loose sleek waves. She looks . . . I try to think of the word and come up with 'untouchable'. Like she has an air of royalty about her. 'Is this Moira?' I ask Denis.

'That's her,' he confirms. 'Nice picture. The little lad looks like her, only not with the brown eyes.'

'Blue eyes,' Lorna says.

I screenshot it, then email it to the Cig, shorthand for *cigre*, the Irish word for 'inspector', telling him that this is the mother of the two children in the house. I email the picture to Kev too, because I know he's in the station sorting out the incident room for conference later. I ask him to do a reverse image search for Moira on the internet and on social media. *To be sure, double-check pictures of her with her children – Ella and Bren – so you'll be certain it's the right feed. She's an artist. She's from Limerick originally*, I type.

I throw out another question. 'Did Moira have any visitors?'

'Sure how would we—' Lorna begins.

'Not many,' Denis answers. 'I saw a man once. Mid-sized fella, dark hair. I asked him who he was and he said he was looking for Moira. He wasn't the friendliest, I remember. Sort of snarled at me. Anyway, I said she wasn't around. He left then. And the day she moved into the house, there was no one with her at all at all.'

As he talks, Lorna's hands still as she turns towards her husband, and I don't know if I imagine it, but the look of loathing in that millisecond nails me to the floor before she wipes it clean with a smile. 'Here we are.' Pulling herself upright, she hands me a page that appears to be torn from a copybook.

To whom it concerns –

Moira Delaney née Flannery is a responsible tenant and I have no hesitation in recommending her to you. She rented my apartment for a year, always paid on time and kept the place in good order.

Barry Jones

24 Newport Street, Newport, Mayo

As I jot down that 'Flannery' is her maiden name, Denis says, 'I rang that chap, the one that wrote the letter. Seemed a nice man, said Moira was wonderful, and I decided we'd let her have the cottage for six months to start with. The woman was desperate, needed a place for herself and the children.'

I pop the letter into an evidence bag, thinking that if she was with this landlord for a year, when was it? Did she and her husband rent a house from him?

'Why are you putting that letter into a bag?' Denis looks alarmed.

'Procedure, just in case . . .'

'Just in case of what?' Lorna asks.

'In case,' I try to choose words that won't panic them, 'in case we're looking at something more than just a house fire and a missing person.'

'Jesus, Mary and Joseph.' Lorna blesses herself. 'Do you think it was on purpose?'

'I don't think anything,' I say. 'This is all procedure.'

They glance at each other, turn to me.

'What aren't you telling us?' Denis asks for them both.

My phone rings, saving me from having to reply.

'We can go in in about ten minutes,' William says.

5

SOCOs have arrived and are in the process of gathering as much evidence from the scene as they can in an attempt to unearth how and why this fatal fire started. The cordon has been extended and a search is under way to try to locate the mother.

Down on the road, the press have begun to gather. RTÉ vie with the local papers for jostling space at the cordon. Jordy, who not only has his shirt tucked in but has donned his full uniform, is ignoring all their calls for a statement.

William, an irritated Joe Palmer, the pathologist, and I are waiting for final permission to be allowed into the cottage.

'They said any minute an hour ago,' Palmer grumbles. 'I've enough to be doing without travelling to the back of beyond to stand around in the drizzle. And I can't even have a cigarette.'

William and I ignore him.

'Oy!' Palmer calls across to Liam, the chief fire officer. 'What's the hold-up?'

'I suppose it's all about trying not to get ye killed when you go in,' Liam calls back pleasantly, making me snigger.

'Easy know he isn't under the pressure I am.' Palmer snorts. 'Still, one more year and me and Jean will be out of this godforsaken place. We'll be sunning ourselves in Spain while you lot are still cleaning up the shite in this country.'

'That's something to look forward to, eh, Lucy,' William says wryly.

'It is.' I try not to laugh.

Palmer eyes us suspiciously, not sure exactly what William means.

'All right,' Liam calls, 'over ye come. Careful now.'

We cross towards him, me finding it awkward in the massive forensic suit. They seem to have no problem ordering gloves in various sizes but never the suits and it drives me mad. It's the only piece of clothing I'll ever be a 'small' in. I shuffle behind the other two as Liam leads us along the safe path to the front of the house. 'We've stabilised the structure,' he says, as he indicates the supports put in place, 'but I'm going to escort ye into the kitchen anyway, just to be safe. I can talk ye through the scene as much as we understand it at this moment. 'Tis one of the worst fires I've ever attended, I'll tell ye that now. It was pure ferocious. There is no way it was accidental, I'll tell ye that now.' A glance at us. 'Are ye right?' Without waiting for a response, Liam flicks on his torch and enters the house.

'The door isn't as bad as I'd expect,' William observes.

He's right. The paint is blistered, and in the small glass pane only a few spiky shards of glass remain. But it's still standing.

'It was open when the fire started,' Liam explains. 'By the time we arrived flames were shooting out from the hallway. The glass from the pane is here.' He toes the ground where shards lie. 'I'll send ye a report on what we observed for conference later anyway. Now, this here is the hallway.' He plays the light of the torch onto a barely recognisable set of stairs. 'You can just see the banister leading upwards. It's not as badly damaged up there, two bedrooms and a bathroom. Thankfully, for that little boy, we managed to get in. We can say for definite that the fire started downstairs. There,' he indicates a gaping hole to the left, 'that's a small sitting room.'

'May I?' William asks and Liam nods. He walks into what is left of the room. Charred wood, metal and glass crunch under his feet. The remains of a sofa and a curtain half off its rail are recognisable, as is a cord in the ceiling, which I suppose was a light. Everything is black and wet and, without the torch, dark. William has a look at melted sockets as Liam says, 'This room was only starting when we got here. It was the kitchen and hall that took the brunt of it. The fire was pouring out, smoke was billowing, so I'm certain it began in the kitchen, not in a basement or anything deep-seated like that. Come on.'

Palmer has already gone ahead, his priority always the body and not the solving of a crime.

The door between the hall and the kitchen is somewhere under our feet and in order to enter what was once a small room, we have to step over a tiny corpse, curled up on the floor.

'There was an accelerant poured on or near the body,' Palmer says, from his crouched position beside the victim.

Liam nods. 'Yes.' He turns to us. 'Can you smell it?'

We nod. Whoever it was had had no chance to escape as the fire has wrought total destruction here. Black walls expose basic insulation, melted appliances, the blackened rafters above what had once been the ceiling. The smell of soot and damp and chemicals. And diesel.

'Typical boxer pose,' Palmer says, snapping a few pictures of the body.

We will have our own pictures shortly too.

'Fire does that,' Palmer continues dispassionately. 'See the way she's curled up? The heat of the fire has caused the muscles to flex. Internal organs exposed.'

The tiny body looks more alien than human.

Finally, Palmer gets to his feet. 'We need to get her to the morgue ASAP because the heat will continue to damage her organs.'

'It's a girl?' That's me.

'Most likely, but we'll know later. Get someone in, take proper pictures and I'll get her removed. You'll have an interim report soon.' So saying, he stomps out of the house.

There's a silence after he leaves. The three of us stare down at what was once a living, breathing, laughing little girl. I feel a pain high in my chest and have to swallow it back, damp it down. It won't do this little one any good if I fall apart. I know we're all thinking the same.

'We need to find a next of kin before the story gets out.' My tone is solid.

'What do we know about the mother?' William asks.

I rattle off what I'd learned from Lorna and Denis, finishing, 'I've got an old landlord's name. I can call and press him for any details. Kev is also trying to track her down on the internet.'

I wait for William to say something else but instead he crouches and scrutinises the child. He spends a long while looking at her, and in the end I turn away: not only can I not look at the body any more, I can't look at him looking.

A few minutes later, he joins me outside, where the air is a bit fresher despite the stench. Taking off his mask, he says, 'First things first. We don't know that that body is Ella—'

'Come on, Cig. You—'

He holds up a hand and I snap my mouth shut.

'But,' he continues, 'on balance of probability, it more than likely is. Let's track the mother's family down, see if they've heard from her. We can ask for a DNA sample for comparison in case she turns up dead too.'

'Grand.' The poor family, I think.

At that moment Kev sends a text. One word: *BINGO!*

6

He has found Moira on Instagram. A reverse image search is a dinky little thing that allows you to upload an image and the program will search the whole of the internet for visually similar ones. Or identical images, if it's online. It's a bit hit-and-miss, there's a knack to using it and some programs are better than others, but when it hits, the surge of adrenaline is powerful.

Kev had uploaded the picture of Moira I found and unearthed an Instagram account called MDel89. Obviously public, he's sent through screenshots of several of her posts. The first is the picture of Moira that I sent him, only this time, lucky for us, she had posted it on her Instagram account and allowed Kev to find her through the search. The post reads, *Thanks to the Arts Council for the grant #onehappyfemalepainter #fun #keepsmiling #keeppainting #love.*

I scroll to the next image. A small boy, about three, wearing a green baseball cap and a blue sweatshirt, being pushed on a swing by a young man, who is laughing at something. The post reads, *Me, Bar and the boy going craziee in the park. #fun #kids #lovemyboy #keepsmiling.*

A second image shows the same little boy, wearing a pair of

swimming trunks. He's giving the camera a thumbs-up and has a big goofy grin on his face. Beside him stands a solemn little girl, furrowed brow, wearing a blue swimsuit and sun hat. *Swimming with my gorgeous boy and my mom – joke – my bossy boots daughter #fun #kids #lovemybabies #keepsmiling.*

Oh, God. The pain in my chest again as I stare at that serious little face. She looks like she's carrying all the worries of the world.

I enlarge the photo, hoping to get a sense of where they are. But all beaches look the same.

'They're the right ages for the children, anyway,' William says. 'Give that landlord a ring, would you? See if he can add anything extra to the mix. Anything else?'

'Yep.' Kev has sent another picture, this time with all three in it. The boy is a little bigger, holding tight to his mother's arm. He's wearing a branded tracksuit and runners and his hair has been spiked up. He looks like a tiny drug-dealer. The girl, still with that inscrutable expression, is staring stoically at the camera. She's wearing a pretty red dress that is so at odds with her expression it's cute. Moira is beaming, her face alight with happiness. She's wearing a tight lime-green dress. The background is dull, grey. *October visiting the father #home #lovinglife #blessed.*

I blow the picture up; there's some kind of sculpture behind her, and further on a building and the stretch of a street.

'That's King John's Castle in Limerick,' the Cig says, peering hard. 'It's right on the bridge. I know that well, lived near there. She's a Limerick girl, right?'

'Yep.'

'Great. I'll contact the stations there and task them to trace the family from our gathered info.' At my look, he says, 'Two

31

children, one dead in a fire set deliberately. A missing mother. Most times these things have a start-up. It doesn't happen out of the blue. There might be a report of something on file. So, you call her old landlord, see what happens there.'

'I can check with the Arts Council too,' I suggest. 'They might have an address for her.'

'She only got that grant within the last four months. My guess is that she was in Achill by then. That's the address they'll have, but worth a try.'

'Okay, I'll get on it.'

As I speak, paramedics, bearing a stretcher with a body bag, pass us by on their way to bring the IP – injured party - our euphemistic name for a victim, murdered or otherwise, to the morgue.

Everyone falls silent as they put her into the ambulance.

'Try to get in touch with relatives as soon as possible,' William orders, as the vehicle drives off, his gaze still on the house. 'The media know something's up. We'll call a press conference for six this evening, so see you back here then.'

Marvellous.

Suddenly there's a shout, a bustle of activity. I hurry behind William as he strides across to where some SOCOs have gathered, just beyond where the front door of the property is.

They've found blood on a patch of grass outside the house. One of the SOCO team is having a closer look.

'What's the story?' William asks,

'Hard to be certain but this blood is fairly recent and there's a lot of it spattered about. We'll take a sample, get DNA.'

'Grand.' William spots me. 'Hop it, would you?'

'On it, Cig.'

***

Five minutes later, having found a quiet spot, I dial first the Arts Council and leave a message, then call Moira's old landlord.

The promise of a sunny day has been rescinded. Rain is falling in a dirty thin drizzle.

A muted 'Hello.'

'Is that Mr Barry Jones?'

'Depends on who's asking. Who is asking?' I hear echoes behind him, as if he's in a warehouse or something.

I don't have time for this. 'Detective Sergeant Lucy Golden,' I stress the 'detective sergeant' bit. 'I'd like to—'

'DS? A guard. Have you news for me?'

News? 'I suppose I have.'

'Well?' he asks.

This is not how I envisaged this conversation. 'Is this Barry Jones of twenty-four Newport Street?'

'Well . . . yeah . . . I guess.' He sounds doubtful. 'Once upon a time.'

'Sorry? Once upon a time?'

'It's my mother's address. I live in Limerick now.'

Is it me . . .? 'Barry, did you ever write a note for a lady called Moira Delaney, saying you were an ex-landlord of hers?'

'Eh . . . yeah. What has that to do with anything?'

I am confused. 'Were you ever her landlord?'

'Eh . . .' He sounds a little panicked now. 'If I wasn't, would I be in trouble?' But he doesn't wait for an answer. Instead, he hangs up. Shit.

I call again but it goes to voicemail.

And again.

Nothing for it but to call out to Newport Street.

7

Fifty minutes later, I'm in Newport but the address Barry gave in his reference letter is locked up tight. I rap on the window, ring the bell, but there doesn't seem to be anyone in. The sound of dogs barking carries from the back of the property.

'Isabelle's away on a break, pet.' A neat-as-a-pin woman appears around the side of the house, wiping her hands on a towel, which she puts into a small haversack. 'I'm minding her dogs in the meantime. If you want to buy one you'll have to call in a day or two when she gets home.'

I show the woman my ID. 'I'm looking to contact Isabelle, would you have a number for her?'

Betty looks unsure. 'Oh, well, now . . . I'm not . . . How about I dial her for you? I'm not sure now it's quite right to go doling out personal numbers willy-nilly. And she's on a break, had a hard year, so she's had. Maybe you're not a policewoman at all.'

I'm a guard actually, but I don't say it. 'This is important. I need to speak to her son.'

'Is it news you have for him?'

News again? There is nothing to do but to come straight out with it. I'm sure it'll be all over Newport in an hour but it'll be on the TV bulletins anyway. 'I'm a detective from Achill investigating a house fire that happened earlier on today. This house was leased to a Moira Delaney and—'

'Oh.' Betty nods sagely. 'I know all about Moira.'

'You know Moira?'

'Well, I don't know her.' She flushes. 'I don't know why I said that. I don't know Moira at all, but I've heard of her. From Isabelle. She says that . . .' she drops her voice '. . . Barry is besotted with her and stupid over her. Apparently, though, she's a very attractive woman and, as I said to Isabelle, you know men and attractive women and—'

'Moira is missing,' I interrupt, or I could be here all day. 'And a little girl is dead so I need Isabelle's number now.'

Barry, besotted with Moira? Now, that's interesting. Maybe he came and—

'A little girl dead?' Betty pales. 'That's terrible, so it is. Right, right. I'll get it for you.' She pulls a battered mobile phone from the depth of her haversack, locates her contacts and calls out Isabelle's number to me.

A few minutes later I'm back in the car, dialling the woman.

She answers promptly. 'Hello?' She sounds as if she's on a ship somewhere as wind distorts her voice.

'Hello? Isabelle? Isabelle Jones, I'm DS Lucy Golden. Are you the mother of Barry Jones?'

'Yes, yes, do you have news for us?'

I explain what I want and there's a moment's silence afterwards. A strange silence, before she finally says, 'I know Moira is originally from Limerick and that she and her husband were living out Louisburgh way but they've separated. Barry had been helping her out. He might know more. I'll call him.'

While I do like straight talkers and prompt help, I find the fact that she didn't ask one single question about Moira or her little one distinctly odd. Five minutes later, she calls back from not such a windy place with Moira's father's address and her husband's address. 'Her husband's name is Eamon and Barry said he's a prick. Said Moira alleged all sorts about him in the past while. You can talk to Barry about it, if you like, he says, but maybe not now. He's very upset, as you can understand.'

'Indeed. Thank you. Tell him we'll be in touch.' Normally, when people are upset, it's the best time to get to them and, honestly, the fact that he's besotted with her and—

'Any news for me?' she says, just as I'm about to hang up. 'Or my son?' There's a harsh edge to her words.

'I'm not following.'

'No one is following, it seems.'

'What?'

'My son, Guard, was knocked down last January. He's in a wheelchair now. The driver who did it said he just walked out in front of her. Barry is adamant he hadn't drunk that much. Your lot are looking into it.'

Ah. 'I'm sorry to hear that.'

She inhales deeply before releasing it in a shaky breath. 'He'll spend the rest of his life in a wheelchair. He's in rehab in Dublin now.'

So, Barry couldn't have done it, then.

There's no point in saying 'sorry' again. Instead, I flip to a new page in my notebook. 'Where did it happen and how?' Pencil poised, I add, 'I'll see what I can find out for you. There might be nothing but I'll ask and get someone to call you.'

'Fine.' She says it without much hope and her negativity makes me determined to prove her wrong. Bad enough that your son ends up in a wheelchair, but to feel that those who might help don't care is not right. 'He was out in Limerick, drinking with . . .' she pauses '. . . Moira. She'd left her husband and Barry was helping her out, letting her stay with him and that. He's always had a soft spot for her despite the fact that – sorry. Anyway, on the way home this night he got hit by a car. The driver maintains that Barry walked out in front of it - now I ask you? He ended up in hospital, paralysed from the waist down. And Moira, she was hysterical and couldn't remember what happened. But she was *with* him – how could . . . ' She pauses, continues in a steadier voice, 'From what we were told, the car hit him as they were walking back to the flat he rented.'

'I'll chase it down,' I promise, as I pocket my notebook. 'It's not that Barry has been forgotten, it's just this sort of stuff takes time and . . .' I'm trying not to sound like I'm making excuses '. . . there's a lot of shit out there.'

'Thank you.' Most of the anger is gone from her voice now.

'No bother. Take care. And thanks for the information.'

She hangs up.

I ring the incident room co-ordinator, Jim D'arcy, to record the addresses and to task him with getting on to Limerick garda station to dispatch two officers from there to talk to Moira's father.

The poor man has no idea that within the next thirty minutes his whole life will be turned upside down and that it will never right itself.

Now, where in Newport can I grab some breakfast before I head back to the incident room? Just as I'm contemplating whether to go for a full fry or a bowl of porridge, I get a call.

Aw, Christ.

It's Susan, one of the guards on my team.

'Susan?' My stomach rumbles.

'Hi, Lucy, I'm at the hospital and there's a man here saying he's the children's father. I—'

'I'll be right there.'

8

The hospital is a maze and it's a while before I find out where to go. At the nurses' station on the third floor the nurse in charge points me towards a set of automatic doors that lead onto a long corridor. Midway down, I spot Mick, a guard from Ballina, lounging against a wall. He's devouring a Snickers bar.

'I'm looking for Susan?'

He jumps to attention, trying unsuccessfully to shove his chocolate bar into a pocket. 'Hi, Lucy,' he stammers. 'Eh . . . Susan's down there. In the family room.' He lowers his voice, 'An Eamon Delaney turned up saying he was the children's father, demanding to see them and demanding to know what happened. We heard you were the DS on the case so . . .' His voice lowers even more. 'He's doesn't know yet about . . .' He trails off.

'He must be out of his mind. Has an FLO been appointed?'

'There's one on the way now.'

Great.

'Thanks. Now finish that bar before it melts all over your uniform.'

With a rueful air he fishes it out of his pocket. 'It's just I had no breakfast,' he calls after me.

Join the club.

***

I hear Eamon Delaney before I see him. His raised voice leads me towards the family room. I take a moment to listen, trying to ascertain the character of the man, bearing in mind what Barry Jones had to say about him.

'I have a right to know what's going on.' Eamon's accent is from this end of the country. He sounds worried, but there's an edge of aggression too. 'I am the father of those children. And where the hell is Moira?'

'Mr Delaney,' Susan says, with just the right amount of sooth-ing and determination, 'if I could tell you what's happening I would, but I wasn't at the scene. I was told to come here and to refer any enquiries to the detective sergeant on the case. I've done that and she'll be with us shortly.'

'What has a detective sergeant to tell me that you can't? What's going on?'

'As I've said, I've contacted the appropriate people, who will answer all your questions. If you could just—'

'Where are these appropriate people? I don't see anyone. And where are my children?'

I take a breath, then push open the door to the room. My first thought is that Eamon Delaney is not at all what I imagined Moira would go for. She is an extraordinary-looking woman, while he is decidedly average. Average size, average shape, aver-age looks. Dark hair, a pale face but strong arms and legs, encased in jeans and a navy sweatshirt. His hands are calloused, and I'd put a bet on him being a farmer of some sort. Beside him, Susan, tall and lanky, looks positively huge. 'Mr Delaney,' I hold out my hand, 'I'm Detective Sergeant Lucy Golden and I'm sorry for not being here. Please, sit down.'

He shakes my hand, looking a little mollified but not sitting. 'No disrespect, Detective, but I just want to see my children.'

'I'm sure you must be worried sick. If you like I can take you to your little boy now. After that, maybe we can have a chat about what happened.'

'And Ella?'

And here it is. The worst part of this job. The horror of a murder scene is one thing, but looking into the eyes of a parent or family member who has lost a person in violent circumstances is my personal hell. And to tell a parent that their child has died muddies all the joy you might ever have. They say you must detach, do your best in the moment, and move on, but I reckon even robots would have difficulty with that. Not for the first time today, I wish Dan was here. He's as terrible as I am at dealing with things like this, but at least we'd be in it together.

'Well?' he asks, eyebrows raised.

There is no anxiety in his expression. He seems not to have a clue about what has happened. I wish the family liaison officer was here. But the man has waited long enough. I can't make him wait any longer.

'Please, Mr Delaney,' I say, 'I really would prefer if you sat down.'

He hesitates, then sits, looking from Susan to me. 'What's going on?'

'It's about Ella.'

'What about her?'

'How much do you know about what happened?'

'There was a fire, that's all I know. I arrived to bring the children out but the road was blocked off. And I could smell the smoke and one of the journalists told me that the house had burned down and I see it was Moira's house. Then another lad told me that ambulances had come and taken people away. How come I had to hear that off the media?'

'I'm sorry about that. We were trying to find the next of kin to let you know.'

'Next of kin? Why didn't Moira give you details?'

'Unfortunately we can't locate her at present.'

'What do you mean you can't locate her? Is she not with the children?'

'No.'

He shakes his head, murmurs something.

'Pardon?'

'Nothing. Just . . . Well, that's typical of her. Typical. Can I see my children, please?'

Behind him, Susan tenses. Waiting for whatever is to come.

'You can see Bren. He's fine. Shock and a little smoke inhalation, I'm told.' He leans forward on the chair, his eyes pinned on me. 'We found the body of a female child of similar age to Ella and we believe it may be her.'

Eamon blinks, like I've punched him. Expressions flit across his face. Disbelief, denial, anger. 'You believe?' he says.

'We need to do a formal identification using DNA but it's almost certain. I'm so sorry.'

He gawks at me. 'I . . . I . . .' The words won't come. 'Oh, Jesus Christ, oh, fuck. Oh, Jesus.' And then he buries his head in his hands. 'Fuck. Fuck.'

Behind him, Susan catches my eye and winces, frowns. I don't react, not yet. 'I'm so sorry.'

His shoulders shake and he rocks back and forwards. Then he peers up at me. 'You must have that wrong. Sure, Moira must have her. Where's Moira?'

'Like I said, we don't know yet, and while we do think it's Ella who was in the house, we need to prove it. So, if you'd be open to giving us a sample of your DNA, we can run it against the DNA from the . . . from Ella at her post-mortem.'

'It's not Ella but, yes, yes, take it.' He holds his arm towards me.

'We only need a cheek swab but we don't need to do it now. I can wait—'

'Just do it. Get it all done. I want to see my son.'

'All right, if you're sure.' I get the kit from my bag and explain to him that it might take a few minutes. 'It's easier if I fill out the labels and the evidence envelope first,' I explain. 'Maybe Susan will get you a coffee while you're waiting.'

'Thanks. Americano, no milk and two sugars, please.'

Susan leaves.

By the time I'm done, she has arrived back with the coffee, which he sips.

I ask Susan to bring us to Bren.

She leads us back up the corridor to where Mick is thankfully standing up straight rather than leaning against the wall. 'Just in there, Mr Delaney,' Susan says, in her soft voice. 'Now the doctor said . . .'

He doesn't wait to hear what the doctor said. He has the door open and, in two strides, he reaches the side of his son's bed. I observe them. I motion Susan to stay with me.

'Brennie!' There is no mistaking the emotion in his voice. 'Aw, baby boy, how are you?' He sits on the bed beside his little son and scoops him into his arms, kissing his head and holding him tight.

Bren immediately bursts into tears, his body shaking. He reminds me of Sirocco, the high childish cry.

Eamon rocks him, whispering that it's all right, that Daddy is here, that he'll be all right now.

I move out of the room, shutting the door quietly behind me.

Through the pane of glass, I observe the way he's cuddling that little boy and how the child is clinging to him, and I feel in my gut that it's real and true and genuine.

But he's off.

He's definitely off.

9

I tell Mick to get Eamon Delaney's contact details from him before he leaves and then, with Susan in tow, I head for the canteen to grab some breakfast. She's hungry too and we both order a full Irish. Finding a quiet table, right at the back, I ask Susan for a blow-by-blow account of her morning.

Kev had called her at six and asked her to be part of the team. 'I'm a specialist victim interviewer,' she explains, 'though, thankfully, I haven't had a lot of cause to use my training, but William knew and told me to come here. And because I came, Mick was sent as well. I haven't talked to Bren yet but, hopefully, when he gets discharged, I'll visit him at home and get to know him.'

'Who's partnering you on it?' There are always two guards assigned to these cases and I don't think Mick has any training in it.

'I'm not sure yet.'

'I used to do it.' I don't mention that it had been my one big failure. The case, which is still open, involved the disappearance of two children from outside their houses. There was no link between them other than that they looked alike. A third child had almost been taken but he had somehow escaped. He was so traumatised that I couldn't get anything out of him. I still call the family once a year to see if he remembers anything. He's a teenager now.

'Did you?' Susan concentrates on cutting the fat off her rasher.

I suppress a chuckle at her lack of enthusiasm. 'Don't worry, I'm not asking to partner you.'

'Oh, I don't mind.' She flushes to the tips of her ears. 'I wouldn't mind at all.'

'Well, you should. You have to be able to call things as you see them and having me breathing down your back wouldn't be productive.' That's why two guards are usually assigned to do the job: neither can outrank the other.

'All right, I would have minded,' Susan admits sheepishly, as she chews the last of her rasher.

I wait for a moment before asking her to tell me about Eamon's arrival.

'He came to the hospital about thirty minutes before you.'

'And what did you make of him?'

She shoots me a sharp look. 'Anxious, a bit aggressive, but that's understandable, and yet . . .'

I sit back and crunch my toast while she ponders what to say. I wonder if she thought what I thought. If Dan was here, he'd have jumped on it, but Dan has years of experience over Susan. Still, she's a good guard, tries hard, and will probably be appointed detective garda one day.

'He didn't . . .' she frowns '. . . he didn't convince me.'

'As in?' I put down my toast.

'Well, my mother, years ago, was killed in a hit-and-run. I told you that before, didn't I?'

'Yes.'

'And when it happened, I remember the guard calling to our door and telling us the news.' She crinkles up her brow. 'And I remember not really being able to take it in. You know, like it wasn't real. Or that I was in a dream. And I remember looking at my dad and he just stood really still, like, you know, like a tree that's been chopped down but sort of waits a moment before it topples.'

She has a way with words, I think.

'And there was this silence, and the guard was looking at us, and then my sister started to cry, just softly, like it was seeping into her, this awful thing.'

'Yes.' And that's a 'Yes, you've got it'.

'Well, when you told Eamon that his little girl was . . . gone, I mean, that's - that's the worst news ever, isn't it? And I know he took that second but . . .' she thinks '. . . it was more . . . well, it was more about *him*, wasn't it? And that "fuck" and "Christ" . . . I think it was weird.'

I play Devil's advocate. 'Everyone reacts differently to news like that, though, don't they?'

'Maybe after a while, but in the moment?' Susan shrugs. 'A sudden death like that? A child? I don't think so.'

I'd had the same thought. Because normally when you tell someone that a loved one has died, it's followed by quietness, disbelief, a terrible sudden shot of sorrow. And while he was certainly shocked, it wasn't the type of shock I've witnessed from other people hearing that news.

But what does it mean?

I observe my fried egg as the yolk runs all over my plate. 'He does love that little boy.'

'And that little boy loves him,' Susan says.

47

'Anything else?'

'No, that was it.' Then, 'Why? Was there anything else?'

'Nah.' I'll run it by Dan. 'What you said is spot on. I thought the same.'

She pokes at her sausage. 'Do you want that? I haven't touched it.'

I probably shouldn't, but I take it anyway, telling myself I don't know when I'll eat again.

'It's great that Kev got appointed detective, isn't it?' Susan comments, after a moment. 'I was so jealous when I heard, but he deserves it.'

'Your chance will come. And that was a really good spot today.'

She beams with pleasure. 'Thanks.'

In silence, I polish off the last of the breakfast. Just as I'm draining the pot of tea, Dan rings.

Susan hops up and bids me a quick 'Goodbye.'

Dan's cheery voice from the other end is like a warm blanket. 'Don't go solving that new case without me,' is the first thing he says. 'I'll be back tomorrow now. I look like I've done ten rounds with Katie Taylor, but it's good for the image. So, what's been happening? There was a fire, they said on the news.'

I fill him in, starting from the beginning, and when I relay to him about Eamon Delaney and his reactions in the aftermath of hearing about his daughter's death, he gets it.

'He's just been told his daughter died and he's able to order a coffee?' he says.

'Americano, no milk and two sugars.'

Dan blows air out of his mouth and I can picture him at the other end, lying in a bed, his notebook open in front of him. 'This guy I want to meet.'

'We'll go tomorrow, when you get back,' I promise. 'We've conference at ten. Tonight, though, I've to accompany the Cig to the press briefing.'

'I shall look out for you on the news.' He chuckles, knowing full well how I hate being on TV. 'I hope William will be kind and put you right at the front.'

'Get lost.'

Another laugh as he hangs up.

10

At six that evening, William, Susan, a new uniformed guard, whom I don't know and who hasn't been introduced to me, and I are assembled just beyond the cordon. The media, with microphones aloft and cameras ready to roll, are gathered in a semi-circle about us. I recognise a few faces, mainly the reporters from the national stations. Stacy, the journalist who used to work on the local paper, is here too. She's a small, squat girl in her mid-twenties with the frizziest off-blonde hair and an impressive ability to ignore instructions to 'ring the garda press office', preferring instead to stalk members of the force. She's even bagged a member of our team, Matt, and they're getting married later this year. In fact, no doubt Matt will be on the team this time because William is obsessed with keeping investigations close so that future court cases will not be jeopardised by leaks or ill-advised pictures. Matt works in the Achill station, though, so I'm sure he'll be beavering away on the fringes.

'Hey, you.' Stacy has spotted William. 'Are you having my Mattie on your team this time?'

William, not used to being addressed as 'hey, you', turns towards her, places her and eyes her up and down in silence, just enough to make her start shuffling from foot to foot. 'Miss Stacy McCann,' he says. 'As you know, I'm not here to discuss the workings of my department.' Then, dismissing her as only he can, he turns to us. 'Right, you three, let's get this done. Lucy, stand to my right.' I do as I'm told and watch as the new guard places himself to William's left and leaves Susan blocked by William. She gives the new guy a glare but he's oblivious. He's an ambitious little fecker, I think, but Susan needs to grow a pair if she's not happy.

'Who the hell is he?' I whisper to her, as William calls the press to attention.

Susan shakes her head, so I don't pursue it.

The noise of the waiting media simmers down as William begins to speak. He talks a little about the fire, saying there has been a fatality but as yet we have no ID. Then, showing them a picture of Moira, he stresses that we're anxious to trace her and that if anyone has any information to call a confidential phone number or indeed the station in Achill. He finishes, 'We can take no questions at this time. Thank you all.'

As they shout after us, William turns to me. 'You had tea yet?'

When does he think I had time for tea? 'No.'

'Grand. Meet me back in the Wanderer. We can get food in there.'

It's just the two of us in the incredibly bleak pub William frequents. Well, us and the elderly, morose barman, Dickie, so-called because he wears a dickie bow. Two glasses of Club Orange are plonked in front of us, along with two sad-looking cheese sandwiches and two packets of salt and vinegar crisps. I can think of nicer places to eat but I daren't suggest it. The pub smells of damp and old dried beer.

The barman, who just smells, holds out his hand. 'Ye can pay now.'

William fumbles in his pocket and pulls out a twenty. 'Keep the change, George.'

George, without even thanking him, shuffles back up the room.

'That's his real name?'

'Yeah.' William sounds surprised that I don't know this. 'Nice guy.' He clinks his glass against mine. 'Cheers.' In three thirsty gulps, he drains his orange and picks up his sandwich. It bends.

Jesus.

Then, instead of asking me about the case, which I thought he would, he says, 'That new guard with Susan tonight. His name is Louis Devine and he's been foisted on us.' A pause as he waits.

Finally the penny drops. 'Devine?'

'Devine,' he confirms.

'As in DCS Devine?'

'Yes.'

'You're joking.'

'I wish I was.' He huffs out a sigh. 'I initially said I had no space for him but who believes that?'

There is always space for an extra body on a team.

'And then Pat goes AWOL.'

'AWOL? Pat?'

'Yeah.' He takes a bite of the sandwich, chews, says, 'PTSD.'

'Aw, no.'

'Aw, no, is right. Now we're stuck with Louis.'

'I meant my "Aw, no" about Pat.' He knows fine well I did but he's uncomfortable with the whole conversation. A lot of guards, in the course of the job, see traumatic things or experience shocking events and most of them bury it deep and push it away. But some people find it hard. And no one ever talks about it, not really. In fact, a lot of the guys who suffer get ostracised because no one on the force wants to look at the poor fecker and think that one day it could be them. 'When did this happen?'

'About two months after the last case we were on, the Sandra Moran one.'

'He handled that well. And he was doing mostly orders and paperwork.'

'That's why Pat does that job, Lucy.' William pops the last bit of his sandwich into his mouth. 'Oh, he's great at it but I never send him out because . . . well . . . he'd been off before with mental-health problems.' He taps his nose. 'That's between you and me.'

'Sure.'

Steady, determined, reliable Pat, who could fire off orders for bank accounts and phone records without blinking, who knew the legalities inside out. Pat who was easy to overlook in an investigation but whom you missed like hell if he wasn't around. He was a good guard, always went above and beyond. We can't afford to lose him, I think.

'So, anyway,' William interrupts my thoughts, 'Mick is doing Pat's job now, he's got a bit of a brain for that sort of thing, and Devine will be with Susan.' He pauses. 'He is a complete and absolute arse-licker.'

I grin. 'Why have you put him with Susan? She looked miserable.'

'She needs to assert herself, and he'll help with that. And they both have training in specialist victim interviewing. It's how Devine senior was able to shoehorn him into the investigation.' He starts on the crisps.

I open mine too. There is no way I'm eating any food prepared in this place.

'Just between us,' William lowers his voice, 'his dad is an absolute bollox. He started in Templemore same time as I did and he would have crawled over the corpse of his granny to go places. Keep an eye on the young fella, just in case he's planning on being like his old man. If he steps out of line at all, you let me know.' He glances at his watch. 'Right, I'd better get on.' He pushes his chair back and stands up. He turns to leave, turns back. 'I'm only going to ask this once more, Lucy, and that'll be an end to it, but are you all right to take the case on?'

I glance up at him. It's me should be asking him. He's the one whose whole family was wiped out in a fire, but I wouldn't have the nerve. 'I'm all right.' The way I say it comes out all wrong. I stress the 'I'.

I see a small tic start at the corner of his mouth. But he gives a curt nod. 'Good, because we don't need to lose another member of the team.'

He strides out, the door slamming behind him.

I wait five minutes before I leave too.

Eamon

Incident 1: Mothers

Eight years old, knobbly-kneed and skinny as a greyhound, standing in the rain outside the school waiting on her to show up. All his pals waving at him as they are driven away by their mammies and daddies and him, standing like a fool, like an abandoned dog, and the weather getting worse.

And he won't take shelter because when she comes eventually she'll feel bad for letting him wait and she'll maybe buy him an ice-cream or a hot chocolate.

Only she must have forgotten about him, he thinks a while later, because it's getting dark. But he doesn't know the way home all by himself. Brother Colum comes out of the school and sees him. 'You've been waiting here all this time.' Brother Colum isn't happy about it. 'And you never thought to come in and we could ring your mammy?'

That's when his tears come, big gulping tears that he'd tried to hide.

'Now, now, no need for all that,' Brother Colum says, pushing him along in front of him. 'I'll call your mammy, and if she doesn't pick up, we'll try your daddy.'

But his mammy didn't answer and his daddy must have been tending the animals or else he's drinking his sleepy tea. So Brother Colum had to drive him home himself and he was cross about it. When they pull up at the driveway to the farmhouse, he opens his car door and says, 'Out you get, and tell your mammy not to forget about you tomorrow.'

Off he drives, water splashing up on the back of his car.

And he and his sister Patti, who had been left alone at her school, had to sit in the porch of the house until his daddy finds them. And then his daddy reads a note that is left on the table and he cries and tells them that Mammy is gone, that she has run off and left them behind, and that it is just the three of them from now on.

From then, he has to walk home all by himself along the roads his mammy told him never to walk.

And no talking about her either.

55

***

Moira. Years later. He used to watch her with the children, so he did, how she minded them, how she read to them at night, and feel a rage, so deep and so red, a jealousy so green that he wanted to smash them all up.

But he wanted it too, he knew that in some deep part of him, and now as he lies there, bleeding out, he wonders why he never asked for it. Why he never became a part of it, why he stood apart, why he spoiled it.

How did some girl from the arsehole of nowhere, from the cesspit of Limerick, learn to become such a good mother?

Why did he never tell her he longed to be a part of it all too?

Rejection: the word comes unbidden.

And he shudders.

11

Sleep fails to find me that night. For one thing, the thought of all my dead ex-husband's stuff sitting just outside my door freaks me out a tiny bit. His whole life in boxes in my hallway, just waiting for my son to unpack them. And as he does so, bits and pieces of Rob will introduce themselves to Luc. I'm not sure I like the idea of that.

Rain hits the window.

I think of William and of what he told me the day we buried Rob.

And the images of what happened to William play in my head so that I just have to get up and make myself a cuppa. I almost trip over Rob's laptop bag, which sits against the fridge. Inside, there's a state-of-the-art machine that I'd say Rob spent a pile of money on. Luc is hoping to locate the password for it by the time he sorts through everything. For lack of anything better to do, I pull out the laptop and flick it on. The screen lights up asking me for the password.

I know Rob will have picked a code that means something to him.

I try everything I can think of but nothing works. Names, dates, old addresses, new addresses.

I flirt with the idea of asking Dan to take a look; he's good with stuff like that, but asking him makes me uneasy. I don't know why. *Because this is Rob's laptop.* The thought slithers into my head. Yes, because this is bloody Rob and leopards don't change their spots.

I must fall asleep because I'm woken some hours later by the blare of the alarm.

Driving to work, the news on every radio station is full of the house fire and speculation on whether the body found is that of Ella and, if so, where is her mother? On *Newstalk*, they chat to some locals and I recognise a few voices giving their twopence-worth. The presenters wonder if Moira abandoned her children and, if so, what must have been going through her mind. Other tragic fires are thrown into the mix. The one sure thing is that Moira Delaney will be one of the most famous people in Ireland today.

Just before I enter the conference room, a number I don't recognise calls me.

'Hello, this is DS Lucy Golden.'

'This is Nick Flannery.'

'I'm sorry . . . who?' The only Nick Flannery I know is gang-land and I would never have had dealings with him.

'Moira Delaney's father.'

I wonder how he got my number. That's so weird. But it's overtaken by my sympathy for the man. 'I'm so sorry for your loss, Mr Flannery. We're doing all we can to locate Moira and find out what happened to Ella.'

'Good,' he says, and hangs up.

Weird.

By conference the rain, which began last night, is pouring down in earnest. Soaked guards and detectives arrive in, hair plastered to skulls, coats heavy with damp. The air in the room begins to steam. The chat rises. The NBCI, our hot-shot national detective unit, have sent a team down but, once they keep out of my way, I don't care. Over the years, I've learned that, like me, many guards are obsessed with crime, with the myriad ways in which people are cruel to each other. It fascinates and repels us all at once.

Kev has done a good job getting the room ready. He's found a picture of Moira, Ella and Bren together, and the image of the smiling trio is projected onto the white screen at the top of the room. In plain clothes for the first time, he's having a bit of a laugh with Larry, our CCTV specialist. Kev, who can't be more than twenty-seven, has been a guard on Achill since he graduated Templemore, and last year, after being run ragged as a 'buckshee' detective, he was appointed detective or DO. 'Buckshee' means 'for free' and buckshees work long hours to prove themselves. It's a rite of passage and quite arseholey if you ask me, but, honestly, that's men for you. This whole force drips with testosterone and machoism, and for years I worked hard to fit in, but I know I never will and I'm fine with that – mostly.

I find a spot near the top of the room and lean against the wall. There's not enough space in here for the conference table that you'd have in the bigger districts. Instead we all just have to cram in as best we can. William is at the top of the room chatting to Jim, who I guess has been appointed incident room co-ordinator or IRC for short. Though I've worked three cases with Jim in charge,

I don't know him that well. But I do know he's brilliant at running an incident room: his attention to detail is meticulous, which is what you need for the job. Across from me, Susan is talking to Mick and it looks, from my vantage point, as if she's having a good bitch about Louis because she keeps shooting grumpy looks in his direction. Oblivious, Louis is chatting to Ben. I'm not sure Ben has been informed of who Louis is because his body language is easy and relaxed. If he knew that the young fella was DCS Devine's son, he'd be as wary as hell. At the door, Matt stands miserably, looking into the melee like a hungry dog barred from a butcher's shop. I know he'd never leak information from an investigation, but the problem is, if there was a leak, he'd be the first one suspected. Still, if he's resourceful, he'll find a way to insert himself.

'Hey, dreamer.' Dan has arrived unnoticed and positions himself beside me at the wall. 'You look . . .' he cocks his head to the side '. . . pensive.'

'I prefer deep and interesting,' I quip. Then I take in the full horror of his concussed face. 'Holy Jesus.'

'Yeah. Right.' He manages a grin, though it looks painful. 'I reckon most people will think I got it apprehending a violent suspect, so it's all good.'

'Let's hope by the end of this week, we'll have someone apprehended too.'

Dan spots Louis. 'Who's the youngster slobbering all over Ben?'

I give him the low-down and he whistles. 'We'll keep him at a distance.'

'He'll be dealing mainly with the boy, Bren, so hopefully he'll be well out of our way.'

'All right, everyone.' William's voice rises over the hubbub, silencing us all. 'Let's get the ball rolling.' He indicates the picture on the whiteboard. 'A few words on the case. Yesterday at around six a.m., officers and firefighters attended a blaze at a house in Slievemore. In the course of extinguishing the fire, they rescued a young boy, Brendan Delaney, from a front upstairs room. The boy is four years old and doing well. He's due to be discharged from hospital and into the care of his father, Eamon Delaney, later today. Susan Blake and Louis Devine will be having a clarification meeting with him and we hope to interview him as soon as he's ready. Unfortunately, there was a fatality. We have not identified the IP yet but it is believed to be the older sister of Brendan. Ella Delaney. This little girl here.' He points to the picture of Ella, who wears a pair of blue shorts and a GAA jersey. Her hair is tied back in a ponytail, and she wears a little unicorn necklace. She's got muck all over her shirt and she looks happy. Happier than she did in the Instagram pictures. 'Ella Delaney. Six years old.'

There's a shift in the room. There always is when a child is involved. A murmuring of disquiet.

William continues, 'We have secured DNA from the girl's father and grandparent and, hopefully, she will be identified today. The parents of Ella and Bren are separated and, according to the landlords of the property, it was just Moira, Bren and Ella living in the house in Slievemore. The children's mother,' he points to Moira, 'is missing. Her car is also missing. We have an alert out on that. We have appealed to the public to keep an eye out for Moira and she will be treated as a missing person until we have evidence to say otherwise. Quite a lot of blood was found outside the front door of the property and samples of that are being fast-tracked for DNA.' He presses a button and an image of the gutted house appears onscreen. 'This is the house.

As you can see, the upper floor isn't as badly damaged. The fire officer at the scene is certain therefore that the fire started here.' A picture of the burned-out kitchen. 'The scene was examined in detail yesterday and the fire officer observed three circular patterns in the vicinity of the kitchen.' A picture of the patterns appears onscreen. 'One, quite horribly, was observed on the IP.'

More murmuring.

'These circular patterns,' William continues, 'give us an indication that liquid accelerant must have been poured and that it pooled in these areas. The kitchen is the only place that these patterns were observed. This was a deliberate act. According to the fire officer, the fire was started in the kitchen. Within a tight timeframe it moved from there into the hall and then to the front room. One thing of note is that the glass from the back door was found inside the kitchen and not outside as you'd expect if blown out by the force of the fire. This leads us to suspect that whoever set the fire broke in through the back door by smashing a window, poured diesel or another accelerant in the kitchen and, after lighting the fire, made an escape through the front door, which was ajar when the fire service arrived.'

A half-melted metal cigarette lighter appears onscreen. 'SOCO found this. It was passed on to the lab and we hope, despite the damage done, to extract DNA or fingerprints from it. A number of items from the children's bedrooms were also recovered and are being tested for DNA to see if they are a match for Ella. As you can see, folks, it's looking likely that the fire was deliberate. A child was killed. It is unlikely that the child set the place on fire so we are fairly certain we have a murder or manslaughter on our hands. The PM will take place today, right after conference and I'll be going along with Garda Louis Devine.'

I glance towards Louis, wanting to laugh at how mean William is yet feeling a bit sorry for the eager beaver. However, he looks thrilled. I think he's seeing it as an opportunity to impress William, which, in fairness, it might be.

'Most of yesterday was taken up with trying to locate Moira, the mother of the children. While no sighting of her has as yet been verified, we managed to inform her father and ex-husband about her disappearance and the fire. In a preliminary interview, her father said that, though he knew Moira had left Eamon, he was under the impression they were sorting things out. He likes Eamon and was unaware of any major issues in the relationship other than that Eamon was a workaholic. Moira had come to stay with him over Christmas but had left soon after to move in with a friend. He says she appeared to be in good form. He hasn't been to her house in Achill.' William pauses, and people look up. 'Moira Delaney is the daughter of Nick Flannery. *The* Nick Flannery.'

That drops into the room like a nuclear bomb.

I am shaken.

Shit.

'Nick Flannery, as most of you are aware, is well known to the authorities. Though he's never been convicted, many of his associates have spent time in prison. Nick Flannery is our number-one suspect in three murders, along with several high-profile robberies. Detectives in Limerick are investigating if this arson is gang-related and I'll have more on that in the coming days. Word on the street is that Moira was his princess. They were quite close. DS Lucy Golden and Detective Dan Brown will talk to Mr Eamon Delaney, Moira's ex-husband, later today. He has provided us with DNA in order to establish the identity of the young girl found in the house. Lucy?' William looks to me.

I take my place at the top of the room. A sea of faces stares back. Most of them know who I am because I was plastered over the papers last year when my house got broken into by an informant I used to run. I push the whole sorry mess out of my head and attempt to give them a succinct run-down of what I learned yesterday. After I do, I continue, 'Someone set the fire. That's not in doubt. What's in doubt is who did it and why. Was this child murdered and the fire set to cover up a crime or was she just unlucky not to be saved?'

I press a button on my laptop and the picture of the burned body of the little girl is displayed on the screen. I see hardened detectives avert their eyes. Louis Devine, however, seems to drink it in. 'Several points of interest did arise. A Mr Johnny Egan, who lives at the next house down from the fire, reports seeing, and I quote, "a big physically strong man" at Moira's house on June the second. Her husband could not be described as such. It may be her father, though according to William just now, he states he was never at her house in Achill. If it wasn't him, we need to identify this man. Second, Mr Denis Long saw a medium-sized dark-haired man at the house a couple of weeks ago. We need to identify him. That may have been Eamon, Moira's estranged husband. He indicated to us that Moira leaving the children alone was not surprising. Denis Long did confirm that he had seen Moira on the beach in the early mornings without her children. We need to find out for sure what her relationship was with her children. Thanks.'

I step down and William starts to assign the jobs. 'Lucy and Dan, you're on Eamon Delaney. Find out his movements the night of the fire and see if you can get a read on his relationship with Moira. You said in a report you filed, Lucy, that someone called him a prick?'

'That was Barry Jones, a friend of Moira, Cig, and I only have it second-hand. He's in Dublin, at the Central Remedial Clinic. He had an accident four months back.'

'Right. We'll wait and see what develops here first. We don't have the resources for you to go haring off to Dublin. As well as Eamon, talk to the landlords, particularly to Denis - he seemed to know quite a bit about Moira. He might be able to offer something else.'

'Sure.'

'Larry, start harvesting any CCTV you can find from near the scene on the day in question and the day preceding it. We've put a call out for dash cam. We're looking, in particular, for Moira's car.'

'I love an Achill murder,' Larry says, rubbing his hands. 'The potential for no CCTV is always a turn-on.'

'Doesn't take much, eh, Lar?' Ben jokes.

There are a few chuckles but Larry has a point. This place is a CCTV black spot, an ideal place for a killing. Something always comes up, though. No crime is ever perfect.

'Kev,' William says, 'I want ye to talk to Johnny Egan. He lives up beside Moira's property. He reported the fire and he also had sighting of a large man at the property in the last few weeks. See if we can get a more detailed description from him.'

Kev is thrilled. It's a bit of a step up for him.

'Mick, we need to try to access Moira's phone records and any bank accounts. Draw up the orders. Get on it.'

'Sure thing.'

'Susan and Louis, hop out to introduce yourselves to Eamon, once Lucy and Dan have talked to him. Get his consent to interview his son. Ben, can you chat to the teachers in Ella's school? And the rest of you on door-to-door.' He outlines the areas he wants covered. 'Jordy, can you co-ordinate that? I want ye to find out all about Moira. I want to know who went in and out of that house, who she was ever seen with. I want to know how she got on with her children. For now, finding Moira is our priority because locating her will unlock this case. Ger?'

'Yes?'

I hadn't spotted Ger up to now. He must have come in late, because he's right at the back. Lucky William never noticed.

'Never be late for conference again.'

'Sorry, Cig.'

'Tic-tac with Forensics, would you? Keep them on their toes.'

'Sure.'

'Anything come on after the appeal for information yesterday?'

'Very little,' Jordy answers. 'A lot of nonsense, though obviously we'll check it all out.'

'Let's not investigate the call about her being forged in the fires of hell and blazing her way back there,' Mick says, to a burst of laughter.

'Sounds like a very personal thing to say.' William cuts the mirth. 'Who rang that in?'

I feel sorry for Mick; he rarely makes a joke about anything, mostly being too terrified of the Cig to try it, and the one time he does . . .

'I'll see if I can find out, Cig,' he says, going bright red.

'Good,' William says. 'Right, everyone. Jim will hand you out the job sheets. Don't forget to return them when the job is done.' He searches for Louis, beckons him. 'Let's go.'

He strides down the room, everyone making way for him as Louis, his jacket on his arm, hurries along behind him, like a butler.

The place starts to empty.

***

While I'm waiting on Dan to collect the job sheets, I take the oppor-tunity to call Pat. He's been on my mind and I don't want him to think we've all forgotten him just because he's not in work. There is no answer so I leave a message that I'll call in on him one day next week if that's all right. 'Text me if you want me to stay away,' I finish. Then add, 'And hope you're well.' Then realise that, of course, he's not, so I add, 'Well, as in, you know, physically and . . .' and stop. 'Damn, I'm making a mess of this. I'll see you next week.'

Within minutes, an answer by text. *Away next week. Day after tomorrow?*

I text back, *You're on.*

Dan and I make our way downstairs to the car park where we pick up a DDU car. As usual, the district detective unit cars are a bit shit, but they're fitted with the essential bells and whistles of the job. Dan slides into the passenger seat. 'Eamon first?'

'Yes. We want to be out of there by the time Susan and Louis show up.'

'Where's he live?'

I glance at the job sheet. 'Louisburgh. Let me question him, Dan, you observe him. He's . . .' I can't put my finger on it. 'You'll see,' I say.

'Can't wait. Do you think the mother is really missing?'

'I don't know.' I pull out of the station and onto the road. 'She might have hurt her little girl and panicked and set the house alight. Until we learn a bit more, we can't rule it out. Mothers have killed their children before.'

'Yes, but they never leave one alive.'

It's a fair point and it gives me the chills.

12

Louisburgh is a typical Irish town, big broad streets culminating in a square. A lot of them can be dour places, grey buildings and run-down shops, but Louisburgh has a buzz about it. It's picturesque, and as we drive through, memories of my childhood tumble about in my head. There were the rare days when we'd leave the strands of Achill and my father would drive me and my mother out to Carrowmore Beach. I was young but I remember the dazzle of sun on sand. We'd set out the rug and the windbreaker and eat our sandwiches and splash in the waves, and I would marvel at the wildlife to be found in the grasslands that surrounded the place. Today, though, with the heavy rain and the glowering skyline and the wildness of the blanket bogs, the town looks haunted and desolate.

We drive through and out the other side to where Eamon Delaney lives, a farmhouse just beyond the GAA club, on the road to Roonagh pier. While it's out on its own, it's still close to the main road. The driveway is well maintained with a semi-manicured hedge lining the route. Beyond the house are barns and fields and I spot some cattle grazing. Coasting to a stop beside an old blue Land Rover, Dan and I jump out, pulling up the hoods of our jackets as we head to the front door. The smell of farm assails our nostrils.

'Jaysus.' Dan covers his nose.

'You can take the boy out of the city but not the city out of the boy,' I tease, as I ring the bell.

'I might just vomit.' He pulls an anguished face. 'What *is* that?'

'Not silage anyway, it's too early.' Dan gawks at me as if I've just spoken another language. 'My mother was of farming stock,' I explain.

He's about to reply when the door is opened by Phil, an FLO we know from other cases. When we ask for Eamon, she tells us, her voice low, 'He's out in the yard talking to Nick Flannery. You know who that is, right?'

Dan flashes me a look. This we hadn't expected. Without speaking, we take ourselves around the back of the house to the concrete square of yard, enclosed on three sides by farm buildings. It's incredibly clean, as if washed down regularly. The murmur of voices leads us towards one of the buildings.

We enter without announcing ourselves and two men turn towards us. Eamon and Nick, who have a look of each other: dark-haired and sallow-skinned. Eamon is smaller, though, and while he wears dirty work clothes, Nick is attired in an expensive-looking pair of jeans and a rain jacket that I know would cost me a month's wages. For a moment there is silence as the four of us regard each other. I break it. 'Nice to see you again, Eamon. This is my colleague Detective Dan Brown. We'd like a few words with you, if you don't mind.' I turn to Nick. 'And you're Mr Flannery, I believe.'

His dark eyes study me and Dan from top to toe. He knows

we know who he is, but he plays along. 'Yes.' His gaze lands on Dan's face.

'Not as bad as it looks,' Dan says cheerily, then follows it with 'I'm sorry for your loss.' That's aimed at them both.

Nick winces. 'Ella was a princess, like her mother.' His accent is the same as the Cig's, which is disconcerting. He crosses to us, gets a little in my face. 'My daughter did not abandon her children. I'd like that noted. I was just saying to Eamon what a devoted mother she is.'

'She is,' Eamon agrees.

That's not what he said yesterday.

Without moving away from Nick, whose breath is close enough for me to inhale, I say, 'As you both know, we're trying our best to locate her and establish what happened. We came to talk to you, Eamon, but,' I gesture to Nick, 'we could do with chatting to you too.'

'I said all I'm going to say to those other guards who came knocking yesterday. I have nothing to add. I don't, as a rule, engage with your lot.'

'Don't you want us to find your daughter, then?' Dan poses the question casually, but the air suddenly sings with tension.

'I'll find her, don't worry. I have my ways and you have yours.'

Behind him, Eamon shudders.

'I would advise you to leave it to us.' My tone is firm. 'We know what we're doing.'

'So do I.'

'Mr Flannery—'

'Nick, please.'

'Mr Flannery, if you do anything you shouldn't and you're arrested, do you think that will help your grandson?'

'I would never do anything to get myself arrested, Detective,' he says, with a smirk, then bids us all goodbye and walks out.

'Oh, God.' Eamon wilts as Nick's footsteps recede. 'Do you know who that was?' In a low voice, he hisses, 'That's Moira's father, Nick Flannery. Fucking psycho.'

'Did he threaten you?'

'No. I've never had a problem with him. But that's not to say I won't if he gets it into his head that I had anything to do with Moira fecking off. Jesus.' He buries his head in his hands. 'As if I'd hurt Ella. Jesus.'

He doesn't say anything about not hurting Moira, though.

'He's off his head,' Eamon goes on, his glance darting towards the door. 'Like he's upset and that. He wants to make someone pay.'

'Is there somewhere we can talk?'

Eamon glances towards the house. 'Bren is inside with my sister and the family liaison officer ye assigned. Things are bad enough without him seeing ye. I don't need him knowing anything too much right now. He's asking all the time about his mother and sister. Have you any news?'

'Nothing.' I add, as delicately as I can, 'The PM has started on the little one.' I choose my words carefully, trying to mitigate the meaning, but really, there is no nice way to impart such brutal information. 'They'll treat her with the utmost care.'

He doesn't seem to know what to do with that. 'We can talk in here,' he says, after a moment. 'This is Moira's studio. Her private space.'

There are half-finished artworks and tubes of paint all over the place. I see now that the two men had been looking at a picture that's balanced on an easel behind Eamon. It's a large one of the

71

farmyard, though it's a twisted, knotted version, like someone has drawn an image and stirred it all up.

'Nice.' Dan stands in front of it. 'It looks a little like my face.'

Eamon is unsure whether that's a joke or not. Choosing to ignore Dan's comment, he says, 'She's good. Has a bit of a following. She was after getting a grant an' all to paint, so she told me.'

'You were on speaking terms, then?' I throw out the question casually.

'Aye, course we were. Had to be for the children. Sit down.' He gestures to the only two chairs in the studio and, folding his arms, leans back against the wall. The light is dim in here, coming as it does through four oblong windows high above while more light filters through the door. There is a bulb dangling from the ceiling, but Eamon doesn't switch it on. How could Moira paint in this space?

I sit down while Dan joins him at the wall. He pulls out his notebook. 'Just taking a few notes,' he says. 'Procedure.'

'No bother,' Eamon replies.

'There is one other thing we do know.'

Eamon looks at me with interest.

'The fire officer has sent us the preliminary reports and it appears that the fire was started deliberately.'

Eamon blinks. 'Someone burned the house down on purpose?'

'Yes.'

'Someone burned my daughter? On purpose?'

'I'm so sorry.'

'Moira?'

'We don't know.'

He makes a dash from the room and we hear him retching

outside. It's a couple of minutes before he comes back in, wiping his mouth with the cuff of a sleeve.

'All right?' Dan asks.

'I'm sorry . . .' he says. 'I just . . .' His expression cracks and he starts to weep. He rocks back and forwards and the sound lifts to the high ceiling.

Dan and I let him cry. There is nothing we can say anyway.

'Sorry.' He hitches his breath, his sobs subsiding. 'It's . . . I can't get my head around it.'

'I know.' I let a pause develop, then say, 'Are you up to—'

'Fire away.' He waves his arm about.

'Okay. There are two possibilities here. One, if it was Moira did this, we need to find her.' He doesn't object, doesn't say that Moira would never do that. 'And if it wasn't Moira, and she's somehow abducted or hurt, we need to check that too, all right?'

'Of course. Yes. Anything.'

'Assuming for the moment that Moira is missing, when was the last time you saw her?'

'The day before yesterday.' Off our reaction, he says, 'I know it makes me look bad but I called over to bring her something for her art. A brush of some sort. I had coffee, as I'd just driven over an hour to get there. Then I said I'd pick the kids up the next day and . . .' He stops. 'That was it.'

'What kind of form was Moira in?'

'Good. Nothing stands out. She looked well. Honestly, she looked very well.'

'How so?'

'New clothes that I hadn't seen before. Make-up. That sort of thing.' A moment before he says, somewhat cagily, 'She was going for a job interview.'

73

'Where?'

'No idea.'

'You didn't ask?'

'Nope.' There is a trace of annoyance in his voice. I let a pause develop. Hairs are standing up on my arms. It's a prickly feeling I get sometimes and have learned not to ignore. The silence grows and Eamon shifts from one foot to the other. He glances down at his wellies. Then, slowly, he draws his eyes to mine, looks straight at me – and it shoots right through me: he's about to lie. 'It was none of my business.'

You bastard, I think. *You know something.*

'What time was the interview?'

'I was there at three so after that anyway.'

'Was she short of money that she needed to get a job?'

'At the rate she spent it, I'd say yes.'

Ouch. 'Was she receiving any money from you to help with the children?'

'I'm not a man to see my children short, Detective.' There's a definite snarl now.

I let the subject drop. If necessary, we'll get a look into his accounts. 'Is there anyone Moira would run to, if she has fled? Any friend?'

'Moira doesn't make friends too easy.' The comment is totally without sentiment. 'She doesn't want anyone finding out about who her father was. Hard to make friends when you have to lie all the time.'

'She lies all the time?'

A flush. 'About her father, I mean.'

'What about a Barry Jones? We heard he was her friend?'

'That deluded fuck.' He gives a short bark of a laugh. 'He's crazy for her. Stalking her almost. I had to order him from the house one time.' A pause. 'Maybe she's gone to him.'

'Unlikely. He was in an accident a few months back. He's in a wheelchair now.'

'Oh, right.' A quirk of eyebrow. 'Well, Moira would have no use for him, then.'

'Can I be frank, Eamon? It doesn't sound like you're too upset about your wife.'

'She left me,' he says. 'And it's hard to be upset if she . . . well . . . if she did what's after happening.'

He has a point.

'You said not five minutes ago to her father that she was devoted to her children.'

'Her father is a psycho. Of course I agreed with him.'

'So you think she's capable of burning her children alive in a house and then leaving?'

To give him credit, he flinches a little at that, but rallies: 'Unless it was some associate of her father's seeking revenge on him, it has to be Moira. Look, she has no enemies wanting to do her harm because she never mixes with anyone.'

'What about you?'

'I'm a respectable man. People like me around here.'

It's the men who say they are respectable that I've learned to be suspicious of.

'Why did she go looking for employment if she was planning on running away?'

'Maybe she got the job and couldn't do it with the children. Maybe she just wanted a new life.'

'Would it not have been easier to leave the children with you, then?'

75

'It would have, of course, but that's not what she did, is it?'

'We don't know yet what she did,' I say. 'Why did she leave you, Eamon?'

'She said she wasn't happy.' There is a shot of regret amid the anger. 'The life of a farmer's wife wasn't suiting the gangster's princess from Limerick.' A bit of a mirthless laugh. 'She hated the farm.'

I'd imagine that wasn't all she hated. 'Where were you that night?'

'Me? You think I did this? You think I abducted my own wife? You think I—' He can't say it. Instead he answers, 'I was here, where I always am. The farm takes up all my time, more so now Moira is gone, and lambs are being born left, right and centre. I'm on call all through the night with them.'

'Can anyone confirm this?'

'I seriously doubt it. There were no complications, so I didn't need the vet.'

Dan makes a note of it. 'Thanks.'

'No bother.' He looks straight at me.

Is he smiling at me?

Challenging me?

'We'd like the name of Moira's doctor and also the names of any acquaintances Moira might have had as soon as possible.'

'I can do that now. Our doctor is John O'Brien, Louisburgh.' He crosses to a small desk, hidden in the shadow of the corner of the barn. Lifting what looks like a paperweight, he turns it upside down, pulls a small key from underneath it and unlocks the drawers. Rummaging about, he hums and haws before pulling out a couple of loose pages. 'There we go, the Christmas-card list.' He holds the pages towards Dan. 'Not too many names on it.

You may as well have it.'

Dan drops it into a labelled evidence bag.

'I'd better be moving.' Eamon lifts himself from the wall and thumbs towards the yard. 'The cows won't milk themselves. If that's all?' Then hastily, as if caught out doing something he shouldn't, 'Work helps, you know.'

I can't argue with that. I'd thrown myself into work ever since I'd been attacked and seen my ex-husband fight for his life in front of me. 'Just a couple more questions.'

A flash of what might be irritation crosses his face.

'You told us that Moira was dressed up, wearing make-up, on her way to an interview. You also say that the last time you saw Moira you had a coffee with her.'

'I did.'

'Sounds very amicable.'

'It wasn't unamicable.'

'Yet you think she might be responsible for what happened to Ella?'

'The apple doesn't fall far from the tree, so they say.'

'Can you elaborate?'

'She could be her father's daughter, who knows?'

'Her father has never been convicted of anything. Do you have proof that Moira has done anything that—'

'No. But still . . .' He eyeballs me once again, silence stretching.

'What was Moira wearing the last time you saw her?' Dan asks, forcing Eamon to turn around.

'A pair of tight blue jeans, faded, rips in the knees. Heels, not too high, black shoes. And a red top, with no sleeves and a low enough neckline. There was a necklace too, one her mother used to have. Red and black stones. She had her hair up in this messy way on top of her head. A black jacket.' He adds softly, almost bleakly, 'She looked lovely.'

'Thanks. Also, just for your information, two of our colleagues will be calling later to get to know Bren,' Dan says. At Eamon's questioning look, he adds, 'It's procedure. They'll explain it to you. Thanks so much, Eamon, and I'm sorry for your loss.'

He shakes Dan's hand but as he reaches for mine, sudden bile rises to my throat. I'm saved by the peal of my mobile. I turn away to answer it.

'Hiya, Lucy, it's Louis here from the PM. William said to give you a bell.' He sounds incredibly cheery.

'Yes?'

'The little girl, Ella? Well, she was alive when the fire started. Apparently, there was soot in her lungs, which means she was breathing when it got going. However, Palmer thinks there is a chance she may have been unconscious as she had had a blow to her head.'

I'm glad about that.

'Palmer— Jaysus, he's a grumpy arsehole, isn't he?' The question is rhetorical because he goes on, 'He says that Ella might have come into the kitchen, slipped on the accelerant, hit her head and fallen unconscious. Hang on, William's saying something. I'll call you back. Yo! Will.'

Jesus! William will love being addressed like that.

I put my phone away and turn back to face Eamon.

He's looking directly at me. His expression unsettles me. Does he know what I've been told or is he just wondering what I've been told?

It's not good to assume anything in an investigation but I can't silence the alarm bells clanging in my head.

'That was one of the guards at the PM. He says little Ella was unconscious before the fire started.' I don't say she was alive because it's too horrible for anyone to hear.

'That's good.' Eamon speaks after a short pause, sounding genuinely relieved. 'Isn't it? She wasn't trying to get out or scared or that.'

'Uh-huh,' I manage.

I have never felt such a strong urge to march someone down to a garda station in my life. There is just something . . . I can't put my finger on it . . .

'Please find whoever is responsible,' he says. 'I'm begging you.'

'We will do our best.' Dan pockets his notebook. 'You can count on it.'

'Good.' Eamon follows us to the door. 'Thank you both, again.'

I say nothing until we are in the car. 'He's bloody lying,' I say. 'I can feel it.'

13

Dan plays Devil's advocate as we tuck into a couple of sandwiches in a cute little pub just off Mulranny's main street. Despite it being June, a turf fire is blazing away and the smell, so old and ancient, wraps itself around me.

'You can't just go assuming because—'

'Because what? His reactions are all off, Dan, you know it. You'd want to be stupid not to see it. Jesus, I tell him that his daughter is having a PM today and he says nothing, no response. He says he and his wife are on good terms yet he also says it wasn't his business where she was going for a job interview. He basically accused her of being a potential murderer. He evaded the question of whether he was in any way supporting his children, and did you notice that even though he said the studio was Moira's private space, he knew exactly where the key to the desk was? And what a crappy painting studio! Who could paint in there? Artists need light. Something is off with him. I'd say he did it.'

Dan lets the words hang there, until I see how thin they are.

'I know it,' I insist.

'You don't, Luce.' His voice is calm. 'You really don't. Maybe he is a shit husband, maybe he was horrible to her, but that doesn't mean anything. Not yet.'

'His wife is missing, his child is dead,' I say. 'And he seems . . .' I shrug, unable even to think of how he seems.

'He's angry at her for leaving him and you know what? Sometimes it's easier to be angry than to break down. I—'

'So? It's just—'

'Let me finish, would you?' Amusement lights his eyes. 'Jesus, you'd never think you were the senior detective.'

I arch an eyebrow. 'Go on so. It'd better be good.'

'He was genuinely upset about Ella - he did get sick. I could smell it on his breath when he came back in.'

'Thank you for that.'

'You're welcome.' He tips me a cocky salute.

I take a moment to think over my reaction to Eamon. It's hard to convey gut instincts properly. 'I know you're saying he was upset about Ella,' I begin slowly, 'but to me it's more . . .' I frown. I'm missing something, some point that had been made to me and I've missed it. 'Susan said yesterday that his reaction seemed more like guilt and I think she's right.' My voice rises a little and an old man, nursing a pint, glances over in disapproval. I wave an apology.'

'I'm sure he does feel guilty.'

'Yeah, but the guilt is more about him than her, you know?'

Dan is unconvinced. 'There's nothing so queer as folk,' he states. 'When Fran's father died, he never cried. Not once. And you know him.'

That does surprise me. Fran is one of those guys who appears totally grounded. A man unafraid of emotion. He'd adored his dad, apparently. 'Never?'

'Well, months later, when he was doing a cull of his contacts he came across his dad's mobile number.'

'Aw, that's hard.'

'Yeah, he cried then for about fifteen minutes and that was it. So, you know, maybe Eamon will react a bit more normally, just not now.'

I'm tempted to ask Dan if he shed tears when his own dad passed away a few months back but I sense he would have referenced himself in the example if he wanted to talk about that stuff.

'Fran's mother now,' Dan goes on, 'she cried rivers. She's still bloody crying rivers.'

'I sense your empathy with her is wearing thin.'

Dan had initially been delighted that Fran's mother had moved in with them. She was going to be cooking dinners for them and looking after the house, and they were going to keep her company at night. Instead she has rearranged the furniture, changed the garden, made quite a lot of friends, and what was once Dan and Fran's quiet little retreat has morphed into, in Dan's words, 'Pensioner City'.

'Thin? It's gone. See this shirt?' Dan tugs at his usual box-fresh immaculate white shirt. 'I had to bloody buy it new this morning before I came in. She flipping shrank all the washing because she refused to admit she couldn't work out the machine. I told her I would take care of it but no . . . she had to have a go.'

'She probably just wants to feel useful.'

'She doesn't listen. She never stops talking. My head feels like it's going to explode some days. And don't you dare laugh.'

I press my lips together. 'Whenever my mother annoys me, I shall think of you and offer thanks to the Lord.'

'Feck off.'

I give him an affectionate punch. 'Fair play to you all the same.'

'She can't be alone. That's what's wrong with her. And she hates silence.'

One day I'll be an old woman, living in a house in Keem, hoping that Luc will have time to visit and only the sound of the sea and the howling wind for company, battling against the elements as—

'There was one thing he did that was a little off,' Dan admits, breaking into my thoughts.

The vision of my future Peig-like self dissolves like frost in sun as I say cockily, 'I bet I know what it was too.'

He opens his palms as if to give me the floor. 'He knew exactly what she was wearing that last day.'

'Yep. Now maybe he's just observant—'

'Aw, come on.'

'I agree. It was a little detailed for a man who doesn't obsess about his wife.'

'I'm looking for a summer job. Is there anything going?' I'm distracted by the familiar voice. I spot Tani, my son Luc's partner and the mother of my grandchild, leaning against the bar, talking to one of the staff. I've barely seen her since college holidays. I'm about to wave her over when a young man comes up behind her and wraps his arms about her waist before dropping a kiss on her head.

'Jesus.' The hiss pops out before I can stop it.

'What?' Dan jumps. 'All I said was—'

Poor Luc.

'Lucy?' Dan asks. 'What's—'

'Isn't that Luc's girlfriend, Tani?'

Dan goes to turn about.

'Don't.'

'Then how can I see?'

'She's with another fella,' I whisper. 'He's kissing her neck.' I jab my knife at him. 'I'm going to go and ask her what she's playing at. Luc's probably off minding Sirocco and meanwhile there she is—'

'Jesus, sit down!' Dan reaches out and grabs my hand, then twists about. 'Yep, that's her,' he confirms. 'Sit down!'

I try to shake him off. The old man from across the way is having a good gawk. 'Luc doesn't even know. This is dreadful.'

'It's not your business.' Dan won't let me go. 'You don't know the full story. Maybe Luc does. Sit.' He glares at me and reluctantly I do, dipping my head so Tani won't spot me if she glances over.

'If I saw Fran at that carry-on, wouldn't you like me to tell you?' I rub my hand. 'You've a hard grip.'

'Sorry. And if it meant his mother would leave as well, I think I could cope.'

'You don't mean that.'

Up at the counter Tani is handing over her CV. She bids the staff member a cheery goodbye and, arm wrapped firmly about her new man, his hand in her back pocket, they saunter from the pub. I have the evil thought that it'd serve them right if one of them tripped.

'Unbelievable,' I say.

'Not your business.'

'I'll have to tell Luc. Sure everyone is going to know before him if she's flaunting herself around like that.'

'Flaunting herself around.' Dan chortles. 'Where are we? The nineteen fifties?' Then, 'Maybe they broke up and he never told you.'

'I'd know,' I say. My heart is broken for Luc. Dan doesn't have kids so he wouldn't understand the - the sheer primal *fury* I feel at the thought that someone would treat him like that. I should have confronted her but the sane part of me tells me sternly that no good would have come of it. So, instead, I call my mother.

'Don't call your mother.' Dan groans. 'Jesus.' He shoves the rest of his sandwich into his mouth.

'Lucy, hello!' My mother sounds in great form. 'This is a surprise. I'm just reading the paper. That Stacy girl, you know the local journalist, well, isn't she only working for the *Irish Herald* now. She's very good. From what she's written today, I think Moira isn't missing at all, I'd say some fella came and—'

'Tani is seeing someone else.' I jam it in or she'll never stop. 'I just saw her with another fellow.'

'No, you didn't.'

'Yes, I did.' I roll my eyes at Dan, who rolls his back. 'And what's more,' I add, 'she's parading him about like she doesn't even care about Luc.'

'Did you tell Luc?'

'No. I just saw it.'

'Well, then, maybe don't until we find out for sure.'

'I know what I saw.' Honestly, she always does this. Makes out I didn't see what I know I saw. When I was a teenager, I used to tell her that she was negating my reality but she didn't know what I was talking about.

'I'll have a word with Katherine.'

'Katherine isn't going to tell tales on her daughter.'

'Leave it with me,' she says. 'You've enough on your plate. You go and do your job and I know you'll do it brilliantly.'

For some reason I get a lump in my throat. 'Thanks, Mam.'

'Luc will be fine. Don't you worry your head.'

'Thanks.'

'Now, I've got to go. The news is on and I might spot you on the telly. Bye.'

After she disconnects, I try to gather my thoughts, focus back on the case, on Eamon. 'Let's get someone to check Eamon out.' I pop the last bit of what has been a spectacular sandwich into my mouth, though since seeing Tani my appetite has waned. 'And—'

'Your phone is ringing,' Dan says, and I scramble to answer it while swallowing a hunk of bread.

'And get this,' Louis continues the conversation as if he'd never rung off, 'the DNA came back on the little girl at the scene. Eamon isn't her father. But the girl is Ella because when they compared her DNA with items recovered from her bedroom in the house, I think a hair in a hairbrush, it was a match. And also the Cig says to say that, in all likelihood, the blood outside the door may have come from Moira because it's not Ella's but there is a DNA close match to Ella. SOCO are seeing if they can find anything with Moira's DNA for comparison.'

And having delivered the bombshell, he hangs up and leaves us reeling.

14

Lorna has taken a half-day from her part-time job in the local sweetshop to talk to us while Denis has cancelled his trip to Knock. 'He'll be able to claim a refund,' Lorna twitters, as she leads us into her kitchen. 'And I'm just as glad not to be going to work because the weather is dreadful. No one buys sweets in rainy weather. Such rain for June. This way.'

In the kitchen, I try not to meet Dan's eye as he takes in all the hen paraphernalia.

'You like hens?' he asks, as he sits down and takes off his jacket.

'No,' Denis jokes, joining us. 'We fecking hate the things, don't we, Lorna?'

She offers a weak titter in response but the atmosphere I felt yesterday seems to have grown a little edgier. From what I can gather, Denis seems oblivious so it's Lorna who's giving off the vibes. She watches him anxiously as he takes a seat at the table.

'What happened to your face?' Denis asks Dan.

'Think of the worst and then think some more,' Dan deadpans.

Denis doesn't know how to respond to that.

'This place is getting weirder by the day.' Lorna pulls up a chair beside me. 'All the murders and the killings and sure you wouldn't know who to be trusting any more and—'

'That's why she was making me go to Knock,' Denis interrupts. 'A few auld prayers and she thinks it'll set everything right.'

'I know it'll take more than that,' Lorna snaps.

A silence follows, which is filled with discomfort.

Denis eventually breaks it. 'What is it ye need, Lucy?'

Instinct makes the decision for me. This was meant to be an informal chat, nothing heavy, enquiring about how they knew Moira and if they could remember anything at all that might help us. But after yesterday and just now . . . 'We'd like to talk to you both separately, if that's all right?'

If Dan is surprised, he doesn't give it away.

Denis and Lorna don't question it. They probably just think that's how it's done.

'Who first?' Denis asks.

'You maybe?'

'Grand.'

'I'll just . . .' Lorna flaps a hand towards the kitchen door '. . . wait outside, shall I?'

'Yeah. Don't worry, I'll give you a shout when we need you. How about that?'

'Grand. Grand so.' She shoots an unfathomable look at Denis before she leaves, but he doesn't notice. Whatever is going on here, Lorna is the one worrying about it.

I wait until the sound of her footsteps has disappeared before I begin. 'Tell me again everything you remember about Moira, from the moment you met her.'

Denis shifts a little in his chair. Scratches his chin. 'Right. Well, she moved into the house in February last, so only four and a bit months ago. She rang about it, told me she had two children, her daughter was in school and she wanted to keep her near her friends. And she gave us a reference when we met her and she seemed like a lovely woman. Me and Lorna agreed to let the house to her for a trial period of six months. I went up to unlock it and put the fire on for her when she arrived, you know, so it wouldn't be cold for the kiddies. I stayed around and helped her that time because she was on her own. That day, there was a bit of chat. Not much, she was quite private. I gathered she'd left her husband. The kiddies were quiet. The little girl was like a mouse, hiding in the corner, shy but watching everything, God rest her,' he blesses himself, 'and the boy was trying to carry things that were too heavy for him and getting cross when he was told he couldn't. But nice children, you know?' He pauses, remembering, and takes a sup of tea. 'After that, I didn't see her again for about . . .' he screws up his eyes '. . . well, not for a couple of weeks anyway. I went up, just to make sure all was well, and she invited me in. I think she was glad of the company and we got talking and that's when she told me she was an artist and she showed me some of her pictures. She said a lot of her things were back at her old house and that she was arranging to get them brought over but her husband wasn't being too cooperative. I got the feeling from her that things weren't great, you know, but then how would they be? Separations aren't great. Then sure, I didn't see too much of her. I might see her around the beach of a morning. She had a habit of rising early to collect seaweed. And she usually brought the young lad for a milkshake in the Moose coffee shop in Keel after she put the little girl on the school bus. I'd just be passing on the road outside and I'd see her there. Sometimes I'd pop in for a chat and other times I'd wave. And she'd maybe be down around Achill Sound getting the bit of shopping in of a Friday morning. I'd see her there too. We'd chat then but 'twas usually about the weather or *Coronation Street*. She loved *Coronation Street*. I'd see her once a month when she'd be paying her rent. I'd call up for it - she liked to pay in cash. The children were a bit friendlier by then, especially as I'd be bringing sweets for them. Sure, look, she was a lovely girl.'

'You saw her most mornings and chatted on a Friday morning, and then you'd see her once a month?'

'That's right.'

'That's quite a lot.'

To my surprise, he flushes. ''Twas only for a few minutes, mind. Sure, we hardly spoke two words.'

'Did you ever feel she was afraid or threatened in any way?'

'I've been thinking about that since yesterday and at first I thought no, but then I remembered one time. It was when we were watching *Coronation Street* and her phone buzzed and she picked it up and looked at the screen and she sort of jerked and dropped it. I think it was messages or something. I asked her if she was all right and she said she was, but she didn't look all right. She looked scared. Or maybe I'm just thinking that now, after all that's happened.'

'Did she say who it was?'

'No, and it wasn't my place to ask.'

'When was this roughly?'

'I'm not sure of the date but I can tell you that it was the day that young wan got her marching orders from the caff on *Coronation Street* and someone painted all the graffiti on the pub wall.'

'That's even better, thanks.'

'No bother. I didn't know the girl well but she loved them children. I don't think she'd let anything happen to them.'

'Was Moira friendly with anyone else around here, do you know?'

'Not that I saw. She kept herself to herself. I think every penny she had went on paying her rent. She was delighted when she got that grant. It gave her some breathing space.'

'Thanks, Denis. Now about the small man you said you saw who was a little aggressive. Would you know what date you saw him?'

'No, sorry. Maybe a month ago?'

I press him a little more but he comes up empty. Disappointed, I say, 'You can send in Lorna now.'

Hands on the table, he pulls himself out of his seat. Hesitating, he asks, 'How's the young lad?'

'He's with his father. He got out of hospital yesterday.'

'And he's happy there? It's just if she left him and—'

'The man is his next of kin.'

There is a pause, then Denis says, 'Aye, suppose so. I'll get herself now . . . She's taken it very bad, so she has.'

'Why talk to them separately?' Dan asks softly, when Denis has left.

'Because there's something Lorna isn't saying and I'm thinking she might if she's on her own.'

'Something about Denis?'

'I don't know. But if it's to do with the case, this will be our best shot.'

'He seems like a harmless auld fella.'

'Yeah. But yesterday, there just . . .' I shrug. 'I can't put my finger on it and then earlier . . .'

Dan doesn't seem madly convinced and I think he's about to say something about all my instincts but Lorna arrives in, closing

91

the door softly behind her. She scurries to a seat, her over-long body making it look like a doll's chair. 'My turn. Fire away.'

'Just what we asked Denis, Lorna, please. Tell us everything you remember about Moira and the children.'

'It was Denis dealt with her the most,' she says, wrapping her arms about herself. 'He accepted her as a tenant, helped her move in, collected her rent. I barely spoke two words to the girl.'

'And when you did?'

'It was about how she was settling in and how the children were finding it. The only time I was up at the house was when Denis asked me to take a package to her. A replacement bulb or something, I forget. She was in the garden, painting the scenery, she said, not that it looked much like scenery, if I'm honest, but that's art, isn't it? Bren was running about and I suppose the girl was at school. Poor little thing. I just said I was here with the package and Moira told me how she loved the house, and all going well, she'd like to stay. I didn't commit. Then we chatted about the weather and said, well . . . she said goodbye and that was it.'

'Any other interactions?'

'Not from me, no.'

Is she hinting at something?

'When she said she wanted to stay and you said you didn't commit, why was that? Was there something about her that bothered you?'

'No.' She says it too fast, a slow redness creeping up her face and neck. 'I didn't commit as it was Denis's decision. It's his parents' old house.'

'All right. Did Moira or the children ever appear fearful or threatened by anything?'

'No, but I didn't see much of her.'

I choose my next words carefully. 'Would you know if she was being bothered by anyone?'

Outside the rain eases and sudden slanted sunlight spills through the window, almost blinding me. Damn, I can't see her reaction.

'How would I know that?' Her voice quivers as she jams her hands under her thighs.

I study her for a few seconds, her brown sparrow darting eyes, her strong arms and legs, her lankiness. She must be at least ten years younger than Denis, in her early sixties, and she keeps herself well. This woman is my mother's best friend, always ready to help out at the drop of a hat. 'Okay.' I leave it there. 'We'll let you get on with your day. If either of you thinks of anything, don't hesitate, all right.' I hand her my card. 'Just in case you don't have my work number.'

She hardly glances at it and, placing it on the table, tells us we can leave through the back. On the way to the car, we pass Denis talking to one of the locals, Milo O'Shea.

'Terrible thing about that girl,' Milo calls over to us, and I'm not sure if he means the child or the mother. 'Girl' is a sort of interchangeable word down here and elsewhere in the country. 'If anyone is going to crack it, though, you will, Lucy. We all know that.'

'Thanks for the vote of confidence, Milo.'

'No thanks needed. After all that hoo-ha at your house last January, you're great to be back doing it again. I'm telling you if some madman burst in my door and threatened to chop me and my family up, there is no way I'd—'

'No one threatened to chop us up.' I'm snappier than I intended

93

but, really, I can't bear the thought that people think I'd put my family in such danger for the sake of my job. 'He was just an angry man who needed to take it out on someone.' Full details have not been released to the papers because of the upcoming trial.

'Nevertheless,' Milo says, 'he—'

The rest of his sentence is drowned out because I've hopped into the car and started the engine. Dan jumps in beside me. 'I think we could both do with some food.'

'The Moose?' I suggest, because it's where Denis had said he'd seen Moira.

'Good thinking, Detective.'

15

On the way to the Moose, I call Matt to dig into Eamon Delaney.
I know the team will be too stretched to do it as quickly as I need
it done.

'Matt isn't on the case,' Dan warns.

'No, but he's going to take it upon himself suddenly to investigate Mr Delaney.'

'The Cig will go mad, Luce. You know what he's like.'

'The Cig will take all the help he can get.'

Dan sits back in his seat, folding his arms. 'You're the boss.'

'How good of you to notice.' I hear a click as my call is
answered.

'Hello, Achill Sound garda station. What's up?'

'Matt, it's Lucy.'

Instant silence followed by 'Oh . . . right . . . sorry, Lucy. I, eh,
well, they like the "What's up?" the locals. Makes them feel we're
human and that, you know.'

'We are human, Matt.'

He has the wisdom to remain silent.

'I have a job for you.'

'Yeah?' His voice piques with interest.

'I want you to dig into Eamon Delaney, the husband of Moira Delaney, our missing woman.'

He doesn't jump on it.

'You'll earn Brownie points if you say you took it upon yourself to do it, might get you on the team.'

'I appreciate it, Lucy, but the Cig—'

'Dig into Mr Delaney, Eamon Delaney.' I give him Eamon's address. 'Now, I know Moira lived in Limerick so you might have to check for him down there too.'

'But the Cig—'

'Up to you, Matt.' And I hang up.

Dan looks at me questioningly.

'He'll do it.'

The Moose is a popular café serving coffee and snacks in Keel. It's got a nautical vibe and even the huge mirror hanging on a wall, facing the window, is covered with decorative shells. The walls are painted in various shades of blue. The food is great.

We hit a bit of paydirt. This is where Moira had come for her interview, the one Eamon had talked about. 'I rang the garda station just this morning to tell them,' the manager, a young man called Con, says anxiously. 'Is that what this is about?'

I pretend I know this already and feel a flash of annoyance that the information hadn't been passed on to us by now. 'That's right. Tell us about it in your own words.'

Con is an earnest, geeky-looking young lad, whose body doesn't seem to realise quite how tall it is. He's all arms and knees. Even his face looks as if it's been made from a million different parts, his mouth long and wide, his nose small, his ears huge and eyes as large as saucers. He wears a shirt with the collar a size too big and a tie that's trying to make the collar fit. He looks like he's being strangled. His blue trousers are too short, displaying skinny white legs.

Who made him a manager? I wonder.

'She used to come in every day,' he says, 'her and the little boy. She'd have a coffee and he might have a milkshake or something. Then a job came up and she applied for it. Like, I never knew it was her until she came in and I thought, Oh, that's the girl who comes in every morning. We actually sat here, as it happens.' He looks down at his chair in dread. 'She sat here, where I am, and I sat there, where you are.' He jabs his finger towards Dan, who is trying to eat his burger and take notes at the same time. 'She had two children with her. The boy and a girl. She was very apologetic, said she hadn't meant to bring them but plans had changed. She put them at another table and, well, the boy was very noisy, very cross about something. She had to keep telling him to be quiet. Anyway, between the long and the short of it, I couldn't take her on.' His tone is apologetic. 'Like I'm sure she would have been amazing, but she wanted to bring the boy with her on her shifts and, sure, we couldn't have that. What if he ran into someone and knocked boiling hot tea all over himself? I had to tell her I couldn't accommodate it.' A second later, he says, 'It was terrible.'

'What was?'

'She was fine about it at first, said she understood, and just as we were finishing off and I was saying again how sorry I was, she just sort of started to cry. Real soft and quiet and, honest to God, I didn't know what to do, so I told her to sit back down and I went and got her a coffee and some tissues and when I got back her little boy was sitting on her lap and cuddling her. I told her again how sorry I was.'

It's eerie, sitting where she sat and now she's gone.

'And then she . . .' the young lad swallows hard and his voice stalls '. . . well, she sort of begged me. Like pleaded. And I said that her child wouldn't be insured, that we couldn't have it, and then the little girl said she'd mind him and that they'd be really good, but like . . .' He stops. 'And then Moira said she'd take care of it and please. And I said' – he rubs a nervous hand over his face – 'well, I said if she could take care of it then yes. I mean, I just wanted her to stop crying.' He looks fearfully at us. 'You don't think she, well, that she . . . that I . . .'

'Nothing that happened is your fault,' I say. 'Now, if you can, think about the moment Moira arrived in for the interview. Tell me everything you remember. Close your eyes if you want.'

He describes seeing her hurry up the steps, pulling her children along with her. 'She stopped and she fixed her hair, looking at herself in the window and then she came in,' he says. Without prompting, he tells us what she was wearing. It's not as detailed a description as Eamon's but similar enough. 'I know she's the candidate because she's all dressed up. I call her name and wave her over and she's a bit flustered. I think she's a bit embarrassed that I see the children. Anyway, she tells me that she wants to buy them a milkshake and she'll be right over. I tell her it's on the house so she sits down opposite me and her voice is shaking, like she really wants the job. She had this air of desperation about her,' he says. 'Like, looking back, sort of intense, wound up. Maybe she was stressed having to bring the children, I don't know. I ask her for her references and she gives me one. It was marvellous and I tell her that, but then she said about the children because it's nearly school holidays. And sure what could I do?' His eyes pop open as he tries to justify his decision. 'I had to let her down and, like I said, she started to cry and . . . hang on . . . she actually grabbed my wrist,' he says, touching it. 'And . . .' he stops, arrested by something '. . . she had this stain on her top. She hadn't taken off her jacket so it was only when she moved that way that I could see it. A huge stain like she'd spilled something on herself. And she must have noticed me looking so she pulled her hand away. And that was when I got up to get her a coffee.' Eyes still closed, he continues, 'I was relieved to escape as I didn't know what to do.' The rest of his story is the same. My heart squeezes at the thought of Ella saying she'd mind her brother while their mammy worked. I wonder why Moira was so desperate for a job. Was Eamon not helping out? If so, what had she done for money? 'Would you have the reference?' I ask.

'I do. I had it thrown out but when I heard . . . well, I dug it out again. Just be a moment.' He hops up, knocking against the table and causing my coffee to slop out over the saucer, before lolloping across the café and into the back somewhere. A few moments later, he comes back and hands me a two-page document.

I glance at it. Then glance again.

'Dan?' I jab the page, at the name of the referee. 'Get a look at this.'

16

On the way back to the station, with Dan driving, I call the guards in Limerick to enquire about the investigation into Barry Jones's accident. I'm transferred to the detective on the case. She sounds stressed when I tell her what I'm looking for. 'Can you refresh my memory?'

'A pedestrian knocked down in the city, not sure where. Barry Jones. He's in a wheelchair now,' I prompt.

'Aw, yes,' I hear her press a few buttons. 'We're waiting on CCTV from the pub Barry was in the night he had the accident.'

'It was six months ago.' My voice is sharp but, honestly, it's no wonder the public sometimes has a bad perception of us. 'You must have it by now. Sure, what premises keeps images for that long?'

There is a pause, where I sense her annoyance, before she says, 'I'll check.'

'You will,' I say. 'And then you'll call his mother and tell her what you find. The woman is out of her mind. Why are you looking at CCTV anyway?'

'Barry couldn't remember much about his accident, which is normal, but he can't remember much about the night that preceded it either. Bloods that were taken in the hospital indicated that he'd taken benzodiazepines, so if he says he didn't take any-thing, it looks like his drink may have been spiked.'

'And you think this has something to do with the accident?'

'I don't think anything. I'm investigating all possibilities.'

She says it brusquely but she's right. Something occurs to me suddenly. 'Was a woman called Moira Delaney a witness to that accident?'

At the other end of the line the penny drops. 'Yes, yes. She was hysterical. Her statement was all over the place. She said that Barry was staggering and that while she was trying to pull him up, this car came at them, she jumped out of the way but he was hit.'

I wonder if the car had been meant for Moira. It's a leap but one that's worth considering seeing as she's missing now, her child dead. 'Who was the driver?'

'A woman says it was a total accident. She claims Barry fell out on top of the road.'

'Can you send me that CCTV from the bar?' I ask on impulse. 'And the CCTV of the accident if you have it?'

'The video does appear to show him stumbling into the path of the car. But, yes, will do.'

'Sorry for taking your head off but I promised his mother I'd ask. Give his mother a ring on progress, will you? Make her think you care.'

'I do care,' she snaps back, a little defensively. 'There's just so much to flipping care about.' And she hangs up.

Back in the station, Dan and I find William in his office. He's on a call and he waves us to a chair. 'I want it TE'd as a matter of urgency,' he says. Then, 'You know what urgent means, do you? It means as soon as yesterday, got it?' A hasty word of thanks before he hangs up. 'They found Moira's car at Keel Beach car park just ten minutes ago. Some fishermen called it in. I'm pressing for technical examination ASAP. So, what have you got for me?'

'A couple of things. We talked to the husband and he's interesting enough to take a better look at, Cig,' I say.

'How so?'

I give him a run–down on what I've noted so far. 'I know it's thin,' I say, 'but he has no alibi for the night and, honestly, I don't like him.'

'All right. We'll get one of the lads to look into him.'

Dan kicks me gently under the table to urge me to tell him that I've asked Matt to do it, but I don't. That'd defeat the purpose and I'd get a bollocking. If William is under the impression that Matt did it off his own bat, he'll be dead impressed with him and it'll be a win–win.

'Has Mick got Eamon's bank accounts yet?'

'He's working on it.'

'Eamon told us he was supporting his family but the manager in the Moose Café, whom we've just talked to, said Moira came to him for a job and that she seemed desperate.'

He makes a note of it. 'I'll kick Mick's arse to hurry it up.'

'Please don't.'

He smiles grimly, not Mick's greatest fan.

'And here's the reference Moira produced for the job.' I pass it across the desk in its sealed see–through evidence bag. 'As you can see, Cig, the referee is this Barry Jones, the guy who also supplied her with the false reference for the cottage.'

'Yes?'

'He was knocked down a few weeks before Moira came back to Mayo. Moira was with him. We'd like to talk to him. Maybe it goes deeper than just an accident – the guards in Limerick think his drink may have been spiked. He's in the central rehabilitation centre in Dublin.'

'We can get some boys up there to talk to him.'

'I'd rather do it myself.'

I don't tell him I've already booked a slot with Barry for seven thirty three days from now.

'I said already that we can't afford for you to be haring off to Dublin.'

He does this from time to time and other detectives will just give up. I know, though, that if I can justify it, I have a chance. 'You can't afford not to. Look, Moira didn't have any friends—'

'Based on what we've been told,' Dan chips in.

'And I bet on the door-to-door you got no one who really knew her or who could offer any information about her?'

His lack of response is answer enough.

'This Barry is the only person, aside from her father and husband, who appears to know her at all. We need to talk to him even if he just gives us an insight into what she was thinking, or into her marriage. He was helping her out. There must be a reason for it.'

William leans back in his chair and studies me with his ice-blue gaze. Beside me, Dan straightens up. At least he's not cowering, like he sometimes does. 'Lucy's right,' he offers. 'It might be our only hope outside family.'

William heaves a loud sigh. 'All right. Go up first thing tomorrow. Don't stay over.'

'Eh, Cig,' my voice is not as assertive as it was, 'we can only get an appointment with Barry for seven thirty in three days' time. They're very strict.' They were like Dobermans, is how Dan described it.

'You've already arranged it.' He's half impressed, half pissed-off.

'We could work that morning and go up in the afternoon,' I offer weakly. 'That way we don't waste the day.'

'Oh, you'll work all right,' he says. 'Ye can both help Larry scan that CCTV.'

He knows we all hate that job. The only one who loves it is Larry because he can sit on his arse and eat crisps while staying out of the rain. Next, I tell him about Nick Flannery and his determination to stick his oar in.

'I'll sort him,' he says. 'Don't worry.'

What does that mean?

Before I can ask, if I even dared to, he launches into his findings. 'Right. As ye know, we've established that Ella is not Eamon's child and the blood found near the front door is Moira's. It was quite a lot of blood, so we're thinking some kind of an assault, though it's impossible to say for certain and we haven't located any sort of a weapon. We'll be checking her car to see if there are any traces there. I'd imagine whoever did this parked her car near the beach to make it look like a suicide or something. Idiot.' He snorts. 'Nevertheless, we're searching the area and we've got divers looking, but all things point to a murder plus a serious assault.' Without waiting for us to draw breath, he continues, 'As for Flannery, we know from intelligence that he had a bit of a falling-out with some of his pals so we're looking at the possibility of a revenge attack.'

'You think this is gangland?' My heart sinks.

'Let's be honest, they're usually not as subtle as abduction or fire but it is an avenue we have to pursue.'

I sneak a quick glance at the wall clock. It's after seven now. I'd been hoping to spend some of tonight with Sirocco. She's coming to stay for two days because Luc has a few days off from his part-time summer job and—

'Lucy, are you listening?' William startles me.

'Sorry, Cig, what?'

'Am I keeping you from something?'

'Sirocco.' The word pops out before I can stop it. 'Sorry,' I gabble.

Dan snorts back a laugh or a gasp, I don't know which.

There's a bit of a silence. I glance up quickly to see him studying the two of us. Finally, after what feels like ages, he says, 'Kev tried to get a description from Mr Johnny Egan of the big guy he saw coming from Moira's house but, sure, he says it was ages ago and you know witness memories? Catastrophic.' He answers the rhetorical question. 'Why people can't remember the simplest details, I don't know. Larry has managed to get the registrations of almost every car that left the island in the hours after the fire started. So far, a big pile of nothing. Of course, the person might still be here, could be a local. The door-to-door, you were right, it was a joke. Sure it's bloody isolated up there. The nearest cottage is that Johnny Egan one and he was next to useless on description. And no one knew her. She was a ghost. Ben is still waiting to interview Ella's actual teacher. She's on leave but, according to the headmistress, the teacher was concerned about her, something about a drawing. We'll follow it up. Nothing turned up with any of the other staff members. Susan and Louis have permission to interview Bren but the social worker has said he's too traumatised to be interviewed yet so it looks like we may have a bit of a wait. And that's it. Ye can go. See ye bright and early tomorrow.'

I can't get out of there fast enough.

17

When I get home, my mother is crouching in the hall with Sirocco, who seems to be playing with a load of dolls and open shoeboxes.

'Before you ask,' she says, casting a glance at Sirocco, 'I haven't yet talked to Katherine about . . .' she mouths '. . . the situation.'

'And Luc?'

'He's staying with friends, haven't seen him.' She stands up with a creak of joints and winces. 'I'll shove your dinner in the microwave. Say hello to your best girl.'

'Hey, Missy.' I tousle Sirocco's dark curly hair and she moves out from under my palm. I point to the shoeboxes. 'This looks interesting.'

Sirocco shrugs absently, her focus on her dollies, which are lined up against the wall. 'This one,' she says, as she picks up a stick-thin doll with impossibly long legs and blonde hair. Mumbling unintelligible words, she places the doll in the shoebox.

'Is she going to bed?' Oh, I want to squish her to me.

'No, she's deaded. She dieded when she felled in a big hole and banged her ear. Bow your head, Nana, and say prayers.' She starts up the mumbling again.

Sirocco has been obsessed with dead people ever since Rob's funeral. Luc told me that Katherine is at her wits' end with the whole thing and blames us. I think it's healthy, I told Luc. Nothing wrong with acknowledging the reality of death. Though, really, it's a bit eerie seeing her there with all her soon-to-be-coffined dolls.

'Did Nana Mags bring you out on the bonfire hunt?' It's an attempt to distract her from throwing water over the doll's corpse.

'Yep. And we got wood and bits of fence. Ack-kill will have the biggest bonfire in the whole wide world next week.' She stretches her arms wide to show me how big it will be. She's talking about the bonfire on Achill-henge, a community one organised by the council. 'When I go, Nana Lucy, I'm throwing my dollies on it and they will come back to life in three days.'

Holy shit. She's getting religion all mixed up in it now.

'No burning dolls on St John's Eve. The fire is to say hello to the nights getting a bit shorter, to hope for a good summer and autumn, and to see who might get married.' That's a simplistic version, but the bonfire on 23 June is a tradition down our way. A pagan feast, it was hijacked by the Catholic Church to celebrate the birth of St John the Evangelist. On the night of the solstice, bonfires are lit all over the island and rituals are performed dating back thousands of years. I used to love it as a child and it's largely died out now, but this year they're reviving it with one large bonfire for everyone to enjoy. I think it's to attract tourists, really. 'Now, enough of your dolls, let's—'

A sudden peal of the front doorbell.

Who can that be? From the kitchen the soothing vocal tones of my mother's favourite radio show float out. 'Mam?' There's an unexpected shake in my voice. 'Are you expecting anyone?' My heart feels like it's going to burst out of my chest. A flashback to the last time someone came without warning to the house zings through my brain.

'Nana Lucy?' Sirocco reads the tension in my body.

I breathe. In and out.

The bell rings once more.

Through the glass in the door I can see a fuzzy shape. It looks like a woman.

'Is no one answering the door?' My mother barrels out of the kitchen and, before I can stop her, flings it wide open.

My legs are jelly.

'Lorna!' my mother exclaims. 'What a— Are you all right?'

The concern in her voice galvanises me. I join her in the doorway, my pulse rate settling slowly. 'What's the matter?'

'This doll is deaded from a fire,' Sirocco pipes up. 'All burned.'

Lorna yelps.

'Sirocco,' my mother chastises gently, 'we have a visitor. Come in, Lorna. Come in.'

Lorna takes a step inside before throwing a fearful glance in my direction. 'I don't know if I'm doing the right thing or not,' she says. 'I feel terrible about it but . . . well, I'd feel terrible if I did nothing either.'

My mother elbows me out of the way. 'What's after happening, a stór? Come into the kitchen with you. Lucy, get Lorna a drink.'

'No, no, I'm driving.' Lorna flaps a hand. 'Hello, pet.' She stoops down to Sirocco.

''Lo, Lorna. Drink and driving will make you deaded.'

'I'd better not so,' Lorna answers faintly.

'You look like you need it and sure who cares? One drink won't matter. Sure nobody bothers with that around here.'

My mouth falls open. 'Mam—'

'A whiskey, Lucy, please,' my mother instructs, as she leads Lorna past Sirocco's line of shoebox coffins and into the kitchen.

I follow them, shutting the door behind me so Sirocco doesn't hear.

'It's actually Lucy I want to see.' Lorna twists to look at me.

'And see her you will, but have a drink first.' My mother pulls out a chair for her.

'Is this about the case?' I ask. 'Have you information?'

'I don't know.' She sounds tearful.

'Mam, if she's going to talk to me about the case, I can't have her drinking. Not yet anyway.'

'Oh, for God's—'

'No.' My voice is sharp and my mother looks affronted.

'Grand, so,' she says, with a sniff. 'Do you want me with you?' she asks Lorna.

'I . . . I don't know. I just . . .' And Lorna wipes away hasty tears. 'I just . . .'

'If you're not ready to talk then don't,' my mother says, and I want to kill her. 'You get yourself together and decide and—'

'Lorna,' I interrupt, before my mother can take away what might be a potential lead in the case, 'just tell me what you have. I'll jot it down and we'll investigate. No prejudice.'

'But will you have to say the information came from me?'

'I don't know. It depends on what it is and who's asking. But we can keep your name out of it unless we need to tell someone.'

Lorna rubs a hand over her face and heaves a shaky sigh.

I knew it. I knew she knew something.

'You don't have to,' my mother clucks, and I glare at her.

I try again, the ruthless guard coming out. 'Someone killed a child and her mother is missing—'

'Mags, do you mind?' Lorna suddenly decides.

'Of course I'll sit with you.' My mother pulls out a chair for herself.

'No . . . I mean . . . this is something I want to say to Lucy in private. It's . . . well . . . it's personal.'

In fairness to my mother, she takes it on the chin. Squeezing her friend's shoulder, she says, 'I understand. Now only answer what you're comfortable with, and when it's done, I'll make us tea and we'll put something in it. And I've made buns for Sirocco but you can have one. And—'

'Mam?' Jesus, we'll be here all night.

'I'm going, I'm going.'

A few seconds later, we hear her in the hallway, asking Sirocco how many of her dolls have died today.

I fish my notebook from my jacket and sit opposite Lorna. I explain to her that I'm going to take some notes but that this is an informal chat. 'If it throws up anything, we can have you make a statement in the station.'

'That sounds very official.'

'I suppose it is.'

She gulps audibly and clasps her hands together in front of her as sudden bright tears stand out in her eyes.

Tearing a piece of kitchen paper from the roll, I hand it to her and she dabs her face. 'Sorry.' She sniffs. 'I've been battling this since it happened, since that poor child was found and the mother gone and I've not known what to do and—'

'Just tell me what you have. Let me take it from here.'

People like to hear that. Someone else taking control of what

they know, or think they know, is a weight off. 'All right.' She
swallows. 'The night it happened, well, Denis wasn't in the
house. He has no alibi, not that anyone asked him for one.' A
scared glance at me.

That doesn't mean much unless there was a reason for him to
harm Moira or if he lies about his alibi when he's asked.

'Do you know where he was?'

'That's just it. He does get up early most days and goes to the
beaches to take photographs of the sunrises and all that malarkey.
He puts them up on the computer and people tell him how great
they are. Load of nonsense.' She snorts, and I sense her rage,
though over what I don't know. 'He told me a while back that he
sees Moira on the beach too and that she does be collecting the
dillisk, which she sells on to make a few bob and that was grand.
I thought nothing of it until I saw the photographs on his camera.
There's a few sunrises but most of them are of her or the children.
Her collecting the dillisk or looking out to sea. Ones of her with
the children, all smiling. Ones of her drinking a coffee. I'm telling you, I got a fright.'

Now that's interesting.

'Do you think Moira knew he was photographing her?'

'I doubt it. Sure there are loads of pictures.'

'But she could have?'

She waits a moment, nods in an offhand way, then adds, 'Look,
he has form.' Then she gasps as if saying the words has somehow
let a demon out of a box.

I wait, trying not to betray any emotion.

Denis? Affable Denis? Easy-going relaxed Denis?

But they can do that, some people. Box things off.

Lorna covers her eyes and her shoulders shake as a sob escapes.

I let her cry. 'He has form,' she repeats. Outside, the innocent happy sounds of my mother playing with Sirocco jar with the creepiness in the kitchen. The juxtaposition makes me shiver. I want to pick up Sirocco and move her away from here.

'It was a long time ago,' Lorna whispers.

Rain, which has been falling all day, hits the window hard as the wind gets up.

The silence deepens. Then softly, 'He became obsessed with this woman I was friendly with. It was before we moved here, when we lived in Galway. She was a workmate of mine in the council. I was her boss actually. Anyway, she was a single mother with two children and, you know, people called her a trollop and all sorts back then. Denis was good to her. He'd offer her lifts and bring her shopping if she needed to get a big lot in. Being friendly. I was so proud to have a husband that was so kind. But then . . .' Lorna is caught in the memory for a moment '. . . one day this woman came to me at lunch break at work. I remember it so clear. I was outside the office, sunning myself, and I was, well, I had just lost . . . I'd been pregnant, you see, and . . .' She inhales, gathers herself. 'She told me that Denis was hanging about outside her house at all hours and calling her, and that she didn't like it, and if he didn't stop she'd report him to the guards. I was sure it wasn't true. I mean, how could it be? This was Denis, for God's sake. So I asked him about it and he denied it and denied it and denied it. Said she was delusional, that she was imagining things, that if anything she'd been coming on to him. And I – I wanted to believe him, but I know my husband and I know when he's lying, and so . . . well, about a week later, when he was out again on some job, I drove to the woman's house and parked in a side street and waited. And I saw him. I was in an alleyway, and he walked past her house

112

and sat on a wall on the opposite side of the road and looked up. I waited about half an hour and then . . . I went home.'

'Okay.'

'I never said anything. It was too humiliating. I just . . . I told him I wanted to move here because he was from here and we both liked it and, anyway, his parents needed help. He agreed. I think he knew he had a problem. I don't think he's done anything like it since. But now . . .' Her voice trails off and her confession leaves her deflated as if all her tension has been released. 'I do love him, but if he did anything to that woman or her children, I'd never forgive myself. Maybe I should have confronted him years ago or . . .' She shrugs. 'I'd just lost my child, well, children actually, and I couldn't bear to lose my husband.'

A tear plops onto the table.

'Lorna,' I reach across and grasp her hand, 'you don't know he did anything. And even if he did, it's not on you.'

'I did think he was getting too friendly with her but . . . well . . . I blinded myself that it was just him being kind and maybe it was but . . .'

'It doesn't mean anything. Not yet. Look, we'll have a chat with Denis, ask him a few questions.'

'Don't say it was me.'

'We'll keep your name out of it.' How I'll do that, I'm not quite sure.

'Thank you.'

'What was the name and address of your friend who complained about him?'

She tells me but adds that she might not be there any more. I tell her we'll find her. I read her notes back to her just to make sure I've got it right.

113

Silent tears fall down her face, and while I feel bad for her, there's the fizzy feeling I get from something breaking.

Much later, after Lorna has left and Sirocco is asleep, her creepy doll coffins laid on the floor alongside her bed, I ask my mother about her time with Lorna and Denis. We've never really spoken about those days a few months back when my mother, Luc and I were separated. She had stayed with them, Luc had stayed in Tani and Katherine's, and I had bunked in Dan's place.

'They were so kind.' My mother wriggles her feet from her shoes and bends to massage her toes. 'Denis couldn't do enough for me, ferrying me about because I was afraid to drive. I remember saying to Lorna how lucky she was to have him. A good man is worth his dinner on the table every night, I said to her. Your father now, when he was alive, I don't think he ever offered me a lift anywhere unless I asked for it. He'd be more interested in reading the weather reports or talking to the lads down at the pier . . . But I loved him,' she tacks on hastily. 'He had other good points.'

'Was there ever any tension between them?'

'What exactly has Lorna said to you?' She peers at me. 'They got on like a house on fire.' Then, horrified, she exclaims, 'Oh, God, what a thing to say. But you know what I mean.'

I'm not sure my mother would notice if two people were at odds with each other. She has a remarkable ability to tune out things like that and she can walk into the most fraught atmospheres as oblivious as a newborn baby. I'm like a divining rod, quivering at the least shift in tensions.

And it also strikes me that when I asked Denis if he had any pictures of Moira he denied it.

That's interesting.

***

After I've rung to inform William about Lorna's revelations, and after my mother has gone to bed, I pour myself a large glass of wine, knowing I won't sleep, the events of the day buzzing around in my head. The rain has finally stopped and the house is blanketed in silence. I open Rob's laptop, determined to distract myself by cracking the password. All I need to do, I tell myself, is to imagine I'm in Rob's shoes. I think better in the quiet, when there's no one around to disturb me. Between the three of us, we've tried everything over the last few weeks. And I know that Rob was not a man to pick a random set of letters or numbers – he'd be too lazy even to try to remember them. In fact, he would rather pick no password than have to remember one.

And there it is.

It has to be something easy. Idiot proof. I press 1234.

Ping.

I laugh as the screen explodes into life, flowers and roses and trees bloom, fade, die and bloom again, and hello, home screen.

Luc will love me.

But I won't tell him, not yet. This is Rob: better check what's on the thing first. I try to open the documents folder but it's password-protected.

Rob. Clever but sloppy.

1234.

Like a deck of cards the documents spill out over the screen. The names are '100%', '50%', '25%', '12.5%' and on and on. I access the 100 per cent folder. It's an Excel sheet of thousands upon thousands of email accounts. The 50 per cent folder has fewer, as has the 25 per cent folder.

Christ's sake, this can't be good. Even I know that storing a lot of email addresses looks suspicious.

I log out of that and into another document. This one is called '100% 2'.

There's also a '50% 2'.

And those are full of email addresses too.

All in all there are about twenty document folders like this.

Further down, I come across a spreadsheet. There are figures and numbers and I can't make out what they're supposed to mean.

But if Rob was doing spreadsheets and there are figures involved, all I can think is that he must have been up to no good. As far as the world was concerned, since he got out of jail, he was a humble photographer. These folders were created in the last couple of years.

I don't understand them but I know someone who will.

Eamon

Incident 2: Girls

Patti, his younger sister. Small, volcanic and with a mouth on her that could cut a tree down. That's what Daddy says and he doesn't mean it as a joke. Patti doesn't care. She just gets Eamon up for school in the mornings, washes his clothes and tells him how great he is.

When she's ten, she cooks dinner for them, telling Daddy she has all her homework done, though Eamon often does it for her along with his own.

They know that Daddy doesn't really care if she has her homework done or not. He just thinks it's what he should ask.

On the mantelpiece in the dining room, Daddy puts away all pictures of Mammy. We must not talk of her again, he says. And he opens a bottle of whiskey and drinks it. Sometimes Patti tries to talk to Eamon about Mammy, but he says it is not allowed and Patti stops trying.

Daddy drinks more and more, and in the end, Patti does all the farm work as Eamon does his studies. It is more important for men to be educated, Patti says.

When Daddy dies, the farm is left to Eamon because he has the family name. Eamon does not want the farm so he tells Patti, 'You have it. It's all right. Daddy is dead, he doesn't know.'

His memory flicks forward, like a snapshot.

First year in college. Anna Byrne. He doesn't even like her but she likes him and that's enough. It's safe. She has a laugh that's like the stream that comes straight from Croagh Patrick and a voice that promises more than she delivers. On their first date, she orders a starter and a main and a dessert. He just orders the main.

He wonders if she would order so much if she was paying. As she eats dessert, he studies her. The way her mouth opens and closes, the ridiculous blue and white plastic bracelet she wears, like something Patti had when she was ten.

'I was just thinking,' he says, as she forks the last of her apple pie into her mouth, 'you'd be a lot prettier if you weren't so fat.'

Her blue eyes widen, her lips part.

'Though if you're happy with how you look,' he continues, 'then that's fine with me.'

There are tears in her eyes.

'I was actually on a diet,' she says, 'but when you asked me to dinner, I thought it would be rude not to eat.'

So she *was* taking advantage.

'Just as well I only had the main,' he laughs, 'or I wouldn't be able to pay the bill.'

She titters a little, unsure, then offers to go Dutch. He tells her that once she has enjoyed it, that's enough for him.

Anna is grand as a diversion. Her friends are arseholes, though.

He buys her size-ten jeans. He cuts off the tags and tells her how much he spent. She can't fit into them. 'They're a twelve,' he says. Then adds, 'Maybe a small twelve.'

She asks can he bring them back.

Not without tags.

She isn't very good at following advice. Her friends keep whispering in her ear telling her she looks great. 'You've such good friends,' he tells her, 'always saying what you want to hear. Though maybe,' he adds, 'they don't want you to lose weight because you'd outshine them.'

She drops those poison friends.

At eight stone, she's a knockout, but then her parents come and they take her away, and though he writes, she doesn't write back.

Women are complete bitches.

Flick.

Flick.

Moira.

Out of his league.

But he can't stop watching her.

His instincts tell him that if he plays it right he can take her from right under the nose of Barry Jones. Dimple Boy, as the other girls call him.

Simple Boy, Eamon calls him. In his head.

Eamon befriends someone in their circle.

In third year, Barry's father dies and everyone goes to the funeral. Eamon doesn't want to but he does because Moira will be there. They all pile into two cars belonging to a couple of lads whose fathers have a penny to spare and off they go, back to Mayo, to Newport, to the funeral.

The chat of them all washes over him. When Moira speaks he listens. All you must do is listen, he knows. Find a way in.

Later, at the graveside, as the priest says the prayers, his gaze is drawn to Barry, who has his arm wrapped protectively around his mother. He hates Barry right then with a fury that scares him. Barry's mother cuddles into him. Barry whispers something to her and she whispers something back and dabs her eyes with a tissue. Their own private world. Then Eamon observes Barry look across the open grave and catch Moira's eye. She blows him a tender kiss. Then Barry says something to his mother, who glances at Moira.

She's a hatchet-faced bitch, that mother.

Later, on the way back in the cars, talk turns to dead parents. They cluck when Moira says that her mother left her and her dad when she was six.

Moira says she is fine with it.

Eamon knows she is lying.

She cannot be fine with it. He knows the deep shame she must feel. The shame of not being good enough, of not being loved enough.

Then Moira says she doesn't have much contact with her father any more.

And Eamon thinks that's good. That's fucking great. Barry Jones had better watch out.

119

18

Day 4

Two days later, just as the dull June day finally shows signs of brightening, we pull up in front of Denis Long's house. I'm overseeing the search while Larry and Dan make the arrest.

Karen Brennan, the woman Lorna alleged Denis stalked a decade ago, was located early yesterday and she's made a damning statement against him. According to her, and backed up by her sister, Denis had persisted in taking photographs of her and her children; he'd followed her, harassed her and sent unsolicited gifts to her children all over a six-month period. Not even the threat of telling his wife could deter him. Based on this, William had had me draw up a search warrant for the property and had ordered Denis to be arrested first thing this morning. 'Let's wrongfoot him early on,' he'd said.

There's nobody on the road other than us as Larry and Dan leave their DDU car and walk briskly up to the Longs' red front door.

There's always a hum of anticipation before any arrest. The threat of violence hangs unspoken in the air because you never know what situation you might find yourself in. There are very few suspects, however, who would mess with Larry's towering presence.

Denis opens the door wearing a pair of plaid pyjamas. I can't hear the exchange but it results in Lorna arriving out. Upon seeing the detectives, she staggers slightly and grabs the frame of the front door for support.

'What the hell did you think would happen?' I murmur. Larry and Dan enter the premises and come out a few minutes later with Denis, dressed and handcuffed and shouting to Lorna that it's all a mistake and to follow him to the station.

I join the search team who have assembled in the garden. Lorna eyes them in terror before spotting me. 'Lucy, what is this?'

'We have a warrant to search your house and farm, Lorna.'

With a tiny gasp of shock, she moves aside to allow the team in.

I ask Lorna to stay with us to make sure that during the search nothing is damaged, or if it is that she should witness us recording it, but she declines. 'I have to go to Denis,' she says, blinking back tears. 'I feel bad enough. I have to go. Do what you like. I don't care.'

'You're happy with me taking charge?'

'I trust you, Lucy,' she says, squeezing my arm before grabbing her coat from the kitchen chair and dashing out of the house.

Turning to the team, I brief them once more on what we're looking for and they move off in pairs to search the premises methodically. The outbuildings on the farm will be covered once the house is complete. To begin, the search is visual: a room is assessed, items of interest are identified and the order in which they can be recovered is documented. Then the team moves in and the examination begins. It can take time and it's picky. Notes are taken on who searched where and when and who recovered certain objects. This is to be sure that nothing is missed and to guard against cross-contamination of evidence.

Lorna's house is a bit of a nightmare. It reminds me of the house from our last case, when Sandra Byrne, a sister of my old school friend, was murdered. In that instance, the place had to be forensically examined but there was just so much clutter and detritus that it was a long job. This is the same. There are so many ornaments, so many bits and pieces, that it will take ages to go through them. And as we are also looking for a potential weapon that might have been used in Moira's assault, we need to move slowly.

We recover the camera almost immediately. It is bagged and tagged, then sent off to the lads to download the pictures on it. Denis's mobile will have been taken at the station, as will his DNA, fingerprints and photograph.

A little while later, in the outbuildings, we find what we hope is the mother lode.

In the afternoon, a shell-shocked Denis is perched nervously on a chair in Interview Room Two, the grimmest, reserved for the people we think are guilty. Despite all the evidence, however, I am having trouble believing it.

He was so good to my mother last year, and she'd made a point of telling everyone how kind he was. He always brought Sirocco sweets whenever he met her or slipped her a few quid. There was never any suggestion of creepy off him. But I should know by now, from doing this job, there are depths to people that you only discover when you wade into them.

My mother, having been tipped off by Lorna, has been calling me for the past hour.

She knows fine well that I can't tell her what's happening.

She'll get the hint if I ignore her.

Outside the station, a few media outlets have begun to gather, news having spread that we've made an arrest in the case. If they find out it's Denis Long, a local, they'll have a field day – the pubs and shops will be buzzing with the information for weeks to come.

Achill is small. They'll find out sooner or later. Someone is bound to have seen the garda presence outside Lorna's earlier.

Of course an arrest means nothing. It's just a very scary invitation to talk that you can't turn down. Many people don't realise that. They think it means 'guilty'. In fact it just implies that there is a suspicion of guilt but unless we get a confession, which we are duty-bound to investigate anyway, or watertight evidence to prove our case we won't get a direction to charge from the DPP.

Dan and I are in the observation room. He's giving me a blow-by-blow account of Delores's latest faux pas and I'm doing my best to look outraged for him when all I want to do is giggle.

'I said to her to leave the tap alone, that it leaks, that we're fine with it, but she went and bought this enormous bloody spanner and—'

'Me and Louis are taking our break now. Can we sit in?' Susan interrupts, shoving her head around the door.

I wave to them to join us. Susan gives a little cheer and plonks herself beside Dan. 'Can I eat my lunch here?'

'Go on,' I say, though the Cig hates it.

She begins unwrapping the foil from an enormous sandwich.

'How's it going with Bren?' Dan asks.

'Brilliant.' Louis pulls up a chair and sits beside me, a little too close for comfort. 'He's a great lad. Ready to talk.'

'He isn't really.' Susan speaks through a mouthful of bread. 'He—'

'I'm good with kids. That's what they said on the course.' Louis talks loudly over Susan. 'He likes me.'

'Yes, but—'

'Did you ever think,' I eyeball Louis, 'that they told you you were good with kids because you're the chief's son?'

In the shocked silence that follows, a red flush creeps up Louis's neck.

Shit. I can't believe that came out of my mouth. I can apologise now or I can stand by it. 'Did you?' I press.

Louis's eyes slide from mine. He stares at his hands and seems to be formulating an answer. Finally, though, without speaking, he pushes his chair back and strides out of the room, the door banging behind him.

'Bloody hell,' Dan whispers, eyebrows raised. 'Talk about the nuclear option.'

'He needs it.' I turn to Susan. 'That's how you stand up for yourself.'

'I would if I could get a bloody word in.' She groans. 'Honestly, he's such an arsehole. Do you know what he did yesterday?' Without waiting for an answer, she says, 'He fined this old woman for not having her dog on a lead. She cursed him from a height, fair dues to her, and he was shocked by that. But he handed her the fine anyway.'

'For feck's sake.' That's Dan.

'It was the old woman - d'ye remember she got really annoyed a couple of years back when Mick and I interviewed her about the night-caller murders? She made a complaint to the station about us?'

124

'Anne O'Sullivan. Small, walks really quickly, cycles an electric bike?'

'That's her. Louis fined her because her dog wasn't under proper control.'

'That dog has three legs,' I splutter.

'I tried to talk him out of it but he loves the power.'

'Little shit,' I mutter.

'I told him I'd square the fine but he said that would be illegal.'

'It kinda would be.' I smile. 'Leave it with me. And sorry, Susan, I think I was a bit snappy.'

'Yeah.' She waves me away. 'Ever since that guy got in your house you've been sort of spacy and all over the place.' Having dropped that bomb, she takes another large bite of her sandwich, which looks delicious. Chewing, she turns to the screen. 'He's such a little man,' she observes, head tilted. 'Could he have overpowered Moira?'

I can't answer, caught up as I am in her previous comment.

I hear Dan say something in reply, then William looks in. 'What are you doing here?' he barks at Susan. 'This isn't the canteen!'

'I was just . . . Can I please watch this?' she says. Then, 'You're the best interviewer and I want to see how you do it.'

I'm amused that he appears a little flattered by that. 'Fine so,' he snaps gruffly. Then to me, 'Matt wants a word with you over something. I told him we're in the middle of an investigation and to leave it for a bit, but he said it was important. And just to let ye know—'

The boppy tone of my mobile interrupts him. My fecking mother. Again. I cut the call. 'You were saying, Cig?'

'You did great in the search this morning, a lot to keep us going, but that camera was a little goldmine as was his phone.'

125

I try to pretend I can't hear my mobile as it starts up again.

'Lucy, are you going to answer that?'

I'm about to tell him no, I'm not, that it's my mother, when I notice Eamon Delaney's name flash up. *Shit.*

'Hi, Eamon, what can I do for you?'

'You've arrested someone,' he snaps. 'Who is it?'

William leaves, the door closing with a click.

'As you've probably been informed, we are not at liberty to say just now.'

'It was my child he murdered. My wife he took. Fuck you and your liberty.'

I leave it a moment. Let him think about what he's said. Wonder if he'll apologise, but he doesn't. I'm not surprised. 'We've just taken a man in for questioning. No charges have been directed yet.'

'Who is it?' he presses.

'As I said—'

'I will find out.'

'Maybe you will but if you do anything to this man or inform anyone else about this man, namely Mr Flannery, you will—'

'I don't give a shit.'

'Do you think that's what Bren needs right now? A father in prison on top of everything else?'

A sudden silence punctured by some heavy breathing. 'You do your job,' he says, and disconnects.

'I really don't like that man,' I say. 'He's going to be trouble if he hasn't bloody caused it all in the first place.'

'Eamon Delaney?' Susan asks. 'You think?'

'I don't know but he's not telling us the truth.' And again the vague notion blooms that I've missed some vital clue and again I can't quite catch it.

'He wasn't exactly welcoming today – we barely got ten minutes with Bren. He said it was too upsetting for him. And Phil, the FLO, said he has a habit of moving outside whenever he gets a call.'

'Does she think he's being evasive or something?'

Susan shrugs. 'She just thinks it's odd.'

'It could be personal stuff. Did she say how he seemed?'

'She said she hardly talks to him, that he's working all the time.'

'But is he upset? Grief-stricken?'

'He could be but, you know, some men just don't engage.'

There's movement on the video as William, carrying a bundle of files, walks into the room, followed by Larry. Denis straightens up and watches with fearful eyes as they take their seats opposite him and introduce themselves.

There's a knock on our door. Matt pokes his head around it. 'Lucy, can I—'

'We're in the middle of something here, Matt,' I say. 'Can it wait?'

'That's for you to judge when you hear what I have.' There's a show of spirit that's unlike him. He waves a slim file about. 'Coming?'

'Go,' Dan says. 'You know what will happen for the next hour. William will charm the pants off Denis and Larry will take notes. We won't get to the good stuff for a while.'

He has a point. 'Come on so.' I follow Matt out of the room and down the corridor to the kitchen. There's no one there. He grabs a glass of water for himself before sitting opposite me at the scummy Formica table.

'I am not going to tell the Cig I did this,' he says, in a low voice, leaning towards me. 'I know you want me to, Luce, but the man is a human lie detector and, besides, you'd be in the shit too. And honestly? If I wanted to get in his good books, I would have taken the initiative myself.'

Is he chastising me? 'I just—' At his look, I mutter, 'Okay. Sorry.'

'It's not that I don't appreciate it,' he says. 'I'll do whatever you want, Luce, but I'm not lying to the Cig.'

That's very principled of him. He isn't after credit or promotion: he just wants to work on the case. 'Fair play. What have you got for me?'

He lays out the file. 'Make of it what you will,' he begins. 'First off, on Eamon, I'm not sure there's much here. I contacted the lads in Limerick and asked if there was anything on record from his time down there. I was just dotting the *is* because I knew they'd have told us by now if there was, but, in a stroke of luck, one of the sergeants, who had been on leave until yesterday, came back to me and said she remembered a couple of incidents with Moira, but those incidents didn't reach the threshold of going onto the system. Moira was a no-show or whatever so they're not recorded on Pulse.' He slides a picture of Moira across to me. 'When I asked her how she could be certain it was the same person she said that her face was not one you could forget.'

Moira stares out at us from the vibrant colour photo. That stunning otherworldly beauty. Once seen never forgotten for most people, I'd imagine.

'Withdrawn incident reports are not evidence of anything,' I say.

Matt nods in agreement. 'I figured then that if she made the reports, then withdrew them, maybe out of fear, there had to

128

be something else. So, I checked with the hospitals in Limerick. And nothing. She was never admitted suffering from any unexplained injuries. Her GP records came down yesterday and there was nothing there either, except about a year ago a prescription for anti-depressants, which she took for a few months and didn't renew. So, unless we think it was a suicide, which we don't, nothing. After that, I chased the bank accounts, trying to have a sneaky look when no one was noticing. Eamon Delaney just has the one in Permanent TSB. As far as I could make out, it was the usual paying-off of loans and that sort of thing. However, there were some odd deposits from a number of individuals.' He runs a finger down the list and I see a payment from an 'Andy Shine' for five hundred euro and another from an 'Imelda Greene' for three hundred. 'I'll come back to them in a minute,' Matt says, cutting off the question I'd been about to ask. 'One thing that struck me was that there were no payments to Moira, so it doesn't appear that he was giving her maintenance, unless in cash. Now, he might have been stingy with money but the man is squeaky clean. I read the door-to-door statements and there were no complaints about him. All the neighbours said that, though she kept herself to herself, he's dead nice, always willing to lend a hand with farming or whatever.'

'They said he was nice?'

'They said he was nice,' Matt confirms.

Feck it anyway. I wonder if my instincts about him are wrong. 'Did Moira have any bank accounts?'

'This is where you tell the Cig that you did this work. Save us both a bollocking.'

'Go on.' I sense a breakthrough.

'Right. The lads couldn't find any and—'

'Hey, guys.' Mick arrives in and pulls a Tupperware carton from the fridge. To me, 'I thought you were in the observation room?'

'Just talking to Matt about one of the locals,' I mutter.

'Is it that fella Eddie?' Mick asks cheerily, ''Cause if it is, I just seen him standing out there opposite the Centra and shouting his head off about Jesus saving everyone. He got rightly soaked in the last shower. And—'

'Yeah, it's Eddie,' I say. 'Look, Mick, no offence but I don't have much time so—'

'No bother.' Mick pulls the local newspaper from his pocket and, taking a seat at the far end of the table, he starts reading while crunching whatever food is in his Tupperware.

'Go on,' I hiss to Matt.

He looks furtively at Mick, and says, in a whisper, 'Mick was trying to locate a bank account for her but couldn't. Then, last night, lying in bed, I thought of Moira's arts grant. That money had to have been paid in somewhere and it wasn't in Eamon's account. They were separated by then anyway so I rang the Arts Council first thing and asked them what bank details she'd given. They were pretty cagey at first, but I served them with a cheeky forty-one and did the "Do you want to help solve the murder of a little girl?" and thirty minutes ago they sent across the information. And here we are.' He pushes another page across the table. 'Last October, Moira Delaney opened an online bank account down in Limerick. I'd say she did it when she visited her father – wasn't one of her Insta photos from last October taken in Limerick?'

'Yes.'

'Various deposits have been paid into it. Altogether she had, before she left Eamon, four thousand euro saved. There's not a lot left now.' A beat before he says, 'Do you notice anything?'

I scan the document and, yes, I do. Heart racing, I glance up at Matt. 'The names of the depositors in her bank account match the weird depositors in Eamon's.'

'They do, and that in itself might mean nothing, so I contacted the bank and through them made contact with the first depositor whose name appears in both bank accounts.'

'And?' I have a feeling this could be significant.

'This guy here' – he points to 'Andy Shine' – 'deposited five hundred with Eamon on the twelfth of November last and deposited five hundred with Moira that same day. He told me that it was in payment for a painting he'd bought from Moira. It had cost him a thousand euro and she told him to pay half into one account and half into another.'

I sit back and wonder what it means. 'Was she hiding money from Eamon?'

'That's what it looks like,' Matt says. 'And she did this over and over until it appears she felt she had enough saved to leave him. Now there's another interesting thing that might throw the cat among the pigeons and it's why I wanted to talk to you before the Cig gets stuck into Denis. Have a look at her outgoings.'

I scan the bank statement. Aside from money taken out here and there, the only other outgoing is her rent. Twelve hundred a month, which seems fairly cheap. At least Denis and Lorna aren't greedy, I think. And then, further down the page, 'It goes down to eight hundred the last couple of months,' I mutter.

'Yep,' Matt says. 'And I wonder why.'

'They might have agreed it.'

'Or he might have. It was him dealt with the rent, I read in one of the reports.'

Across the way, Mick turns another page of his newspaper.

'Thanks, Matt.' I gather up the documents. 'That's great work. I owe you one.'

'I'm just doing my job.' He stands up. 'I enjoyed it. Thanks, Luce.'

'I have to let the Cig—'

'No. But give me more stuff to do and I'll do it.'

'Thanks, Matt.' William will wonder where this information came from, but he'll only wonder for about five minutes.

Time for Denis to answer the hard questions.

19

William hadn't taken well to being called out of the interview, but when he sees what I have, he beams. 'Great work, Lucy.'

A big worm of guilt unfurls in my stomach. 'It wasn't just me, I—'

'We're about to get to the meat and bones now. I'll rework our interview plan.' Another grin and he's gone back into the room.

I join Dan and Susan. She's finished her sandwich and they're sharing a monster bag of salt and vinegar crisps. 'This isn't a movie.' I dig my hand into the bag. 'Have I missed anything?'

'Just Denis talking about the house and how he met Moira and all the stuff we already got out of him. It turns out he and the Cig have an interest in old houses and history.'

'My arse.' I snigger.

'Your arse is not that old.' Dan sniggers too and I thump him as Susan giggles.

On the video, Denis is looking a little more relaxed. He even has a cup of tea in front of him and he's lying back on his chair. Dangerous.

William comes into shot as he sits back down. I notice that the exhibits officer has joined them. 'Sorry about that, Denis. Just getting some documents from my colleague.'

The interview resumes with William saying pleasantly, 'This is a fine how-do. You've told us how you met Moira and how you became friendly with her and the children, and how you think she was getting a series of threatening calls and texts because when you were there watching *Coronation Street* with her one evening you witnessed it happen. And from the information you gave us this would have been between seven thirty and eight on the fourteenth of March last.'

'Yes, and I don't see why ye think I had anything to do with what happened to Ella. Oh, God, tonight, like, that's awful. And as for Moira, sure she was a great girl altogether and I'd never harm her either.'

'Noted,' William says. 'Tell me, is this yours?' He produces the camera, wrapped in a clear evidence bag. 'For the purposes of the recorder, I am showing the suspect exhibit MD10.'

Denis visibly wilts. He knows what's coming. 'Yes, if you found it in my house. Yes.'

'And is this your phone? Exhibit MD11.'

'I can explain. I can. And—'

'Is it yours?'

'Yes, but let me explain.'

'Please?' William gives him the floor.

Denis takes a huge swallow of coffee and wipes his mouth on his shirt sleeve. His hand trembles. 'Do I need a solicitor?'

'If you want one, we can provide one,' William says casually.

Denis does what they all do: calculates if engaging a solicitor makes him look guilty. Finally, he heaves a sigh and begins, 'It's like this. I always go to the beach on fine mornings to get pictures of sunrises or whatever catches my eye. My wife will tell you that. I sell a few of the good photographs here and there, and in December I bring out a calendar with the best pictures and sell it for charity. *Everyone* will tell you that. And one morning, down on the beach, around about February, I seen Moira there and we got talking and she said she was collecting seaweed to sell to Andy Mac – he's the man that dries the seaweed out, have you got me? Anyway, after that I'd see her most mornings. She was a worker, got up before anyone else and collected the dillisk until she couldn't fit any more into the sack she brung with her. I admired that. I did wonder about the children left alone in the house but I suppose they were sleeping and it's a safe place.' A pause. 'Or was.' Another pause. 'Anyway, I never asked her. I didn't want her to think I was judging her.'

'Very noble.'

Denis shoots a quick glance at William, unsure if he is being sarcastic or not. William gazes innocently back and Denis, encouraged, continues talking. 'And then one morning, as I arrived, the sun was just coming up and she was on the beach, facing into the sun and she had her hand on her head, holding back her hair and, sure, the photographer in me couldn't resist it and I just took the shot. I gave it to her later.'

'Just the one shot?'

Denis squirms. 'That day. But, sure, you know there's more. She was the perfect subject. My camera couldn't get enough of her. Each time I took a picture, I'd see a better one and on it went.'

'And what about these?'

One by one, he places an array of pictures in front of Denis. Moira in the cottage garden. Moira and her children crossing the road. Moira in the Moose drinking coffee with Bren. Moira waving Ella off on the school bus. Moira swinging Bren around. Moira looking pensive with the children playing in front of her. Hundreds of pictures. 'I didn't . . .' Denis closes his eyes '. . . I didn't realise there was so many.'

'That's just the tip of the iceberg.'

He buries his head in his hands and moans. 'I know what it looks like.'

'What does it look like?' William asks, ever so gently. Ever so concerned.

'It looks like I was obsessed with them.'

'I suppose it does all right.'

'But I wasn't!' Another moan. 'I wasn't.'

William doesn't respond; he lets the silence work for him instead.

'I just liked looking at her. At the children. And not - not like that,' he shoves in. 'I'm not a pervert. They were . . . they were a lovely little family.'

'Did she give you permission to take the pictures?'

'Yes.'

It's a lie and it lands with a clang.

Denis shifts uneasily but doesn't take it back.

'You followed her about taking pictures of her and the children and she didn't mind?'

'I used a zoom lens so it wasn't intrusive. She was grand with it all.'

William quirks an eyebrow.

'She was grand with it,' Denis insists.

More silence but Denis doesn't bite.

'Did you pay her?'

'No.'

'Tell me, do you know a Karen Brennan?'

The change in subject makes Denis flinch, sending his cup spinning across the table. Coffee splatters onto the floor. 'Oh, shit! Shit!' Though whether at the mention of the name or the spilling of coffee, I don't know.

'We'll wipe it up,' William soothes. 'Just answer the question. Do you know Karen Brennan?'

'I want a solicitor.'

'Interview concluded at sixteen oh-five,' William narrates, flicking the recorder off before reading over Denis's interview and having him sign it.

The video feed goes to fuzz as Denis is returned to his cell and William and Larry leave the room.

It'll take a couple of hours to get Denis sorted with a solicitor and then he'll want to talk to him, so I tell Dan I've someone to see and use the opportunity to drive over to visit our missing colleague Pat. It's a typical Mayo day of soft rain and shifting light. I have to pop on sunglasses when the slick wet road is illuminated by the glare of white sunshine. On the radio, they're wall-to-wall discussing the murder of Ella. The country is full of it, people standing in judgement on things we may never understand. I flick it off. Twenty minutes later, I'm driving up a grassy track, my poor beautiful new car rocking from side to side as I ascend. Three minutes later, outside a modest bungalow, Google tells me I've arrived.

'Lucy.' Pat, sounding delighted to see me, answers the door, 'Come in.'

He looks dreadful, his face hollowed out, grey shadows under his eyes. He's lost weight too. I disguise my shock and embrace him, saying how good it is to see him and telling him how much we miss him.

I'm wondering if I should have come.

With a slight stoop to his walk, he leads me down the hall.

'You can say it.' His voice is as mellow as ever. 'I look like shite.'

'You look like shite.'

He laughs a little.

'How've you been?'

'He hasn't been well.' Pat's wife, Selena, appears in the kitchen doorway. 'That job ground him down until there's nothing of him left for this family.'

'I'm—'

'And has anyone come to see him? Has anyone rung to see if he's all right? No. No, they haven't. They took all he had to give and discarded him.'

'Isn't Lucy here?' Pat says mildly.

I feel instantly bad.

She harrumphs and marches back into the kitchen, the door slamming behind her.

'I'm sorry.' Pat winces. 'She's taking it very bad and I can't blame her. I'm not the man I was.'

'You just need rest.' Then I add, 'I thought William visited.'

'He did but he didn't stay long enough in Selena's opinion.'

He leads me into his front room.

It's beautiful, all leather and wood and brass. It puts my tatty sofa and scraggy rug to shame. 'Wow. Fabulous room.'

'Selena's great at the decorating.' Pat waves me to a chair as he takes a seat. 'D'you want tea?'

'No, thanks.' I decide to abandon my reason for coming. It wouldn't be fair. 'Just . . . called to see how you're doing and to say we miss you on the case.'

'I'm getting there. How are you?'

'Me?' I laugh a bit. 'I'm grand.'

'Even after . . .?' He lets the sentence hang.

'Yes.' I over-compensate with a wide smile. 'Sure, you just keep going. It never ends.'

'You making any progress?' He leans towards me. 'I've been following it. That Eamon Delaney is a chancer if ever I saw one. He's loving the attention.'

I glance at the door, not willing to risk Selena's wrath. 'He is. Though we've nothing to tie him to the scene. We miss you for the paperwork.'

'I used to be good in the field,' he says, his voice tinged with what I think may be regret. 'Years back, like. Before your time. But there was one case, with children - Jesus, what was done to them.' He hitches a breath. 'Some lads block it out and they carry on. I did that for a while, but it gets in somewhere. With me, I started dreaming of it and seeing it and hearing it all over again. I was drinking and, sure, I was a complete mess. No one wanted to work with me. I took time off and found it hard to get back in. William looked after me. Brought me on board.' He waits a moment. 'You need to mind yourself, Lucy. You've seen a lot in the last couple of years and what happened at your house last—'

'I'm looking after myself.'

He's a guard. He knows a shut-down when he hears it. But it's true: I am doing well.

'Good. Because at the end of the day, it's your family that suffer.'

That I do not want to hear. 'I'm grand.'

'What's in there?' He nods to the laptop bag.

'Nothing.'

I'm saved from an interrogation as Selena enters, bearing a tray with two mugs and a plate of biscuits. 'Tea,' she announces.

I leap up to help her lay it all out.

'I'm sorry for earlier,' she apologises, a little tearfully. 'We appreciate your visit.' And before I can reply, she's gone, footsteps clicking down the hallway.

'You're a terrible liar for a guard.' To my dismay, Pat picks up the thread of our interrupted conversation. 'What's in the bag? D'you want my help with something?' There's no mistaking the hopeful note in his voice.

'Only if you want. It's nothing to do with the case. It's something I'm looking into myself. I just thought if you'd nothing to occupy yourself that maybe . . .'

'What is it?'

I unzip the bag and take out the laptop. Handing it to him, I say, 'Password is one, two, three, four.'

He enters it, muttering about idiots who don't password-protect things properly and, as before, the screen springs to life.

'I have a zip drive here of the files.' I give it to him. 'Have a look through it. You'll see a lot of spreadsheets, and I can't make head or tail of them. There are also files with lists of email addresses and other stuff I don't understand. I want to know what this laptop was used for.'

'Any reason you haven't turned it over to Computer Crime? Or asked Dan? He's a bit of a computer whizz, isn't he?'

'I don't know if what is on this is a crime,' I explain. 'And, Pat, I want this just between ourselves for now.' Am I crossing a line?

I don't know. I won't even think about it. And if I find out that what Rob has been doing is illegal, what will I do about that? If I turn it in as evidence, Luc will never forgive me. And he needs to believe that Rob was a good man. 'If you're uncomfortable with—'

'I'm just a friend who's good at this stuff.'

'Thanks, Pat.'

'Pleasure.'

In the house somewhere a door bangs and he jumps, the computer sliding from his grip. I catch it.

We both ignore what just happened.

20

Two hours later, having fielded calls from my mother and Eamon Delaney, who has moved on to threatening fire and brimstone on me if I don't pick up, I'm back in the observation room, this time with Kev. Dan has had to race home because Fran's mother has somehow managed to cause a bit of bother to the washing machine and it's flooded the kitchen. Dan was fuming. 'It's Fran's mother but he won't answer her calls,' he'd said, as he yanked on his jacket.

At that moment MAM had flashed up in my caller display. 'What a very clever son he is,' I'd joked. Dan had merely glowered and stalked off.

'How's your end going, Kev?' I ask, as we wait for the interview to kick off. 'Anything turn up?'

'Nope. Though Johnny Egan, the guy we talked to a couple of days back, he said he knew you from way back and—'

'I'm sure that wasn't your reason for talking to him.'

'Well, no, but he said . . .' At my look, Kev smirks. 'Right. I'll stop. I was up at the school, talking to parents who had children in Ella's class. Interesting thing was none of them mentioned a sleepover, and Denis and Lorna both said to you that the children were meant to go on a sleepover. Isn't that right?'

'That's right.' I wonder who was taking them: they'd never come forward. Maybe Denis had mixed up the days. 'Anything else?'

'Ben managed to talk to Ella's teacher today at last. There was something about a drawing, I don't know, he said he'd have it for conference tomorrow.'

'Okay.'

'And a couple of the teachers had met Eamon once or twice when he picked Ella up. He was always late, always apologised and blamed a mix-up at home. Still,' he waves a hand at the monitor, 'it'll all be moot if this lad is guilty.'

On screen, I watch Denis say something to the solicitor at his side. The older man pats him reassuringly on the arm. I know that guy. He's a family friend too. My mother went on an ill-advised date with him years ago. Said he was as wet as an Irish summer.

Kev's phone pings with a text. He reads it, then looks at me with a delighted expression. 'Kylie only went and won her weightlifting competition last night. She's sent me the video. D'you want to see it?'

I should ask if this is his work mobile or not, but I don't because the whole station is dying to see Kev's six-foot-three, weightlifting, uniform-loving girlfriend. 'Go on.'

He shoves the phone under my nose. On the screen there is a still of a scary-looking person with their mouth wide open in what appears to be a silent snarl. Pressing play, this huge, muscled girl, with what looks like a twenty-four pack, heaves an impossibly large barbell from the floor and after a bit of heavy breathing and hefting, stands with it over her head. Her legs, the width of tyres, strain under it, and she staggers about a bit before thumping it back to the ground with a loud 'Huh'.

'That's my girl,' Kev says proudly.

'She's amazing.' I wonder how a lanky, skinny kid like him could have attracted such an Amazon. 'What weight was that?'

'Three times mine,' he says.

'What's that? Ten stone?'

'Ha. Ha.' Kev chortles good-naturedly.

'My client wants to cooperate.' We both jump at the voice from the TV.

'Fireworks,' Kev says, rubbing his hands. 'Wouldn't it be great, though, if this was it? If he pleaded guilty.'

I'd hate Denis to be guilty.

'I don't think he is, though,' Kev remarks. 'I know him a bit from coming into the station every year. Me, Matt and Jordy always buy his calendar. My mother loves it.'

On the video feed, William lays a bundle of files on the table, deliberately slowly, letting Denis get a good long look at them.

Larry reminds Denis that he's under caution and starts a new interview.

'Tell me about Karen,' William says.

Denis stalls for the longest moment. 'She was a friend of Lorna. My wife,' he clarifies to William. 'Who told you about her?'

'We have our ways of investigating,' William answers. 'Now—'

'What ways? I want to know how you found out about her.'

'Karen told us,' William says, which isn't an untruth. 'Now, unless I heard wrong, I thought you were going to cooperate.'

Denis hesitates, wondering, I suppose, if it's something he wants to pursue, but eventually he bows his head and the whole story of how he'd become 'a little fascinated' by Karen and her two children pours out of him. He talks of how he, Lorna and Karen were all good friends until Karen started to think he was being creepy. 'She told me she'd tell Lorna if I didn't stop but I knew

144

she wouldn't. She wouldn't like to upset Lorna. And, anyway, I wasn't doing anything wrong. Like, it wasn't as if I was texting her all the time or sending her horrible messages or anything. I was just . . . watching. Watching out for her. For the children. And then Lorna took a notion to move down here and this house came up for sale and she suggested we buy it. It was near to my parents' cottage and they were getting on and I was making the trip home most weekends anyway so it was just handier. And that, honest to God, is it. I never bothered Karen after. Did she tell you that? Did she say I'd moved and that I'd never bothered her after?'

William doesn't answer the question. 'She said you'd taken unsolicited pictures of her.'

'I don't remember that at all.'

'She does.'

'I helped her out whenever she needed it. Fixed things around her flat. Me and Lorna babysat at the drop of a hat.'

'And did you take pictures of her?'

'I don't think so.'

'Why did she think you were creepy, then? Why did she think you needed to be reported to your wife?'

'You'll have to ask her.'

'We did. She said you took pictures, you followed her, you stood in the street and watched her flat.'

'That's making it sound worse than it was.'

'Her sister confirmed it. She saw you one night, waiting.'

'I did nothing to her.'

'Going back to Moira, you admit you watched her too. You took pictures of her.'

'Moira let me.'

'And what did she get in return?'

'Nothing.'

'Denis.' William says it as if he's disappointed.

'What?'

'Come on, now. Tell me the truth. Help us all out here.'

Denis looks at his solicitor, who looks at William, who frowns. Solicitors are not well tolerated by William if they so much as open their mouths. This one knows it well.

'Right.' Aware that nothing more will be forthcoming from Denis, William flicks open the folder I'd given him and spends a moment or two staring at the page.

Beside him, Larry flexes his fingers and we can hear the crack.

'Ouch!' Kev remarks. 'Hate that.' He pulls a bag of toffees from his jacket and offers me one.

'Have I missed anything?' Susan comes flying in and spots the sweets. 'Oh, good, toffees.'

'The Cig is going in for the kill.' Kev unwraps one and pops it into his mouth.

Very slowly, like a magician about to astound his audience, William pushes the copy of Moira's bank statement across the table to Denis. This is followed by him pulling a photograph of Moira with her children buying fish from a man in Purteen harbour. 'Explain.'

Denis looks baffled. 'I don't . . .'

'May I?' William asks.

Denis gulps, his eyes round in his chalk white face.

'This picture here, this was taken,' William taps the top corner, 'on the second of February last. As were fifty more. Fifty pictures, Denis. This goes on and on and on. Now, this here,' he taps the bank statement, 'shows that Moira's rent was reduced two months ago. A whole almost three months after you started taking copious pictures of her. By my estimate, that's ninety days of pictures taken at an average of fifty pictures a day, how many pictures is that?'

'Four thousand five hundred,' Larry pipes up, and William's look of surprise at Larry's amazing computation skills makes the three of us chortle.

'You just multiply ninety by one hundred and divide in half,' Larry explains helpfully.

'Four thousand five hundred pictures, Denis,' William says ponderously. 'To us it looks like she didn't know you were taking them and then she found out . . .'

Denis shakes his head. 'No. No way.'

'No way, what?'

'She wasn't blackmailing me if that's what you're thinking.'

William sits back, folds his arms and studies Denis from top to toe.

Kev claps in admiration. 'Nice one, Cig.'

Denis breaks. 'She needed a drop in rent and I gave it to her and that was it.'

'And how did your wife feel about that?'

'She didn't know.'

'Your wife didn't know you had just gifted your tenant four hundred quid a month? That's quite the secret.'

'It was my cottage. My parents' house. I could do what I wanted.'

'That was very generous.'

'I couldn't see two kiddies out on the road.'

'Exhibit MD11 was your phone, wasn't it?' William asks.

Denis emits a mew of horror. He stares at William from the rubble of his defence. 'Yes,' he whispers.

'There were a number of texts on it,' William says, 'and I'm going pass them to you now. Can you read them for me?'

Denis looks like he might be sick.

'The first one that rang alarm bells with us is from Moira,' William says. 'It was sent on the fourth of March. Will you read it?'

Denis moans and shakes his head. 'I did nothing to her.'

'"I appreciate all you've done, Denis, but please don't follow me any more,"' William reads. 'You reply that you're just taking pictures. She then texts, "You are not to take any more pictures of me or my children." You reply that you are not. Finally, at the end of March, she—'

'All right!' Denis cries. 'All right! Yes, yes, she said she'd tell Lorna. She said she would. And so, to stop her and to show I'm sorry, and I was sorry, I let her have money off the rent. But that does not mean I killed that child or harmed her. I never would. I loved her. I loved those children.'

Oh, good God.

'Holy fuckaroo,' Kev says, sucking on a toffee. 'People are mental, aren't they?'

'Just when I think I know what someone is going to say, they say something totally different,' Susan agrees. 'Mostly weird stuff.'

'Welcome to the shit show that is this job,' I mutter.

On screen, William sighs. 'How did her blackmailing you make you feel?'

'She wasn't blackmailing me. I was just showing her I was sorry.'

'And yet you continued to take her photograph. Not as many, but still . . .' William pushes more recent pictures across the table. 'You just couldn't help yourself, could you?'

'I never laid a finger on her or those children. Never. And there is no proof, isn't that right?' He turns to his solicitor, who nods.

'You're right,' William concedes. 'The fact that you were blackmailed by this lady for taking her picture, for stalking her, for harassing her children, the fact that you've done it before, the fact that you reduced her rent and kept it a secret from your wife, none of this is hard proof that you had a part in hurting her or her children. However, your last text does say . . .' he finds the spot on the page '. . . "Please don't report me or you will regret it."'

'I meant regret it that she'll have nowhere to live, that Lorna would want her out. Lorna's a very jealous woman, you know.'

William steeples his fingers and eyeballs Denis. 'It could be read as a threat,' William says. 'And honestly, Denis, Moira is an attractive woman. I'd say it was hard not to take her picture and it must have been galling for you to have your kindness thrown back in your face. There you were, doing odd jobs and babysitting, and she threatens to report you for taking a few pictures. It must have made you angry?'

'No. I could see her point but I could also see my point. I was doing nothing wrong.'

'What happened to Ella?'

'I don't know. I wasn't there.'

'It's hard to believe you, Denis. You've told us outright lies time and again.'

'I'm not lying.'

'Do you know where Moira is?'

'No!'

I glance at my watch. By my reckoning Denis has about two hours left in custody. If we don't get something on him by then, or if he doesn't admit to anything, we might have to let him go.

And just then the lads in Forensics call.

'Well?' I ask.

And the answer sends me haring down to William.

The accelerant we found in Denis's yard matches the diesel found at the scene.

149

21

'You've arrested Denis.' My mother meets me at the door, calling out into the night as I lock my car and trudge towards the house. It's been a long day and I've to go to Dublin tomorrow, though I'm not even sure it's worth it now. Still, we must be sure we've exhausted every avenue of the investigation, and despite what happened in Denis's interview today, there is still nothing definitively tying him to the crime.

'He's been released for now but might be called in again,' I mutter, passing by her into the kitchen. I drop my coat on the chair and shove on the kettle.

'And what does that mean when it's at home?' She follows me in.

'Exactly what it says. We have evidence but not enough yet.'

'Thank God for that,' she says, as she ladles some stew onto a plate and lays it on the table for me. 'I never heard of anything so ridiculous in my life. Denis Long a murderer. Sure that's like saying Ireland is a terrible country.'

Hmm. 'Thanks for the stew. Is Sirocco gone home?'

'She is. Eh . . .' She hesitates. 'I have some news. I had a chat with Katherine when she came to pick Sirocco up.'

'Oh, yes? Did she apologise for her cheating, two-timing daughter?'

She ignores that and calls, 'Luc! Your mother is home!'

'Leave him out of it for now.' I am appalled. 'He doesn't need—'

A very downtrodden Luc slides into the room. One look at his face and I know he knows. 'You've told him.' That's to my mother. 'Oh, Luc, I—'

'Go on, Luc!' My mother sounds uncharacteristically sharp as she glares at him. She never glares at him.

'Fine,' Luc mutters. 'Tani and I broke up about two weeks ago.'

'And you never said?'

'No.' My mother answers for him. 'I wonder why. I wonder—'

'There's no need to drag it out, Nan,' Luc snaps. He turns to me. 'Tani found out that I was with another girl in college.'

My world tilts. My Luc . . .

'Now,' my mother says, and in that word there's a whole world of judgement.

'What does that mean, "with"? Did you have a coffee *with* this girl or did you—'

'You know what "with" means,' Luc cuts me short. Then, to my mother, 'I don't know why everyone is so surprised. Tani and I were never going to spend the rest of our lives together. She's great, I really like her, but we weren't exclusive and we have nothing in common and—'

'You have Sirocco in common,' I snap.

'Except Sirocco,' Luc says. 'And I'm not going to ditch Sirocco.'

'I should hope not!' This is dreadful, I think. I liked Tani. I liked the idea of Luc and Tani.

'And Tani has a horrible mother and I can't be doing with that.'

'That's ridiculous,' I bark. 'Katherine is really nice.'

They both look at me.

'She's got better,' I amend.

'I was never good enough for Tani in her eyes.' Luc sounds resigned. 'I was always going to be my father's son. I was always going to be your son, Mam. That would never change. There's too much history for it ever to work and I told Tani that but she kept crying and begging me and—'

'Don't make excuses,' I interrupt him. 'You can blame everyone else, but the bottom line is if you loved that girl, you would have made it work. You wanted someone new and you cheated on her. That's it. Just own it.'

He dips his head.

'I hope you apologised to her and to Sirocco.'

'Sure, hasn't she got someone new herself?' my mother says, feeling sorry for Luc now. 'And isn't it better for everyone to be happy?'

I take a half-empty bottle of wine from the fridge. 'I'm going to bed.'

'Katherine definitely has a new man,' my mother says, apropos of nothing, about thirty minutes later, poking her head around my door.

I don't respond.

'She's looking very well, these days.'

I know a barb when I hear it. 'Meaning I'm not.'

'I never said that. But seeing as you—'

'Katherine isn't out mixing with the dregs of the earth,' I say.

My mother tries out a joke: 'She was married to Johnny.'

Then, in a terrible segue, she says, 'Talking about dregs of the earth, Denis isn't guilty, is he?'

'I don't know.' He'd explained away the diesel, told us that he'd lent Moira some to get her lawnmower going. In order to get a charge we need to place him near or at the scene on the night in question and so far we haven't been able to.

'They won't like it here if he's in trouble.' She takes the bottle from me and gulps a mouthful. 'He's got a lot of friends.' A look at me. 'Including us.'

And with that, she makes to leave. 'Go easy on Luc,' is her parting shot. 'He's young.'

Always the light sleeper, especially these days, I jerk awake.

It's four a.m.

Someone has sent me a text.

Denis Long, the text reads. *I know who he is. I'm watching.*

It's from Nick Flannery.

Eamon

Incident 3: Girls continued

Moira.

His mind zigzags like a kite flown too high in cross winds.

Pain zips through his body but he holds fast to the image of charming, gorgeous, funny Moira.

Calculating, deserting, bitch Moira.

Two for the price of one.

He love-bombs her. Secretly follows her back to the flat she shares with Barry, leaving notes in her door. Unsigned notes

153

telling her she's beautiful. Her girlfriends wonder who it is. Some weirdo, they say. Creepy, they say. He knows they're just jealous. And Moira likes it, as he'd known she would. Him and her, peas in a pod.

He sends flowers and sniggers when Barry, who hasn't a pot to piss in, tries not to be jealous.

He knows she keeps those flowers until the petals fall off and they turn grey. Until they rot.

He remembers the blonde woman behind the counter in the college canteen handing Moira a tray saying, 'Your mystery man bought this for you. He hopes you like it.'

She looks around. He can still see it, so long ago now: the room was full of chattering and craic and no one looking in Moira's direction. Only him, but she never noticed. And as she takes the tray, she beams from ear to ear because she wants him to know, whoever he is, that this sort of thing makes her veins fizz.

And in the end it was just him. Maybe she was disappointed, she never said. Until he revealed himself, she barely noticed him, passing him with a brief 'Hi' now and again. But now, now she knows he has hidden depths, an untapped source of creativity running inside him, and she is mad for him.

Eamon is aware that he's nothing special but he made himself so. For her.

He tells her that, like her, his mother has left him. That he had never got over it. He tells her this, his deep shame, not because it's true, though it is, but because it will bind them.

And it does.

She breaks up with Barry, moves in with him and two weeks later she is announcing her pregnancy.

It was golden.

And Barry, fecking idiot that he is, still wants to be her friend. But Moira ghosted him.

He didn't even need to coax her to do it, so he knows she loves him. When Barry leaves college soon after, Moira feels bad because he won't have a degree. Does she not know, he asks her, whispering in her ear, that Barry only left to *make* her feel bad? He tells her that if Barry was a decent friend, he would have told her in advance that he was leaving. Instead, he had fecked off without telling her. Friends don't do that.

Mothers don't do that.

Wives should never do that.

She is from the arse end of Limerick City. From the infamous Estate. No name other than that.

It regularly makes the news.

She won't talk about it.

Good.

No family means no ties.

He rings her multiple times a day just to say hello. If she is out, he wants to know where and with whom.

He realises that his obsession with her has left him wide open.

When Ella is a year old, when he's working in a shit job, he decides to go back to the farm. To where they won't be bothered. Moira is having meltdowns. The guards came out one time and it was infuriating to have them ask puerile questions over what was a misunderstanding about dinner. He convinces her to relocate to Mayo. He paints his home place in blues and greens and browns.

The artist in her can't resist.

He tells Patti to leave the farm, to find a place for herself, because he and his family are coming home.

22

Day 5

After Nick's text, I can't go back to sleep, so I decide to get up and make it count. I take a hasty shower, throw on a black trouser suit with a white blouse and slip my feet into a pair of comfortable shoes.

I make some fresh coffee and a ham sandwich, and bring them with me as I leave the house. Outside, it's still dark, the full moon standing out like a shiny gold coin among the scatter of stars. Nothing stirs and I can't hear a thing except the heave of the ocean below on Keem Beach.

The thrum of my car engine shatters the silence as I drive away, out along familiar roads, the twists and turns like a tune my heart plays each time I travel them. I descend the mountain into Keel, zip past the pubs and the shops and the holiday homes, past the caravan park, which is beginning to fill nicely for the summer season. Finally, I turn towards Slievemore, driving the long road up to it, the mountain growing in my windscreen, a darker shadow against the dark sky. I pull up in front of the graveyard, where Rob lies buried. His headstone hasn't been erected yet but his sister, Clara, told me that it was to go in any day now. For the moment, there's just a wooden cross hammered into the earth. I walk on towards the deserted village, a rubble of stones and shells of old booley houses where, in generations gone by, farmers lived temporarily when they took their livestock to the mountain to graze during the summer months. That's the thing about this island: the past is everywhere. There is an acknowledged truth when you live here that your life is a speck in the chain of time. That one day you will be the past and the future will arch on without you.

And it's comforting in a weird way.

But Ella left the chain way too early.

At the cottage, garda tape still flutters around the cordon and the guard on duty, a young lad, yawns widely as I approach.

'Here.' I hand him the coffee and the foil-wrapped sandwich. 'It'll keep you going.'

'Aw, you're a saint. Thanks a million.'

I smile, don a suit, give him my name, and he allows me onto the scene. I walk towards the house. Sometimes it's nice to return to a scene on your own minus the chatter of a team. In the silence of the space, your thoughts can surprise you. This house, once so pretty, looks hellish, a yawning front door, the broken windows, the room above from which Bren was rescued.

I stand for a while, envisaging what might have happened that night. Walking the perimeter, putting myself in the shoes of the victims and the perpetrator. I think about Moira getting ready to go to the beach, packing her car, sneaking out, trying to be quiet.

Bren was rescued wearing his dressing-gown.

Ella was downstairs.

They were going with her.

Of course they were. She wouldn't have left them behind. They probably slept in the car and Denis would never have known.

Ella must have seen or heard something that caused her to run back into the house. And . . .

Suddenly I know what happened, or at least part of it.

'I think Ella saw the SO,' I say to the room. 'Or else . . .'

Dan slides in at the back. He seems to have ditched the sharp suits for a luminous orange and yellow shirt, which looks like it belongs in the seventies. There's a moment of communal 'Holy shit,' but because the Cig is there and because it's a murder conference, no one says anything. Ignoring the attention, Dan stares straight ahead with stony concentration. 'As I said, I think Ella saw the suspected offender.' I fight to contain my giggles. 'Or else she saw the fire, which we know started at the back door. I think she ran into the kitchen, slipped on the diesel, which explains why it was found on her body, banged her head and was knocked out. Bren was upstairs, getting ready to leave, he had his dressing-gown on. Moira was bringing these children with her. Now, either the SO was deliberately trying to kill the children or the person believed that the children were away on a sleepover.'

Which lands Denis Long neatly in it.

William mulls it over.

In the middle, Kev waves his hand about like a schoolboy.

'Kev?'

'One of the parents I talked to yesterday, Cig, did say that Ella came to her house for a playdate once and fell asleep.'

'Her teacher said Ella always seemed tired,' Ben agrees.

'Okay, good,' William says. 'So her brother, Bren, he might have information for us. How's it looking with him?'

'It'll be another while,' Susan pipes up.

'It'd better not be,' William warns. 'We can't afford it. Denis

158

Long is walking about free and I do not want him out there if he's a danger to anyone.'

'You can't hurry a child.' Susan's voice wavers only a small bit. 'That's too traumatising for them and—'

'Louis, what's your take on this?'

Louis looks from Susan to the Cig and back again. Susan is glaring at him, daring him to go against her. But, hey, the Cig is the Cig. That's what he's thinking.

'That's my thoughts exactly,' he says. 'The sooner the better. We don't need Denis Long at large. We'll push the social worker as hard as we can to bring it forward.'

'You can if you like.' Susan folds her arms. 'This is a four-year-old boy you're talking about.'

'Yeah, and—'

'Just sort it out.' William turns from them. 'But, Susan?'

She looks up.

'You conduct the interview with him. It's obvious you have his best interests at heart.'

'I do,' she says pointedly, in Louis's direction, as he flushes and mutters something under his breath.

'Anything else, Lucy?' William asks.

'No, Cig.'

'Dan?'

'Nothing else, Cig.'

'I think there is.' He contradicts Dan. 'Are you planning on changing that shirt anytime today? It's not quite the image we need.'

A smattering of laughter.

'Have you worn it for a dare?' Larry asks. 'Or are you raising money for your favourite charity?'

159

More laughter.

'The charity will be "Let's help Larry walk again after Dan hit him,"' Dan shoots back, amid applause. Then to William, 'All my shirts were ruined when my washing machine went rogue. I'll buy one in Dublin later today.'

'Good,' William says. 'Right, Ben. I believe you had something from the school.'

'Not sure how relevant it is, Cig, and it'll throw the cat among the pigeons, but I was talking to Ella's teacher and she said that earlier in the year she expressed concern over Ella's home life with the principal and she also called Moira in. She says Moira didn't seem too bothered by it but that she could have been putting on an act to save face.'

'How so?'

'Apparently, last October, the teacher had asked the class to draw a picture of their families and Ella drew this.' Ben taps a button on the projector and Ella's picture pops up on the screen.

There's an 'oof' as everyone reacts.

Ella had talent, there's no doubt about it, but her depiction of her family is chilling.

Three small figures, presumably Moira, Ella and Bren, are placed in the very corner of the page. Moira is slightly larger than her children. Bren wears brown shorts and a red T-shirt, Moira a red dress and Ella a black dress. Taking up the whole length of the page and most of the rest of the width, Eamon is labelled 'DADDY'. He's a monstrous, twisting, wraith-like creature in a pair of brown wellies, brown jeans and jumper, and a blue hat. His mouth is open, exposing a huge red tongue and teeth.

'The teacher asked Ella to explain the picture and she just said that it was Daddy, Mammy, her and Bren. Daddy was the biggest one and he was in charge and everyone had to do what he said, especially Mammy, because she wasn't very good at lots of things. The teacher thought it was alarming.'

'It is,' William agrees, 'but what does it prove? That Eamon Delaney might be a bit of a bully. That maybe he gave out to Ella that morning and to punish him she drew this because she was angry.' He turns to Mick. 'Any luck on accessing Moira's mobile records?'

'Later today, Cig.' He tacks on, 'They promise.'

'If we see anything on those that seems threatening, we might invite him in for questioning. The bank statements show he didn't pay any money to Moira for the children and it also appears that he was taking half her earnings from her painting, though he might have thought it was the full amount. Moira also had a bank account that we suspect he didn't know about. And while it's sinister, it proves nothing. We have no record of his car on the island that night. Push for those records, Mick.'

'Yes.' Mick is notoriously bad at pushing for things. He's too polite by half.

'I mean it,' William grinds out, and Mick blushes. 'Larry, CCTV?'

'I did check for Eamon Delaney's car at the times he said he was here, which was on the day Ella was murdered, at around three thirty. I caught him coming over the bridge onto the island at three and leaving again at four.'

That's interesting. I take a note.

'I also have him arriving back on the island at seven the next day, which presumably was when he found out about the fire, although his car wasn't here. Of course, he may have hired or borrowed one, but so far we have no proof of that.'

161

'There is no suggestion of him paying for a hire car on his bank statements,' Mick pipes up.

'Okay.' William nods. 'He has no alibi, though, so it's still up in the air. Anything else?'

'There is.' Larry beams in satisfaction. 'Just this morning I caught Moira's car on dashcam heading in Keel Beach direction. Have a look.'

He presses play and footage appears onscreen. 'The owner of the footage was travelling in the opposite direction to Moira's car,' Larry says. 'There.' He uses the mouse pointer to show a red speck appearing in the distance. 'That's the car. I'll slow it down and you'll be able to see the reg plate.' Slowly the car crawls forward and Larry stops the playback just in time for us to make out the registration. It's not clear but good enough. Larry lets the playback continue until the car is almost on top of the dashcam car. 'Unfortunately, it's difficult to get eyes on the person behind the wheel as they seem to have taken precautions. You can make out a red scarf here,' he shows us with the mouse, 'but height wise, I'd estimate someone of five foot seven at least. Moira, as we know, is only five two. So, not Moira.' He projects an enlarged image onto the screen but it's fuzzy and unclear. 'The only thing identifiable in this picture is that red scarf.' He lets the footage run on. The car streaks by and then it's gone. 'That was it for Moira's car that morning. It was taken at about four thirty and the owner of the other vehicle can't recall anything about that car. It was speeding, going in the direction where we found it. That much we do know.'

'All right. Good work all the same. At least we know it wasn't Moira driving. Ger, forensics?'

'Moira's car was TE'd yesterday, Cig, and I got the preliminary results in at about eight last night. Interesting stuff, actually.' He pulls out a sheet of paper. 'Just a summary. Trying to understand the forensic emails wrecks my head.'

There are murmurs of sympathy all around.

'There was blood found in the boot, which was compared with the blood found on the grass outside the house. They are a match. And it's also a match for DNA from saliva found in Moira's tooth-brush at the cottage. Moira was in the boot of that car. And from what Larry says it appears that our SO drove Moira's car to Keel and transferred Moira from the boot to another car, or our SO may have disposed of Moira before driving to Keel. We don't know which way it went yet.' He looks to Larry.

'I'll put a call out for video going in the opposite direction within that time frame,' Larry says.

'It also appears, from the blood in the boot, that Moira was struck again while in or near the boot, so she wasn't actually dead from the altercation at the cottage.'

How awful. If it was Moira in the boot she was probably kick-ing and screaming and no one heard her.

'Another thing of interest,' Ger continues, 'is that a number of plant spores and pollens were found in the front of the car with traces also found in the boot.'

'Plant spores and pollens?'

'Yes, Cig. And pollens and that kind of thing. They're unsure if they were deposited by the person in the boot or by the SO or, indeed, if they were in the boot all along. They've sent samples off to a forensic botanist to identify them. For instance, if they came from Moira, they'd be the plants that might be found out-side the cottage or maybe from a place she had recently visited. If they came from the SO likewise. We just need to ID the plants.'

'I'm not following,' William says impatiently.

Ger winces. I get the feeling he barely follows the thinking himself.

'Cig, if I may?' I raise my hand.

'Please.'

'I was reading a book by a Patricia Wiltshire - she's a forensic ecologist and botanist. She does a lot of work analysing plants and pollen at crime scenes. In one case she had, two men had kicked a third to death and dumped his body in ferns. They then came back and tried to burn the body but people called the police. The men were arrested and this woman matched pollen from the men's shoes to pollen found at the scene. In fact, the pollen found on the shoes was so specific that she was able to say exactly—'

'So, pollen is unique to the area and by tracing what pollen comes from what plants you can identify an area?'

'Eh . . . yes.' I hadn't actually finished my story but that is the point I was making.

'That's pretty amazing. So, if the pollen comes from the SO his garden might have those plants in it, or it might be from a place he visited recently.'

'Exactly,' Ger and I say together.

Denis and Lorna's garden is a shambles. Eamon Delaney's garden, however, was all neat and tidy with a lot of flowers.

'Anything else?' William obviously doesn't hold out much hope on the spore front.

'Just on the lighter that was located at the scene,' Ger says. 'There are no decent prints or DNA on it but it's not a run-of-the-mill cigarette lighter either. I'll let Kev fill you in.'

'Before it was damaged in the fire,' Kev says, 'it was a unique lighter. That much was obvious. With the help of jewellers, we

164

narrowed it down to . . .' he unfolds a piece of paper '. . . an antique S. T. Dupont lighter, gas, and that it was manufactured between 1953 and 1960 under D57 code mark, so we are looking at something worth a couple of grand. The jeweller also spotted that at one stage there must have been an inscription on the lighter.' An image of the lighter pops up. 'See, just here,' Kev points to a spot, 'where the S. T. Dupont mark is, you can make out some lettering. I had it blown up again and the letters we can identify with certainty are W, T, O, S, T. Not much but back between 1953 and 1960, there were only a handful of shops in the country selling anything like this. We're tracking vendors down now to see if they have records of who might have bought one and had it inscribed. Hopefully, it may allow us to trace its journey from shop to Achill. Long shot but it's all we have.'

'All right. There can't have been too many people who could afford that sort of item in those days. Good work. Everyone keep at it. Lucy and Dan, I want a report from Dublin the minute you talk to this Barry guy and—'

'Cig!' Matt shouts from the doorway. 'You need to see this, Cig.' He's waving an iPad around and people make way for him as he stumbles over feet in his haste to make it up the room. He shoves it into William's hands and stands beside him, panting as if he's just run a marathon. 'Eamon Delaney's only on the telly saying we aren't keeping him informed,' Matt tells the room, 'and that the man who murdered his wife and child has been released.'

'Jesus Christ.' William's face is a thunder cloud. 'Lucy? Were you talking to him yesterday?'

'I told him I wasn't at liberty to give him any information until we knew ourselves, Cig.'

'The stupid idiot, he'll bloody prejudice the trial if he keeps

165

this up. What TV producer decided to put him on?' And he's gone, storming out of the room, Matt following, half afraid to ask for his iPad back.

There's a small silence before the chatter breaks out.

'Anything else?' I take charge of the conference.

'I couldn't find anything on the call that came in the first night,' Mick says. 'The one telling her to burn in hell.'

'Anything else come in on the lines?'

'Nothing we deemed useful, though we are checking things out.'

'Fine. That's it, so. Jim will give out the job sheets. Don't forget to return them.'

When I'm done, Dan is waiting for me outside the room. 'Leave the shirt on. It'll cheer me up.'

'This is Fran's only shirt,' Dan mutters, striding alongside me towards the office where we've been ordered to help Larry with CCTV for an hour or two before we set off. 'Honestly, Lucy, the whole wash turned red and I don't know how because there was nothing red in the bloody wash. I shouted at her.'

I gawk incredulously at him.

'I know.' He winces. 'Stop. I feel awful about it but then Fran shouted at me and sure now no one is talking to anyone. And today, right, in an effort I guess to make peace, do you know what she said to me?'

'Go on.'

'Red suits you. Red suits you,' he repeats, as I laugh. 'Jesus, Lucy, I'm losing my mind.'

I'm still laughing as I enter our office. Immediately, the theme music of *Saturday Night Fever* blasts out of Larry's computer and he and Ben crack up laughing. Dan gives them the fingers, but he's grinning.

Larry uploads some footage and soon the three of us are staring at crap pictures taken in dim light on empty roads. 'Such a dead-end shithole,' Larry murmurs.

'This in my hometown and it's very beautiful, thanks.' I poke him in the arm. 'Easy to know you've never climbed the Booster.'

'I'd rather eat my head, thanks.'

'I wish you would. Then we wouldn't have to look at it.'

Larry laughs good-naturedly.

My mobile rings.

'Hey, Lucy, it's Eileen here.' Then realising I haven't a clue who she is, she says, 'The guard who's dealing with Barry Jones's accident.'

'Sorry. I don't think I got your name the first time we talked.'

She gets straight to business. I like Eileen. 'I've got some interesting footage from the bar that night for you. Moira Delaney is there so I thought you might be interested.'

'Absolutely.'

'And just FYI, if you roll the footage on, you can clearly see a woman put something in Barry's drink. She's older, maybe thirties, forties.'

'Grand.'

'I'm sending now. I'm setting up an interview with Barry in the next week or so. He might be able to offer an ID on this woman. If it's useful to you, I'll pass it on.'

'I'm seeing him this evening in connection with the Moira Delaney case. I can ask him for you, if you like.'

'That'd be great.' There's definite relief in her voice. 'The last thing I need is a trip up to Dublin.'

'Consider it done.'

Two minutes later the footage drops into my email.

23

Dan and I arrive in Dublin around four, having stopped off for food and a shirt in Maynooth. As we turn onto the M4, and after he's had a moan about Delores, I tell him about Luc.

My story is met with silence. 'I'm so . . .' I pull into the fast lane '. . . pissed with him.'

'It was a bit of a shit thing to do, all right,' Dan agrees. 'But Tani looked happy enough the day we saw her. Eh, don't keep accelerating.'

'It might be just a rebound guy.'

'And maybe it's not. Luce, they're both young. I mean, would they even have lasted this long if it wasn't for Sirocco? Jaysus' sake, slow down.'

'Sorry.' I take my foot off the accelerator. 'I just thought Luc had more integrity.'

'No one has integrity when they're young.'

'I had.'

Dan smirks a bit at my self-righteous tone.

And even as I say it, I think that my integrity had allowed Johnny Egan to humiliate me with Katherine because I'd clung to that relationship even when it was publicly crumbling. I jab

168

Dan's arm. 'You're useless at comforting me, d'you know that?'

'Luc is a good lad. He's a good dad. He'll be grand.' Then, with a wink, he adds, 'Better?'

'Better.'

'Drop me off at the Central Criminal Court,' Dan says, as we turn onto Dublin's quays. 'I'll meet you at the Central Remedial Clinic at seven, unless you want to join me?' Dan loves a good trial.

Normally I'd jump at it. I enjoy the spectacle of courtroom too: the drama, the reveals, the showmanship of the barristers. I like it better again when the accused gets sentenced. It means we've done our job right. But today I have something else I want to do. Something I haven't told anyone about. Something that's been at the back of my mind since Rob died. 'I'll catch you over there at seven,' I say.

He doesn't ask why I'm not accompanying him. Instead, as I drop him off, he tips me a salute, tells me to have a good day and we go our separate ways.

Forty minutes later, using Google, I drive the M50 motorway en route to Dundrum. As signs flash past of all the places I used to be so familiar with, there is an unexpected pang in my stomach. I'm not sure if it's grief at what was or apprehension at what I might find.

At the large roundabout on the turn-off, it takes me a moment, and an annoyed blast of a horn from the motorist behind, to get my bearings. I take a left, towards Ballinteer where I lived with Rob and Luc for nine whole years. Another lifetime. I never kept in touch with anyone from back then, being too ashamed of what

Rob had done to allow myself any memories of a place where I had been so happy – falsely, as it turned out. I had lived a lie and not even known it, telling everyone that Rob was a property salesman. And telling everyone that I was a detective inspector, overseeing the hard cases, running informants, cracking the whip. Some detective I was. I couldn't even see the rot under my own nose.

The demotion that came with it, back to guard, back to the arse end of Mayo, was humiliating but not unexpected. The scar on my face that came soon after had sent me spinning, but I'd rallied, clawed my way back, working every hour, taking all the shit jobs, and I'd done well. But it came with a price. Luc had been reared by my mother. I'd done my best but work was the one thing I understood. The rest of life was just too unpredictable to dip my toe in again. But lately, what with the dreams I'm having and the fact that Rob once again confounded my certainties about things, I've been hankering to just . . . I can't explain . . . go back to where it started. See if it's as I remember.

I drive past the church and turn left again, driving on down the road and into a small car park beside another church. I take a breath. I'll walk from here.

The weather is mild, damp, not like the wildness of home. I spot things I'd forgotten. The old oak tree at the top of Sycamore Lane is still there. The cracked wall that divided one road from the other is still cracked, worse than I remember. The fields and sports pitches are there, some kids kicking around a football, running about in T-shirts and shorts even though it's chilly. And it's not as green as in my memory, maybe because now I'm so immersed in large open spaces, in the emerald grass and golden brown of the bogs. The colour here is dulled, the fields too manicured, sculpted and carefully controlled, a sanitised version of nature. Turning from the ad-hoc soccer match, my heart picks up pace and I can feel it hammering against the walls of my ribcage as I cross from Willow Lane into Birch Avenue. A long road of large, semi-detached houses, with big driveways and birch trees planted in every back garden. Thankfully, it's deserted, people not yet coming back from work and kids inside doing homework maybe. Taking what courage I have, I stroll as casually as I can down to number twenty six. Past the Byrnes' – they put Christmas lights up all over their garden each year – and the Rabbitts', who had the breeding prowess of rabbits with their eight kids. That's what Rob used to say. I can hear his voice now, rich and teasing. Cum, rabbit, cum, rabbit, cum, cum, cum. I laughed at it every time. Next was Bennetts', then Coles', Reillys' and O'Briens'. The names come back to me easily.

And there it is.

The Ganleys'. Our old house.

St Fiacre. I'd forgotten that.

The patron saint of gardeners. Rob had christened the house for a joke one night after we'd had a row about him not cutting the grass. 'There's the man to help us,' he'd said, as he drilled the sign onto the wall.

The new owners had kept the name.

The door has changed from black to red. And Fiacre must have worked some magic because the garden blooms with roses and poppies and is so full of colour that I'm glad these people, whoever they are, live here. Cream blinds on the windows, one car in the driveway. And, too late, a woman in the garden of O'Briens' straightens. I hadn't seen her behind the low wall that runs around the gardens of the houses. She'd been pulling weeds from a flowerbed.

171

She recognises me immediately, as I do her. Debbie O'Brien, my best friend back then. Luc and her little lad loved running in and out of each other's houses. They had played for the same soccer team, gambolling about pitches in their oversized kit and performing forward rolls whenever they scored a goal. Debbie would always mind Luc, and Rob would mind her young lad. I was always busy working. But if I had a free ticket for the cinema or a concert, it was always Debbie I called on. She looks the same, if older. A few more lines around her eyes and a droop to her shoulders that hadn't been there when I'd left. She regards me, I regard her. I wonder what she sees.

The silence stretches.

I lift a hand in a half-wave. 'Hi. Just . . . just seeing the old neighbourhood.'

I don't know what I expect her to do but when, after holding my gaze for a moment, she bends to resume her weeding, it cuts me to the quick.

It's what I deserve.

I can't get away fast enough.

24

Pat rings me as I'm waiting for Dan outside the hospital and he wastes no time on small talk. 'I had a look at that zip drive, Luce,' he says, and there is a grave note in his voice that makes my heart plummet.

'And? Good or bad?'

'I'd like to tell you these files are old, Lucy, but they were created just over a year ago. And, yes, bad.'

'Shit.' And it's not a 'Shit' because Rob had been scamming again. I think I half expected that. It's a 'Shit' for Luc. It's 'Shit' because I'll once again be the one to expose his dad as a bad guy, just when he believes Rob was a hero and someone to be proud of.

And yet Rob was both, I suppose. Though if he had thought he was going to die, I doubt very much he'd have jumped through the window in the first place.

'What was he doing?' I ask.

'In simple terms, he buys email addresses and sends out unsolicited stock-market predictions to them,' Pat says. 'To half of the list he writes that shares in, say, gold are going up next weekend and to buy and to the other half he says that shares are going down. This means that to fifty per cent of the people he's right. He disposes of the emails where he'd got it wrong. With the emails where he predicted correctly, he sends another prediction. He tells half that silver is going up and the other half that silver is going down. Once again he's correct with half of the list. And then he does the same thing a third time. On the fourth go, he sends emails out asking for payment for predictions and, of course, if he's got it right three times in a row, people will risk twenty quid. And he just keeps going and going and going, collecting twenty quid each time he's right.'

'Shit.'

'There is, wait for it, over three million in the bank accounts I've managed to locate.'

'No, no, no, no, no,' I whimper.

'My advice?' Pat says.

'Go on.'

'If this is what I think it is, Luce, the person is dead. This person can't be prosecuted. You could turn it over to Computer Crime and, really, what can they do?'

I could also get rid of it, I think. Not have any reminder of anything any more. Let Luc believe his fairy tales.

'People have been swindled out of their savings,' Pat goes on. 'They might get something back.' He waits for me to respond and when I don't, he asks, 'All right?'

'Thanks, Pat.'

He bids me goodbye and I hang up.

I need to get rid of the bloody thing. I am horror struck at the thought of turning it over.

Dan, knocking on the car door, startles me. Pulling on my coat and scarf, I join him outside.

Deep breaths, Lucy, I tell myself.

'A slam-dunk today in court,' Dan tells me gleefully, as we walk at a brisk pace towards the hospital reception. I listen with half an ear as he gives me a blow-by-blow account of how the prosecuting barrister had delivered his closing remarks standing beside an old woman in the public gallery. 'As he's telling everyone about the defenceless old woman who was tied up and robbed in her home, they're all looking at her in her seat and thinking, My God, she's so tiny. That could be my mother or aunt or whatever. The man is a genius.'

At Reception, there's a form-filling exercise to go through. Then, twenty minutes later, armed with three cups of coffee, we are escorted to a beautifully bright, cheerful reception room, where Barry Jones is waiting for us at a table. Barry Jones. The 'Bar' from Moira's Instagram.

I'm taken aback at how impossibly young he looks for a twenty-nine-year-old guy. Wiry, with wide blue eyes and a riot of loose curls framing a baby face. A dimple punctures his left cheek. I'd imagine women flock to him. He wears a tracksuit, and despite the wheelchair, he looks fit and healthy.

Dan pulls up a couple of chairs and I hand Barry a cuppa.

'Thanks,' he says, taking a sip. 'Any sugar?'

I pass him two sachets and he uses both. 'That's better,' he says. Then, with pain in his voice, he asks, 'Any sign of Moira?'

'Nothing yet that we're aware of,' Dan answers. 'How you doing?'

Barry indicates the wheelchair, says with a hint of humour, 'I've been better.'

'Bloody terrible luck,' Dan acknowledges. 'A car ploughed into you, I heard?'

'So they tell me. I don't know.' Barry shrugs. 'All I remember is knocking back a whiskey. Last drink of the night. After that, it's a blur. They think drugs or something but I never took anything like that ever.' There's a pause before he says, 'What is it you want to know about Moira? How can I help?'

'Anything you can tell us, really. Start off with the last time you saw her.'

'She came in to visit me last weekend with the kids. She was in great form, chatting away, fixing up my room, eating all my sweets, having the laugh.' Sadness flits across his face. 'Bren was all chat - he loved their little cottage and . . .' he gathers himself '. . . Ella, she was loving being in school. Loving their new house.' He brings a hand to his face and rubs his eyes hard. 'Moira was so happy. Her life was moving on, and I can't believe . . .' He looks at us. 'And Ella? She's really . . . gone?'

'Yes. And we're wondering if Moira—'

'Look, I don't know Moira as well as I used to, all right. But I do know, from when she stayed with me and from our conversations since, that she loved those kids. And I knew her way back in college and she was . . . she'd never have . . .' He shakes his head. 'No. No way.'

'We think she may have been abducted. Do you know of anyone who would want to hurt her or Ella?'

'Yes,' he snaps, without hesitation. 'Him. Eamon.'

And even though I knew he was going to say that, the word is a bomb in my head. I want to fist-bump Dan. I want to jump up and say, 'Yes! See? I told you!'

'How so?' Dan's voice betrays nothing of his emotions.

'He's a creep. Tries out being nice in the beginning but it's just a ruse to get what he wants.' His voice rises. 'He was a sneaky

176

bastard. He took Moira from me and I didn't even notice. It was like he saw her, figured out what she wanted and became it. For a while anyway.'

Lots of people do that, I think. Usually the ones with no self-esteem. Or, part of me whispers, the ones who want to entrap.

'Moira was great in college, good fun,' Barry continues. 'We were together. She was even going to have our baby but . . . well, she lost it at six weeks.' Even now, remembering, he looks devastated. 'After that everything changed with us. Maybe she realised she'd had a lucky escape. I don't think she ever wanted a humdrum life. She was waiting for security – she wanted a guy who had money.' He laughs a little bitterly. 'That's like – not being mean about her, it was understandable. She never had much security growing up, I don't think. Eamon was right there – he'd been there all along, spending money on her, sending her gifts, and didn't he have a farm coming to him? That was all Moira needed to hear. She took up with him.'

'But how does that mean he would want to harm her?'

'Because once they got together and it was soon after the baby thing . . . Moira ghosted me. I hadn't her pegged as that type of person. I took it bad.' He glances at his hands and a shadow crosses his face. 'Very bad. My poor mother, Jesus, I put her through hell. But once I got myself together, I accepted it and tried to be happy for her and all. But I saw her once, when I was down visiting my mother. It was maybe about a year after she moved to Louisburgh. I was in Westport and there she was, and I was going to say hi to her but . . . well, she was pushing a buggy and she looked . . .' he tries to think of the right word '. . . beaten down. I just, well, I had a weird feeling, looking at her. She didn't seem like the Moira I knew. I didn't go near her but I couldn't shake the feeling that all was not right for her so I tracked Eamon's place down and eventually plucked up the courage to call in to her a good few months later. And maybe she thought it was odd, me turning up on her doorstep, but it was more than that. She was so on edge, jumpy, and when Eamon arrived into the room, she just . . . well, she became downright unfriendly. He was nice enough but it was for show. That man buried her alive. The next thing is she contacts me in January, out of the blue, asking for a place to stay as she had left Eamon and didn't want her kids in her father's place as it was too rough. She'd kept my number all those years.' He gulps down his emotion. 'Tell you one thing, when she left him, he didn't take it well.'

'Really?'

'He messaged her every night. He was threatening all sorts against her. That's why she moved to Achill, so he could see the children and maybe he'd calm down. Plus it would look good in court. But the texts didn't stop. He even bought a phone with a different number, she said, and pretended it wasn't him. And the things she told me that he did, honestly, I wanted to kill him.'

'What things?'

'That he'd check her texts at the end of every day. He'd go through her call logs and she'd have to answer questions about why she rang this person or that person. Then she'd have to tell him what she said to them. And it was never the right thing. In the end, she said it was just easier not to call anyone. And if they ever went out, which wasn't much, she had to keep her eyes down and not talk to anyone, because if he thought she was even glancing at a man, he'd pinch her arm and totally go off on one when they got home. Anything she'd wear had to be run by him first because he wasn't having her dress like a whore and she a respectable farmer's wife.' He looks distressed. 'Like, it was everything and yet nothing. That's what Moira said. She knew if someone challenged him on it, he'd explain it away. In the end she was doubting her own mind, thinking maybe that she was imagining it all or that she was overreacting.'

'Did she say if there was any history of violence?'

'She never said, but he didn't have to hit her, did he?' He doesn't wait for us to answer, he goes on, 'She was a nervous wreck by the time she eventually left him.'

'When we talked to Eamon, he said they were on good terms.'

'Well, they weren't.' He sounds angry at the idea of it.

'Did you ever witness any of this?'

'No.'

If Moira had wanted Barry to give her a reference for a cottage and for a job, she might have embellished things. She might just have been a woman who'd left her husband.

'We'll be checking her texts,' I say. 'And if we do find threats or intimidation, we'll talk to him. Now, other than Eamon, is there anyone else who would hurt them?'

'Just him.' Barry is adamant.

'You're saying he killed his daughter?'

For a second, he hesitates. 'Maybe it was a mistake on his part. I don't know.'

'You liked Moira a lot yourself?' Dan asks.

Barry flushes. 'Yes, yes, I did. But that's got nothing to do with anything.'

But of course it has. It colours everything. No matter how nice a lad Barry is, Eamon with his farm and house and money had taken away his relationship with this girl. It's bound to affect his perception of the man.

179

'You gave her false references for the cottage and for the job.'

'Yes. She needed them. That fucking bastard even wrecked that for her.'

And there it is. I can almost hear a click. The timings, the mystery of the sleepover. That piece I'd been missing slots beautifully into the narrative.

'He was meant to take the kids for the night so that she could go for the job interview, but once he found out what she was up to, he bloody refused. She rang me that day and she was crying.' He swallows hard. 'She was certain she'd get the job and then she didn't. It was her only hope of providing for the kids. Bastard.' He swipes a hand across his face, lobbing his empty coffee cup at the bin.

'These are people we believe Moira was in contact with.' Dan shows Barry the photocopy of the Christmas-card list Eamon had given us yesterday. It was disappointing, really: there were only about ten names on it. Most have been identified and questioned. 'Anyone there with a grudge that you'd know of?'

Barry scans it. 'The only name I know on that is her dad, sorry.' He hands the list back to Dan. 'But, trust me, it's Eamon you need to be looking at.'

'Thanks, Barry. Now, on another subject entirely . . .' I pull out my laptop and call up the CCTV from the pub. 'The guards in Limerick passed this on to me today. It's harvested from the pub you were in on the night of your accident. There's a woman on the video they're keen to identify.'

He takes my laptop from me, presses play, and footage of a packed pub appears onscreen. Barry is immediately recognisable at the bar paying for a pint of Guinness and a glass of whiskey. We watch as he pockets his credit card. He is just lifting the pints from the bar when his attention is caught by a woman saying something to him. 'She asked if I'd dropped some money,' Barry remembers.

We see him look down and shake his head but as he does so, the woman drops something into the whiskey.

'Did you notice that?' I ask.

Barry has paled.

'Play it again,' he says.

I slow it down and we watch it for a second time.

'How long was she there, in the pub?' Barry asks.

Dan looks at me and I shrug.

'Do you recognise her?' I pull up an enlarged image.

Barry shakes his head. 'The whiskey was Moira's. I drank it as she'd had enough and didn't want another. That pill was meant for her.'

25

On the way out, as I update William, Dan retrieves Barry's coffee cup and places it in an evidence bag. I am fizzing with excitement as I fill William in. If this woman was prepared to drug Moira, what else would she be capable of? And though Barry didn't recognise her, perhaps Eamon or her father would. I try not to think about how this new information complicates the case.

'That's great work,' William says. 'And don't worry about Barry not being able to prove his statements about Eamon. It corroborates Anna Byrne's account.'

'Who?'

'She saw Eamon on the TV this morning and had a few tales to tell about him. That little stunt of his backfired,' he adds, with satisfaction. 'Plus, Mick managed to use his big-boy voice today and he kicked some arse. Moira's phone records came down and they're very interesting. Hop it. Get some sleep. Long day tomorrow.'

Three hours later, Dan and I collect our cars from Achill station. Though I'm buzzing, the thoughts of Rob's laptop taking up space in my boot burns away at the back of my mind. I am so focused on it that I almost run over some teenagers dragging

182

wood and branches across the road to a raggy bonfire they've erected.

'Shit.' I wave an apology at them as they give me the fingers.

Only another couple of days until the fires are lit across the county, I think, as I spy a small one higher up on a hill. I can't wait to see Sirocco's face as she watches the massive one burn up at Achill-henge. The henge is a horrible-looking but compelling monstrosity that was illegally built on a hill overlooking Achill more than a decade ago. Constructed in one weekend, the man responsible for it had lost a lot of money in the Anglo Irish debacle. He christened the structure, which is fashioned on Stonehenge, the Tomb of the Celtic Tiger. There was a lot of legal wrangling, and he was told to take it down but he refused. The council were to demolish it but they still haven't. Apparently, if it had been brought to completion, it was engineered to capture the solstice, so it's kind of fitting that St John's Eve is being celebrated there. Lorna and my mother had been the brains behind the idea and pushed it with the council, who, I think, were too scared to say no. A makeshift car park will be in operation on the night and there will be jeeps and vans to ferry people to within two hundred metres of the henge. They'll have to walk the rest of the way themselves or, if fit enough, they can walk from the car park. Refreshments will be served at the barn, where the jeeps stop. At midnight, the fire will be lit, and when it burns down, embers will be taken from it to be scattered across the land to ensure its fertility for the coming year. When safe enough, couples with hands joined will leap across it to see if they'll stay together. Luc and Tani had jumped a bonfire last year amid much cheering.

And that's when the idea presents itself.

I turn sharply and take the road for Achill-henge. I urge my car up the appalling track but eventually it becomes impassable for all but the hardiest of vehicles. I pull in, get out and take the laptop from the boot.

There are only a handful of houses up this way. I trudge onwards, my legs aching with the effort.

This is illegal, my brain tells me. *You're destroying evidence.*

But who will ever know? It'll be burned to ash.

Oh, God, am I really doing this?

As I round the bend, the bonfire rears up in front of me. It's an impressive creation, though there is a lot of junk on it, people coming in the night to get rid of their crap rather than paying for a skip. Mostly, though, it consists of wood, including branches from felled trees. The council have outdone themselves as there is a hoist with a basket attached so that things can be thrown directly onto the top of the bonfire. I take the laptop from its bag and stand on it, smashing it with the heel of my shoe. The keyboard crunches and the glass smashes and the keys fall out. Guilt flattens me, causing me to freeze with the shock.

What am I doing?

I think I might be sick.

But Luc will hate me for ever if I don't.

And I'll hate myself for ever if I do.

Later I'm in a daze as I watch Luc go through a box of his dad's belongings. I've made feeble attempts to talk to him about this girl he said he kissed but, unsurprisingly, I've been met with monosyllabic answers.

In silence, he pulls out a grey and red cardigan and holds it up to his chest.

I can't help myself: 'You're not keeping that, are you?'

184

Sensing my disapproval, he answers, 'Yes.'

'But it's . . .' His flat-eyed gaze warns me off. I change tack. 'Are you having Sirocco tomorrow?'

'Yep.'

'You'd want to see her with her dolls the last day she came. She had them in coffins and—'

'Nana told me about it.' He makes a big deal of examining a blue T-shirt that has seen better days. 'That's the night Lorna came to you for help and now Denis can't go out of his house. The guards told him it's not safe.'

'Lorna made a statement to me, Luc, a statement against her husband. I was only doing my job. And, frankly, if Denis did go off and kill someone, he should be in jail.'

'You just care about putting people in jail. Sure, look at Dad.'

I freeze, inhale a breath of calm, resist the urge to tell him about the laptop. 'Rob was a thief.'

'Only because he felt he had to match up to you and your brilliant career.'

'Ah, here now—'

'And it wasn't so brilliant, was it? Sure, you made a perfectly nice man be an informer and then he came and broke into our house and killed my dad.'

'Perfectly nice man?' My voice rises.

'He probably was before you took his wife and kid from him and then he killed Rob.'

'Do you believe that? Do you really believe that?'

He drops his gaze. 'Yes,' he mutters. 'It's what happened.'

'What also happened is that your father ripped off thousands of people, left them penniless, Katherine and Johnny, Tani's parents, among them. He also—'

185

'He only ripped them off because you didn't like them. I heard Nana say it to Lorna once and—'

I ignore that. 'Remember Mrs Mills who used to—'

'My dad died and he shouldn't have.' With that stunningly simple observation, my son dismisses me. He hefts a box onto his shoulder and marches down to his room.

'I did nothing wrong,' I yell after him, like a five-year-old.

'Only me!' my mother calls, the front door slamming behind her, distracting me from marching down to his room and yelling it again. 'Oh, Lord, Lucy, you won't believe what's after happening.'

'What?' I hop up, on full alert.

'There's a petition going around about Denis Long being arrested. "Clear the name of Denis Long" it's called.' She frowns. 'It's not very catchy, is it?' Without waiting for me to answer, she pulls a sheet of paper from her bag and lays it in front of me. 'Do you want to sign it?'

Is she for real?

I push the paper back to her. 'First, Denis Long's name is clear because at the moment we don't have enough to charge him and, second, no, I can't sign it because, as you know, I'm a guard and guards investigate and, honestly, if people in this house can't understand that, well, tough.'

Offended, she piously tucks her petition back into her bag. 'I'm sorry if I want to support my friend.'

'And what about your daughter?'

'I always support you.'

'Well, in this instance, you can't do both. Lorna is the one who reported him and—'

'She never thought it'd go this far.'

I don't dignify that with a response. 'Can we not do this?' I pour myself some wine. 'I just had Luc take my head off. Jesus, he's made me into a villain and Rob into some sort of a saint.'

'Of course he has,' my mother says, as if that's normal. She pulls a glass from the press and helps herself to the wine. 'Sure, the poor lad feels terrible guilty. God love him, the last time he talked to Rob, didn't he insult him terrible? And in the middle of Rob's photograph exhibition too. He knows he ruined his father's big night. He has to take the guilt out on someone. You should be flattered it's you.'

'Does he blame me for letting him do that?'

'No.' She's not convincing, but I let it go.

Settling down at the table, she says, 'I saw Katherine tonight. She was coming out of the hotel in Mulranny,' her voice dips, 'with a man.' Before I can respond, she adds, 'I told you she had someone. I think I'm the one should be a guard.' A little laugh. 'From what I could see he was a fine thing. Tall and broad, not like that weasel of a husband. Are you going to bed already?'

'Busy day tomorrow,' I drop a kiss onto her head.

Eamon

Incident 4: Family

Patti doesn't like Moira. Patti comes three times a week even if she isn't invited and she sits in the kitchen, carries food into the TV room and takes meat from the freezer. It was her home first, she tells Moira and him.

Patti tells Eamon that Ella is too skinny. Moira tells her to mind her own business.

Eamon likes it. These two women going into battle.

He likes the way Moira looks to him for help and all he can do is shrug. 'She is skinny,' he says. 'You need to feed her more.'

Then he tells her that Ella looks a little fat.

Patti agrees.

On and on, round and round.

Like a funfair.

Flick.

Flick.

One day, just before they moved to the farm, Moira is tired. Eamon says she shouldn't be trying to paint pictures: it was making her exhausted. He is worried about her, he says. It's high time she concentrated on Ella instead of trying to do it all. 'You missed your mother not being there,' he tells her. 'Don't do the same on little Ella. She loves you. She depends on you.'

Moira says she will miss painting but he tells her that will pass. Things pass, he says. And new things come instead.

Moira thinks of her mother a lot now, maybe because she is a mother too. Eamon is pissed off listening to her. 'Don't keep going on and on about it,' he says. But one day, when he is out, she calls her father. He knows because he sees the call on her mobile when he asked to look. 'I just want to know if he knows where Mammy went,' she explains to him.

Eamon thought she didn't talk to her father.

'I do now and again,' she says. 'And I want to know about my mother.'

'You have your own family now.' Eamon pokes his face at her. 'Are we not good enough for you? Are you not happy? Have I gone looking for my mother? No.'

But she gets worse and no amount of discipline helps. One day, in winter, she doesn't light the fire for him coming in from work. So he has to discipline her, then makes her sit outside in the cold in her pyjamas.

It was for her to see what it was like for him all day, that's all. There was no need for her to go ringing the guards.

But she withdrew it after he'd told her how sorry he was, how he had just had a bad day, and don't you always take bad days out on the ones you love? He was so sorry. He loved her. If she wanted to call her da and get him to explain, she could. He wouldn't advise it. Once things are out of a bottle, you can't put them back in – and what if she found out something that made Eamon not love her any more? What about that? But he loves her and trusts she will do what's best.

One day, when they moved to the farm, Moira's dad just came and visited the house, which was annoying. He couldn't even blame Moira because he knew she hadn't answered his calls when he'd rung. He'd finally convinced her that she didn't need to know about her mother to be a mother. But there he is, Mr Flannery, pulling up in their drive on Sunday afternoon. Stepping out of his old Merc, wearing a suit with style. Moira's dad looks like Moira, only taller and leaner and meaner.

Eamon doesn't want to cross him, he thinks.

He just needs to keep him at bay.

'I don't want to see him,' Moira says.

Her dad knocks on the door and shouts through the letterbox that he is ready to tell her the truth about her ma. 'Princess,' he says, 'I'll tell the truth.'

Eamon makes a gesture. 'Let him in if you want. If you're happy to let him in.' And she does, the stupid bitch.

He pours Nick a drink, which Nick refuses because he's driving.

'I like to obey the law,' he says, and breaks his hole laughing.

Moira laughs a little at that too. 'Nice to see you're obeying the law, Dad,' she says, and he laughs and Eamon is LEFT OUT.

It's only later he understands the whole of it.

It's only later he realises who the fuck he married.

Her dad says what a nice house Moira has and Eamon says it's his parents' house. Her dad says, 'But it's Moira's house too now, yes?' And there is something in that look that forces Eamon to agree. He says Moira is a great wife and her da says that Moira is a princess and Moira says, 'What is it you want to tell me?'

Her da looks at the floor, at the ceiling, at her. 'You were too young at eight to know,' he says. 'But now you have a little girl and a good man to help you and it's time to tell. Your mother walked from the Estate to the Shannon and drowned herself. She filled her pockets with rocks and sank. Sorry now.' And her da puts down his tea and shuffles to his feet, and Moira rushes out of the room. Eamon promises Nick that he will take care of her.

Soon after, her da leaves and Moira sobs into her pillow and Eamon hisses in her ear, 'Well, you pushed and pushed and now you know. You wouldn't listen to me. Your mother was a selfish cow to do that. At least mine only left me.'

And they never spoke of it any more.

But he thinks about Moira's mother now in the fading life he has left. What she did made Moira the best mother she could be.

Moira didn't leave her kids. She left *with* her kids.

26

Day 6

The Cig wasn't joking when he said it would be a busy day. He's given me and Dan the job of questioning Eamon when he's finally arrested. Before that, though, we must get as much as we can on him. As we pore over all the information, new details coming in bit by bit, we plan our strategy. We identify our objectives, things we want to probe, and figure out how to use the information we have to its best advantage.

We also run through some of Eamon's expected responses, to ascertain if we can pick them apart.

I know I won't be able to build much of a rapport with him, so Dan will be conducting the interview.

As with Denis, we don't have enough to charge him, we can't place him at the scene on the night of the fire, but we do have plenty to suspect him of an offence. The hope is he'll inadvertently give us what we need. And if we can get enough we may be able to persuade the super to let us detain him for another six hours.

At four o'clock, having been arrested at his home amid a lot of shouting, Eamon, wearing his farming gear complete with boots that smell of shite, is waiting for us in Interview Room Two. His solicitor sits neatly beside him, hair parted, legs crossed, sharp suit. As we enter, the stench assails us but we're prepared for it. Or, at least, I am. Dan is quite anal about dirt and muck, and if I didn't think Eamon was quite so repellent, I'd probably laugh.

'Hello,' Dan says cheerily, before inserting three DVDs into the recorder, cautioning Eamon once more and informing him that everything is being recorded. Then he introduces both of us by rank, and asks Eamon and his solicitor to introduce themselves, too, for the purposes of the recording.

'You all right for everything, Eamon?' Dan arranges his files in a neat stack on the desk as I slide in beside him, flexing my fingers in readiness for all the note-taking. It won't do any good, though: they'll still cramp afterwards. And, honestly, I have yet to meet one person in the force who thinks writing down interviews makes any sense.

'D'you fancy any more tea or coffee?' Dan asks.

'I fancy knowing what the hell I'm doing here.' Eamon leans across the table, eyeballing Dan. 'Is this some sort of payback for my going on TV yesterday? Can the guards in this country not take a bit of criticism? She' – he jabs his finger in my direction – 'she wouldn't tell me anything. My child was murdered. My wife is missing. And I really don't need my father-in-law getting wind of me being held here or I'll be wiped out too.'

'At the time, DS Lucy Golden wasn't legally able to tell you anything. Believe me, if we had charged someone, you would be the first to know. All we did yesterday was we brought a man in for questioning, same as we've done with you. He said he wasn't guilty, same as you're saying. And unless we can prove it, we are not going to go naming people. You wouldn't like it now, would you?'

'Because I'm not guilty.' He sits back and folds his arms.

So much for rapport. I can see Dan wondering where exactly he should bring the conversation to now and, just as I would have done, he decides to go for it. 'All right, I can see you're anxious to get started, so we'll fire ahead. There are a few things we need you to clarify for us. Now, I know we've gone through this before but would you tell us about the last time you saw Moira. In as much detail as you can. Time you arrived, what you talked about, that kind of thing.'

Eamon heaves a sigh that seems to come from his filthy boots. 'I called over at three thirty,' he says, in a monotone, as if we're stupid. 'She answered the door. The children were inside watching TV. She was looking well, all dressed up. She was going for a job, she said. I wished her luck and I had a coffee and then I left. That was it, really.'

'I just have a few questions on that. Can you clarify for us what time you left?'

'No, I can't clarify that.'

'How long roughly is the journey from Louisburgh to Slievemore?'

'About an hour and ten.'

'And, finally, why did you call over that day?'

'I was, eh, just checking in.'

'But you were there again the next morning?'

'I was. I was there to collect the children. Ella had a day off school and I was bringing them out. Getting them off Moira's hands. She told me to come early.' A beat. 'She couldn't wait to get rid of them.'

'I see.' Dan pretends to consider this. Then he flicks through some paperwork as if he's searching for something. 'Ah,' he says.

'That's what I thought.' His gaze flips to Eamon. 'You originally told us you called on your wife to bring her a paintbrush or something to do with her art.'

Eamon stares somewhere over Dan's head. He shifts slightly in the seat. 'I did. Yes, I did. That's right. I forgot.'

Liars forget. We all know that.

'Easy to do,' Dan agrees. Then asks, 'So, why not bring her the rest of her things?'

'I'm sorry?' He jerks.

'The rest of her art supplies? They were in that studio on your farm, weren't they? Why not bring her those too, save you future journeys? It's a long way.'

'She didn't ask for anything else.' There's a small defensive note in his voice now. 'Small cottage, no space for anything anyway.'

'Of course, that makes sense. Yeah, I didn't think of that.'

Eamon's shoulders relax slightly.

'Let's talk about the timings then,' Dan says pleasantly. 'Is this your vehicle? Please note that I'm showing Exhibit MD15, a CCTV image of a dark blue Land Rover taken at Achill Sound at fifteen ten on the fifteenth of June last.'

Eamonn examines the picture. 'That's mine.'

'It's approximately a twenty-minute journey from the Sound to the cottage,' Dan says. 'So you're right when you say you got there at three thirty. Now, here is an image, Exhibit MD16, of your jeep leaving the island that same day. Would you agree that's the same vehicle?'

'Yes, which means I left and wasn't there that night.'

Dan ignores this. Eamon is right, but that's not to say he didn't travel back in another car. 'This image was taken at four o'clock that day.' Dan pauses, shrugs, 'So you see our problem, Eamon?'

'No.'

'Let me explain,' Dan says, as if he is doing Eamon a great favour. 'If you got to the cottage at three thirty and you were back in Achill Sound at four, it means you had less than ten minutes to talk to Moira and the children, have tea, and then leave. Pleasant conversations tend to take more than ten minutes. Arguments, however—'

'I did not argue with my wife. Maybe it did only take ten minutes. She was in a hurry out, I told you that already.'

'D'you know what I think, Eamon?'

'I don't give a fuck what you think.' His voice rises: 'This is a guard set-up. That's what it is.' He turns to his solicitor. 'What are you sitting there like a dummy for? I'm not paying you to wear a suit and stay shtum. I've had enough of this.' He stands up, sending his chair toppling over. 'I'm leaving. I'm leaving now.'

'You can't,' Dan says calmly. 'You're under arrest. Your detention period is for six hours unless we get it extended, which we just might do.'

Eamon's eyes narrow and the silence builds, like an elastic band about to snap. Finally, he turns around and looks pointedly at his upturned chair. His solicitor picks it up and Eamon sits down.

And here we go. Belt up, Eamon, I think. You're in for a rough ride.

'I believe,' Dan begins, and Eamon starts to hum, 'that Moira had to be in Keel for four thirty and she asked you to take the children that afternoon for a sleepover. You know why? Because no one, not her landlords, or her neighbours or any of the parents at the school, said they were taking the children that night, no one. And we know the children were to go on a sleepover because her landlords told us and her friend Barry Jones told us.'

195

He stops humming momentarily upon hearing Barry's name but starts up again.

'Were you having the children that night, Eamon?'

He presses his lips together. Hums louder.

'How did you feel when you saw your wife all dressed up and you heard she was going for a job interview?' Dan produces another statement. 'Another witness told us that Moira apologised for bringing the children into the interview, that her plans had changed. Did you change those plans, Eamon?'

'Fuck off,' Eamon hisses.

'It would do you good to cooperate with us. Our colleagues still have to chat with Bren so he might shed some light on what happened that day. Moving on—'

'That stupid bitch never told me she was thinking of getting a job. Why would I help her? If she got the bloody thing, it'd only make it easier to live away from me. I'm not a patsy for anyone.'

Yes!

'So, you admit that she had asked you to babysit.'

'When I got there and found out what it was for, I suppose I was annoyed. I told her she could fecking well get a job without any help from me and I left. I shouldn't have but I did and . . .' to my surprise, his voice breaks '. . . the children suffered.' It's quite horrifying to witness the tears in his eyes. He seems such a harsh man. 'It's hard to live with,' he says eventually, his voice muffled. 'It's so hard to live with.'

His solicitor glances at us, then at his client.

'Is there anything you'd like to say, Eamon?' Dan asks, after a small silence.

We know he didn't kill her during that argument because she was at the Moose at four thirty. We also know he left the island.

'Just that if I'd taken the children when I should have, Ella would still be here,' he says. 'But instead she died. And that's my fault. Me and my fucking temper.' And sobs tear out of him, and I think that if he's pretending he's a bloody good actor. I feel my certainty slipping away.

'I think we'll take a break now,' Dan says, and while I think we might get more out of him if we keep going, it could also land us in trouble come any trial. 'We'll kick off a new interview later this evening after you've had something to eat. Interview stopped at sixteen forty-five.' He presses the button on the recorder.

'Thanks be to Jaysus.' Dan inhales a lungful of air once in the corridor. 'Jesus, the stench of these boots. He's a total gouger.'

'Yeah, but is he guilty?'

'I thought you said he was,' Dan teases.

I wince because, really, it's a thing no guard should ever say. 'Let's see what happens later.'

'D'you think it's Denis?'

'I find that even harder to get my head around,' I admit. 'Maybe I'm too close to it. Maybe it's this CCTV woman.'

'Let's brief the Cig, grab some food and see where we're at.'

Music to my ears.

The food in the local hotel is great and, because they know us, they generally give us extra. Today, though, the portions are miserly. Dan's face is comical as he takes in the spoonful of pasta on his enormous plate.

'Is this gone fine dining or something?' he whispers across the table, as he manages to fork his entire dinner into his mouth in one bite.

'I'm not sure but it may have something to do with Denis,' I whisper back. 'He's got a lot of local support and my mother seems to be leading the charge.'

Dan chortles just as my phone rings.

Why does my mother insist on calling me at work? 'I'm busy,' I answer shortly.

'And hello to you too.' There is a lot of noise behind her. It's like she's at a party. 'I wouldn't normally ring but you'll never guess who I've just met. Delores McGuigan.'

I have no clue who Delores is.

'Fran's mother. Fran Dan's partner's mother.'

'How on earth have you met her?' I put my hand over the receiver and tell Dan the news.

'She's hosting the Denis Long committee in her house.'

Oh, for God's sake. 'Dan and Fran's house,' I correct, 'and she doesn't even know Denis and, sure, Dan doesn't even live on Achill.'

Dan looks alarmed. 'What's she doing?' Then, 'Tell her not to do it.'

'Dan says to tell Delores not to do it.'

'She's a very nice woman and injustice is not just local. It affects us all.'

'I am a detective!' Despite myself, my voice rises. 'I do my job. I don't do injustice. You're attacking me with this nonsense.'

There is a long silence. 'It's not nonsense. And I'm not attacking you. No one is attacking you. You're very good at your job. You're one of the decent ones. But poor Denis, he got a threatening letter delivered to his house last night and someone threw an egg at his window. That's not nice for him. And—'

'I have to go.' I shoot Dan an anguished look but he's busy

dialling Fran, I suppose, judging by the panicked look on his face.

'Me too. Just thought you'd like to know. There in a second,' she calls to someone, before returning to me, 'Delores is cooking us all lunch and she's just putting it on the table. Bye.'

The line goes dead.

'I can't get hold of Fran,' Dan says. 'Damn. What's happening in our house?'

'Nothing much.' I brush it off. The last thing he needs is the distraction of Fran's mother feeding the hungry hordes of Achill in his pristine kitchen. 'Are we ready to give this arsehole another jolt?'

'Yep.' Dan snaps into detective mode as he stands and brushes down his suit. 'If he thought this morning was bad, I cannot wait to slam him with the rest of the stuff we have.'

'Lead on.'

27

'It looks to us as if you weren't paying your wife maintenance.'
Dan pushes Eamon's bank statement across the desk.

Eamon barely glances at it. 'I was giving her cash.'

'Really? When?'

'Whenever I saw her.'

'So, when she left first, you drove down to Limerick to give
her cash. Is that right?'

'Yeah.'

He knows we know he's lying.

We can't prove it and he knows that too. Dan takes a stab at it,
though. 'Your phone shows no record of any trips to Limerick.'

'I don't bring it everywhere.'

'So you may indeed have been in Limerick.'

'I may indeed.'

'In the last few months.'

'That's when she left me.'

Lovely, Eamon. That helps us further along.

'There are no records of cash withdrawals on your bank statement,' Dan says.

'People paid me cash for work I did for them, on their farms and that. I just didn't lodge it.' He beats Dan to it. 'So do me for tax evasion.' A snort of laughter.

'Why would your wife feel the need to open a bank account in Limerick, in her own name, last October?'

Eamon's lip curls, 'She did not. I would have known.'

Like a magician puling a rabbit from a hat, Dan produces Moira's bank statement. 'Exhibit MD45. Bank statement in your wife's name. And look.' He goes on to point out that the depositors in Eamon's bank account are the same ones as in Moira's. 'What was all that about?'

Eamon stills, his whole body tensed as he realises his wife's deception. 'Well, it looks like she was squirrelling off money, doesn't it?'

'Her money,' Dan says. 'From her art.'

'Our money,' Eamon says. 'We shared everything, me and Moira. Sure wasn't she living in my parents' place? On a farm I inherited.'

And I'll bet he never let her forget it either.

'Our problem is,' Dan says, 'that though you say you didn't harm Ella or abduct or harm Moira that night, and fair enough,' he holds up his hands in supplication, 'we can't find any car belonging to you crossing over that night, we can't yet place you at the scene, but we do have an argument between the two of you in the hours beforehand. We have your wife making plans to leave you by opening a secret account and, as you say, squirrelling away sums of money. We also have, Eamon, two witnesses who give quite damning accounts of your treatment of women. One of them, a Mr Barry Jones—'

'Barry Jones?' Eamon makes a dismissive gesture. 'Scraping the bottom of the barrel, aren't ye? Barry Jones hates me because I

201

got Moira and he didn't. Simple as. I told ye before he was always sniffing around her. I had to tell her it was either him or me, she had to make her choice, and she did. Barry Jones knows how to carry a grudge, I'll give him that.'

Dan says nothing. DNA tests carried out on the cup we'd taken from Barry's room had proved that he was Ella's father, though neither Barry nor Eamon is probably aware of it. Ella had to be the baby Barry thought Moira had lost. If this case goes to court, we probably won't be able to use Barry's testimony against Eamon.

'Barry Jones did say that you sent Moira threatening texts after she left that—'

'He's lying.'

'Not about this,' Dan says. 'We checked your device when you were arrested. On a preliminary search, we discovered that three days after your wife left you, you called her one hundred and thirteen times.'

'I didn't know where the hell she was. And I wanted to talk to my children.'

'You didn't know where she was?' Dan lifts one eyebrow, which is quite a talent. 'Are you sure?'

Eamon reddens so much, he goes purple.

'You knew exactly where she was, didn't you? You down-loaded a tracking device for yourself, didn't you? But you didn't go down because you didn't want to tangle with her auld fella.'

'I just wanted to talk to my children.'

'Can you read out the text you sent to Moira three weeks before the house fire?' Dan passes a transcript across the table with the text highlighted.

Eamon skims the words. 'That was just because she had the

cheek to inform me that I was not to collect Ella any more from school. That the teachers had been told to put her straight on the school bus. Do you know how humiliated I felt?'

'"I will pay you back for this you stupid cunt,"' Dan reads.

'I was angry,' Eamon says. 'For God's sake, have you never written something in anger?'

'Moira made peace with you, didn't she?' Dan ignores the question. 'We've seen her texts too.'

'Only because it suited her,' Eamon says. 'She wanted it all nice as pie for when she took me to the cleaners. And she wanted to use me to set herself up in her new life, asking me to mind the kids while she went off to get a job.'

'Maybe she just wanted the best for her children,' Dan says. 'Maybe she wanted her children to have a good relationship with both of you.'

For a second Eamon looks confused. Then he says, 'My arse.'

'She was allowing you access to the children on Fridays, and you could bring them out. She suggested that you get counselling and she'd go back to you.'

'Counselling! Load of rubbish. It was her needed counselling. She just hadn't got what it took to be a farmer's wife. Always wanting new clothes and to be entertained. A farm doesn't lend itself to that.'

'Would you say you treated her well?'

'Like the princess she thought she was.'

'Did you treat Anna Byrne well?'

And there it is. The tell. The shift under the eyes, calculation. The found-out look. Half surprised, half admiring at the guards he didn't rate finding out something that mattered. 'That fat bitch. What's she been saying?'

'She saw you on TV tearfully appealing for the safe return of your wife.'

'A lot of people saw that.'

'And she called in to say that she went out with you about nine years ago, a year or so before you met Moira.'

Eamon stills, a chess player waiting for the next move.

'She alleges that during your eighteen-month relationship you bullied her into believing that she needed to lose weight, that you checked her fitness apps to see how many steps she did every day, that you denied her food when she didn't do what you thought she should and that you regularly flew into a rage with her.'

Eamon laughs softly. 'Anna Byrne. She was the original snow-flake. She'd been told she was diabetic, that she needed to get healthy. I was only trying to help her. She was just weak-willed and quite annoying.'

'How do you respond to the following statement from her?' Dan picks up a page and reads, '"Eamon Delaney got into my head. Anytime I did anything, I could hear his voice so that I didn't know where I started and he began. He told me what to wear and how to behave, and if I stepped out of line, I was pun-ished. Food was withheld. If he thought I was looking at another man, he'd spend hours questioning me about what I liked about this man. I wouldn't even know what man he was talking about. I was too scared to look at anyone. If I went out I'd spend most of my time staring at the floor."'

Dan looks at Eamon.

I look at Eamon.

Eamon looks impassively back at us. He shrugs.

'It's just that it echoes a statement by Mr Barry Jones—'

'Barry Jones has a vendetta against me, I told you. He was

obsessed with my wife. I believe she even stayed with him in Limerick. She probably fed him a load of lies.'

'According to Barry,' Dan flips some pages in his notebook, 'Moira said, "If I even looked at another man, he'd sit me down and question me for hours."' A glance at Eamon. 'That's two women saying the same thing.'

'The first one is lying and the second, as you well know, is hearsay. Tell me, Detective,' he says mockingly, 'is there any garda report of me mistreating women?'

'No,' Dan answers.

'There you go then, whiny women, that's all.' He sits back, hands clasped on his lap, looking very satisfied with himself.

I want to reach across the table and punch him.

'Coercive control is a crime nowadays,' Dan remarks casually. 'Just saying.'

'Accusing someone of something they didn't do is a crime always.' Eamon smirks. 'Just saying.'

Dan studies him, lets the silence build. He knows that if he keeps pushing, it'll go around and around in circles. 'So, you're angry with Moira, you're sending her nasty texts, phoning her multiple times and keeping track of her whereabouts.'

'Yes. I'm not proud of it but I can't deny it either.'

'Tell me about this phone here.' Dan pushes a list of texts retrieved from Moira's phone across the table. Texts from an unidentifiable phone number.

Eamonn peers at the texts. Reads some of them. 'Not mine. She accused me of sending her stuff from another phone. It was bollox. She was only saying it to keep Jones onside, make him think she was persecuted.'

Dan leaves it. We haven't uncovered that phone in our search of

Eamon's property so far. 'And you say you made trips to Limerick to give her money.'

'I did.'

'Without your phone.'

'Obviously. As I said, I don't bring it everywhere.'

I put down the pen and stretch my fingers. Eamon's solicitor is picking some dirt from his fingernail. Eamon doesn't know he'll be tied up in a knot in the next few minutes.

'Were you there on the nineteenth of February?'

'I may have been. I don't know the exact dates.'

'You admit you know Barry Jones and that, in your words, he has a grudge against you.'

'Yes.'

Just then, there's a sharp rap on the door and Ben slides into the room. 'DS Golden, if you wouldn't mind, just a second.'

We pause the interview as I join Ben outside the door.

Mick is with him, grinning from ear to ear. 'That video,' he says, 'the woman who tried to drug Barry. It's Eamon's sister. I recognised her just now. Ask him if it's his sister.'

28

We have to wipe the grins from our faces before we start the interview again.

Dan takes his time sitting down, Eamon glaring at him, cocky.

I have to bury my head in my chest and pretend to concentrate on the writing. I cannot wait for this. After we once again go through the preliminaries, Dan pushes the CCTV still of the woman who drugged Barry towards Eamon. 'Do you recognise this woman?'

The change of tack blindsides him. He studies the picture and then there's the double-take they all do, that you can't help doing if you recognise someone but you don't want to tell. 'No,' he says, but it's too quick.

'Are you sure? Look hard now,' Dan pushes the still image further across the table and Eamon rears back from it. 'We have her on video too, so we could show you that if it helped.'

'I don't know who it is.'

'Is my client a suspect or a witness here?' the solicitor asks.

Dan ignores him. 'If you know this woman, it will be very bad for you, Eamon, because this woman, we believe, deliberately tried to drug your wife four months before she disappeared.'

Eamon winces. Groans. Drops his head in his hands.

'Do you recognise her?'

'Patti,' he says, his voice faint. 'But you must have it wrong. She'd never do the like of that.'

Thirty minutes later a decision is made to arrest Patti first thing in the morning.

We also ask the super for permission to extend the period of Eamon's detention, which is granted. Even if Patti had nothing to do with Ella's murder or what happened to Moira, she is still potentially guilty of a crime and, if proven, will be charged with that anyway.

In the meantime, we pull out all the stops to see if we can catch her on CCTV on the night that the house was burned.

It's after nine when I finish up for the day. In the incident room, Mick is holding court, regaling anyone who passes with how he suddenly recognised Patti Delaney. 'It was the hair,' he says to Susan, who's helping herself to a slice of pizza. 'I had to talk to her, she was on the Christmas-card list, and I remember thinking as we chatted that her hair was a weird colour. It's a strange sort of red. And then when I saw the CCTV I thought, Oh, there's another person dyed their hair that colour. It must be very popular. And then I was eating me lunch in the canteen today, a banana sandwich, and I thought, Jaysus, I'd better get a look at that CCTV again because maybe it's the same woman, and it was.'

'That's great, Mick.' Susan licks her fingers and offers Mick the last slice of pizza. 'You're a brilliant detective. D'you want to go for a drink?'

'I'm saving myself for tomorrow night. Me and my nephew are

heading to the henge. There's a massive bonfire going up. Should be great.'

'How old is your nephew?'

'Twenty-five, three years younger than me.' He spots Matt. 'Hey, Matt, did you hear what I did today?'

And he's gone, trotting down to the front desk where Matt is closing up.

'I hate bonfires,' Susan says to me. 'Honestly, you'd think with a fire and a murder, they'd have had enough of bonfires in this place. That was great work today, Lucy.'

'Dan did most of it but, yes, bring on tomorrow. How's Bren doing?'

Her expression darkens. 'Poor little lad, he's with his aunt Patti at the minute, but who'll take him tomorrow when she's arrested? I don't think Nick Flannery would be that great.'

'Any word on when he'll be interviewed?'

'In a couple of days, the social worker said. Bloody Louis is driving me nuts, pushing for it.'

'Don't bend to his pressure.'

'I don't, though Louis is trying to tell me—' She stops, flushes, as Louis, white-toothed and fresh-faced bounces into the room.

'I'm heading for a drink, anyone coming?'

'No,' we say together.

I feel a bit mean at the disappointment on his face.

Later that night, as I drive home, I rerun everything that happened that day, step by step, word for word, like a chess player wondering how they can improve their game.

Eamon insisted that he didn't know what his sister was doing in Limerick, that he didn't know she had even been there and, surprise, surprise, he remembered that that weekend he had been nowhere near Limerick. In fact, if we checked his phone, he'd been somewhere entirely different.

'But you don't always bring your phone with you,' Dan said. 'Isn't that right?'

Boom.

Eamon

Incident 5: Erosion

One time there was a programme on the TV. There was a cliff and the sea ate away at it and the house that was perched on top of the cliff fell into the sea, and he laughed at the way it tumbled in, walls smashing and crashing against the rocks.

One time Barry Jones calls to visit. Out of the blue with no invite.

When he tackled her afterwards Moira swore that she hadn't invited him.

He might never have known about the visit only one of the neighbours wondered who owned the strange car that was parked outside the house. Eamon was not a man for surprises.

The first thing he sees is Ella, his daughter, who hides away whenever he's in the room, hugging Barry, who, it seems, has bought her a ridiculous purple ball.

Moira is smiling, saying that Ella has taken a shine to Barry.

'Ella must take after her mother so,' he says, striding into the room, making Moira jump. And he puts his hand on the back of Moira's head and tousles her hair and pulls, just a little.

Moira is unsure now. Meanwhile he is perfectly nice. Laughing, shooting looks from Simple Boy to Moira and back.

Barry says he's calling because he's passing by. After all his mother is from Newport, and he often sees the house, and sure, he just said, 'Why not?'

He's over-explaining, Eamon thinks, as Barry starts filling Moira in on the lost years.

Moira nods along, coiled uptight like a spring, acting out her role.

Eamon acts affable but his eyes ask questions that only Moira can see.

Ella has retreated to her corner, sucking her thumb. Quiet as the dead.

After half an hour, when Barry is in the middle of a sentence, Moira tells him he must go. There are things to do. Eamon says, 'What a pity.' Moira says she knows but she has things to do.

'Keep in touch,' Barry calls, as he leaves.

Eamon stands, still as a statue, after Barry drives off. He watches silently as Moira clears up the teacups and the uneaten biscuits. She tries to chatter away, like Barry calling is not a big event. He knows her game. As she peels potatoes she prattles about Ella's achievements. He says nothing. She puts the potatoes on to boil, first asking if he is happy with mash. But Eamon doesn't answer, just keeps his eye on her and, finally, she just has to break the tension. 'What is wrong?' she asks.

He says, his voice quiet, 'You know what's wrong.' He comes closer to her, he has a spoon in his hand. 'You know what's wrong,' he says again, stirring the potatoes, 'bringing strangers into the house. Don't you know I never liked Barry? What's wrong with you?' he asks. 'How can you not understand that I don't want to

211

chat to the man that fucked you before I did?'

And he stops stirring the potatoes, takes her hand and presses the hot spoon onto her arm. His eyes are cold. He takes the spoon away. 'There now,' he says. 'There's a lesson for you.'

When Bren was born, Eamon was filled up. He was a prince, he says. Carrying Bren in his arms, he marches with him across the fields. 'One day,' he says to the baby, 'all this will be yours.'

But the sea doesn't stop washing at the cliff face and one day the smallest wave makes the house topple.

That bitch of a daughter.

29

Day 7

My mother is up when I stumble into the kitchen early the next morning. Without saying a word, she puts on the kettle and places four slices of toast under the grill.

'Use the toaster. It's quicker.'

'Grilled bread is always nicer.'

I could go down a whole rabbit hole there, but I wisely keep silent.

'About Luc,' she says, as she flips over the toast.

'Ah.' I knew there had to be a reason for the royal breakfast treatment.

'He doesn't mean to hurt you. He's just trying to find himself.'

'Find himself a new girlfriend more like.' I lean against the sink and regard her. 'Honestly, I feel ashamed of him.'

My mother stares at me for ages, but I'm a guard and I do silence very well. She waits until the toast is done and the tea is made before she begins her defence. 'Put yourself in his shoes. He became a father at nineteen, he was attacked in his own home at twenty-one, his father died a few weeks later. Just give him a break is all I'm saying.'

'I try talking to him and he blanks me. Or says awful things. He has to give me a break.'

'You're the adult.'

'I liked Tani.' God, I sound about ten.

'Me too.' She covers her hand with mine. 'Katherine must have been ready to swing for him.'

I can't even bear to think about it. First off, my husband swindled her and Johnny out of their savings; second, my son gets her daughter pregnant; and now this.

'Our children make choices we'd rather they didn't, but if you want to keep him, you have to go with it,' she says.

'So I—'

'You married Rob and it broke my heart.' And with those words, she picks up her teacup and says, 'Now.'

As in 'I've got you there.'

And she has too, so as I slather butter onto my toast, I ask, trying to sound accepting, 'Who is this girl and is he still with her?'

'Her name is Cherry and, yes, I think he is. They'll be at the bonfire tonight at the henge. I think he wants her to meet Sirocco.'

'For God's—'

'He's telling Sirocco she's a friend.'

'Wonderful.'

'So, we'll meet her later.' My mother ignores my tone. 'I take it you're still coming?' Then, before I can answer, she goes on, 'Lorna said she'd drive me. She's got the jeep so she can get close to it. Have you seen the size of the thing? People have been coming all week and adding to it. It's going to be great altogether.'

'I'll definitely be there.' I wouldn't miss it for the world now.

214

***

Dan arrives at work at the same time as me. My 'Hello' is drowned out by the slam of his car door. 'Oh, has the mammy annoyed you again?'

He whirls around. 'Your mother and her friends ate us out of house and home. Fran and I had to go off to a restaurant last night.'

'Oh, no!' I feign horror. 'A restaurant? You're so brave.'

'Shut up.' A smile tweaks the corner of his mouth. 'It's okay for you going home to a nice normal mammy. This woman is on something – she has to be. Fran says she was always like that. Honestly, I like my own mother better and that's saying a lot.'

I follow him into the building and let him bitch for a few more moments. When he's exhausted the subject, I proffer, 'Well, my trauma is that I'll be meeting Luc's latest girlfriend, Cherry, at the bonfire tonight.'

'I don't fancy her chances of surviving if she stands too near you.' Dan chortles, pushing open the door of the incident room. 'Roasted Cherry.'

'Ha-ha.'

Conference begins and the strain on William shows in the overly controlled way he chooses his words. 'Today Larry and Ben will question the latest suspect.' A shake of his head. 'I'm not sure we've had as many strong suspects in a case ever. Patti Delaney has been positively identified as the woman who dropped something, we don't know what, into Moira Delaney's friend Barry's drink in a ham-fisted attempt, we think, to drug Moira. Barry denies any drug-taking on the night but toxicology reports from him at the time of the accident show benzodiazepines in his blood. Did Patti Delaney drug him and, if so, why? Was she in league with her brother or acting alone? Did the sister have any beef with Moira and, if so, what was it? Great work recognising her, Mick.'

His blush lights up the whole room. 'It was nothing.' He brushes it away.

'Jesus, if it was nothing why were you hell bent on telling us all about it yesterday so?' Ger quips as everyone laughs.

'Lucy, can you give everyone a rundown of Eamon's interview?'

I do and finish with, 'We got an extension on Eamon's detention. It means we've a bit more time to trawl through his mobile records.'

'And on that?' William looks to Mick again.

'I just started looking through them yesterday. I passed on the pertinent ones to Lucy and Dan. There are a good few calls and texts between Eamon and Patti, which I'll pass on to the lads. On a quick look, they're mainly things about the farm and how he's managing, and a good few texts where he calls Moira the C word. Moira's phone records have her receiving nasty texts from an as yet unidentifiable number. I gave that information to Dan and Lucy yesterday and Eamon denied knowledge of it.'

'As expected,' I say.

'No such device has been found on Denis's property,' William says. 'Or on Eamon's. But maybe it had already been disposed of. Keep at it. Double-check Eamon and his sister's bank statements to see if any purchases were made from the Carphone Warehouse or other mobile providers. You never know, we might get lucky. Larry?'

'I've checked PULSE and there is only one car registered to Patti Delaney. So, I re-examined some of the footage taken on the day of the murder, fecking déjà vu, looking for her car reg or even the same make of car, but nothing. I can't find a trace of her on the island for that day. I'm going to re-examine the day beforehand just to see if maybe she came then. Now, I did come across one other interesting thing. Very interesting, I think.'

He pauses for dramatic effect.

'Is he the cleverest man in the world or what?' I whisper to Dan, who grins in amusement.

'Moira's car on the day of the murder,' Larry intones. 'Previously we caught it on camera heading from the cottage, with her in the boot, we think, towards Keel Beach. Or so we thought.' He presses a button and replays the footage. It's really bad and grainy. 'I was having a think yesterday. This person shoves Moira in the boot. Then we know when this person arrived at the destination, Moira was whacked again. Her body was presumably dragged from the boot, put into another car, disposed of . . . who knows?' He taps the screen, where Moira's car is a frozen image. 'This car is found at Keel Beach. SOCO went to the scene, and correct me if I'm wrong, Ger, but no blood was found on the ground near the car. Moira was whacked and there was no trace of her at that spot, am I right?'

'That's it. They thought maybe she was packed up in tarpaulin and transported to another car but what with all the tyre prints up there it was impossible to say.'

'All the tyre prints,' Larry says. 'In other words a busy spot. Who disposes of a body at a busy spot? I began to think Ger could be right. What if . . .' Larry lowers his voice and we all lean in to hear.

'God, he's loving this,' Dan murmurs in my ear.

'. . . Moira's car was driven somewhere first, the body disposed of and then the car taken to Keel Beach?'

'A lot of bother,' someone says.

'Maybe,' Larry agrees, 'but look.' He presses play and more footage appears, the time twenty minutes earlier than it was on the previous video. And, more tellingly, the car is travelling in completely the opposite direction, away from the cottage and away from the beach. 'Our SO drove that car somewhere else, disposed of the body and abandoned the car at the beach car park. Then,' Larry shoots a look at the Cig, 'they either hopped into their own vehicle and made their escape or, if local, they walked home.'

He means Denis. He's a fifteen-minute walk to Keel Beach. Or he could have parked his car there and walked to Moira – a half-hour at most.

Denis could have done that.

Could Eamon?

Maybe with help.

William rewinds and replays the footage again. 'That's great work. Any chance we could get a clearer image of whoever is driving the car?'

'That's as good as I could get,' Larry says. 'The footage is actually from the same dash-cam as the previous lot.'

'Damn. All right. Let's take the door-to-door further afield. We need to start canvassing homes in that area. From beyond Keel Beach to . . . ?' He looks at Larry.

'Based on the timings and the speed at which the car was travelling, I'd say at least ten miles further on.'

There is a stifled groan from all those tasked with door-to-door. William glares at them. 'This is what being a guard is,' he says. 'Layer upon layer of hard graft. Anyone who thinks an investigation is like *CSI* or fecking *Line of Duty* can leave now. Anything on forensics?'

'Some of the plant spores have been identified, Cig,' Ger says. 'I have a whole load of Latin jargon here but when I looked them up, they are the ivy-leaved bellflower, purple saxifrage, stiff sedge and least willow. There was also rhododendron.'

'I'm unimpressed, Ger. What do we do with that?'

Ger winces at William's tone. 'I guess if we find a suspect and they live near those plants, then hey presto.'

'I hope going to court we'll have stronger evidence than a few plants. What's the story with the lighter?'

'"With love, your love,"' Kev says. 'And that's not me looking for promotion, Cig. That's what was inscribed on the lighter.'

People chuckle. Kev always manages to inject humour into whatever he's investigating.

'There was this auld lad in Sligo, been selling lighters since he left school. High-end ones. Mad about his lighters this fella is. Anyway, he went back through all his records, an auld fella like . . . like Jordy, and—'

More laughter.

'I'm only fifty-five, ya bastard,' Jordy wheezes.

'Okay, well, this lad must be in his eighties or whatever and he says he remembers every lighter he ever sold. He was like yer man Ollivander in *Harry Potter* the way he went on.'

'Who?'

'No one, Cig, sorry. Anyway, that's what he said and I was, like, sure you remember them all, but as Ger would say, "Hey presto," and he starts reading out to me from a page about a lighter he sold way back in the sixties to a man called Gerald Greene. Had an address for him and everything, so yesterday I tracked Gerald down and he was dead, so I tracked his son down and he says, yeah, his dad gave his ma a fancy lighter one time for her birthday and it had passed on to him but that it had been stolen in a burglary in 2019 and never recovered. And do you know who got done for that burglary?'

There are blank looks all around but I think I can guess and I groan at the new layer Kev has just uncovered.

'An associate of Nick Flannery,' Kev says.

'You're joking?' William says.

'Nope.'

'So, what are we thinking? That he was there that night?'

Kev shrugs. 'Maybe. Sure what's another suspect?'

William groans. 'I suppose we have to ask him. On that note, Detective Lorcan Brown is here from Limerick where he talked to Nick Flannery. Sorry, Lorcan, but your job isn't finished yet.'

A smattering of laughter.

Lorcan stands, looks around. 'Hi, yez.' He runs a hand through his hair. He's quite cute, though way too young for me. 'We interviewed Nick Flannery and the man he argued with, Bertie Hannigan, at length over the last couple of days. Their row, believe it or not, was over Nick parking in Bertie's space. It was a question of respect, apparently. Anyway, Nick apologised. I don't know how that came about, but I'm assured by both parties that it was all sorted out. I don't believe either man had anything to do with what happened. When Nick was told that his daughter was missing and of his granddaughter's death, I can testify that he was genuinely shocked and broken-hearted. They were close. I do believe that if he gets his hands on whoever did this, there will be trouble. Nick was a suspect in the murder of an Adam Lewis ten years ago. This was a young man who was dating Moira, and when they broke up, rumour has it Adam hit Moira. Well, he was found with his heart cut out. Make no mistake, Nick will be looking for whoever did this as well. The fact that the guy he rowed with is still on the streets means his alibi stands up.'

'That's not to say he didn't pay someone else,' William says.

'Agreed,' Lorcan concedes.

'Can I ask,' I put up my hand, 'if this Bertie guy is a large fella with dyed black hair?'

'That about sums him up.' Lorcan smiles.

Gosh, he has a dimple.

'Good point.' William grins at me. 'Lorcan, could you ask Bertie if he visited Achill on the second of June? And, Lucy, get a picture of the man and bring it up to Johnny Egan this morning, would you? Ask him if he can identify him.'

Great.

'Jim will give out the jobs. Dan, help Mick with the phone records. If you get anything, straight in to Larry and Ben with it. They'll be questioning Patti later on. Lucy, when you get back, give them a hand too, would you? Larry and Ben, make sure that prep is meticulous. We'll be bringing Patti Delaney in very shortly. Ger and Kev, keep on forensics. The rest of you, door-to-door. Hop it.'

The room empties but not before I ask Lorcan to email me a picture of Bertie. He fires it off without looking at me, wishes me luck and strides from the room, eager, I guess, to get back to Limerick. Nice arse.

'Eh, Lucy,' Matt jolts me out of my reverie on arses, 'I need you at the front desk. Mrs O'Sullivan is down there and she is demanding to speak with you. Like she's shouting. I can't get rid of her.'

'Is this about a dog fine?'

'Yes.'

'Right. Where is Louis?'

Like a dog hearing his name, Louis pops his head out of the kitchen. 'You want me?'

'There's an old woman down there you gave a dog fine to. Her dog is probably older than she is. She wants to waste my time by giving out about it. So, you are going down in my stead to apologise to her. And you're going to tell her you'll pay her fine and that you were just being too enthusiastic because you don't know what you're doing yet.'

Matt slides away, back downstairs, happy to face the anger of Mrs O'Sullivan rather than what might be coming here.

'I can't do that.' Louis tilts his head. 'It's illegal.'

'Admitting you made a mistake? No, that's honourable.'

'You're asking me to square a fine.'

'I'm telling you to pay it.' I turn away. 'Hop it.'

'I'm not paying.'

I ignore that.

'You've just got it in for me because of who my dad is,' he shouts after me.

I whirl around, advance on him. He takes a step back, and for one tiny moment, I feel a bit sorry for him. 'You're right,' I say, 'but not because your dad is who he is but because he used his position to shoehorn you into this investigation. There were other guards, fine guards, who have done their time and would have loved a chance like this. But you,' I look him up and down, 'what have you done with this chance? Fine an old lady for her dog. Brown nose everyone you've met who you think can help you. You've even managed to fast-track a little boy's interview, forgetting that he's lost his mother and his sister. You won't get far here on your name, not with me anyway. Do a bit of proper work, for God's sake.'

222

He looks like he might cry.

As I turn, I hear him mutter, 'Bitch,' under his breath. The measure of him now will be how he reacts to this. Will he go about whimpering and whining, or will he pay that fine and knuckle down? I don't care if he tells his father because that will only make him look more pathetic and, honestly, I've been through the worst this job has to offer: I've been demoted, moved sideways, had my name all over the papers.

And I've come through it.

30

Johnny meets me in Mulranny where he's working on a house for a newly married couple. The site is a mess and he really should have warned me to wear rubber boots. 'This way,' he says, helping me to cross a trench. I fizz at the touch of him.

'The kitchen is free.' He lets go my hand. 'Come on in and show me what you've got.' He chortles a little at his wit.

'Did you ever grow up?'

'Yep, but I didn't like it so much.'

'I'm with you there.'

The kitchen is full of muddy boot-prints and knocked-down walls. Further out, through the window in the remaining wall, there's a new extension being constructed. 'We'll knock that wall once that part is built,' Johnny explains. 'Aw, it'll be gorgeous. Loads of space and full of light. They'll get the best sunsets sitting in here in the evening.'

Johnny was always good at art. I think he got an A in the Leaving. I remember his finely detailed drawings of buildings. He has found his true vocation in this job and I'm stabbed with sudden envy.

He clears a mess of unwashed cups and half-eaten sandwiches to one side as we take seats at the table. 'Is this about the big fella I saw that day? I told the other lads already I can barely remember him.'

'Take a look at these.' I flick on my iPad and open Viper, the facial-recognition software we use with witnesses now. 'Are any of these the man you recognised? They may not be.'

Johnny flicks through the pictures. 'They all look kinda the same.'

'That's the idea, so we don't prejudice the identification.'

'And it was weeks ago.' He groans. 'If I had to guess—'

'Please don't.'

'All right, if I had to say, I'd finger this lad.' He points to Bertie and my heart sings. 'Or it could be this lad.'

I can't breathe as he ponders his decision.

'Right. Him.'

It's Bertie.

'Can you sign and date that ID?' I hand him the stylus.

'Was I right?'

'It's not a test but, yes, that's the man we're thinking it was.'

'Yes!' He fist-pumps like he's just scored a hat-trick. Hopping up, he says, 'That calls for a coffee. D'you want one?'

I probably shouldn't but, hey, I've got a positive ID, so my work here is done. 'Go on.'

He potters about, making himself at home in this kitchen he's half demolished. I find myself thinking that, if life had taken a different turn, I could easily have ended up with this guy. This preening, vain, funny, talented, flawed man for whom I've been carrying a half-lit torch from for ever.

When we're sitting nursing two horrendous cups of coffee, I broach the subject of our offspring. 'Luc and Tani broke up, did you hear?'

'Last week,' he confirms. 'Sure, isn't it as well? They're way too young for all that malarkey.'

Jesus, it seems I'm the only one who actually cares.

'Your fella now,' Johnny says, 'he could have done it differently, though.'

'Like you did?' Oh, God, not the thing to say, Lucy. But my mother and I are the only ones allowed to give out about Luc.

'*Touché.*' Johnny winks at me. 'I deserved that. But Tani is my daughter and I swear I was ready to plant Luc when I heard what he'd done on her, but Katherine told me she was glad and I guess it's for the best.'

'Why was Katherine glad? Is Luc not good enough for your family?'

'Aw, Jesus.' He snorts. 'What do you want me to say? Luc is a grand lad, mostly. But what he did, no, it's not good enough. Anyway, we don't want our girl settling down young. Me and Katherine didn't work out so well.'

I pass a hand over my face. 'You're right. Sorry. I'm a bit all over the place. Honestly, I feel really annoyed with what he's done too. I was really fond of Tani.'

'Thanks.'

Outside, someone turns a machine on and the roar of it fills the air.

'I'm sorry for way back when,' he says suddenly, over the noise. 'You know, when we were kids and Katherine came all gorgeous down from Dublin and I dumped you. Sure, look, we were young as well, but I know I owe you an apology. I always felt, you know, that it hung between us.'

I wave my hand about, as if him stomping all over my heart was nothing. 'Oh, that? Forgotten.'

'Good. I'd hate to think you were carrying it around like a big burden.'

'No way!' Oh, God, he was only joking I realise too late. But I can't take it back.

He looks faintly embarrassed.

'Life is gas, though, isn't it?' he says, after an awkward moment. 'Katherine's only gone and found another fella and guess what his name is?'

'What?'

'Johnny.'

'Feck off.' I giggle.

'I said to her, do you have a thing for Johnnies?'

Like two adolescents, we both find this hilarious.

'Have you met him?'

'Nah.' He suddenly doesn't seem as okay with it. 'Sure, what's the point? Tani says he's a pain in the hole so Katherine will dump him.' He fiddles with the handle of his cup, running his finger up and down it, then glances at me. 'How are you doing?' The question comes out of nowhere. The look of concern comes out of nowhere. It's like he's been longing to ask me all along.

'Fine. Why?'

He stands and takes our empty cups to the sink. His back to me, he says, 'You don't look fine, that's why. You look tired and wrung out and sort of stressed.'

'I'm trying to solve a murder. Two murders maybe. I'd better go.'

'Don't kill yourself in the effort.' His back is still to me.

I manage a slight laugh. 'Oh, God, I'd swear you actually care about me, Johnny Egan.'

He turns. 'Course I do. I've known you a long time.'

I study his forty-seven-year-old face. Properly. All trace of the boy I remember is gone and he hasn't aged as well as he should have - too much drinking probably - but he's got the craggy sexy look down well. It's me who's been stuck in the teenage cycle. 'I'll be grand.' My voice is a croak.

'See you are.'

I tap my iPad. 'And thanks for the ID.'

He waves me off.

Once in the car, I have to blink back tears.

I don't know why.

31

I fill William in, finishing, 'So, will you get Lorcan in Limerick to ask Bertie why he was knocking on Moira's door, please? And thank you.'

'I will.' He pauses. 'I believe you had words with our new recruit.'

'He'd fined an old lady for her dog.'

'He was within his rights, though.'

'Maybe, but that's not how you police a place like Achill.'

William bows his head. He knows the lines blur sometimes, even in small things. 'He's a pain in the hole, I'll give you that,' he says, 'but I do think he's trying.'

'Very trying.'

He smiles, a rare thing. Waves a hand to dismiss me. 'Go on. Mick and Dan are drowning in work next door.'

By lunchtime, we've managed to isolate the number of times an unidentified number texted Moira.

The messages are vicious.

'"I hope you die,"' Dan reads out.

'"I will watch you burn in hell,"' Mick contributes.

229

'"Go back home to your husband, you bitch,"' Dan says.

They look at me for guidance.

'I remember Denis telling us he was present when she got a bad text, d'you remember? He said he was watching *Coronation Street* with her. What was that date again?'

Dan finds it and Mick checks Moira's records. 'Yes, here's one,' he says. 'Same number. Right time. It says, "I'm watching you, bitch."'

'So, Denis wasn't sending those,' I mutter. 'Are they texts from our SO or another person entirely? There seems to be quite a queue at this stage.'

'Denis could have sent them,' Dan offers. 'We only have his word for it that he was watching *Coronation Street* with her. He could have been watching it with his wife and fired off the text.'

'Fair enough. Though we didn't find anything to back that up at his house. Ring the number, Mick, see if anyone picks up.'

'I did already but I'll try again.'

None of us are is surprised when it rings out.

I throw down the list of numbers and rub my eyes with the heels of my hands. 'At the end of the day, the texts were just words.'

'"I hope you die"?' Dan says.

'"I will watch you burn in hell"?' Mick adds.

'I know it's bad. But what we need is Moira's body, if she is dead. Without her we can't even prove we have a double murder. For all we know, for all we can prove, *she* could have set that place alight. Wasn't the lighter stolen by an associate of her father?' I turn to Mick. 'Where would you hide a body up beyond the beach?'

He looks uneasy at the question. 'Well, first off, she wasn't completely dead going into the car, was she? So whoever it was might have made her get out, stand in a grave, hit her again to finish her off, then buried her. And driven off.'

'You've given this some thought.'

'Honestly, these cases are so bad, I bloody dream about them.' Mick rubs the bridge of his nose. 'How can you not? It's all you're doing all day, talking about it with people. One time, my flat-mates threw cold water over me in bed to stop me roaring out. Last night, I dreamed that whole scenario I just told you. Larry is right. Where the car was found is not where the body was dis-posed of or moved from. Anyway, Keel Beach is too open.'

'Dan?' I ask.

'I don't dream about it,' he says easily. 'I go home, switch off the brain cells and eat good food. That's what you do, Micko.' He slaps him on the back. 'Right, where would I bury a body? Tell you what, a freshly dug grave, even right out on the bog here, would be noticed. There is no way she was brought out to sea because that would have been noticed too.'

'Unless it was dark?'

I'm thinking of our last case. That SO had been able to navi-gate the dark.

'Denis isn't a sailor, is he?'

'No. And Eamon Delaney is all about the farm. But we can check.'

'So, I reckon,' Dan returns to the problem, 'you'd have to get rid of the body in plain sight. Like, I don't know, say you ran a butcher's shop, you'd hang it from a hook with all the animals. Or embalm it and put it in a waxworks museum.'

'There are no waxworks museums in Achill and, honestly, if

231

our local butcher, Frank, had it in his shop, he'd probably sell it at a profit. Be real. Where?'

Dan thinks some more before huffing out a sigh and asking us if we want a coffee.

'Go on.'

He leaves.

'What about you, Lucy?' Mick asks. 'You know this place better than any of us. Where do you think it is?'

'Most murderers, unless it's some gangland thing, tend not to go too far to bury their victims,' I say. 'Usually within ten kilometres of the last sighting of them. So, yes, I do think she's still here. We've searched Eamon's farm and Denis's farm, so I think she's out on the bog somewhere. I think we'll find her or some walker will. But I don't know where I'd go.'

Dan arrives in with Patti's phone records under his arm while also trying to balance three mugs of coffee on a tray. 'Jesus, the sister is worse than the brother. I just saw her down at Reception. She was steaming.' He lays the tray on the table and we grab a mug each before dividing more work between us.

'First thing is to find the date Patti was in Limerick drugging Moira,' I suggest.

We find no texts between her and her brother on that date. Nothing the following day either. Then finally, the day after, Eamon texts:

9:10
Did you enjoy the weekend?

PATTI
10:05
Limerick is a kip. How's things with you?

EAMON
10:20
The cunt is still playing hard to get.

PATTI
10:25
Not with everyone she's not.

EAMON
10:26
?????

And then she'd made a call to his number.

'Does that mean Eamon knew she was following Moira or not?' Dan asks.

'Your guess is as good as mine.'

'The records put her in Limerick at least,' Mick says. 'So that's a nail in her coffin as far as dispensing drugs are concerned. When we get her mobile we can check its locations. At least Barry's mother will have some answers as to what happened that night.'

'Yeah, and the woman who knocked Barry down will know it wasn't her fault.'

Larry pokes his head around the door. 'Interview is about to kick off,' he says.

We gather up the records and the coffees, then hurry down to the observation room.

32

At first glance, Patti Delaney is milk-and-waterish. Small, petite with the sort of looks that probably got her bullied in school. But scratch the surface and there roars a tiger. Her posture is all defiance, from her jutted-out chin to her pursed lips. Her foot, in a pointy-toed boot, jiggles up and down. Her fingers tap the table.

And Mick was right: her hair colour is unforgettable.

Larry has just asked her to talk about her time in Limerick.

'Limerick? It's a shithole. Is that what you're looking for?'

'Our boss is from Limerick,' Larry says pleasantly. 'He won't like that.'

'Well, I don't like the fact that, on the orders of your boss, I'm in here and my brother is detained somewhere else. And poor little Brennie is being minded by strangers.'

'That is terrible,' Larry agrees. 'So, in the interests of everyone, maybe you'll help us out. Is this you?' He jabs his finger at the CCTV image and recites the exhibit number for the sake of the recorder. 'Bear in mind that your brother already said that it was.'

'It's not the most flattering picture but, yeah, that's me. Is it a crime to go out and enjoy yourself these days?'

'It is not,' Larry says, with heart. 'Sure I only wish I could do it myself from time to time.'

We all snigger. Larry has a better social life than the rest of us put together.

'So, this is you,' Larry continues. 'Right, let's just roll this video on here.' He pretends he can't understand how to do it and then, after it restarts, with an easy charm, says, 'There we go. Now, tell me what's happening here.' He lets the video run, then freezes it.

'I was telling that fella, the one with the drinks, that he'd dropped money on the floor. He looked and said he hadn't, then walked off.'

'Aren't you honest,' Larry rewinds the video to the point at which she drops something into the whiskey. 'But what about here?' He slows the video so that her actions are unmistakable.

Patti frowns. 'It looks like I was raising my hand. Oh, that's right. I was saying hi to someone and then I dropped my hand because it wasn't the person I thought.' Another jut of chin.

Keep quiet, Larry, I say in my head.

And he does.

On and on the silence goes.

Patti starts to shift on her chair.

'What person?' Larry asks.

'What?'

'What person on the video?'

'Can't remember now.'

'But you can remember almost waving to this non-existent person?'

'After looking at the video, yeah.'

'Did you know your sister-in-law was there?'

'Really? No, I didn't.'

'That guy you talked to, Barry is his name. He was with her.'

'Really? I see.' There is something fragile in her now, like she might break.

Larry senses it too. He leans across the table, Patti pulls back. Larry talks softly: 'I'm going to be straight with you, Patti. The court, if they see this CCTV, are unlikely to believe you. You say you went to Limerick on your own for a break. You went drinking in a packed pub on your own. You didn't spot your sister-in-law but you managed to have a conversation with the guy who was with her. Let me tell you something, that guy there, someone put something in his drink that night and he stumbled out in front of a car, got knocked down and is paralysed and—'

She shakes her head. 'That's a lie. He did not get knocked down.'

'He did, Patti. His name is Barry Jones and at present he is in the Central Rehab in Dublin. He has lost the use of his legs.'

'But that's not my fault!' The words burst out of her and she clamps a hand over her mouth. 'That's not my fault.' Her edginess is gone. 'I didn't knock him down. I didn't even mean to drug him.'

Dan claps as Mick and I laugh.

'Aw, now we're getting somewhere,' Larry says, as if she's his prize pupil. 'Tell me what happened and why.'

Patti looks like she might resist, then starts to sob, soft, gentle, hiccuping sobs. She pulls a tissue from her sleeve and scrubs her eyes. Sometimes when the truth comes out, especially when things had been accidental, people cry with the relief of having confessed.

'Do you want water?' Ben, the softie, pipes up.

'No. No, thank you. Look, I'm sorry. I didn't know the man was paralysed. That's not what I was trying to do. I was only trying to help out Eamon. That's all.'

'Go on.'

'Moira left him, as you know. She took his children one night when he was away and snuck out of the house. The next thing he knew, she was telling him she wasn't coming back. Eamon was devastated. He didn't know what he'd done. He rang me and he was in tears. Can you imagine, my big brother in tears? The last time I ever saw him cry was when he was eight. I came right over and started to look after him and we discussed what to do. He tried ringing her, rang her day and night, but she wouldn't pick up, and the next thing is he gets a message from her saying she wants maintenance. He said that if he gave her anything he'd never see her again, she'd be off, and I agreed. So he told Moira to come back and discuss things like adults. Well, that went down like a lead brick, or whatever it is. It didn't go down well, is what I'm saying. So, then it got worse. He got more upset and angry, and she said that if he wouldn't support the children, he wasn't entitled to see them. Oh, she grew a pair of horns for herself, so she did. He said that was downright illegal and she said he could see them once he gave her half the farm.' Patti stops to draw breath. Her whole body is shaking now, but with indignation. Her voice, when it comes again, is full of repressed fury. 'Half of the farm,' she says, as if she fully expects Larry to be outraged too. 'That farm has been in our family for generations. When Eamon took it over, he made a solemn pledge on Daddy's deathbed that it'd be kept in the family. Sure that's why he was so delighted when Bren survived the fire. Well, he was devastated about little Ella, of course he was, but Bren carries on the family name.'

237

Beside me, Dan lets out a slow breath. I think I might be sick.

'And Eamon was so upset over this, well, I thought, and I was stupid, I know I was, but I thought if I could show that Moira was an unfit mother, I could give the video to Eamon and he would be able to use it in court if and when the time came. So I took myself off to Limerick where I knew Moira was because Eamon had told me. She'd told him she was with a friend and Eamon suspected it was Barry Jones because Moira had no friends. The only friend she had was me, actually, and we got on all right, though she was a bit too arty. Anyway, Eamon knew that Moira was staying somewhere in the Shelbourne Road area there and sure enough I found her. And I followed her into that pub and, yes, I did pop the tablet into the drink. It was my own Valium and I used a bit of it. I swear I didn't mean for anyone to get hurt. The minute I saw what was happening with the drinks, I left. I came straight back to Eamon. Never told him a thing about the tablet but I saw for myself how she was carrying on with that Barry fella. And I told Eamon about that.'

'It sounds like you were very angry at Moira.'

'Who wouldn't be? There she was, living in my parents' house, having a whole farm to herself, then threatening to take it away. No way was that happening.'

'We did a preliminary examination of your mobile when we confiscated it,' Larry says. 'We'll be looking at it in more detail later, but where were you on the night of the fire?' He tells her the exact date.

'I was away with a friend. Having a break from all the drama. I remember Eamon rang. He had been over at Moira's earlier and, well, he was supposed to collect the children but he was annoyed with Moira and he didn't take them. But I said to him, "Go and

238

get those children first thing in the morning. Don't have her say that you refused to take them. She'll take the whole shebang off you if you let her." He agreed that he would and we chatted for a bit, and then he said he had to go for a few hours and not to call him for the rest of the night.'

'He went out?' Larry says.

'Yes. He had things to do.'

'That's not what Eamon told us,' I say to the screen.

33

After they wrap up with Patti, and Mick and I finish checking the contents of her texts, which mainly consist of her bitching about most of her 'friends' to other friends, moaning about her ungrateful cow of a sister-in-law and how she was trying to destroy the family farm, and her friends texting back that, yes, Moira is a complete bitch, who didn't know how lucky she was and how lovely Eamon was, we have to let her go.

Aside from her attempt to drug Moira, for which a file will be sent to the DPP, there is nothing to tie her to the crime we're investigating.

I head into the Cig at the end of the day to get an update on Eamon's interview, which I had missed.

'We got nothing new.' William sounds a bit stressed. 'He says he told the truth to you the first time. He didn't go out. He only told his sister he had to go because he wanted to end the conversation. She does his head in, he says, and he also says Patti was delighted when Moira left because she thought she could get her feet under the table in the farmhouse because she's resented Moira ever since she arrived. So, he thought a night without her yabbering in his ear would be good.' A pause. 'Believe it or not.'

'That man can invent stories at will.' But, I have to admit, that explanation is plausible. His sister is a pain in the arse. 'It does set Patti nicely up for a motive to want to harm Moira, doesn't it? Hating and resenting her sister-in-law?'

'That it does.' William sits back in his chair. 'But we can't prove it. We also told him about the DNA on Ella. Thought maybe it might break him.'

'How did he react? Does he realise it puts him squarely in the frame, his unfaithful wife and a daughter that isn't his both gone?'

'He was gobsmacked, actually,' William says slowly, as if teasing it out. 'I really don't think he knew. In fact, I believe he didn't know. Watching his reaction, the evil part of me was delighted.'

'You have an evil part?'

He doesn't respond immediately and it's disconcerting. 'Doesn't everyone?' he says, after a bit, then goes on to tell me that Susan and Louis have finally been given the green light to interview Bren. 'Day after tomorrow,' he says. 'The room is all set up and Susan says he's quite excited, poor little chap. He'll find it tough. It's not easy to talk about bad stuff happening in your family. We'll have something from that and, you never know, it might break the case.'

William must have had to give a statement when he was a boy and his family were wiped out. Back then, people were not aware of trauma and how it affected children in the way we are today. 'I don't think that little boy has a hope. If Eamon is guilty, what a burden for the child to carry, and if he's not, imagine growing up with him for a dad.'

'People said that about me.' William shrugs.

241

I don't know how to respond to that and he looks faintly embarrassed that he said it. He pushes a bunch of bananas towards me. 'Have one. Good for energy. Tell me your thoughts?'

They look fresh enough. His usual fare is the mushy ones. 'Thanks.' I peel one while considering my answer. 'Eamon, Patti and Denis all look good for it. The evidence, though different, is compelling for all three. I'm probably biased about Denis because I know him and he's never struck me as that kind of a man but, then again, he never struck me as a stalker either.'

'A sad, pathetic stalker, though,' William muses. 'Not the other kind, I don't think. Eamon, though, I've seen men like him before. He's a monster. A clever one, because he's covered his tracks well with regard to how he treated Moira. It's so bloody hard to prove controlling behaviour. He explains it all away and it sounds so reasonable. Even his sister and her friends were on his side.'

'Yeah, because Moira had no one to confide in. He made sure of that.'

'And the person she does trust ends up in a wheelchair.'

'I believe that was accidental.' I don't add anything else because I want to leave. I need to talk to Isabelle Jones, then head along to the bonfire. If I say any more, I could be here for ever.

He must read my mind. 'Go on. Enjoy the night. You're heading out with your granddaughter, yeah?' He peels another banana, tosses the skin at the bin and misses.

How does he know that? 'Yes. It's bonfire night. What about you?'

Shut up, Lucy.

'What about me what?'

'Are you doing anything?' *Shut. Up. Lucy.*

242

'Paperwork.'

'You can't miss bonfire night on Achill.' I feel a bit sorry for him. 'Join us later up at the henge. It'll be great.'

Then I think, Jesus, this man probably hates fires after what happened to his family. What the hell am I thinking?

'Okay.' He surprises me by agreeing. 'How do I get there?'

A little faintly, I reply, 'You drive past Keel Beach and you'll see a makeshift car park. Pull in and I'll wait for you or you wait for me. A jeep can bring us to within two hundred metres of the fire or we can walk if you're feeling energetic.' I glance at his clothes. 'You might want to wear a pair of boots and definitely not a suit.'

'Noted. I'll finish up here, brief the super, tell him what a wonderful chap his young lad is and I'll be there probably around half ten, eleven.' He seems surprised at his own decision.

'Great.' Then I wonder, Is it? This is Sirocco's night and here I am dragging my boss along. God knows what my mother will say to him. Probably bang on about Denis Long. But it's too late now.

'See you later, Cig.'

He raises his hand.

I'm forgotten for now.

There are a couple of things I have to do before I head to the henge. The first and more pleasant one is to update Eileen. She's buoyant with the news that we've managed to wrap up Barry's case for her. 'I'll call on Barry's mother and let her know,' I offer. 'No point in you coming all the way up.'

'Thanks, Lucy.' She sounds incredibly grateful. 'You're an absolute star.'

'No bother.'

I hang up. Seeing Mrs Jones is not a visit I'm looking forward to, but as I was the one who promised her results, I want to be the one to deliver them.

Isabelle Jones is a strong-looking, nervous bundle of energy, and I arrive at her house just as she pulls up in her driveway. I wait until she and an energetic spaniel hop out of the car before I approach her. She's dressed in heavy-duty trousers and boots and pulls a hunting rifle from the back seat, the dog alongside her.

'Can I have a word?' I show her my ID. 'We talked a few days ago.'

She takes my card and has to hold it close to her face to read it. Passing it back, she says, 'This had better be about Barry because I'm beat. I've spent all day hunting muntjac and I'm done in.' At my blank expression, 'They're an invasive species of deer.' She reaches down to rub the spaniel. 'Now, unless it's—'

'Yes, it's about Barry.'

She jerks like a puppet whose string I just pulled.

The spaniel, sensing her shock, presses his white and liver body closer to her legs.

'Let's go inside, shall we?'

'Okay.' Her fingers are unsteady as she unlocks her door. 'This way.' She ushers me through a shining hallway into a kitchen with windows that sparkle. Unlocking a cabinet she places the gun inside and locks it again. Her dog finds his basket and curls up, his eyes on her.

Out the back, dogs bark wildly.

'Ignore that,' she says, as I take a seat. 'It's just my dogs. I train spaniels for hunting and as sniffer dogs.' She opens a window. 'Quiet!' she calls, before slamming it closed again.

244

I make a comment on how cute her dog is to which she doesn't respond. Instead her gaze flits across my face. 'Well?'

'As I said, we've found out what happened to Barry and we've apprehended the person responsible.'

'You've got someone but I . . .' Her mouth hangs open, the thought unfinished. 'I'm sorry . . . I didn't . . . I just . . .' She sinks into a chair. 'What happened?'

I inform her as gently as I can about Patti's confession and of how she was very remorseful, especially when she realized he'd been in an accident.

'But why would she drug him?'

'The drug was meant for Moira.'

The news is greeted with silence. Then her gaze, which had been full of anxiety, hardens and she stands up slowly, turns her back on me, her spine rigid. 'Of course,' she breathes, and there is a world of bitterness in it. 'Of course.'

'I'm sorry?'

She turns to face me. Jabs a finger in my direction. 'That woman, the one you're all so concerned about, she has caused me and my son nothing but heartache since she came into his life. I always thought she was like one of those sirens that lured fishermen onto the rocks.' Tears spill from her eyes and I don't think she notices. 'My son, Detective, had a breakdown years ago over that girl. If it wasn't bad enough when his father committed suicide, I ended up having the same fear for my boy. Have you any idea what it's like for a parent to worry about their child night and day?'

'That must have been terrible.'

'I knew when she came back into his life that trouble would follow.'

There is no point in telling her that Moira had nothing to do with the accident. I let her cry, steeling myself for the next bit. I've come here to deliver news and deliver it I will. 'There's more, I'm afraid.'

Her eyes cloud with fear. 'What?'

Her dog looks from her to me, and comes to stand at her side. She reaches a hand down to its head. 'What?' she asks again.

There is no easy way. 'Ella, the little girl who died, we did DNA and . . .' I stop, thinking maybe she might know but her face is blank.

'She was Barry's little girl.'

Her look of horror is stark.

'I know it's too late and I know this—'

'Why did you tell me this?' Her whole body shakes. 'Why? What good can it possibly do now? What good?'

I'd wondered about the wisdom of it. What is the point? But the way Patti talked about Ella, as if she was somehow less than, made it important to tell someone. A family who might have loved her. 'I just want Ella to be claimed by decent people. Eamon Delaney has already been informed and we thought you might like to tell Barry in your own time.'

She stares at me without even seeing me.

'I'll let myself out.'

Outside, I exhale.

Inside, she starts to wail.

I get into the car and drive off.

34

By the time I get to the car park, it's jammed. Eleven o'clock, an hour before the bonfire, and vehicles are parked haphazardly all over the road. A few people, wearing bright yellow jackets with the words *Car Park Attendant* emblazoned on the back, have given up and are having a glass of wine as they sit on a wall.

'This is dangerous,' I call to them, from my car window.

They shrug, go back to their wine.

'Well, this is a mess, eh?' William, dressed head to toe in Regatta hiking gear, peers in at me. 'I thought you said it was all organised.'

'I suppose they weren't expecting so many people.' I reverse my car onto a grass verge, blocking about ten vehicles in, and climb out.

'That's not going to be great later on,' William observes primly.

'I'll worry about later on later on. Where are you parked?'

'This taxi fella came into the station complaining about the state of this road, and when I said I was hoping to go he offered me a lift. He's gone back to complain to Matt now but sure the main door will be closed.' He chuckles at his cleverness and nods towards the track where masses of people are now ascending. 'Are we climbing?'

I need to wipe the meeting with Mrs Jones out of my head so I agree. When you've been responsible for ruining someone's day, you need to decompress before mixing with friends and family.

William is surprisingly fit, and after about five hundred metres, I'm puffing a lot. Four jeeps full to the brim sway past us, carrying those who don't want to walk. Irish music blares out of speakers, which are hooked up to huge transformers that whirr and hum. Vans that have somehow managed to drive part way up the road are selling hotdogs and chips and the smells snake through the air. The atmosphere is buzzy, and as I puff and pant behind my boss, I allow myself to be carried on it. Halfway up, there are plastic glasses of free mulled wine with big signs telling people to throw the glasses into the bins provided. Finally, my legs aching, we reach the barn. People are hopping off the jeeps and making their way towards the enormous unlit bonfire. Safety marshals patrol its perimeter.

'Lucy!' My mother spots me and waves wildly. Pulling Sirocco along, she hurries towards us. She's wearing a luminous yellow jacket with 'Steward' on the back. 'There you are! What took you so long? And— Oh.' She spots William. 'There you are,' she says. 'Well.'

'He was at a loose end so I thought he deserved to see a St John's Eve.' I crouch down to my granddaughter, who is wearing some kind of druid costume and looks adorable. 'Hi, Miss, are you having a great time?'

'They haven't lighted it yet,' Sirocco says, sounding bored. 'And Lorna bought sweets for me but they've got raisins in them and they are . . .' She makes a puking sound. 'And the music hurts my ears and I told Nana but she said she can't do anything about it even though she said she is in charge and—'

'So, not good, then.' I pick her up and squeeze her tight. 'How about we go and get you a big can of Coke? The man over there is selling them.'

'Yes!'

'I told her she couldn't,' my mother shouts after me.

I buy three cans: one for me, one for Sirocco and one for William.

'I don't suppose I have a mouth on me,' my mother mutters, so I buy her one too.

'There's my girl.' Luc bounds up and grabs Sirocco, who squeals in delight as he spins her around. Her Coke fizzes everywhere and people jump out of the way.

'Luc!' my mother yelps, though fondly.

I look over his shoulder. No sign of Cherry. Maybe she didn't come. Maybe it's all off.

'You loving this, Siroc?' he asks her.

'They haven't lighted it yet.' Sirocco pouts. 'And the music hurts my ears and Nana said—'

'Five more minutes, Munchkin.' Luc hefts her onto his shoulders. 'Hold on to me now and you'll see everything. Ready?'

'Yes!'

'Micko and Jay are over here. And a girl with a cool name.'

'A cool name?'

'Cherry.'

'I like that name.'

'Well, come and say hello.'

'Micko and Jay and Cherry! Yay!'

'Yay.'

'I want to throw my dollies on the bonfire,' Sirocco declares loudly, making Luc crack up as they move through the crowd.

A couple of people look at her in horror.

'My granddaughter,' my mother announces proudly. She starts to tell William all about Sirocco's game with the dolls and the coffins.

I stand on tiptoe but Luc has vanished into the melee and, knowing him, he'll keep as far away from me as he can.

'Two more minutes,' the loudspeaker announces. 'Gather around, everyone. You're very welcome. With this large bonfire, high on a hill, contributed to by all the community, we go back to the traditions of pagan Ireland when whole villages would turn out to celebrate this feast. The fire marked the summer solstice, and it was lit to protect farms from harm. It was a night of singing and rejoicing. Originally called the Bone Fire, animal bones were used as a sacrifice. This bone fire . . .'

Holy shit.

Slievemore to Achill-henge and Achill-henge to Keel Beach. The timings would fit.

'I'd bury her in plain sight,' Dan had said.

What better place than this bonfire?

Didn't I come here with the laptop?

Both Denis and Eamon possess the type of vehicles that can drive up to this place. They'd have had to haul Moira the last two hundred metres but she was tiny. Good farming men both, it'd have been like carrying a dead animal. And, sure, if they'd concealed her with a blanket, in the dark, who would have noticed up here? All it would take would be a few bits of wood thrown on top of her and she'd be hidden in plain sight. People have been bringing bits and pieces for the fire all the time in the last few weeks. What if Moira is in there? In the middle of the bonfire.

What if our biggest piece of evidence is about to go up in flames?

'One more minute!'

People cheer.

Two men walk to the edges of the bonfire with unlit torches.

More cheering.

The crowds are huge. People have come from all over the county to see this. The roads are jammed with cars. The craic is in the air. Vendors are making money hand over fist.

What if I'm wrong?

'Forty-five seconds.'

The torches are lit.

Oh, crap.

Luc will disown me if I stop it.

And if Sirocco was disappointed before now, what will she be like when she has to go home?

And what if I'm wrong?

The thought makes me shiver.

William looks down at me. 'All right?'

If I say nothing he'll never know that I suspected it.

But I can't do that to Moira.

I tug at his arm. 'Cig.'

'Thirty seconds!'

'It's William,' he calls over the noise. 'We're not in work now.'

'We just might be.'

At his look, I indicate the bonfire. 'I think that could be where Moira is.'

'What?'

I gabble out about the timings and about how it could be done so bloody easily. I'm not sure I even make sense but the fact I'm saying it at all is enough to convince him.

'The murder weapon,' William says. 'What's the bet it's on there too? A piece of timber.'

'Ten seconds!'

The crowd begins the countdown.

'We'll be lynched. You know that, don't you?' he says to me.

I nod.

'Ready?'

'Ready.'

Eamon

Incident 6: Artwork

He does not understand why Moira packs herself and the children up one night and leaves him.

A note.

On the fucking table.

A long, explanatory note.

The words dance in front of his oxygen–starved brain.

He sees that note, clear as this morning.

Outside, leaves falling in the October air.

Inside,

When I was six years old, I thought my mother had run away. When I was twenty-six years old it was pointed out to me that my mother hadn't run away. In fact, as you know, my mother had committed suicide. And when I was told that, I could clearly see how it was true. Because after the day when I hadn't been picked up from school, Da cried a lot and then he sent me to a friend of his to stay for a 'holiday'. And I had a great time, and when I came back, life just went on. But in the street, for a long time after, people came up to Da, shaking his hand and saying, 'Sorry for your trouble.'

I realise now, Eamon, that even if you have all the facts, sometimes things just need to be pointed out. Especially to me, who seems to have blinded herself to reality somehow.

Ella's teacher called me in last week. She wanted me to see a picture Ella had drawn of our family.

When she laid it out on her desk for me, my first thought was that Ella has talent. An abundance of talent. I was so proud.

Then the teacher asks if everything is all right with Ella, with our family.

And I saw it. Not the picture, not the talent, but the drawing. You took up most of the page, Eamon, looming over us all. And I was there, in the corner, cowering with our children.

I told the teacher that Ella has a good imagination.

Then I left the room and now I'm leaving you.

I won't be walking into the waves like my mother, Eamon. I will make them.

That's what mothers do when they love their children.

The words enrage him even now as the blood flows out of him. Even now when his mind dulls and his senses slow.

35

Day 8

We don't quite get lynched but someone spits at poor Mick, who'd been at the bonfire too, and I'm called a lot of unsavoury names. My mother pretends she doesn't know me as she gets into a jeep to be ferried back down the mountain with a load of strangers.

Of course, before anyone could leave, they had to queue up to give me and Mick their names so we could log them off the site while William called the powers-that-be to explain our theory and ask for the resources to check it out. I'm sure a few people dodged off but there is only so much three guards can do with a thousand people on a wide-open plain.

Finally, after three hours, at three in the morning, the site has been secured. William, Mick and I stand in front of the unlit bonfire, whose towering form is etched against the dark night sky.

'I hope you're right, Lucy,' William says.

'Thanks, Cig.'

He laughs drily. 'Don't worry, I'll back you. It's a good deduction. We'll come back first light and start the search.'

'I'll stay. Just, you know, if she is here, I wouldn't want to leave her another night on her own.'

'She's dead, Lucy. You can do more good tomorrow.'
'Still.'
'I'll get someone else.'
'If she's there, I found her.'
He looks slantways at me. 'All right. I'll be here in the morning. Mick, you take over from Lucy at eight, okay?'
'Sure thing.'
They leave me then, alone with the bonfire and Moira.
I know she's here.

By two o'clock the next day, the search is in full swing. I'm unable to tear myself away now and William has allowed me to supervise and report back on any interesting finds. The weather is dry, the sky blue, temperature average. By any standard, a good day on Achill Island. There's something serene in watching the search team go about their work. It's in the methodical, calm way things are done, a ballet of order. The bonfire is examined carefully and the best way of deconstructing it is discussed. The last thing they want is the whole thing collapsing in on itself. We all agree that we want to preserve the body in the condition it was when she was murdered.

After a while, equipment is brought up onto the site and I wonder, not for the first time, how on earth this structure was built in a weekend. It's such an inaccessible place. It takes time to figure out where each piece of machinery will be positioned, but once this is decided upon, the recovery of Moira begins.

How high was the bonfire a week ago, they want to know. I ring my mother, because as one of the organising committee, she might have an idea. She's surprises me by jumping in with an apology. 'I was out of order last night,' she says. 'My God, if that poor girl is there, of course you couldn't have her going up in flames. I'm sure everyone will realise that in time. I tried to explain it to Sirocco but sure she's just a child and she was inconsolable.'

I'm not sure if this apology is meant to make me feel better.

'How high was the bonfire a week ago, Mam?'

'I'm not sure. I do think now that a dead body might have been noticed on it.'

I hang up. 'She hasn't a clue,' I tell the officer. 'So go carefully all the way.'

'Grand. Okay, lads.' He gives a thumbs-up to a crane operator. 'Let's get going.'

A text alert pings.

Let me know if you find my daughter.

I ignore it.

Another ping.

Please.

I text back OK.

William arrives around five with some cold coffee and some nice sandwiches.

'Progress was slow at the start,' I tell him. 'But they've got into a rhythm now.'

The bonfire is half the size it was earlier.

'Have you been here all night and all today?'

'I got a lift to my mother's, had some lunch and came back.'

'Come on.' He takes the sandwich from me. 'That's not a way to last long in this game. We'll grab a bite. If Moira is here, she's not going anywhere. I'll fill you in on what's been happening and we'll get the lads to call us if they've got anything. Deal?'

'Grand.'

***

Twenty minutes later, we're in the Anville restaurant with two gorgeous dinners in front of us. We've both gone for the salmon.

William looks at his with suspicion. 'I'm not a man for sauces.' He moves a ramekin to one side.

I pour the white wine sauce all over mine.

I watch covertly as he pokes at his food, before lifting a piece to his mouth. He chews, looks mildly surprised, takes a bigger forkful. 'This is pretty good,' he says to me, in approval. 'Well chosen.'

'Yeah, well, there are places to eat on Achill other than Dickie's.'

'That man is legend,' he tells me. 'Take the time to know people and they'll surprise you.'

'That they do.'

He glances sharply at me and is about to reply when his mobile rings. 'Yes?' he barks. Then to me, 'Come on, they think they've got something.'

36

Moira's been found. I can see her, where she was thrown, apparently haphazardly, into the middle of the pyre. She's wrapped in a blanket – it looks like a Barbie one, maybe Ella's – taken from the house or the car. Other than this, there has been no attempt to conceal her body, so the SO must have just dumped her and piled wood on top of her. Because it's out in the open air, and she's in the centre surrounded by wood, tyres and people's rubbish, the smell of her decomposing body was minimised. William and I wait as discussions take place about how to get her safely down.

An hour later, she lies on plastic sheeting on the ground. She'd been dressed in black jeans and a red rain jacket, her hair pulled back in a scrunchie. Blue shoes, one missing. The smell of decomposition is overpowering and her body is green. William and I stand in silence over her, and my objectivity is punctured with grief for the life she never got to live, for the children she won't see grow up. I'm sure she wants better for Bren than the path that may be laid out for him. She's unrecognisable as the laughing artist on Instagram. And yet the way she was murdered is obvious. One massive blow to the head, which cracked her skull.

'We also found this,' Joe shows us a plastic evidence bag with a phone inside. 'It was close enough to the body, and if you look over there, I think we may have found our murder weapon.'

'Bonanza day, eh?' William strides to where a bloodied piece of firewood lies on the ground.

'It came from a pallet,' Joe says. 'There's lettering on the side, look.'

'That might make things easier. We can trace the pallet and maybe find someone in this investigation who chopped it up.'

'William,' someone calls. 'We've a selection of bits and pieces over here, not sure if they're relevant to the investigation or not.'

I follow William to where several items are laid out on plastic sheeting.

Thank God the laptop isn't there, is all I can think.

I turn my attention back to Moira. 'I'd like to go to the PM with her.' I can't let her go on her own to be poked and probed by the weirdo that is Joe Palmer.

'I don't—'

'This woman saw her child run back into a burning building,' I interrupt William. 'She knew her little boy was upstairs. She must have known she couldn't save them or herself. I just . . .'

'Lucy.' William pulls me away. His hands on my arms, he bends to look into my face. 'She's dead. We can't change it. The only thing we can do for her is to get her justice. Go home, get sleep, and come in ready to do that tomorrow. We're getting closer. You've minded her all night.'

'Then send Dan to the PM, will you?' Dan is good at PMs. He'll make sure Joe is kind to her.

'I will.'

I can ring Dan when it's done and find out what's happening, I decide.

'Go,' William orders, then heads towards one of the SOCOs to ask a question.

I text Nick Flannery. *We have found your daughter.*

He doesn't reply.

37

Lights are on in the house and my mother has the door open before I even have my key out. 'Just to let you—'

'Yes, we did find something up at the bonfire,' I say, pre-empting her. 'No, I can't go into details. No, I don't think—'

'Lucy, I—'

I push open the kitchen door and stop dead.

Luc is there with a strange girl.

'I did try to tell you,' my mother whispers. 'Isn't she gorgeous?'

'Hello.' I throw my coat over the back of the chair as I take in the exotic creature who has taken up space in my tired little kitchen. Tall, long-legged, with a mane of curly blonde obviously dyed hair, she's wearing a pair of impossibly small shorts and a belly top that shows a taut midriff. Her make-up is flawless though very heavy, her nails sparkly and long. Her gaze, as she eyes me up and down, is languid and assured.

'You must be Lucy.' She oozes confidence.

'And you must be?' I raise my eyebrows and walk past her to put on the kettle.

'Cherry.' The name sounds slightly comical with Luc's Mayo accent. 'She's come for a visit, she's staying in Achill Sound for a few days. She's from Dublin.'

Those Dublin girls, I think, with a wince.

'Hi, Cherry.' We shake hands. Hers is smooth and slim. 'Luc hasn't mentioned you. How d'you know him?'

'I have mentioned you,' Luc grinds out, with a glare at me.

Cherry isn't bothered. I admire that. 'I know Luc from college.' She tosses her mane of hair. 'What did you find at the bonfire?'

'Probably a body,' Luc says, in a pathetic attempt to impress her. 'That's what my ma does. Solves murders and that.'

'That's not really something to discuss,' I look at their glasses, 'over vodkas and beers.'

Luc throws me a murderous look and I feel a bit mean. Just as I'm about to say something nice to Cherry, Luc stands up. 'Cherry is going now. Nan, will you drive us back to the Sound?'

'Of course.' My mother, without looking at me, bustles past to get her car keys from the drawer. 'Come on, Cherry, love.'

Turncoat, I think.

Cherry downs the full vodka before standing gracefully up. Bending over, giving me an eyeful of arse, she picks up a shiny tote bag. 'Bye, Lucy.'

'Bye.'

'I'll see you again, no doubt. Come on, Lukey.' She hands him her jacket, slings her bag over her shoulder and shimmies out of the room. Luc trots after her like a faithful puppy.

The fecking eejit.

'Tani didn't stand much of a chance against that, did she?' my mother remarks, when she returns *sans* Luc. 'He's besotted but, mark my words, it'll end in tears.'

'As long as it doesn't end in another grandchild,' I mutter

darkly, and my mother gives a horrified gasp. I take in the house through Cherry's eyes. At the mess of Rob's boxes. 'And did Luc mention when he's going to finish sorting Rob's things?'

'Tomorrow after Cherry goes home. I think Luc is taking his time because he's afraid of what he'll find.'

He should be. 'Rob had terrible taste, I'd be scared too.'

My mother chuckles. 'Honestly, if that girl hurts him, I think I'll hunt her down and kill her. She's the hurting type.'

And much as Luc has done wrong, I agree with her.

'I remember one time, when you started going out with Rob.' My mother puts her keys back in the drawer as she speaks. 'Now, I never told you this, Lucy, but it was the first Christmas he visited, before ye were married. You were in your room changing and he was in the hall, just waiting on you. I can still see him. Clear as day. And I said to him that if he hurt you I wouldn't be responsible for what happened to him.'

I splutter out a laugh. 'You didn't!'

'I did too. You were all I had, Lucy, and I could see how you felt about him and I just knew, like, I had an inkling.'

'Rob never told me that.' I admire that he hadn't because it would definitely have resulted in a row between me and my mother. I would have sided with him. I loved him and he knew it, and he hadn't exploited it.

Eamon Delaney would have exploited it. The thought pings in my brain.

'I know. That was nice of him.' Her mind has moved on. 'Have you seen Rob's laptop? Luc says it's disappeared.'

'Nope.' Then, just as she's about to say something else, probably about the laptop, I tell her that I've an early start tomorrow and I have to get to bed.

263

Eamon

They all knew that she had left him. Patti and the neighbours. They're all wondering what happened. They're all talking about him. Some are sorry for him. They bring him food and he pretends that he's grateful. They pat his hand and tell him that these things happen in a marriage, that people leave.

More fool them that accept it, he thinks.

Moira can't leave him.

She had been pliable, grateful for the house and the land, as he'd known a girl brought up on the mean streets would be. He had given her everything and she'd never given him one clue that he wasn't good enough for her.

But now, now she'd made it perfectly clear that he was easily discarded, easy to walk away from.

The BITCH.

He texts her while having a coffee, taking his time over it: *I miss you, I need you and please let me see my children.* Those words have always been the best way to get Moira onside.

But this time, Moira texts back. *You need to get help, Eamon. Anger management or counselling. If you love me and the kids, then you'll give it a shot.*

Fuck you, he thinks, as he throws his cup against the wall, brown liquid spattering everywhere. What's she's really saying is that he's not good enough the way he is. That unless he changes, he won't measure up.

Patti is a comfort. She says Moira doesn't have the right to take his children. Patti looks it all up online and hands him pages and pages of advice. He should go to a solicitor. He should sue her. He should just turn up outside her door and have it out with her.

If those kids had to live with his da, they'd know what anger was. The drinking, the chaos that followed his mother's leaving. And him and Patti trying to keep a lid on it. Is a bit of control in life too much to ask? A bit of certainty? A fire lit when you come in from work, for God's sake. How hard is that?

His breathing grows shallow.

His light is dimming.

He can hear the crunch of footsteps as the people who did this to him walk away.

38

Day 9

I wake up about six. All is quiet as I slip my feet into my shoes. I'd slept in my clothes, being too exhausted to change. My head spins. There was a time it wouldn't have knocked a feather out of me. Age is a curse. The hall is in darkness but the light is on in the kitchen.

There's a bowl of porridge on the table with a note from my mother telling me to eat it. She adds, *Sirocco left a card in for you yesterday, I forgot about it. It's on the table. PS I think she might take after you.*

Smiling, I put the porridge in the microwave and open Sirocco's card. She's drawn a bonfire with a woman in the middle of it. The woman looks like she's screaming in agony, and then a very unflattering figure, fat with grey hair, a massive scar down her face, seems to be riding in to save the day. 'Well done, Nana,' Sirocco has written in a big scrawl.

I pin it to the fridge.

I'm glad I haven't let her down too badly.

Just as I'm stirring some honey into the porridge, Dan calls. He's early.

'Hey,' I say.

'You sound rough.' There's a faint note of concern in his voice.

'I'm just up, eating porridge. Were you at the PM yesterday?'

'Yeah. It was late last night when we finished so I didn't call. Just preliminary findings for now. She was hit at least three times, blunt-force trauma to the head. Preliminary examination of the plank of wood thought to be the murder weapon seems to match the wounds on her skull. Palmer reckons, too, that she would have half walked, been dragged the last two hundred metres to the bonfire, forced to climb into the bucket and been dropped. Now brace yourself, he also thinks that the blows to the head and the drop would not have killed her, just rendered her unconscious. She would probably have been alive when she was first on the bonfire.'

'Aw . . . no.'

'Yeah.'

I wish he hadn't told me that.

'There were some historical fractures too, on her arm, about five years old, Palmer reckons.' We're silent for a moment before he adds, 'Her clothing has been sent for testing but so far nothing much of interest showed up.'

'Okay.'

'How could you stuff a woman in the boot of a car and drive to a place like that, hit her again, drag her, whatever, to a bonfire and not be seen?'

'It was early. It's fairly isolated and whoever it was knew that that bonfire was there.'

'I know you don't want to hear this, Lucy, but to me it screams local.'

'Not necessarily. It's been advertised all over the regional

267

papers and Midwest Radio did a section on it during the week. How's Delores?'

I think he welcomes the change of subject. Sometimes a case makes you feel grubby.

'Fran clipped her wings over the whole inviting everyone to dinner whenever she feels like it. She was leaving, she told us, then changed her mind and offered to cook us an apology lunch.'

'I think I love Delores,' I declare. 'What a woman.'

'You're welcome to join us. I'm sure she'll cook too much, insist we eat it and get insulted if we don't.'

'Aw, no, I couldn't.'

'I'm begging you.' He sounds deadly serious. 'Just be there, it'll relieve the tension.'

'What an enticing invite. When?'

'Lunchtime.'

'Okay. I'll look forward to that, I think.'

He hangs up with a laugh.

39

The news is full of the Bone Fire Murder. That's the name the media have given to it so they can grab the headlines and sell their papers. Moira's identity will be lost now, and whoever murdered her will become a story that people tell. Maybe the Bone Fire Murderer will have a documentary made about them or they'll write a book about why they did it and how it made them feel, and Moira's voice will be forgotten.

Not on my watch.

I'm surprised to see Stacy, Matt's reporter girlfriend, in the station as I pass through on the way to conference. 'Hi, Lucy,' she calls. 'I'm having a premonition that you and I are going to be a big help to each other.'

Ignoring her, I take the stairs two at a time, eager to be there early so I can find out what progress we've made since last night. The room is full, which isn't a surprise. It's probably due to the fresh developments. William hails me, and I join him and Dan at the top of the room.

On the dot of ten o'clock, he calls everyone to order and gives a run-down on what has happened so far. Dan talks about the PM. Then he calls on Kev and Ger for forensics.

'That lighter,' Kev says. 'It turns out Moira's father left it behind one time he visited her in Mayo. She'd had it ever since. So, mystery solved. It may have been used to light the fire, but it doesn't belong to our SO.'

'Disappointing but good work anyway,' William says. 'Ger? You've got the rest of the forensics, I believe?'

'Well, yes.' Ger flushes red. 'Moira's clothes were examined as a matter of urgency. The main thing of note was the presence of . . .' he gulps '. . . plant spores, Cig. Just a few. Not as many as were in her car. They reckon they were deposited by the SO touching her or wrapping her in the blanket, you know, leaning in and over her and—'

'I know how to wrap someone in a blanket.' William says drily. 'Is there someone in that lab in Dublin who's obsessed with bloody plant spores? Anything else?'

'There was a hair found on her sleeve but there was no root so no DNA. They said it's from a European person, though.'

'That narrows it down. Marvellous. Have you got results in from the phone that was found?'

'They are doing that today. But there was no SIM in it. It was destroyed. I'll let you know as soon as we get anything on that. As for the wood pallet, we believe it was taken from Moira's store because the letters on it match up with some other planks in the shed there. Denis Long would have chopped it for her but that doesn't mean he used it.'

'Nothing so.' William looks as if he can't believe it. 'How's the door-to-door coming along?'

'The search will be narrowed down to the houses along the route today, Cig,' Jordy says. 'We've a lot of guys on it but nothing coming from it at the moment. Thankfully, there aren't too many properties out that way.'

'Any interesting calls?'

'Nothing of interest,' Mick answers.

'That call on the first day, did you ever find out who made it?'

'Eh, no, but it was a woman, so . . .'

'So?'

'Well, I thought we were looking for a man and—'

'You have information that the rest of us don't, is that it? We don't know it's anyone. Get on it.'

I feel sorry for Mick. William is just frustrated that we haven't got more from finding the body. Right now, over a week in, we're in trouble. Every lead seems to give us a new suspect.

'This woman,' William is hell bent on proving his point, 'did you recognise her voice? Did it sound like Patti, for instance?'

'I can't remember what the voice sounded like now. I'll have another listen.'

'Do that. Detective Lorcan Brown has kindly come back up from Limerick. He talked to Bertie, Nick Flannery's nemesis, for us. Lorcan, what have you got?'

'I'm afraid I can't add to anything, William. According to Bertie, yes, he did come down. He found out where she lived and took a picture of himself standing outside her house and sent it to Nick. It was a threat, I'd imagine, though Bertie would never admit it. And that, I believe, is how the argument between the two men was resolved. I don't think he did it, because if Nick Flannery thought he had, Bertie would not be around right now. And guns are more that lad's style anyway. This whole bonfire thing, it smacks of amateur.'

'Thanks,' William says. 'We won't discount him but it's a good point. Susan and Louis, all set up for Bren's interview today?'

271

They both nod. 'Yes.'

'Right, all, Jim has the job sheets there. Make sure to return them. Susan and Louis, anything of interest today, get back to Lucy with it.'

As everyone starts to pick up their job sheets, Matt tugs at my sleeve. He looks faintly mortified. 'Can you come with me for a second?'

'Why?'

'Just . . . come on.' Then, 'You owe me one.'

I guess I do so I follow him out of the room, calling to Dan to collect the job sheet for me.

Matt leads me into the scraggy yard behind the station, the one that was meant to be a pleasant place to sit, but what with the weather down here and the salt from the sea, the one bench we have is rusted and falling apart and all the foliage is dead. Stacy is leaning against a wall at the far end, out of sight of any windows. She straightens when she spots us. 'Great, Mattie.' She blows him a kiss and, after flinging an apologetic look at me, he disappears.

I'll kill him. I turn to leave.

'Hear me out,' Stacy says. 'I think we can help each other.'

'This isn't a film, Stacy. I do my job and you do yours. I like Matt but I'm not telling you a thing.'

'I'm going to tell you a thing, actually,' she says, 'something your other garda friends won't find out because only I know it.'

'Withholding information from an investigation is a crime.'

'I'm going to tell you.' She says it like I'm an idiot. 'And if I do, I want the rights to this story when it's done. The exclusive.'

'If I'm caught talking to you now . . .'

'Then hurry up and agree.'

'What have you got for me first?'

She cocks her head to one side and regards me cheekily. Stacy is not afraid of anything. She is a proper newshound and will go anywhere a story brings her. 'You seem to see me as your adversary,' she says, 'but I'm not. The media are not. Honestly, we are only ever after the truth, the same way you are. We are the servants of the public's right to know.'

'What have you got?' I'm not in the mood for her trying to justify her job. Though, in fairness, she has made a valid point. 'Tell me or I'll walk away. I'll find out anyway.'

'You won't, actually,' she says. 'And me telling you won't help. But here it is. Yesterday, after hearing what happened up at Achill-henge, I took it upon myself to canvass houses along the route to find out if any of them saw or heard anything that night. My aunt lives up there, and she convinced people to talk to me. But the best of all is she's the only one who spotted the car that night.'

It's like she's punched me. We'd put call-outs for anyone who saw things. 'Why didn't she come forward?' I keep my voice steady.

'She's old. She didn't realise what it was she saw.'

'We'll be canvassing people today, so we'll be talking to your aunt.' I turn to leave.

'She won't talk.'

'What?'

'Unless I tell her it's all right, she won't talk.'

'That's . . .' I cannot believe it. 'You want exclusive rights to this story when it's done in return for your aunt talking?'

'Yeah. Worked for the night-caller case.'

'That was way different.'

Stacy looks a little abashed.

'Tell me what she saw and I'll see what I can do.'

'She saw a woman,' Stacy says. 'That's what she saw.'

Mick had heard a woman on a call that first night.

I shrug as if it's not enough. 'Anything else?'

'She says it was very early. She gets up at four most mornings, and that morning she saw a red car and it was having trouble on the roads. It's not easy to get a car up those roads. She said it was a woman driving because she got out of the car, had a look and got back in again.'

'Description?'

'Her eyesight isn't great, you know old people.' She tosses out that remark as if I'm the same age as her aunt. 'But she said that the person had on black trousers and a black hooded top. It was dark, though, that time in the morning. Maybe it was navy. About twenty minutes later, the car came back down.'

'And she's sure of the day?'

'No, but the time fits. I've worked it out and that was the first car she ever saw up there at that time in the morning, so it's got to be it. It had got busier, though, with people trying to sneak all their crap on the bonfire.'

'If I send two guards up to take your aunt's statement, will she talk?'

'Only if I tell her it's okay.'

'You're skating along the thin edge of the law here.'

Stacy seems unconcerned.

'Okay. You've got your story. But only when we tie it all up.'

'Thanks. Pleasure doing business with you. Here.' She hands me her aunt's address.

And, light as a feather, she dances off, no doubt to tell Matt what a coup she's got.

I return inside and ask Jordy to get someone up to this lady. Handing him her details, I say, 'She may have something for us.'

As Jordy huffs off, I try to locate Mick, who seems to have wandered away somewhere. I eventually find him making toast in the kitchen. 'The grill in our place is broke,' he attempts to explain. 'So—'

'The call that William told you to locate. Make it a priority, and when you find it, send it to me.'

Could it have been Patti Delaney?

Though both Eamon and Denis at five feet seven could have been mistaken for women. Especially by someone with bad eyesight.

Jesus.

40

Delores is a charming woman, warm and welcoming and very glamorous. No wonder my mother loved her. She's also completely hyper as she whirls about setting an extra bowl and plate, knife and fork for me, chattering all the time about Dan and Fran and how impossible they are to live with. 'But we knock along,' she chirrups gaily, as Dan throws her a sour look behind her back. 'Right, lovely to meet you, Lucy, I'm off.' Standing on tiptoe, she plants a kiss on Fran's cheek. 'Bye, pet.' She turns to Dan, hesitates and mumbles, 'Bye, Daniel.'

'Thanks for this,' he says to her.

'You're very welcome.' And she's gone in a blitz of perfume and clacking heels, the front door slamming after her.

Dan flinches. 'She'll have the door off its hinges if she keeps doing that.'

'And I'm sure she'll fix it too,' Fran says pleasantly, though with a bit of grit as he dishes out the salad.

Dan is obviously not allowed to criticise Delores.

Once we're all seated, Fran asks, 'How is the case going?' To me, 'That was great work finding her on the bonfire, Lucy. When Dan told me how she'd been alive when she'd been dumped

276

there, I got chills. I did.'

'You told him that?' I gawp at Dan. 'That's confidential.'

'Sure he's not going to tell anyone and it's good to bounce stuff off him. Actually, Fran, you might be able to help us. This weird thing keeps popping up in the investigation.'

'Dan.' This really isn't on. I tell my mother nothing. In fact the one time I did it by accident, it was all over the papers the next day.

'Plant spores were found in the car of the IP and on her clothes. We don't know if they were deposited by her or by the SO. William doesn't set much store by the find but it's weird, yeah? What's the story with them? Would they be important?'

Fran chews, thinking. 'Spores from what plants?' he says, through a mouthful of coleslaw.

'I can't remember, can you, Luce?'

They look at me. I shake my head, trying to convey how unorthodox this is, then decide to go with it and fish my note-book from my bag. I find the page where I'd jotted it down. My writing is a bit of a scrawl. 'Ivy-leaved blueflower—'

'Bellflower,' Fran corrects. 'Lovely thing. What else?'

'Purple saxifrage?' I'm not sure I've pronounced it right.

Fran raises his eyebrows at that one.

'Stiff sedge, least willow and rhododendron.'

'Interesting.' Fran is intrigued. 'Rhododendron is all over the place on Achill so that's not a biggie. But to find it with all those other rare plants, that's quite the feat.'

'Rare?'

'Yeah, the ivy-leafed bellflower is difficult to find. And these spores and pollens were all together on the victim? And in her car?'

'Yep.' Dan chomps on a cucumber.

'Interesting. I'll check that out for ye.'

'Great.' Dan beams.

I'm not sure the Cig would see it as great, getting a civilian involved in the case.

At five o'clock Susan and Louis arrive back at the station with Bren's recordings. They both look a little subdued.

'Anything?' I ask.

'I'll play you the relevant parts,' Susan says. 'He was very good, really cooperative.'

'That was the sad part,' Louis mutters, flashing a look at me, then making himself scarce.

'How was Eamon?' I ask, as Susan sets up the video.

'Actually, he was all right, the arsehole. He adores that little lad, told him not to be afraid and that he'd be waiting outside for him with a surprise.' Video set, Susan explains, 'The early part is just me building rapport. You know the drill, Lucy. Making him feel at home and able to question things. I did the whole do-you–understand–what–is–right–and–what–is–wrong and I tested him and made sure he did. Then I made sure that he knew it was all right not to know things. He didn't have to try to please me. Will I play from where he talked about his family or do you just want to go straight to the night of the murder? I think you need to hear it all, though.'

'Play it all so.'

She flicks the switch and Brendan appears onscreen. I haven't seen him since the day in the hospital when he was rescued, but he looks thinner here, his face pinched, his blue and green T-shirt a little large for him. He's perched on a colourful blue, red and green chair, sitting on his hands. The room is a special one, away from garda stations and designed specifically for children, full of posters they like and bright, cheerful things.

Susan, her voice pitched exactly right, says, 'First, Bren, it's okay not to know something. So, if I ask you a question and you don't know, just say, "I don't know." And if you ask me a question and I don't know, I'll say I don't know. Do you want to practise it?'

'Uh-huh.'

'Okay,' Susan says. 'How many Smarties are in a box of Smarties?'

The little boy frowns. 'Probably about fifty.'

'But do you know for sure?'

'Well, if you think of the size of a Smartie and the size of the box then it's a good guess.'

Dan and I laugh for the first time in this investigation.

'That part is too early, hang on, I'll just . . .' Susan rolls the footage on a bit.

'Tell me about your family,' Susan says.

'Mmm.' Bren kicks the back of his shoes against the steel legs of the chair. 'Well . . . I have a daddy, his name is Eamon and he's big and strong, and my mammy . . .' he falters '. . . I think she is real pretty for a mammy only she is gone for now, and my sister.' He stops. 'Is a person who is died still in your fambily?'

'Yes.'

'Good. My sister is dead and she is Ella and she is very quiet.' He whispers 'very quiet'. 'And then me. I am Brendan like my granddad Delaney, only he is dead too. I am called Bren.'

'Good. Anything else?'

Bren shrugs.

'Tell me more about your daddy.'

'He makes the rules.'

'Tell me about the rules.'

Bren screws up his eyes. 'Like no food in the TV room, no shoes in the house, no painting for Mammy until it gets dark outside, dinner at five on the very dot, ironing on Tuesdays . . .' he frowns '. . . and lots more.'

'And would you all obey the rules?'

'Yep.'

'What happens if you didn't obey the rules?'

He pulls his hands out from under his thighs and plays with his fingers for a moment. 'Lots of things,' he sing-songs. A sigh. 'Mammy didn't obey the rules.' He looks right at Susan as he says indignantly, 'She kept making his dinner all wrong.' Then, as if he's reciting a mantra, 'Too many peas on the plate, too small an amount on the plate, the wrong dinner, dinner too late. She just would not get it right.' Then, with a swing of his legs, 'Daddy told me she just did it to annoy him. Also she didn't 'preciate Daddy and all the hard work he did. She just painted pictures and didn't care. But she made nice dinners for me and Ella so she liked us. And we love her very much.'

'I'd say you do.'

'Yep.'

'Anything else you can tell me about your family?'

'I don't think Ella liked Daddy either because she hided when he came into the room. Daddy didn't like that. But Ella liked me and Mammy, and I liked everyone, and Mammy liked me and Ella, and Daddy liked everyone.'

Gently, like a surgeon, over the next fifteen minutes, Susan gradually unfolds the story of life in the Delaney household. Bren charts it in all its horror in bright, oblivious tones.

'What a bastard that Eamon is,' Dan says. 'Making Moira kneel down on all fours so he could rest his feet on her.'

'Yeah.' Susan looks upset. 'Just listen to this bit.'

'Aunt Patti doesn't like Mammy either,' Bren said. 'Only me and Ella like Mammy. Aunt Patti told Daddy that she hates Mammy and the sooner she was put in her place the better, and when I heard that I hit Aunt Patti, because you have to hit people to make them behave and now she doesn't like me either.'

'It goes on like that for a while,' Susan says. 'But Patti is a very powerful presence in Bren's world. From what I could make out, and you can read the transcripts later, Patti has a say in everything that happens in that house, from changing the light-bulbs to what colour to paint the walls. What I want to get to is this.' Another fast forward. 'Now, the day before the fire, his account is fairly similar to what we believe happened, so after that, I led him on to the night of the fire. Here we go.' She presses play.

'Mammy goes out seaweeding – that's what she calls it. Me and Ella say sea-weeing.' He giggles. 'She gets up in the dark and she wakes us up and we have to pull on our dressing-gowns and get in the car and then she drives to the beach and we sleep in the car and she gets the seaweed and a man pays her for it and maybe Denis is there sometimes and he might give Mammy a lollipop for us to eat after our breakfast. But we stay in the car and don't talk to anyone, never, never talk to anyone. Never, never get out of the car.' He wags his finger in imitation of his mother.

'That sounds exciting,' Susan says. 'Now, the day of the fire, can you tell me what happened?'

'We didn't go seaweeding that day a-cause of the fire.'

'Okay.'

'I wasn't scared or anything.'

281

'Wow.'

'I know. Ella was a-cause I hearded her scream. She was downstairs. I didn't want to go a-cause I was supposed to be on a sleepover in my daddy's but Mammy ruined it and I was cross and I said I wasn't going. Then I heard the car started, to warm us up, and then Ella comes into my room and says that Mammy would buy us sweets and she helps me pull on my dressing-gown and then outside Mammy shouts, I don't know what, and so Ella goes out and then more shouting, and Ella screams and then someone else shouts, "Get out, get out," and I stayed in my room, thinking Mammy would come but she didn't and then the car drives off and Mammy is gone, and I smelt the smoke and then I don't remember but Daddy says Fireman Sam came and brung me to hospital.'

There is a silence after that.

Then Susan asks, 'You heard someone say, "Get out, get out."'

'Yes. A lady's voice.'

'Okay. Do you remember what the lady's voice sounded like?'

Bren looks at her blankly. 'Like a lady.'

'Okay.'

Susan presses pause.

'A lady?' Dan quirks his eyebrows.

'Yep. But he didn't say if he recognised it. I didn't want to ask just in case . . .'

'You were right.'

'But he was certain enough it was a woman.'

'Just one second.' I dial Jordy. Putting him on speaker, I ask, 'Any news?'

'Just finished with that witness now.' Jordy is huffing and puffing as he walks. Then he coughs chestily and we all wince. 'She lives right opposite the part of the road where it gets nasty so good line of vision for any car stopping. She was ninety if she was a day,' he croaks out, 'but sharp as a tack. She says she saw a red car that morning and a woman was driving it. She's adamant it was a woman because she got out and pulled at the bumper, and she said men don't walk like women. Now, she's an alert old dear but her eyesight isn't the best and she was about twenty feet away at four in the morning, so make of it what you want. But that changes things, eh?'

'It certainly does.' I hang up. 'I'll inform William,' I tell the other two. 'Great work, Susan.'

'Louis wasn't too bad either,' she says.

Hmm.

To my horror, the super, Louis's father, is in with William.

He's a slimy fecker with a slimy reputation. He wasn't exactly nice to me when I got transferred west. Told me he didn't appreciate getting Dublin's cast-offs.

He's a bit more civil now that I've managed to solve a few high-profile cases.

'Aw, DS Golden,' he says, his voice round and plummy. 'I believe my boy is doing well.'

I shoot a look at William and manage, 'He and his colleague got a good interview out of Bren Delaney today. That's why I'm here. I was wondering if we could bring Patti Delaney back in.'

'Louis specifically requested to be let come here,' the super goes on, ignoring the urgency in my voice. 'He has a great admiration for you, Lucy. Ever since the night-caller case, he has followed everything you do with relish.'

'Aw, we all have our problems,' I deadpan.

'My boy has no problems.' He glares at me and I remember too late that this man is famous for his lack of a sense of humour.

'It was a self-deprecating joke,' I explain. 'I'm really flattered that Louis hero-worships me and thinks I'm fantastic. I could give him a signed poster if he likes.'

William stares resolutely ahead, arms folded.

'That won't be necessary,' Superintendent Devine says. 'He's not five.' He thumbs to William. 'I was just explaining to Will that I want Louis to travel with you for the next couple of days. He'll learn a lot from a woman of your experience, and what's the point of being in my position if I can't call in a few favours? Will and I go way back.'

There is no way that little shit is travelling anywhere with me.

'I wiped the floor with him in Templemore but he's not done so bad for himself, have you, Will?'

'No,' William says calmly. 'Thanks for dropping by.'

'My pleasure, my pleasure. And if the lad is any trouble, you sort him out, eh, Luce.' He beams at me.

'Oh, I will, I promise you that.'

His smile falters a tiny bit.

'Good one.' He laughs. Then, to William, 'This bonfire case, let's get it done in the next week or so. The media will not let it go.'

And he's gone, back to his lair.

'Louis Devine travel with me?' I whirl on my boss. 'I presume you said no.'

'I said yes, actually.'

'I can't stand the little prick.'

'Exactly,' William says. 'If you'd liked him, I would have refused point blank, but we all need to be able to work together and I have the awful feeling that Louis might be here for the long haul. I thought it was a good suggestion and, honestly, Lucy, it makes my life easier just to agree with him. After all' – he cocks an eyebrow – 'I can't give him too much of a progress report so far, can I?'

'That's not my or the team's fault. We're working our arses off and we've narrowed it down.' I rein in my annoyance and focus once again on the case. 'In fact, both Bren and a woman who lives out by Achill-henge describe a woman driving Moira's car that morning.'

'Really?' He sits up straighter, interested now.

'Descriptions are sketchy at best,' I admit. 'Black clothes, black hoodie. But as Patti is our only female suspect and Bren describes her as not liking Moira at all, it might be worth calling out to her.'

'Any other proof? Her alibi for the night is strong. She was with a friend and her friend corroborated it.'

'She's the only woman suspect we have.'

William shrugs. 'Lucy, we've questioned her up and down and sideways. Even before we knew or had a strong suspicion it was a woman, we treated Patti as a suspect. Unless you can prove her friend is lying, we have no cause to go bringing her in.'

And, damn it, he's right.

'Can I just go and talk to her?'

'No. Look, the bits of the puzzle we have yet to check, check them out. See if Mick has isolated that call yet. It might be nothing, totally unrelated, but if we can identify Patti's voice, we may have something. Alternatively, if we find her prints on the phone, that might help us too. Or if we can trace the plant yokes to her.'

'Bren was pretty damning about her in his—'
'No.'

Mick is laughing about something with Matt at the front desk. When they see me, Mick goes bright red and Matt bends over, pretending to write something in a ledger that isn't there.

'I'd say it might help if you got a piece of paper, Matt,' I call, then beckon Mick towards me. 'Any progress with the call?'

He surprises me. 'Yes. I was just coming to get you but Matt caught me and was telling me this story that happened to him and Stacy last week and I—' The stony expression on my face stops him in his tracks. 'Right, you don't want to hear about that. Fair enough.'

I keep the amusement from my voice as I ask, 'Where's the call?'

'I lined it up for you on my computer.' We climb up the stairs to the incident room. It's a hive of activity and I'm gratified to see Louis helping Ger.

Mick offers me the chair in front of the computer and, leaning over me, sets up the audio file. 'I had a listen myself,' he says, 'and it sounds like she's trying to disguise her voice.'

He presses play and hands me a set of earbuds.

That trollop was forged in the fires of hell. Let her burn her way back there.

My heart thuds in disappointment. It's not Patti. But there is something . . .

'I think it's just a weird randomer.' Mick is leaning against the desk.

'Play it again.' I think I know that voice. And that word. Trollop. Who used that word during the investigation? Someone did. I'll have to look up my notes.

That trollop was forged in the fires of hell. Let her burn her way back there. 'Just – just hang on,' I call to Mick, as I rush to pull my notebook from my jacket. I know that voice. I bloody know it.

I flick through all the statements I've taken from the female witnesses and I find it.

And, with a sinking heart, the pieces of the jigsaw start to click–clack into place.

41

Day 10

Early the following day, I take Louis with me to pick up Lorna. William had agreed that, rather than arrest her, I could invite her in for questioning as, other than the written statement against her husband, which we hope to use against her, we have no proof that she carried out any crime. And yet it all fits.

Voluntary interviews are handy because they cut out the need for all the formalities of an arrest. The paperwork alone takes a few hours, so it saves us and the witness quite a bit of time. But they are still carried out under caution, still recorded and only conducted on people we think are strong suspects.

Voluntary does mean voluntary, though.

Lorna can walk out at any time.

If Lorna refuses to attend, we'll either have to think about arresting her or more likely go back to the drawing board and try to find something.

Yesterday, Bren Delaney and Stacy's aunt had been shown Viper images, one of which was Lorna, and asked if they could recognise anyone. We had one moment of hope when Bren picked out Lorna, but it was just because he knew her.

No other evidence has popped up. Lorna and Denis's joint bank account shows no extra charges for a mobile phone. The call she'd made to the station and on which I recognised her voice was traced to a sweet shop in Mulranny, where she works.

'This is a blast,' Louis says, as he hops from foot to foot outside their door.

I think he thinks I like him.

'This.' I point to my mouth. 'Zipped.'

His face falls but he complies.

On my second ring, Denis opens the door a crack and peers out. 'Lucy,' he says, with some relief, 'it's you. We've been harassed with people throwing things in the garden. And I've been getting threatening texts. Not the locals, mind, they've been very supportive, especially your mother and . . .' His voice trails off. 'If I was guilty, I'd deserve it. I wouldn't complain even, but I'm not guilty and—' It suddenly dawns on him to wonder what I'm doing at his door so early in the morning. 'What is it you want?'

'This is my colleague Garda Louis Devine,' I say.

Louis puffs himself up, clearly thrilled.

'We're here to invite Lorna down to the station to answer a couple of questions.'

'Lorna?' Denis frowns. 'Why would you want to talk to her?'

'Is she in, Denis?'

'Upstairs,' he says faintly. 'Lorna,' he calls.

'What is it?' Lorna appears at the top of the stairs, then spots me and Louis, him in full uniform. 'Lucy.' Surprise floods her face. 'What do you want?' She joins her husband at the door. 'You haven't come for Denis?' An anxious look from me to him. 'He hasn't done anything. He swore to me he hadn't done anything. Have you?' she barks at Denis.

'It's actually you we want to talk to, Lorna,' I say. 'Down at the station.'

'Am I under arrest?'

'Not at all. We've just a few questions to put to you. Now, you can come with us, it's nice and early and no one will see, or Denis can drop you down at a pre-agreed time.'

'But why?'

Denis wraps an arm about her.

'We think you might have information about the murder of Moira and Ella Delaney.'

'Me?' Her eyes dart to her husband. Presumably she never told him she was the source of information on him. 'But I told you all I knew.'

'What did you tell them?' Denis looks down on her. 'When did you talk to them?'

Lorna looks desperately at me.

'When we arrested you, we had questions for Lorna.' The lie slips out easily.

'That's right.' Lorna flaps her hand at Denis, like he's an irritating fly. 'I have nothing to add to what I told you then.'

She's a good liar, I notice.

'We appreciate that.' I keep my voice level, professional. 'But we think, well, my boss thinks that you might be able to add extra information. Now, do you want to come with me?'

'If you can help, I think you should go,' Denis says. 'Sure Lucy wouldn't ask you if she thought you couldn't help.'

Holy shit. I feel like a heel. My job manages to do this to me time and again.

'I suppose.' She looks nervously at me. 'But your mother never said this would happen.'

'My mother isn't privy to the things I do in my job.'

'I'll get your coat,' Denis says pleasantly, as he wanders off. He arrives back with it.

'Thanks, Denis.' She takes it from him and joins us in the car, beside Louis at the back, as I drive us to the station.

The car journey with a suspect is always interesting. Because they've been cautioned, anything they say is admissible and can be taken down in writing. Each suspect is different. The scariest are the still ones, who sit, rigid with anger and righteous fury, ready to explode, the air in the car growing ever more oppressive. Then there are the criers, glad to be caught, the tension of constantly looking over their shoulders finally over. There are the mutterers, who throw out words like breadcrumbs for birds. And then there are the ones like Lorna, blabbering and fretting. All the way to the station, she worries away at me, like she's nipping at a fingernail. 'How is it you think I can help? Has Denis said something? What use am I? I only told you what I thought at the time. How can I help? What is it you want to know?'

And on and on.

Before Lorna's interview, I head to the incident room. 'Have Forensics come back on that phone, Ger?'

He looks up from some witness statements. 'Not yet, anytime this morning. The good thing is Lorna's prints are already on the system as we took them for elimination purposes at the beginning of the investigation, so if they match, I'll let ye all know.'

'Good. Push for it, won't you?'

'Yep. Who's going to be talking to her?'

'Dan and Larry.'

'I hope I'll get to see some of it,' he says.

The whole team will probably cram into the small observation room to have a gawk. If we've got it right, this could be the break we need. There will, of course, be a whole lot of other work to be done before it makes court, but once we have a confession, it's 70 per cent there.

I wonder how long it will be before the jungle drums start up. Someone is bound to have seen us arrive at the station.

Matt appears, his face flushed. 'Eamon Delaney is down in the reception area looking for you, Luce.'

Jesus Christ, how on earth . . .?

When we arrive down, Eamon is pacing to and fro like a caged animal. Up to the door, back to the desk, up to the door, back to the desk. Matt eyes him warily. Just as Eamon turns back to the desk, Malachy, another local, for whom the phrase 'misery guts' was invented, slides in.

'Going to be one of those days,' Matt murmurs.

On the steps outside, a few media heads have gathered. They've no doubt been brought here by Eamon.

'Eamon, hello.' I struggle to keep a professional tone.

Turning, he strides back up the length of the waiting room. 'I believe you've arrested someone.' He wastes no time on small talk.

Menace rolls off him in waves.

Matt, sensing trouble, stands beside me.

'Hello?' Malachy raps the counter with his knuckles. 'Guard?'

'We haven't arrested anyone,' I answer pleasantly. 'You must have got it wrong.'

His eyes glitter, his fist curls. 'I haven't got it wrong. I've—'

'I'm sorry for your trouble.' Malachy shuffles over, oblivious.

'Losing your wife and daughter like that. This place is gone to the dogs.'

'The person we have is not under arrest. She is helping with enquiries. Now, as I said before, you will be told any news when we have something to tell you.'

'You think it's a woman now, eh?'

'I can t—'

'You thought it was me.' He leans over the desk and smirks.

Malachy takes a step back.

'Sir,' Matt tries to intervene. 'If you—'

Holding Eamon's gaze, I lean towards him. 'I'm not paid to think, I'm paid to investigate.'

'Indeed.' A laugh. 'I loved my wife but she was like a lot of women, very hard to satisfy.'

'It's a pity that you couldn't satisfy your wife.'

The air in the room vibrates with tension.

Eamon stares at me, for what seems like ages, as if he's committing me to memory, before righting himself. 'You make sure and keep me updated.'

I don't reply, and after a moment, he stalks off and into the media melee, waving them away, as if he's too upset to engage.

'You wouldn't think he'd just lost his wife and daughter,' Matt observes.

'Just as well,' Malachy huffs, 'because yez are doing nothing to help.'

My legs have turned to jelly. The animosity in Eamon's eyes brought me back to that night in my kitchen. Nausea fills me. I run into the ladies and vomit into the toilet.

Lorna, neat as a pin, sits upright, knotting her fingers in and out. She looks totally bewildered and, despite what she may have done, I feel sorry for her. Dan and Larry take their seats opposite her and apologise for the state of the room.

'It's fine,' Lorna gulps out. 'What is it I can help you with? I just want to do that and go home.'

'As this is voluntary,' Dan says kindly, 'you can go whenever you want, just up and go, but it would really help if you talked to us.'

'Yes, well, I promised Lucy I would. Is she not here?'

Shit. Maybe we should have put a woman in there. Lorna might have felt less intimidated and been more able to explain herself. People who commit murders generally don't mean to do it. Most of them aren't all bad, they're simply people who have made a catastrophic mistake. Once they admit it, they need to tell us why and how things happened, and generally it's just sad crap.

I'm not sure Lorna will relate to two large men.

'Maybe we should have got a female in there,' William remarks, coming into the room, which is already packed.

All the banter and chit-chat stops.

'Dan is a bit of craic,' Susan pipes up, after a moment of silence. 'He'll have her eating out of his hand.'

'Women like gay men,' Mick agrees.

'Dan is gay?' Louis gasps.

And there follows a discussion on poor old Dan, whose ears would burn if he could hear it.

Finally, the interview starts properly with a caution.

Dan starts off in the usual way and Lorna seems to relax with the two men, telling them a little about herself, about Denis and of how she met him.

'Children?' Dan asks.

'No.' Lorna's eyes cloud. 'A source of grief for us both. Look, really, this is all very nice but how can I help?'

'Can you just humour us by telling us what you did the night of the fire? Not your husband, because we know that, but you.'

Lorna, looking surprised, shrugs. 'Well, I was out at a meeting for the Tidy Towns and then I came home about ten and watched some TV. Denis was in bed. He gets up early to watch the sunrise and take pictures and . . . Sorry . . . me?'

'Yes, you.'

'I went to bed about eleven thirty. I heard Denis get up about three-ish. Then I fell asleep again and only woke up when Mags, that's Lucy's mother, Lucy the detective, her mother rang me to tell me about the fire. Well, I thought she'd got it wrong but then Lucy called in and we learned the whole horrible thing.'

'Thanks.' Dan jots a few notes. 'Anything else?'

'No.'

'Right. Going back. What prompted you to go to Lucy about your husband?'

'I wish I hadn't now. I just thought I was doing a good thing. I never thought he'd be arrested and everyone would know, and we'd get things thrown at our house. I was worried in case he might have done something. I know I shouldn't have been but, anyway, I thought Lucy might have a quiet word with him about it. But instead it was a big hoo-ha and he got arrested and everyone found out and it's been terrible. Really terrible.'

'So, you're saying you went to Lucy because you thought you were doing a good thing and were worried in case your husband had done something?'

'Yes. I wanted to find out if he'd done it, for my own peace of mind. I had seen all those pictures on his camera and it scared me because he'd done something like it before.'

'Murdered someone?'

'No, stalked someone, become obsessed with someone. And I was worried.'

'When did you discover these pictures, Lorna?'

'Maybe six weeks ago.'

'So, you discovered pictures six weeks ago, well before Moira and Ella were murdered, and you weren't worried then?'

She hesitates. 'I was. Yes.'

'Did you say anything to your husband?'

Lorna flushes. 'No.'

'Why?'

'I don't . . . I don't know really.'

'So, you're saying you found the pictures, were worried and yet you did nothing?'

'Yes.'

'And yet when Moira and Ella were murdered, you went straight to Lucy and told her everything?'

'Yes.'

Dan sits back, lets her think about it.

'Look, I thought it was just . . . well . . . harmless. But when Moira disappeared and— I had to do something.'

'You say you heard Denis get up at three in the morning?'

She starts at the change in subject. 'Eh . . . yes.'

'And that you fell asleep and only woke when your phone rang.'

'Yes.'

'Can you prove this?'

'Sorry?'

'Can you prove that you were in bed all that time?'

She gawks at Dan in horror. 'What do you mean? What are you suggesting?'

'Let me tell you what I'm suggesting,' Dan says, 'and then, sure, you can tell me if it happened that way or not. Do you want to hear it?'

I half expect Lorna to get up now and walk out but, like passing a car crash, she can't tear herself away. Yes, she wants to hear it. Yes, she needs to know what they're thinking. Yes, she thinks she can refute it.

'This murder – these murders,' Dan corrects himself, 'were carried out at four in the morning by someone we believe knew the area. Someone who walked to the cottage. This person concealed themselves, attacked Moira, set her rented house on fire, hid Moira, still alive, in the boot of her car and drove it to Achill-henge. This person – we have two eyewitnesses who say it was a woman –'

Lorna gasps, half stands up.

'– hit Moira again before pulling her from the boot of the car to the bonfire where she was dumped in the middle of it. Wood and debris, including the murder weapon, were piled on top of her. It was sloppy but it worked. Moira's car was then driven by this woman back to Keel Beach car park and left there. We believe this woman walked home as we have successfully traced and ruled out all the other cars driving at that time in the morning.'

Lorna glares at him. Tears stand bright in her eyes. 'Did someone say they saw me?'

'No.'

'Do you have my prints on anything?'

'No.'

'Any proof?'

'Accelerant found at your property matches the accelerant used to light the fire.'

'Denis explained that. We lent diesel to Moira for her lawn-mower, not that she bothered with the grass. She left the can there, right outside the front door. She never bothered putting it in the shed.'

'We also have a recorded call to the station the day after the fire.'

Lorna turns white, makes to stand up. 'You said I could leave, didn't you?'

'Yes.'

'Then I'm going.' She gulps back tears. 'How dare you? You're trying to stitch me up for this because you can't do your job.'

'Like you tried to stitch up your husband,' Dan says mildly, and a little cruelly.

And that does it. The dam bursts.

'Yes!' she says, and there is viciousness in her tone. 'Yes! Yes! I did! I reported him because he needed teaching a lesson. He needed to know that taking photographs of women and their children was not on. He needed to be shocked into thinking about his behaviour. I had no idea the accelerant matched. I didn't want him in jail – God, how humiliating. I don't even want people to know about it. I told Lucy because I wanted her to have a quiet word with him. I wanted her to warn him off. But it grew too big and he's not the better of it and I feel terrible.'

'Did your anger at him extend to Moira?'

'No. Never. And you're so stupid, you can't even work out that it wasn't even her he was obsessed with. Not really.' And now she breaks down, head on the table, sobs racking her body. Larry and Dan are at a loss. They look at each other and then at Lorna.

'Pass her a tissue, for Jaysus' sake,' William mutters.

Ger bounces into the room. Bright and cheerful, he announces, 'Bad news, Cig. The fingerprints from the phone on the bonfire are not a match for Lorna. Looks like just some random device.'

'Remind me to get you to announce the garda budgets for next year,' William remarks drily as he takes the page from Ger and skims it. 'Brilliant. Yet more non-evidence.'

'Has she folded anyway?' Ger looks at the TV – Dan has eventually pushed the tissues across.

'No.'

Ger settles against the wall.

'Get back to the incident room, Ger,' William says. 'We can't all be in here.'

Looking aggrieved, he slumps out.

My phone buzzes. Stops. Buzzes. Stops. Buzzes.

I don't look at it because I know it's my mother again.

'It was the children.' Lorna ignores the tissues and wipes her face with her sleeve. 'He loved the children, not in a bad way, just – just the way I love them. Oh, he told himself it was the women, but it was the children. We couldn't have any, you see, and we tried to adopt but we were just not lucky enough or we didn't give the right answers, I don't know what it was. IVF was a disaster and the one time I did get pregnant, I lost it. Five months in, a little girl. That's when it started, when we both lost hope. And I buried the pain. I carried on. Denis, too, until he met women who were alone and had children. It was irresistible to him. Oh, he'll tell you how he took photos of Moira on the beach doing this and that, but it was the children. He just wanted to feel part of it all, watch the kiddies playing or messing about. I think he thought he could fit into Moira's family, be a sort of uncle figure. And for a while she let us babysit and play with them, and it all might have worked if he'd just stopped himself being too involved. But he was up there morning, noon and night. And I know he scared her a bit but I thought it served her right. If she and her children were going to take my husband's attention, she deserved what she got. It hurts, you know – it hurts to think that I'm not enough for him.'

This has gone way too personal for the two lads.

This is not a confession, it's a counselling session.

'Right, well,' Dan swallows hard, 'to summarise, you're saying that you had—'

'Lucy,' Ger pokes his head around the door, 'there's a call for you.'

'Who is it?'

'I didn't ask. He just said he'd been trying to reach you on your mobile but you haven't been answering.'

Great.

At William's disapproving look, I say defensively, 'I thought it was my mother.' I fish it out of my pocket.

Fran. Ten missed calls.

Shit. What's happened? I dial quickly.

'Fran?'

'Ballycroy National Park,' he says. 'That's the one place you'll find all of those plants.'

42

Jonathan, the elderly, bespectacled man behind the visitor's desk in Ballycroy National Park, gawps at my ID. 'A detective.' He looks at me in disbelief. 'But you're only young and you're a woman.'

He should have stopped while he was ahead. 'Nevertheless, I'd like a list of your employees and their rotas for June. And if you have a visitors' book, I'd like to examine that too.'

'Have you got clearance?' Jonathan bristles a little at my tone. Drawing himself up to his full five foot two, he asks, 'Isn't that a GDPQRXYZ matter?'

'Some might say it is a GDPR matter,' I agree. 'Others might think that a murder investigation after a child and her mother died trumps all that. What do you think?'

He flushes a little. 'Well, I—'

'D'you have grandchildren?'

The haughty look is replaced by a hundred-watt beam. 'One. Born yesterday. Eleven pounds four ounces. A girl.'

'Congratulations.' Bingo. 'How exciting for you. Grand-children are great. Look, I'd really love it if you can help with that list.' I lower my voice: 'Data protection is a pain, you have to agree.'

'I suppose that was a terrible tragedy, poor little mite and the mother.' He taps a few buttons on a computer in front of him. 'I'll get you a list of employees, no bother. One list has their pictures too. Would you like it?'

'I'd love it, Jonathan.'

'No visitors' book,' he continues, 'but I may be able to get you names if people paid for things in the coffee shop and visitors' centre by credit card, if that's any use? That might take some time, though.' Another beam. 'Credit cards is how you lot track people, amn't I right?'

'Very good. We'll also be harvesting any CCTV you have for the following dates.' And I read them out to him.

'I can send that on if we have it. I'll get one of the girls in the office to sort it out.'

Half an hour later, sitting in the coffee shop with a free coffee provided courtesy of Jonathan, I'm skimming the employees list.

Nothing.

No one who works here has come up in our enquiries. But Fran was definite. Rare plants from Ballycroy National Park, he'd said.

Ballycroy.

Whoever it was had visited here or been associated with the place in the couple of weeks before the murder.

Needle in a haystack, though, if they've no records.

'Not going too well, eh?' Jonathan appears silently beside the table, startling me.

I rub my hands over my face. 'I'll get there.' I'm not sure I believe it.

'Good.' He hops about a bit. 'We're closing in fifteen minutes, just, so . . .' He looks embarrassed. 'I have to get home, like.'

'Of course. Sorry. I'll just . . .' I indicate my coffee. I may as well finish it, enjoy the peace. It's then that I spot a map of the park, hung on the wall just behind his head. Something about it makes me pause. I move towards it, Jonathan trotting anxiously at my heels. It's the notice underneath that has attracted my attention. 'You closed off some parts of the park?'

'Yes. We give out amended maps. That farmer there,' he points to a parcel of land that straddles the borders, 'he's restricted access for the last three weeks now.'

In my opinion there is only one reason that farmers restrict access. But I ask anyway, 'Why?'

'He's having terrible problems with deer, I've heard. Feckers are destroying the place. He has to cull them.'

A shiny bright penny of information.

'Would you have the name of that farmer?'

'I suppose somewhere.' He peers about his reception area before picking up a phone and dialling someone else.

In the meantime I call Fran. 'Do spores travel, Fran?'

'They can. But honestly, Lucy, if there were a lot of spores, whoever did that was in Ballycroy or on its borders. No question.'

All I need to do now is to ask the farmer who did the culling of the deer for him.

But already I know.

William has taken charge of the room.

'All right, everyone, settle down.'

He waits until we're quiet, though we're buzzing with the new information. It doesn't mean that the case is solved, but it does mean we have a brand new, unexpected suspect. One we have to start working on from scratch. But one who might fill in all the blanks.

303

'For now,' William says, 'we're ruling Lorna Long out of the investigation.' He turns to Ger. 'Would you like to tell them why, Ger?'

'Because the pollen traces and spores found in Moira's car are from very rare plants. Very rare plants that grow near each other. Our suspected offender would have had to be in contact with those plants in the days leading up to the murder as deposits were found in Moira's car and traces were found on her clothes.'

'Indeed, well done,' William says, making Ger pink up. 'This breakthrough came about because Daniel told his partner about the investigation. Not recommended by the way. However, we have been on to some other experts who have confirmed that, yes, indeed, these rare plants are all to be found in Ballycroy National Park. Lucy?'

I explain to the room that Isabelle Jones's name has come up as hunting on the border of Ballycroy National Park. 'She has spent the past month hunting deer on behalf of three farmers whose lands cross with the park's. They provided me with her name – she's the best in the business apparently. Shoots game during the year also. We'll get a positive ID on her later today. However,' I continue, 'Larry will be checking CCTV images to make sure that Moira and her children were not at the park in the days leading up to her murder as that might explain the deposits too. We'll also be making sure that none of our other suspects was there either, though there were no traces of pollens found in the Longs' car or indeed Eamon's vehicle. Mick?'

'Yes?'

I hand him my ID in a clear evidence bag. 'Take that and see if the prints on it match prints found on the phone we located at the bonfire. Mrs Jones handled that at one point.'

'Sure thing.'

'The race is on to find out whether Isabelle Jones is guilty or innocent,' William says. 'We need to hurry - we don't want her getting wind of it. I have to stress this is not yet proven so keep an open mind. But we also have to build this case tight so that if we get her there is no wriggle room. And if it can't be proven, it can't be proven. Susan, Louis, I know there are guest lists from every B&B, Airbnb and hotel in the vicinity of Keel, and that they have been sitting on desks for the past week and a half. They've only been partially checked. Get on it now. We do know she was away somewhere the night Moira was murdered. She told her neighbour that she was away for a few days so we're checking accommodation here, though chances are she may have used a false name and email address anyway. Worth a shot, though. Lucy, do we have a picture of Isabelle?'

'Yes, we've got one from Barry Jones's Instagram page,' I say.

'Good. Get that done up now, and I want you all out knocking on doors to see if anyone can ID her. Is Matt here?'

'He's on the desk.'

'Get him involved, too. He did good work tracing Moira's bank accounts.' A glance at me. 'I'm not stupid, Lucy. Don't ever pull that one again.'

'Ouch.' Dan chortles softly.

I flush. Being reprimanded in front of the whole team is embarrassing.

'The aim here, folks, is to find some trace of Isabelle Jones on the island on days leading up to and including the sixteenth of June. Chances are, if she was planning to harm Moira and the children she might not have used her real name, she might have paid for things in cash, so we need to ID her. How did she get here? We haven't had her jeep pop up, have we, Larry?'

'Nope.'

'She may have come by bus or taxi. Ben, can you check that out?'

'Sure.'

'Right, everyone, get the job sheets and no sloppy work. Focus. Right.'

And he strides off, no doubt to give an update to the super.

Dan and I are on CCTV with Larry. We are scanning street footage from the day before outside one of the shops at Keel. It's feeling like a waste of time.

Finally Larry says, 'I think what we need to do is find Moira on the footage because this woman probably followed her now and again. How else would she know Moira's routine?'

'Worth a shot,' I agree. 'Better than what we're doing now.'

'Would Moira not have recognised her?' Dan asks.

'She wasn't expecting to be followed so she may not have noticed her. She may not even know what she looked like either. It could be years since they met. Right.' Larry taps his pen against his teeth. 'We know Moira sent Ella off on the school bus each morning from Keel, so let's try to find her on that.'

Half an hour later, Larry has located Moira as she stands apart from the other parents at the stop. Moira is stunning, even in black and white. She's diminutive, but there is a gracefulness in her movements as she wraps her arms about Ella and kisses her. Then, with Bren, she waves Ella off. We watch Bren run after the bus a little way as Moira laughs.

She looks happy.

The other parents drift away and Moira catches Bren by the hand and leads him back to her car.

'I can't see anything there,' I comment.

'The camera focus is narrow enough.' Larry muses. 'Where else did Moira go?'

'She was in the Moose at four thirty on the fifteenth.'

'But how would our SO know she was going there?'

'Barry wrote her a reference. He may have told her.'

'Worth a shot.' Larry scrolls through reams of images he has harvested and eventually finds one taken opposite the Moose. 'I looked at this already,' he mutters, 'but let's go again.'

Moira arrives into shot, Bren screaming and crying and dragging his heels. Annoyed because he couldn't go on his sleepover, I suppose. Ella chivvies him along as Moira stops to study herself in the glass. We watch as she adjusts her hair. It's so weird, knowing what transpired in the next few minutes. How all her preparations would come to nothing, thanks to that bastard Eamon. She bends to talk to Bren but he's having none of it. Moira braces herself, hitches her shoulders back, and steps into the Moose.

'No one.' Larry throws down his pen in frustration.

'Just leave it for a few minutes.'

Onscreen, people drift by the café, some going inside. And then someone wearing black passes just under the camera, opposite the café. This person stares across the road. Moves slightly forward into the frame and stops.

It's a woman and she is definitely looking for someone. Finally, she walks on.

Larry rewinds the video and freezes it so we get a bit of profile. 'Recognise her?'

'With the hat and the bulky clothes, it's impossible to know.'

'Fast-forward until Moira exits,' Dan says, 'see if she's around then.'

Larry does, and we watch as Moira leaves the café. Her body language is despondent. My heart fractures a little as Ella tries to wrap her little arms around her mother. They appear to be ignoring Bren, who sulkily stomps behind them. As the trio disappear from shot, the black-clad woman reappears, this time on the far side of the street. She hesitates before walking into the café.

'Any footage from the café?' I ask.

'No.'

'Bollox,' Dan says.

'Let's just keep tracking Moira and see if we can spot this person again,' Larry offers. 'I'll go to the bus stop the previous day now.'

Three hours later, we have had no success. The woman in black, as we've christened her, has only appeared once, at the coffee shop.

'Where else did Moira go?' Dan wonders.

'Beach, collecting seaweed?'

Dan and I head off for a coffee and leave Larry hunting footage from around or near the beaches. I don't have much hope of him finding anything.

My mobile rings and, wary of missing any other important calls, I whip it out.

'Susan, what's up?'

'We're here at the Lodge Hotel in Keel. The owner ID'd Isabelle for us. She stayed in the hotel for four nights, one of which was the night of the fire. She says she remembers her because she asked for her room to be changed to one overlooking the street.'

I call up the Lodge Hotel on Google Maps. It's right opposite the school bus stop. No wonder we didn't catch her on CCTV: she was probably looking out of the window.

'She also told me that the rooms on the other side of the hotel are nicer so it was an unusual request.'

'Does she have a record of it in her book or on the computer.'

'That's the great thing. She does. Isabelle Jones called herself Izzy Murphy and she paid in cash.'

'Can you ask her if Isabelle was spotted going out late or coming back early on the fourteenth and fifteenth of June?'

'I did. The reception is open from nine a.m. to midnight. Guests have a key and can come and go as they please.'

'No CCTV?'

'It's wiped the next day.'

'But she definitely ID'd Isabelle?'

'Yes.'

'That's brilliant, Susan. That's great.'

And then it hits me, a long shot at best, but one worth trying. Denis and his camera.

As Larry continues to trawl the CCTV, I download all of Denis's photographs of Moira, starting with the ones taken in the weeks leading up to her death. I rope in Jordy and I think he's glad because he really isn't fit enough to be walking from house to house looking for an ID.

'What have we got?' he asks.

'We're trying to spot anyone suspicious in the background of Denis's pictures. And don't ask me what looking suspicious is, Jordy, I don't know. But keep the photo of Isabelle in front of you. Go slowly.'

'Sure thing.'

It's quiet in the incident room as day passes into evening. Jordy shifts in his seat every now and again.

'Not a bad photographer, this guy, is he?' Jordy comments, after a bit. 'I used to like taking pictures back in the day.'

'Yeah?'

'I got a few printed in the nationals until I was told it conflicted with the job so . . .' A shrug.

'I didn't know that about you.' People are always surprising me.

'It was maybe twenty years back when I was working in the midlands. Not a lot to do there.'

I laugh. 'You've just insulted half the country.'

'I was a wild man in me day.' He gives his chest a thump. 'Paying for it now.'

'You must have hated being moved here. It's even quieter than the midlands normally.'

'The wife had left me and a change was as good as a rest.'

'Sorry to hear that.'

'Hard to keep a marriage going when you're working all day and drinking all night.'

'I'd imagine.'

He coughs, slurps some tea, and returns to the job.

Lorna was right: these pictures are more about the children than Moira. Bren and Ella, heads together, talking. Ella in pink wellies looking at a starfish. Bren laughing, the sun lighting up his hair. Moira is there, of course, but as a background figure and—

There.

The photo is dated 13 June at 15:30 and Moira and the children are in the cottage garden. Denis must have been perched on a slope above the house because, although the camera is pointed at the garden, the road in front of the house is in the picture too. And there's a figure, impossible to make out at first, but Denis was obsessed. And in each shot the figure becomes clearer because it's nearing the cottage. In the final shot, the figure is looking directly at the children and also staring directly into the zoom lens. I isolate the figure and magnify it. The pixels blur. It could be her.

There must be more. I keep at it, and other guards move in and out of the incident room, filing reports and handing in job sheets.

At eight, Jordy stretches. His neck cracks so hard, I do an 'ouch' for him.

'I'll come in early and get back on it.' He yawns.

'Go home. It's grand. I'll hang on.'

'You want me to stay?'

'Nah, you know me, obsessive. I'll do a hundred more images and then I'll get going.'

'You'll get going now.' William speaks from the doorway. 'No point working when you're tired. Night, Jordy.'

'Cig.' Jordy rushes out.

'Any luck?' As he peers over my shoulder, I show him the image I isolated.

'We can check that against the CCTV that Larry found and do a comparison of weight and height. It's not very clear, though, is it?'

'No. Just let me do fifty more.'

'Fine. I'll do another fifty, can't have the staff outshining the boss.' A grin.

He takes over Jordy's computer and we work in silence for about fifteen minutes.

'Hello,' he mutters, pressing some buttons. 'Lucy, over here.'

On the computer, there's a picture taken from the opposite side of the street to where the Moose coffee shop is. Through the window I can see Moira with Bren, both at a table, Bren with a huge glass of something in front of him. Outside the café, a black figure is looking in, back to the camera.

'I can see the figure but their back is to camera.'

With a chuckle, which melts the ice blue of his eyes, William zooms in on the tilted mirror in the café. Facing the window, it reflects the street outside. The woman's face is visible in it, though at a distance. 'We'll get it enhanced,' William says confidently, with a wink at me.

'And that's why you're the Cig.'

He smiles, picks up his jacket from the chair. 'Get home, for God's sake. We'll meet in the morning and go through what we have. The only thing I don't understand is why. Sure, she barely knew the girl.'

'From talking to her, I don't think she was overly fond of Moira, but what she did . . .' I shudder.

'Maybe we'll discover why tomorrow. Hop it, go on.'

'William?'

He glances absently at me, as if I'm already out of his mind.

'I was wondering, and tell me to get lost if you like, but do you ever get, you know, nightmares or panic attacks to when . . . you know . . .' I flounder a little, then say crassly '. . . to when all your family died in the house fire?'

He appears a little taken aback at my bluntness, then throws me a shrewd look and I wilt a little under it. 'Have you been feeling that way?'

I notice that he hasn't answered my question.

'No!' I laugh. 'Just, you know, I'm still a bit shaky, I think, after what happened, but I can do my job and—'

'Because if you are,' he interrupts, and he sounds deadly serious, 'you cannot do this, Lucy.'

'I know that,' I gabble. 'I totally know that. I was just asking. But you're fine?'

'I would not be heading up this investigation if I wasn't,' he says, but I think he would. 'Now go home.'

I can't get out of the door fast enough.

43

Day 11

By ten the next morning, the picture the Cig found has been enhanced and there is no mistaking Isabelle Jones. In fact, the detail is so good that you can even see the brown mole on her chin.

'Isabelle Jones stayed at the Lodge Hotel from the twelfth to the sixteenth of June. During her stay she asked for her room to be changed to a street view, presumably so she could keep an eye on Moira and the children. From this room she was able to observe Moira in the morning and in the afternoon as she picked up Ella from school. It is also in the vicinity of the Moose coffee shop where Moira brought the children for treats. From the hotel she would have been able to walk to Moira's cottage comfortably. She had the strength to overpower Moira, and we know she holds a firearm, so she may have threatened her with that. She would also have been aware of the bonfire at the henge as it was widely reported in the local media. We have accessed her credit-card accounts and she purchased a mobile device in Westport Tesco three months ago, crucially two days before Moira's first nasty text. The phone number of that device matched the phone number the texts were sent from. Also, partial prints found on

Lucy's ID were a match to prints on the phone. We also believe that the SO was at the scene because we found plant spores from the Ballycroy National Park in Moira's car and on her body. Isabelle Jones was working in lands on and adjacent to the park for the three weeks before the murder and also for these last two weeks.'

Someone whistles.

There's a fizz of excitement in the room.

'And, yes, spores from the plants found at the scene are located on the western edge of one of the fields Isabelle was hunting in. So, to sum up, we have proof she was in Moira's car, we know she was on the island the day of the fire and we also know that she never mentioned it. We have opportunity but the intent still eludes. Why would the woman do this?'

'I dunno, Cig. I guess we'll have to arrest her to find out,' Kev pipes up, and everyone laughs.

'Exactly. We have drawn up a search warrant. Lucy, head on out there and bring her in. There is a firearm on the property so proceed with caution. DDU will assist you. Louis, go with Lucy.'

There's a bit of a murmur at that and Dan looks distinctly put out.

I beckon Louis to follow and he skips alongside me, like an eager puppy, as I fire off a list of instructions for him. 'Do not open your mouth. Do not offer an opinion. Do not get involved with any altercations that may emerge unless I instruct you to. Do not—'

'Is there anything I can do?' Louis asks sulkily

'Yeah, put your cap on.'

He does as he's told without comment and we get ourselves a DDU car. Soon, with the armed detective unit following and the search team, we're on the road to Newport. Normally with Dan we'd be having the craic, delighted with ourselves to see the end of an investigation, but it's impossible with Louis: you just don't know how much of it will go back to Daddy.

'I'm not going to say anything to my dad, you know,' he says, looking at me sideways. 'I'm not a complete arsehole.'

We cross the bridge to the mainland.

'Why don't you like me?'

'I never said I didn't.'

'You didn't have to.' He pokes at a fingernail. 'You're not at all like I expected.'

I clench the steering wheel tighter and take a deep breath. Giving him a sideways glance, I say, 'It's nothing to do with whether I like you or not. As I said before, it bugs me that other, better, guards would have killed to be on this investigation and you just think you have the right to waltz in.'

'That isn't my fault.' He glares at me.

'You could have said no. You could have said you hadn't earned your stripes. You could tell—'

'Have you ever tried to tell my dad no?' At my look, he smirks. 'Exactly.'

'You'll get to the top,' I floor the accelerator, throwing him a little back in his seat, 'and it won't be because you're any good. It'll be because of who you are. People wonder why the garda management is so shite. It's because the likes of you are at the top. And—'

'I knew you were talented,' Louis narrows his eyes, 'but I never knew you could see into the future.' He turns to gaze out of the window,

A little bit of admiration for him blooms in my chest.

44

I pull up outside Isabelle Jones's house in Newport. Behind me the search team and the DDU assemble. Before we knock, I order Louis to stand behind me. The last thing I need is for anything to happen to him.

'Isabelle Jones?' I call, as I rap on her front door. 'This is DS Lucy Golden and Garda Louis Devine. Can you open up, please?'

Nothing. The only sounds out here are the call of the birds and the smash of the ocean. There's a twitch of curtain in a house across the road.

In the back garden, the dogs start barking.

I rap again but there is no answer.

I'm just about to pop around the back when Isabelle, barefoot, wearing a tracksuit, pulls the door open.

'This is a surprise.' She doesn't sound surprised. 'What's going on?'

'Isabelle Jones, I'm arresting you on suspicion of murder. You are not obliged to say anything unless you wish to do so but anything that you do say will be taken down in writing and may be given in evidence. Do you understand?'

She takes us all in, her gaze roving over the armed detectives.

Behind me, the leader of the search team gives a run-down on what we're looking for in Isabelle's house, his voice carrying on the breeze.

'Do you understand?' I ask Isabelle again.

Irritatingly, I can feel Louis's breath on my neck because he seems to have taken 'stand behind me' literally.

'I understand.' She doesn't protest her innocence, which is unusual. Maybe she's too shocked. 'I need to get my shoes.'

'That's fine. I'll accompany you. Louis can you—'

All of a sudden, she turns and sprints towards the kitchen. I take after her but Louis, two decades younger, is quicker. And then, he pulls to a halt and I slam into the back of him, both of us tumbling to the floor.

Fuck!

Isabelle looms over us, a hunting rifle in her hands. 'Up,' she says.

Behind me, I know one of the lads from the armed DDU probably has her in his sights.

'Drop the rifle,' someone calls.

Clambering to my feet, hands raised, I say, 'Isabelle, this is not a good—'

She positions herself directly in front of Louis. The blinds have been drawn in the kitchen. There's a suitcase packed. She was ready for us in case we came, I realise.

'Make them leave.' She jabs her rifle in the direction of the DDU and search team.

'It's not a good idea.'

'Get out of my house, all of you, or I'll blow his brains out.' With icy calm, she points the rifle at Louis, who whimpers slightly.

'Lads,' I call, without taking my eyes off her, 'you need to leave, right now. Right now.' I crack out the order.

'That's right,' Isabelle shouts. 'Get off my property. If I see anyone, anyone on it, I'll kill this boy.'

'You heard her,' I say, and in silence, the teams vacate the premises.

'You too,' she says to me. 'Go.'

'That guard is my responsibility and I'm not leaving him. Swap him for me.'

She thinks about this as my heart ratchets up. Never for one moment did I get a sense of crazy off this woman. But then again, I only ever talked to her to give her news about Barry's case. Please, please, please let him go, I mentally beg.

'I'll keep the two of you,' Isabelle says, and my heart sinks. 'More leverage. If I accidentally kill one, I'll have another. I know you detectives carry guns. Throw it my way. Now.'

I take my gun slowly from its holster and hand it to her. 'You don't need to do this.'

Outside the dogs are barking up a storm.

She backs towards the bin, the rifle trained on us, and drops my gun into it. 'Both of you, throw your phones on the floor.'

A clatter as they fall onto the tiles.

Louis looks terrified, the cocky confidence gone to be replaced by a pale, scared youngster.

'Sit down at the table,' Isabelle instructs. 'Any false move and I will blast you, young man, to kingdom come.'

I sit and scan the room to see if I can use anything to help us. But with a gun pointed firmly at Louis's head, I'm reluctant to take any chances. But I must do something to end this because she means business. She will shoot us, I have no doubt. She's already killed twice. I reach for my belt as I pretend to adjust my position on the chair. Just a fingertip, just a tiny motion, just a fraction of a second and I'll have it in my palm. I have to do something before the regional support unit arrive and take action because she will unleash carnage.

'Sit still!'

Louis jumps.

Damn! My finger slips.

'Move the chairs closer together so I can keep an eye on ye.'

'Over here, Louis.' I use his name, trying to humanise him for her.

He picks up his chair, the barrel of her hunting rifle following his every move, and scoots in beside me.

'Let Louis go.' My voice is steady. 'He's not much younger than your Barry and—'

'My Barry is in a bloody wheelchair. That fella there,' she waves the gun at Louis, 'he's hale and hearty. Shut your mouth.'

'You don't want to do this, Isabelle.'

'Yes, I do,' she says. 'What does it matter? I'll go to jail either way.'

Shit.

I know by now the boys outside will have radioed for backup; plans will be put in place. The RSU will have arrived and be moving in. The trick is to keep her talking, to keep her from going off on one, keep her from panicking, but the truth is I'm panicking. My mind is whirling with images from last year. I'm seeing that madman again in my kitchen.

Isabelle pulls a seat for herself and sits opposite us, the rifle resting on her lap. She's still barefoot, her tracksuit riding up to reveal thick ankles.

'What now?' I ask, careful not to panic her. 'What do you want?'

'To catch the flight I booked. I knew you were coming, see, because they were all talking about the visit from the guards in the national park when I popped in to tell them on whose land I was working that morning. I came home, packed and I had this,' she pats her rifle, 'all ready in case I wasn't quick enough to get away. How did you figure it out?' She looks at me.

I sidestep. Gently poke her on every mother's tender spot. 'You'd be leaving Barry if you ran.'

'Once he found out I'd killed Moira and Ella, he wouldn't want anything to do with me. But I was prepared to take his anger because I love him.'

'I know you do.'

For a moment, her expression softens. Turns sad. 'I do.' It's a whisper. 'Everything I did was for him but no one will understand that. No one will understand how evil that girl was.'

'I have a son.' I seize the opportunity to build a tentative rapport. 'I'd do anything for him as well.' And I think about what I have contemplated doing and I say, 'I'd break the law for him too, if I had to.'

I can feel Louis's gaze on me.

Isabelle's lip curls. Anger flares in her dark eyes. 'Don't bullshit me.'

'His girlfriend did the dirty on him. I was ready to kill her.' I apologise to Tani in my head.

'Like that bitch Moira.'

'Yes.'

For a second, I think I have her, but she's playing with me. Her lip curls. 'Fu—'

'D'you know what I did?' I interrupt her, before she has a chance to sneer, throwing my career away, knowing that this is all I have to offer. 'A few days back, I tried to get rid of evidence just so that Luc, my son, could think well of his father. My husband, Rob, was—'

'I know who your husband was.' Isabelle smirks. 'The whole country knew. Did you get rid of evidence for him the time he almost bankrupted the country?'

'No, and do you know why?'

She narrows her eyes, shakes her head, studying me like a curious specimen. 'No.'

'Because my husband wasn't my child. But this time . . . this time I broke the law to protect my boy.' Jesus, anything to connect with her. Anything to save the boy sitting alongside me. Anything to save myself.

'Fucking. Liar.' She relishes the words.

'D'you want me to prove it?'

The loud brash tones of her mobile startle us. The gun jerks in her hand and instinctively Louis and I flinch.

I curse at the timing, but say, 'You should get that.'

She holds fast to the gun with one hand and, keeping her gaze on us, presses 'answer'. 'What?' she barks out. Then, 'I'm not handing myself in. I am not going to jail for the bitch. She ruined my boy twice. Three times if you count Ella. I have a flight booked. I want to be brought to the airport and not followed. Then the two guards here can go.' She disconnects.

'You,' she motions to Louis, 'move even nearer to Lucy.'

'Sure,' Louis says, his voice only shaking a tiny bit. 'Though Lucy doesn't like me, so she may not want me so close.'

What the hell had I told him about not talking?

322

'Why doesn't she like you?' He has her attention now.

'Sometimes people don't like each other,' he says.

'That's true,' she answers. 'I didn't like Moira and somehow it's a crime. Closer now so I can keep you both in sight.'

Another call. She listens to the voice at the other end, then hangs up with a titter. 'They think Barry will be able to talk sense to me. Pathetic. He'll hate me because he was bewitched by that one.'

I don't speak. Maybe she'll keep going.

Thoughts of Moira make her hitch her breath and her face flares red. 'She destroyed my Barry. Destroyed him.'

There's a roar in my head as that night, the night Luc was tied to a chair, sparks bright. The noises of the shouting, the smell of the fear. The yawning horror that was the threat to my family. I plant my feet on the floor, feel the hardness of the kitchen chair in my body and tell myself that I'm not back there. Instead I'm in Isabelle's kitchen. I need to stay clear if we're to get out of this. I need to stop the thoughts. 'You only did what you thought was best for Barry, didn't you?' The images in my brain start to settle like the white on the top of a Guinness. So many perpetrators like to unburden themselves: they like to justify their actions in the hope that they make sense to someone. 'I get that.'

'You get that.' She copies my voice.

'Yes, because, like I said, I broke the law for my son.' My voice is steady, my eye contact firm. 'I get it, Isabelle.'

'You're just saying that.'

'I can prove it.'

'How?'

'You have to let Louis go first.'

'No way,' he says, and I glare at him.

323

'You prove it right now and I'll let the boy go.'

It'll have to do. If it's just me and her, I might find a way to move this on, get her to disarm. With Louis here, it's too risky. 'Okay. First, I'll need you to call William Williams, he's the detective inspector on the case.' I recite his number. 'Ask him to look in the boot of my car. There's a laptop in it that I was in the process of getting rid of. Tell him to take the hard drive from it. It may be too broken to be any good, but they should get something.'

'What will they get?'

So I explain to her, slowly, about the laptop, about how I uncovered the accounts, leaving Pat out of it. I recount how I attempted to destroy the evidence so that my son will revere his father. I tell her that I just hadn't quite done it yet. 'When examined, the hard drive will reveal a set of dodgy accounts that my husband set up a year ago.'

I can't even look at Louis as I tell her this. Saying it aloud makes me ashamed and embarrassed.

'What if this William Williams is in on it?'

'In on what?'

'What if this is just a ruse to—'

'How can it be? We didn't know you'd hold us up with a gun, did we? If you ring that number you'll get him. Don't tell him what's on the hard drive, let him tell you, and when he does, you let Louis go.' I can't think of a better reason for throwing my career away, though there's a sick feeling in the pit of my belly that has nothing to do with being held hostage. 'Ring him.' I am on the verge of shouting, so I rein it in.

She picks up the phone, dials the number I call out to her. He answers immediately. 'I want you to do something,' she says.

'Not until you reassure us that Lucy and Louis are safe,' he says, as she puts him on speaker. To hear his voice is comforting. 'I want to talk to them.'

'Say hello.' Isabelle waves the phone in our direction.

'Louis here,' Louis says. 'We're both grand.'

'Lucy?' William barks out.

'Grand, Cig. Isabelle needs you to do something. It concerns a laptop in the boot of my car.'

'She says she was in the process of dumping it,' Isabelle cuts me off. 'Get into the hard drive, tell me what's on it, and if it's what she says, I'll let the boy go. That's it.' A look at us. 'Now we wait.'

Two hours later, my arse is numb from the chair and Louis shifts uneasily beside me. The dogs are still barking but the noise is drowned out by the sound of a helicopter chopping the air. Outside on the road, I know a cordon will have been established and within it there will be a command unit. People from the neighbouring homes will have been told to leave, armed gardaí will be positioned around the house, waiting on their moment to strike.

Isabelle seems content to remain seated, the gun pointing at us. Further efforts to engage her have failed. She's ignored all attempts at outside contact, obviously waiting for William to ring back. She's resolutely ignoring the approaching storm. I find I have to tell myself to breathe. The air crackles with tension. Finally, at about lunchtime, she gets a call. Putting it on speaker she says, 'Well?'

'Tests have revealed a set of accounts from a Robert Ganley. We'll need to examine them further, but they look suspicious.' There is no emotion in William's voice. I want to cry because I have let him down. When I was demoted, William was the only one on the force who had faith in me. He put me on the night-caller case, although he was advised against it by the very man whose son is sitting beside me now. I proved William right back then, and Devine hasn't interfered too much since. But this will fracture our partnership. And to me, the fact that he knows I've betrayed his trust is worse than the thoughts of losing my job. I'll have let the whole team down. There will be no coming back from it.

'To be clear,' Isabelle says, 'is that the Robert Ganley who was married to the woman sitting in front of me?'

'We believe so, yes.'

She's distracted. My hand goes to my belt.

'Why do you think she tried to destroy that laptop?'

William remains silent.

'It's all right, Cig,' I call.

'I believe Detective Sergeant Lucy Golden or a member of her immediate family did it in an attempt to destroy evidence of Robert Ganley's wrongdoing.'

'I did,' I admit.

Isabelle gleefully disconnects the call. 'Isn't that dreadful?'

Off it comes, neatly into my fist. Sweat beads my forehead. 'We aren't all that different, you and I.' I think it may be true. 'Can you let Louis go now, please.'

'I'm not going anywhere,' Louis pipes up. 'No way. I'm a guard and we stick together.'

Oh, for Christ's sake, this isn't Power Rangers. I may have just blown up my career for him. 'I'm ordering you to go. I'm your boss.'

'I'm not going. You just sacrificed yourself for me, and if I have to do it for you, then I will.'

326

'Louis, please. I need what I did to mean something. If you get killed, I've just . . .' I can't even think it. 'Just go.'

'You've got thirty seconds to decide,' Isabelle says. 'I don't care either way.'

And she doesn't. Goosebumps pop up on my arm.

'I'm begging you.' I can't have the disposing of evidence plus the death of an officer charged against me in one day.

A brief hesitation. His gaze falls to my right fist and he looks questioningly at me.

'Go now,' I order.

'Okay.' Then, heavily, he adds, 'If me doing this will help you out, I'll take the plunge.'

What the hell is he talking about? Does he think we're in a film? 'Just get out of here.' My tone is sharp.

He stands up.

'Can you call and let them know that he's coming out?' I ask Isabelle. 'We don't need any misunderstandings.'

Without taking her gaze from me, she rings a number outside and imparts the information to the lads. I think by now some of them should be surrounding the house. Though the dogs would give her ample warning. But once they surround the place, it won't be long until they draw up a plan to rescue us and I don't fancy my chances with Isabelle then. I'll wait until Louis is gone and—

She hangs up and looks at him. 'They're expecting you.'

Louis, hands in the air, walks towards the door but just as he reaches it, he falls forward, tripping dramatically and letting out a yell.

The idiot.

But it's enough to distract Isabelle, her gaze swivels from me to Louis, who is rolling all over the floor.

327

Springing up, I try to cover the space between us. She spots the flash of movement, turns back and pulls the trigger.

The muzzle flashes at the same time as I pepper spray her.

There's crashing and banging as the house is flooded with guards from the RSU shouting, 'Armed gardaí!' In the crazy, noisy blur that follows, I hear Isabella shriek as the burn hits her skin.

I know I've been hit in the arm because I am on the floor. There is no pain.

Not yet.

Light and sounds from everywhere.

Louis is on the floor, beside the door, curled in a ball.

Oh, no.

I watch, my vision greying as Isabelle is pulled up from the floor and cuffed, still shrieking, clawing at her face.

In the melee, William, shouting orders. Standing over me. Calling for an ambulance.

45

Day 14

The days blur. Or maybe it's just a day, I don't know. There are voices and chatter, which seem to happen over my head, people pulling at me. Images dancing in and out, too nebulous to grasp. One day, red under my eyelids. I blink and the red grows. It's the window. Sun is setting. White sheets. A figure in a chair by the bed. Tall, dark, long-limbed.

Luc.

'Luc.' My voice is a whisper. I try again. 'Luc!'

His head, which has been resting on his chest, pops up and he blinks awake. He stares at me for a second of what I think is disbelief before he crosses properly into my line of vision. His eyes are bloodshot, he's unshaven, and he looks as if he hasn't slept. 'Aw, aw, Mam.' Bright tears, which he hastily blinks away. 'You're awake.'

'Looks like it.' Oh, it hurts.

He doesn't seem to know what to say. He just stands, arms dangling by his sides. And his tears fall. I don't think he notices. And then he leans forward, rests his head on my shoulder and sobs. 'I thought you were dead too,' he gulps out. 'I thought you were dead when they took you off in the ambulance, but William said—'

William. The whole night crashes in on me. What happened. What I did. How I let everyone down. I wonder how Louis is doing. Please let him be okay.

Luc is still talking. I'm inhaling him. His tears are dampening my hospital gown. 'It's okay,' I soothe. 'I'm all right now.'

I must have been shot in the left arm because it's painful when I try to move it.

After what seems only a moment, though in reality is longer, he gathers himself, wipes a hand across his nose. A rueful smile. 'I don't have a tissue, so don't say it.'

I move my good hand to caress his cheek and he doesn't resist. 'I love you, Luc,' I murmur.

'I'll call Nana.' Embarrassed, he pulls away. 'She'll want to know you're awake and—'

At that moment, there's a tap on the door and William's voice: 'Okay to come in, Luc?'

'She's awake,' Luc answers. 'Will you hang on with her? I'm just going to call my nan and a few others.'

William arrives in as Luc, flashing one of his gorgeous smiles at me, leaves, his fingers flying as he dials numbers.

Shame crawls up my body and I can't even look at my boss.

'Hey,' he says, pulling the chair alongside the bed. 'How are you feeling?'

'How's Louis?'

'Lucy, don't be worrying about—'

'Please?' Ever since the memories had barged in, I'd been afraid for the boy. He was supposed to leave, God damn it. He was supposed to go.

Fecking idiot.

'He's fine. Shook up.' Wryly, 'Apparently, according to Louis, you and he have a good understanding of each other.'

'He decided to be a hero. There wasn't much I could do about it.' Oh, my throat hurts.

A soft chuckle.

I broach the subject. 'About the laptop—'

'Later.'

'No. Now.' I try to pull myself up but the pain is too much. I fall back onto the pillows. 'Look, I'm sorry. I know I let you down and—'

'I know you stood on the laptop by mistake.' His gaze pins me in place. 'Louis attests that he believes you invented the other story to build rapport. We all do it, clever move.' His eyes beg me to agree.

I don't think I can.

I say instead, 'I am not sure what I would have done with the laptop.'

'I am.'

His faith in my better judgement causes me to blink away tears.

'I'm dealing with it. Just . . . just leave the investigation with me, all right?' His voice brooks no argument.

I don't know what that means, but from now on he'll have something over me. Is that a good thing? Do I trust him? Is he doing this for me? For himself? Is that just me being the cynic I always am?

He senses my hesitation. 'I can help you but you'll have to help me do it. You stood on the laptop by mistake.'

I swallow. Why would he . . .?

'Lucy?'

The seconds stretch. 'Okay.'

'Good.' A tiny smile.

I have to move this on. 'And Isabelle? What happened with her.'

'Do you ever stop thinking about work?' Then, 'Isabelle, pardon the unprofessional analysis, is one crazy weirdo.'

That's so unlike William that I manage a painful gulp of laughter. 'She confessed?'

'It took three days but because she was under caution when you were being held at gunpoint, it meant that she'd already confessed. Hadn't she said that she'd done it all for her boy because she loved him?'

'Yes. What happened in the interview?'

'You sure?'

'Go on.' I'm not sure really. I'm scared to hear the story because I can understand the murderous urge to protect your child. I'd happily gut the gouger who threatened my mother and Luc. So does that make me the same as Isabelle? What's the saying about fighting monsters? Making sure that in the process you don't become one yourself. Maybe it's already happened.

'Well, the woman was so out of it when she was arrested that we had to get a doctor in to assess her. And when we finally got permission to talk to her, she denied, stalled, lied, but she finally broke when Larry agreed that it was terrible Barry ended up in a wheelchair because of his night out with Moira. And I mean broke. She cried like she was never going to stop.'

I wonder how Larry dealt with that.

'Funny, yeah?' William reads my mind as his eyes crinkle up in a grin. 'But it did the trick. It all came out. First she cried and then she vented. And it was like watching Vesuvius erupt. Her rage at Moira was off the charts. Moira always had her eye on the main chance. Moira had only gone out with Barry to get her hands on someone who might have money one day. Moira was from nothing and all she wanted was a man to get her hooks into.'

'With her looks, she could have aimed a bit higher,' I say.

'Moira got pregnant to trap Barry. And when Barry told her Moira was pregnant and that he was hoping to propose, she visited Moira in secret and gave her a lot of money to have an abortion.'

'Jesus Christ!'

'Yep. Her Barry was too clever, he was destined for great things, and if Moira loved him, she'd let him achieve his potential. Moira took the money and, as far as Isabelle was concerned, she had the abortion. But then, according to Isabelle, Moira turned the tables by telling Barry she'd lost the baby and began ignoring his calls and treating him like shit and taking up with other men. With Eamon. She did it all on purpose, according to Isabelle, to make Barry drop out of college and not achieve his potential. It was Moira's way of getting back at Isabelle. It was Moira's fault that Isabelle had to nurse Barry for two years after his breakdown. And then,' William continues, 'after years, Moira comes back into Barry's life and, according to Isabelle, he jumped to attention. He let her live in his flat, he paid for things for her kids. And Isabelle said it was all Moira's plan to ruin her. She was terrified, terrified in case Moira told him about her paying her for the abortion.'

'But she never did, did she?'

'No. Instead she called Isabelle one day and told her that she was an evil bitch and to leave the two of them alone or she would tell Barry everything.'

'Nicely played.'

'For a while. But it also fuelled her anger. Moira had come back to take revenge. Moira had somehow pushed Barry in front of that car. Moira was getting away with the attempted murder of Isabelle's son. After the accident, Moira rang her and told her that she was sorry, that Barry needed her. But that, according to Isabelle, was only because Moira had no more use for her son. She knew then – her words – that Moira was going to dump him and cause him to have another breakdown. She would be left to pick up the pieces once again and she wouldn't do it. Moira was not going to win. It was better to kill Moira because at least then Barry wouldn't feel rejected. He'd be upset but at least he'd be spared the knowledge that Moira had abandoned him.'

'Christ.'

'She'll plead that she's insane,' William says. 'And, honestly, she is. Her reality is skewed. She did try to wriggle out of the murder charge for Ella saying that Barry had told her about the children going to Eamon's on a sleepover, so she hadn't known they'd be there but then . . .' William looks upwards and I see him gather himself before his gaze falls on me again '. . . then she said . . .' he swallows '. . . that she'd paid Moira to get rid of Ella years ago and it was karma.'

I can't invoke a response to that level of hate.

'No doubt the defence will produce all sorts of bleeding-heart reasons for why she did what she did and maybe they'll be right.' William heaves a sigh. 'But at the end of the day, she killed two people who didn't deserve it.'

And left Barry, the son she convinced herself she was protecting, worse off than ever. So what if Moira had been trying to trap Barry? So what if she was after money? It was up to Barry to see that for himself. Just like it's up to Luc to deal with whatever happens with Cherry, and it was up to me to deal with Johnny and Rob.

That is life, in all its shitty glory.

'Part of me is bloody sorry it isn't Eamon we're putting away, though,' William says. 'He shouldn't be allowed near another woman. Ever.' He pauses to pull a bag of sweets from his pocket. Opening it, he offers me one. 'But we'll get him somehow, one day.'

I smile, lifting my bonbon in a toast.

'No matter what happens,' he says, 'you did a good job on this case.'

And to have him say that means a lot.

Bleep.

A text.

Standing up, William puts the bag of sweets on my locker. Tipping me a salute, he says, 'I'll let you answer your well-wishers.' With a brief smile, he leaves.

I click into the message. The same person has sent me three messages every day, I notice.

And you thought it was me. Well, well . . . who's sorry now? ☺

46

Day 15

On the day of my discharge from hospital, I order a taxi to take me home. My mother kicks up a bit of an unconvincing fuss but I know she's relieved to be off the hook because she has a book club meeting.

When the cab arrives, I ask the driver to ferry me to Eamon's house in Louisburgh. Thankfully, he's a monosyllabic man who doesn't ask any questions and forty-five minutes later pulls up outside Eamon's door.

'Can you wait here, please?' I hand him fifty quid.

Climbing from the car, I'm hit with a shot of light-headedness as I step into the fresh air of the open countryside.

I take a moment to steady myself but before I get a chance to ring the bell, the door opens and Eamon, dressed in jeans and a check shirt, stands there. His polite look of enquiry morphs into a sneer.

'Come to apologise, have you?' He leans against the door frame, arms folded, looking amused. 'Making an innocent, respectable man like me into a suspect?'

'You were a suspect. When you texted that I thought it was you—'

'I don't hear the word "sorry" in there,' he interrupts.

'—you were right,' I continue, 'because you know you would have been more than capable. You, Eamon Delaney, are the lowest of the low. We know you bullied your wife and—'

'Why don't you fuck off?' He attempts to shove the door closed.

I jam my boot into it. I'd been expecting him to do that. 'I'll be watching you,' I tell him. 'I'll be waiting for you to slip up with whoever you end up with next. You think—'

'I'll be watching you, Lucy Golden, with the one son and the one grandchild and the—'

Terror claws at my belly as he rattles off the details of my life. Part of me knows they've been splashed about in the newspapers, especially after the assault on me and my family at my house, but it's like he's been following me. Stalking me like . . . like before. All I can hear is the shriek of ambulances, the stomp of feet as the RSU broke in my back door. Sweat pops out on my forehead and then, from behind Eamon, Bren peeks out.

Has he been here all along?

Has that man let him listen in?

Eamon tousles his son's hair, pulling him in front of him, a smirk playing on his lips. 'Which is better, Bren, boys or girls?'

He's mocking me with the question.

'Boys, silly!' Bren says, with a delighted laugh. 'Stronger, smarter, bigger.'

'That's right.' Eamon eyeballs me. 'Boys. Men. Women just run away and die, don't they?'

Bren's smile falters and I can't bear to witness it.

I turn to go.

'I'll be seeing you,' Eamon calls after me, and his front door slams closed.

47

Day 16

Moira and Ella are buried two days later. William and Dan, representing the investigation team, are there in full uniform. I slink into the back of the building. I'm wearing black trousers and a black jacket. Dan spots me and waves me up the church. I'm reluctant to go but he'll keep waving until I do so I slide in beside him and nod a hello to William.

'How's things?' Dan whispers, just as the organ begins to play. Then before I can answer, 'You look like shite.'

William glares at him, and I don't get a chance to respond because the coffin has arrived.

As it passes us on the way up the church, we bless ourselves. I watch as Eamon and Patti, with Bren in tow, take their places in the front seats. Eamon mops his eyes with a handkerchief.

My stomach churns.

Nick Flannery slides in beside Eamon, grief written into the story of his face.

He turns around and, to my surprise, he and William lock eyes. Nick gives a brief nod and turns back to face the altar.

Dan seems not to have noticed, and William remains impassive as if nothing happened. Maybe I imagined it.

There isn't enough space in the building for all who want to attend. Where were all these people during Moira's short life? Pushed away by Eamon most likely.

A loudspeaker in the churchyard allows the mass to be broadcast to those standing outside.

Eamon is called up to do a reading and I have to damp down the urge to shout from the rooftops that he is partly responsible for what has occurred. His bullying made Moira run away to protect her children. His bitterness and jealousy caused Ella's death. Patti, who'd wanted to drug Moira, does the second reading, and my heart almost breaks for the woman in the coffin. Bren sobs through a prayer of the faithful. Finally, at the end, Nick gets up to speak.

And though he's a bloody thug, right now he's a father who has lost his daughter and grandchild.

He must be devastated and of them all, apart from Bren, at least his grief is real. At least he deserves a place at the funeral.

'I've been asked to say a few words to ye all on behalf of the family. It's not an easy task for a father to bury his only daughter, his only child. It's not easy for a grandfather to bury his only granddaughter.' A moment as he gets himself under control.

'I pity the woman who murdered his daughter,' someone whispers behind us. 'She won't last long in prison.'

Tit for tat. Always.

No. Not always. An idea that has been floating somewhere just out of consciousness hardens and sticks.

'Moira was born to me and my late wife twenty-eight years ago and from the beginning she was our joy . . .'

He talks on and on about his daughter, his voice rising and

falling and faltering in places. 'And then she met Eamon and seemed so happy,' he says, and it's as if someone has planted a fist into my solar plexus. How can he get up there and talk about his daughter and not know that she'd married the Devil himself? He throws in a few stories that make people chuckle and then, his voice quivering, he bids her farewell and stumbles from the altar.

After that, Moira and Ella are borne from the church as the choir sings 'You Raise Me Up'.

I have to get out. I can't stand to watch as people cluck in sympathy; I almost retch as Eamon embraces his father-in-law. I push my way out of the seat and exit by a side door. I move past the throngs towards the road and sit on the stone wall that borders a field.

It's a nice day, almost warm, and small clouds float high above. The crowds pour out of the church, and as they congregate in little groups, the noise rises. Moira is placed in one hearse, Ella's little white coffin in another.

People offer condolences to the bereaved.

He crosses the road towards me.

Like I hoped he would.

He stands in front of me, hands in his pockets. 'I hate the fucking guards,' he says, 'but thanks.'

I look at Nick Flannery, take in the danger that rolls off him, the smell of volatility even in the way he regards me. 'Don't think of getting your minions to hurt Isabelle,' I say.

He *pfts* out what might be a laugh before turning away.

'You're no different from her.'

'What?' I've got his hostile attention now.

'She went crazy and killed your daughter because she believed, in her exhausted mind, that your daughter was about to hurt her and her son. By all accounts you did the same to an Adam Lewis some years back when you heard that he'd hit and dumped Moira.'

'Never been proven, Guard,' he says, spreading his palms wide.

'Maybe not.' I pause, say carefully, 'Isabelle Jones is not your problem. We can deal with her. Your problem is still out there.'

He looks at me like a tiger that's been unexpectedly offered a treat.

'Moira never told you anything really, did she?'

He remains silent.

'She told you nothing because she felt responsible for the death of Adam at your hands.'

I turn my gaze to where Eamon is, alone now, holding Bren by the hand. 'Sometimes we can't always get the real bad guys.'

The birds sing, the breeze blows.

The world turns.

And Nick walks off, back across the road.

Eamon

Eamon feels he is being dragged now, his mind spinning and free-wheeling towards something. Towards that day. The sixteenth of June. He's in his car, his rage a snapping, crackling loose wire, determined to burn down all before it. Patti had advised him to talk to her.

Oh, he'll talk to her all right.

There's a knife on the seat in case she should get smart with him. He will force her to listen. He will get her to apologise for making a fool of him after he sacrificed so much for her.

He's been too soft on her, too scared of her gangster father.

But not any more.

From now on she won't be going to any more job interviews.

That's for sure.

He doesn't bloody care if her father is Satan himself, she won't be visiting Limerick ever again.

A few bloody RULES!

But the mountain is alive with media at seven in the morning. Eamon pulls in, shoves the knife under a seat, joins the crowd and asks what has happened.

He's pumping with adrenaline.

A fire, he hears. Maybe a fatality.

He sees the cottage. HER cottage.

Hope flares. Maybe she's dead, the bitch.

Maybe someone just saved him a job.

He had come close, so close, and now it frightens him.

And apart from Ella, who had never been his anyway, who'd been the cuckoo in the nest, the whole thing couldn't have worked out better.

Why does everything always fall apart when life is good?

When he has his son and heir and while his sister is dancing attendance on him the way his bitch of a wife should have done.

That dragging and pulling.

Eamon braces himself against the pain.

Why? he wonders.

And then somewhere, maybe inside him, maybe outside, maybe in the wind, he hears the word 'justice'.

And the world turns and he is gone.

Acknowledgements

To everyone who bought, spoke, wrote, posted, sold, read and championed my books – thank you.

To my family – best in the WORLD!

And my dogs – also the best in the world!

My friends – I'm lucky to have some wonderful buddies from all areas of my life, school, college, drama, writing, running, and the ladies who drink coffee on a Wednesday!

My agent – a wonderful, straight-talking woman, Caroline Hardman and all at Hardman Swainson.

My publishers, who are a pleasure to deal with and who work hard to get the books to such an amazing standard - Krystyna Green, Rebecca Sheppard, Peter Jacobs and Hazel Orme.

Thanks to Hachette Ireland – especially Siobhan Tierney (she knows why!) for all her hard work on the last book.

To the lads in Achill for being so welcoming and for ordering and making such a fuss of me and the books – thank you, John, Mary and Caroline.

Finally, to three people who have given this book a realism and a truth that I would never have achieved on my own: Ellen

Sharpe, who taught me so much about being a specialist victim interviewer; Brian Willoughby, who answered my research questions with such patience and kindness; and to the detective who reads my books before anyone else – without his forensic eye for detail, many of my villains would probably have walked free from court due to lack of sufficient evidence.